A MUTUAL ADDICTION

MERMAID ASYLUM BOOK 1

MARY WIDDICKS

ABOUT THE AUTHOR

Mary is a former cognitive psychologist turned suspense writer. She is a firm believer in strong, twisted female characters and unhappy endings. Born and raised near Portland, Oregon, she now lives in Illinois with her three kids, two dogs, and two rowdy cats.

Join Mary's reader group for an exclusive, free copy of *Insomnia.* Go to marywiddicks.com

---

"*Insomnia* delivers Widdicks' usual bone-chilling dose of creeping dread and atmospheric lyricism."

-Wendy Heard, author of Hunting Annabelle

"Lyrical and hypnotic...an ominous journey into sleep-deprived madness."

-Meghan O'Flynn, bestselling author of the Ash Park series

ALSO BY MARY WIDDICKS

The Mermaid Asylum Series

Insomnia: A Mermaid Asylum Short Story

A Mutual Addiction (Book 1)

Born Under Fire: A Mermaid Asylum Short Story

Folie à Deux (Book 2)

Mermaid Asylum Book 3- Coming early 2020

Short Stories

Come Away With Me: A Short Story

Vice: A Short Story

First printing, January 2019

This is a work of fiction. Names, characters, businesses, places, events and incidents are either the products of the author's imagination or used fictitiously. Any resemblance to actual persons, living or dead, or actual events is purely coincidental. Opinions expressed are those of the characters and do not necessarily reflect those of the author.

Distributed by Outmanned Publishing, LLC

For anyone who has ever believed in me...

For my writing partners for believing in my work.
For my family for believing in my worth.
For my children for believing in my immortality.
For my friends for believing in my soul.
For the fools that have believed in my heart.
And for me for believing in myself.

"What I want is to be needed. What I need is to be indispensable to somebody. Who I need is somebody that will eat up all my free time, my ego, my attention. Somebody addicted to me. A mutual addiction."

-Chuck Palahniuk, Choke

CHAPTER 1

It had been 3,684 days since groundskeepers lowered Max's body into the ground and as many nights since Cressida last dreamed. Ten years. Each time Cressida gasped her first breath in the morning it was like being pulled from the water, her lungs fighting for air, her body learning to live again. It was rebirth without the transformation, without the novelty. The doctors called it Aphantasia, but Cressida called it purgatory: slow, torturous emptiness.

The stiff leather of her wingback chair groaned as Cressida leaned forward to straighten a magazine on the coffee table in front of her. On the other side, Mr. Hamish drummed his thick fingers against the wooden arm of the couch. There was dirt ground under his nails that looked like it had been there for a decade. He could have been one of the men who buried Max that day, except, like most of her patients, he'd lived in Silverside all his life and Max had died thousands of miles away.

The clock on the office wall read 6:52 a.m. Cressida nodded her head in time with Hamish's thumping and sank into the mahogany leather, her eyelids as heavy as her thoughts.

Sunlight streamed through the bay windows behind the sofa. Dawn was the only time of day when her office was alight with color: the red wood of the couch, the gold lettering on the spines of her books, the auburn of Cressida's sleek, shoulder-length bob. Cressida tipped her face into the warmth. The beautiful view wavered and was replaced by Mr. Hamish's opaque silhouette rocking back and forth against the sofa.

He stopped pounding and raised a hand to his sandy beard. "What d'ya think it means, Dr. Dunhill?"

Cressida's eyes flicked to his face. "Which part, exactly?"

"The whole damn thing. It don't make no sense." His brown eyes narrowed into his tanned face. "I fall off my pa's crabbin' boat and at first I'm just in m'skivvies, but the water ain't cold. I'm swimmin' to shore when summit pulls me under. I take a swing, thinkin' it must be a fucking tiger—"

"A tiger?"

"Shark. And a big'un too."

Cressida nodded. "Go on."

"So I'm kickin' an' fightin' but I ain't felt nothin'. No teeth or nothin'. So I turn 'round and alls I see is this fluffy pink cloud." His eyes were wide enough to see the pale sclera around his irises, milky white and tinged with red. He'd been sleeping worse than usual lately. Usually the vivid dreams were merely a nuisance to the no-nonsense fisherman, a force to be reckoned with and healed by a doctor like a cancer, but today something was different. His hands shook in his lap.

The leather chair whimpered its excitement as Cressida selected a pen from the Mason jar on the tall end table beside her, straightening the container ever so slightly when she was done. For once, it might be worth taking notes. The pen was faded black metal, and heavy, with a silver band around the middle and a silver clip at the top. It was the same pen she'd admired her first day in therapy, the one Max had used to describe Cressida in his notes: *angry, suicidal, alone.*

Cressida wrapped her fingers around the pen. The familiar contours of the instrument were comforting, a talisman of the power Max had passed on to her. He once used the pen to label Cressida, to literally define her, but now she was here and he wasn't.

Now the pen belonged to Cressida, and she wasn't angry anymore.

She scratched the worn pen across the notepad in her lap, the sound like white noise in her brain. Comforting and focusing. "So you're being pulled into the depths by a pink cloud?"

Hamish released his breath and it whistled through the straggly hairs above his top lip. "No. That's what I'm tryin' to tell ya. It was a dress. A big fluffy one like my wife wore at our weddin'."

"A dress?" Cressida's eyebrows peaked. Hamish didn't know how lucky he was to have unfettered access to his subconscious mind, to all the pieces of himself that were too overwhelming to process during the bright, waking hours. A life without dreams was like snow-blindness.

"Yeah. Is it a bad sign, Doc?" Hamish wrung his callused hands together and bounced his knee against the coffee table. The smell of perspiration and Pacific sea water filled the room like he'd squeezed it from his pores.

Cressida rolled the pen along the seam of her notebook. After weeks of banal, stress-induced insomnia, Mr. Hamish had finally presented a proper puzzle. Cressida's tired brain sputtered to life. "Dreams, Mr. Hamish, can mean a lot of things, and they aren't always the most obvious interpretation of events."

"What d'ya mean?"

"Dreams are often a backdoor to our consciousness. A filter through which we can deal with things that would otherwise be too scary. Like wearing special glasses to look at the sun during an eclipse." Cressida's voice trailed off. Interpreting dreams was a lot like piecing together a puzzle upside down. She loved the moment she was able to flip it over and reveal her handiwork to her patients.

Hamish shifted. "So you're sayin' it might not really be 'bout me wearin' a poofy dress?"

A smile pulled at the corners of Cressida's mouth. "I'd say there's a good chance that's the case, Mr. Hamish."

His hands dropped to his lap and he wiped the sour sweat onto his brown corduroys. "That's good 'cause my wife an' me just found out last week that our oldest boy is gay. That's about all the bad news I can handle."

Cressida's legs sagged beneath the notepad, upsetting the pen and sending it skittering to the floor. Such a splendidly intricate dream reduced to a paltry show of casual homophobia. Some veils were thinner than others. A cloud passed across the sun and the office dimmed again. Almost into obscurity. The promise of another day was gone.

"Then again," Cressida said, "sometimes dreams are exactly what they seem."

His face blanched. "What do ya mean?"

Cressida stared at the black pen that had settled onto the sea of beige carpet. The exhaustion crept back over her like the shadows across the office. It was all wrong, the pristine rug contrasted against the antiquated pen and Mr. Hamish's muddy shoes bouncing behind it. It was going to be another day like all the rest. Cold, monotonous, and endless. Dreams belonged to those who felt the warmth of the sun, to those who occupied the land of the living. Death was the opposite of dreaming. Cressida was something else entirely: too broken to dream and yet too human not to hope for more. It wasn't fair.

Hamish coughed into his sleeve and used it to wipe his nose. Along with the chill came the thoughts of Max. He moved with the shadows and the wind. Max would have hated Hamish the way Cressida hated the mud on the carpet, both blemishes on their otherwise orderly worlds. She glared at the pen. Hamish might be simple, but at least he wanted to change. They had that in common.

Cressida raised her eyes and pinched a half smile into place. "Well, obviously you're having some trouble accepting your son's sexuality and it's seeping into your subconscious. Maybe next week we should spend some time talking about why you feel that him being gay is dragging you down into the water."

Hamish coughed and the sound rattled in his lungs. "But it don't mean I'm queer too, then?"

Cressida squeezed her hands tight in her lap. All her patients wanted was a connection, just a small moment in a sea of anonymity when they could feel known. It was why they came to her. They couldn't make her flinch. That was her gift to them.

Cressida stood, and stepped around the table to lay a hand on his tense shoulder. "No, I think you're probably safe there." It had taken her years to appreciate the power of human touch to pull the desperate back from the edge. Max never taught her that.

A sigh of relief wafted past the edges of the magazines fanned out on the table behind them. His cooled breath stank of stale beer and cigarettes. *Everyone has their vice.* Her eyes dropped to the pen lying by her feet. She turned her back to the mess, but even as she bid the burly fisherman goodbye she could feel Max breathing down her neck.

When she finally closed the door between them, she bent forward and pressed her forehead against the polished wood, and her eyelids sagged. The restless nights had taken their toll on her sleep. The emptiness wasn't always so bad. There were times she felt almost normal, but the pain and the loss seemed to ebb and wain like the cycles of the moon. Lately it was all she could think about. She squeezed her eyes shut. Exhaustion was bleeding her dry and soon she would disappear completely.

But not today.

Cressida stalked back to the place where the pen had fallen to the carpet and stooped to pick it up.

"No, Max, not today." She laughed out loud at the absurdity of her own voice bouncing off the barren walls of an empty office, squatting beside an inanimate object, imagining it held a power her rational brain knew to be impossible. Ridiculous. If she couldn't rest soon, she might have to consider sleeping pills again. The pen was cold against her skin, and a chill ran down her spine as she recalled the first time she touched it. The night Max died.

The air in the car that night had been frigid and her breath had swirled from her open mouth like smoke from the jaws of a dragon. She hadn't even needed a pen at the time, but she had wanted it. And her heart had fluttered when she'd taken it from Max's pocket. Crouched now in her office, her pulse quickened again. Every sensation leading up to the moment she stole his pen lingered in her mind, crisp and new—and then nothing. Snow-blind.

Fast forward ten years and she was still lost, floating through life in a haze of sleep deprivation. And yet somehow she had washed up on the shores beneath a sand-blasted psychiatric facility the residents of Silverside, Oregon referred to as The Mermaid Asylum. Nestled against the beach, the former inpatient psychiatric hospital was once home to a patient who believed she was a mermaid, complete with a seashell bra. She had tried to swim home to the mermaid kingdom one night, and her body had washed up on the beach behind the building, drowned.

The legend of The Mermaid Asylum hung over the town like a fog, but tragedy called people to the building like a siren. It was the kind of place Cressida might have ended up in another life. If it hadn't been for Max. Working there every day was almost like living in her very own, very vivid nightmare. And it was the main reason Cressida had chosen Silverside to start over. To search for the cure to her Aphantasia. The way back to the land of the living.

Cressida walked the pen back to its place on the side table beside her day planner. She wasn't feeling very hopeful that morning. She was still alone, apart from during her sessions. Only then did she feel the healing power that her profession had bestowed upon her. She was indispensable to her patients. Important. That was going to have to be enough. She could fix them even if she was beyond saving. Besides, she could think of no better place to disappear than an old mental institution turned psychology office.

Keys jangled on the other side of her office door. Must be the therapist across the hall. Dr. Roger Banks had housed his mental health practice in that same building for the last thirty years, almost as long as Cressida had been alive, and had lived in the apartment above for almost as long. Cressida had never been upstairs, but the peeling walls and creaking floors of the ground level were a reminder of the institution's checkered history. Roger's living arrangements seemed an unhealthy lack of boundaries between the personal and professional, but he appeared largely unaffected.

A knock from the office door broke the silence, making her jump. "Just a minute, please."

Cressida quickly leafed through the moleskin appointment book. Her 7:00 a.m. was early. A new patient. Sparse notes in the margins gave almost no information about who was about to walk through the door: *29 year old Viola Marquis, paranoid?* The handwriting was Cressida's, but she couldn't remember speaking with the patient; it must have been another referral from Roger.

Cressida gripped the brass handle hard and swung open the door. "Sorry for the wait. Come on in."

Her limited notes had described the girl on the other side of the door as being twenty-nine, three years younger than Cressida, but this girl was dressed like a teenager. Her tie-dyed tank top and floor-length skirt billowed as she whisked into the room, giving the impression she had jeweled wings on her shoes. Cressida shut the door behind her and leaned her back against it as she watched the girl float toward the sofa.

The girl's skin was bronzed, and her eyes were haloed by the subtlest hints of creases, like she'd spent her short lifetime squinting out to sea. She plopped onto the pale sofa with a fluttering of emerald and ruby fabric. There was glitter all over her. On her eyes, in her short, blond hair, and spilling down the front of her low-cut top. She wasn't wearing a bra. This girl was not Cressida's typical clientele of rough townies and disenfranchised youths. She was raw and exposed like the fresh, pink skin that emerges after you pick an old scab.

Cressida concentrated on the feel of her long sleeves against her arms and tugged the concealing fabric over her wrists. She could hear Max's voice in her head. *You shouldn't pick scabs. It's how scars are formed.*

"Am I early?" The girl's voice was breathy like she'd run up a flight of stairs even though they were on the first floor. Her cheeks were flushed.

"No. You're right on time." Cressida took her seat in the leather chair opposite the girl and stared at the floor. There were tiny shards of glitter working their way into the carpet fibers, grinding down so deep that no vacuum could recover them. This was worse than the mud. Her heart thumped against her chest in a way that was distantly familiar and yet beyond her conscious recollection. Like hearing a lullaby from childhood. Max would not have approved.

Cressida reached for the table without taking her eyes from the girl and retrieved her pen. She was in control now. "Do you prefer Ms. Marquis or Viola?"

"Just Vee."

"Ok, Vee. Would you like to tell me a little bit about yourself?"

The girl pursed her lips to one side and shrugged her shoulders like a child. "There's not much to tell. I was born and raised here in Silverside. Just your average, boring, small-town girl."

"I'm sure that isn't true." Cressida followed the flickering glitter hovering around the girl like a crown. "What do you do for a living, Vee?"

"I teach part time at the local preschool and I've been helping out on my father's fishing boat most mornings to earn some extra cash."

"Commercial fishing? That sounds like a very unique vocation."

Vee scratched her nose with a long fingernail that must have made it very difficult to haul fishing nets out of the ocean. Raised on the wild sea, the girl was like a goddess cursed to walk the earth even though she had no idea how to blend in. Practicality was not a priority for this girl. "Not around here it isn't."

"Okay. Then why don't we start with why you're here?"

The light from the rising sun cast a rainbow of shadows across the girl's face. Cressida's small office was a dreary ocean of sand and dirt, perpetually bland until this water nymph of a girl splashed so much color into every corner that it was almost blinding. She was the dawn on two legs.

Vee tucked her feet under her on the sofa, her shoes scraping against the rough fabric. "Well, like I said when I called the other doctor, my boyfriend thinks I'm paranoid, and I finally decided to call his bluff." She giggled, and Cressida's ears pricked. She was lying. Or he was an idiot. Someone who was paranoid would want to hide their emotions for fear that others might misinterpret them, or they might mask their fears with what they deemed the "correct" response. This girl was doing neither.

"Paranoid is a pretty strong word. What do you think?"

"I think he's a liar and a fucking cheater." Bingo. A flutter of excitement gripped Cressida's stomach. She exhaled with as much control as she could muster. She counted the seconds between breaths. *One. Two. Three.*

Finally, Cressida inhaled again. "Then why come here? Why not just break up with him?"

Vee tipped her head as if that were a satisfactory response to the question. Clearly, the girl wanted Cressida to wonder about her, to yearn for more. Around here, people must have thought she materialized from another planet.

Cressida gripped Max's pen hard, and she could feel him itching to darken the clean, white page of her notebook with thoughts about this girl: a diagnosis, a treatment, a judgment. Max was always logical. Always thinking. Cressida's mind was no longer sticky and sluggish. The promise of the dawn had finally delivered. This girl wasn't so easy to decrypt as Hamish had been. Vee was something new, and her dreams had yet to disclose her secrets. Cressida held her tongue and waited for Vee to tell her more, to reach out for that universal connection. Even the darkest mysteries eventually revealed themselves, the most willful eventually begged to submit.

Vee's eyes wandered the room as freely as her skirt had flowed when she'd entered the office. She was completely without restraint and yet totally in control. Her eyes danced from Cressida's face to the floor-to-ceiling bookshelves and finally landed on a row of tattered books along the top shelf. Her eyebrows lifted. All the classics were there: Homer, Sophocles, Virgil. Shakespeare and Chaucer. The ancient volumes were the only literature among the shelves of crisp, new textbooks, diagnostic manuals, and academic journals: worn islands among a sea of the unsullied.

The girl stood from the couch and approached the wide shelves that spanned the wall of the office. Cressida's spine stiffened as Vee browsed the shelves, running her fingers along the tidy rows of journals and textbooks. Most patients barely glanced at Cressida's shelves, as if their contents were merely a backdrop before which to play out their fantasy of what therapy was supposed to be like. The books provided façade of safety and control that allowed her patients to see Cressida as she wanted to be perceived. She was a healer.

But Vee's fingers—searching, intimate, and violating—probed the illusion like no one had bothered before. It was as if Vee had walked her hands over each of Cressida's vertebra as well. Cressida wanted to stop her, wanted to shout at her to sit back down, but that wouldn't have been professional. It wouldn't have been allowed. The excitement in Cressida's stomach soured and the air in the room tasted stale. The girl touched everything, leaving her oil, her skin, and her fucking glitter in her wake.

"You don't have any photos around." The girl spoke more to herself than to Cressida. Vee tipped a book away from the shelf and frowned at the cover. Not enough color, perhaps. Twenty-nine years old. This girl was more like a child.

Cressida spoke softly through gritted teeth. "This is a place of business." She folded her arms, sweat tickling the back of her neck, and hugged her shirt to her chest. "I like to keep it that way."

Cressida was not prepared, not in control. She was at the mercy of this impulsive girl, helplessly watching as Vee trapesed across her borders and dragged long hidden feelings along with her. Cressida's skin prickled with cold sweat. The Emptiness from earlier that morning might have been preferable to this.

Vee stretched onto her toes, pulled down a blue leather-bound copy of *The Aeneid* and flipped through the pages. Dust sprang from the thin paper as her fingers traced the words. Cressida sucked clean air into her lungs and held her breath. It had been years since she'd touched those particular books. Not even to clean.

Unable to part with the books completely, she'd laid them to rest on her highest shelves. Reminders of her past. Like Max's pen. Souvenirs were the closest thing she had to dreams, but now their filth invaded the room, trickling down from the ceiling like black snow. Cressida scratched deep trembling marks across the page with the tip of Max's pen. *Boundaries.*

"I wouldn't have pegged you for a fan of the classics." Vee closed the book and curled around it on the sofa as if she was lounging in her own living room. Her dirty feet rested on the sofa cushion, real sand meeting the sandy hue of the fabric.

Cressida's skin crawled. Cressida had never encountered a patient like Vee before, never been tested so mercilessly. Was this how Max had felt about her that first day in his office. *Angry.* Maybe Cressida had shaken Max the way this girl had unsettled her. Vee. What kind of name was that, anyway?

Cressida took a deep breath and focused on the task at hand. She tapped the back of the pen to the paper and with each thump she repeated two words. *No past. No present. No future. Just this.* Just Vee, the puzzle now scattered across the sofa. Calm shimmered over her like the glitter that emanated from the girl. She had come here for a reason, for a connection. Just like everyone else. She was nothing more than Hamish wrapped in glittery paper.

Cressida needed a way into her mind. Just a foothold. "What do you think the books imply?"

Vee ran her fingers along the gold embellishments on the front cover of the book. Her long nails scraped across the worn leather with a soft hiss. Cressida held her breath and the tension between them hung in the air like a poisonous fog. Vee finally met Cressida's gaze with savage eyes.

"That you're a fraud."

CHAPTER 2

Blood rushed to Cressida face, hot and unwelcome. Her fist clenched around Max's pen, the silver clip gouging into her palm. Words rasped in Cressida's throat like they weren't hers. "Why would you say I was a fraud?"

"Because..." Vee's sapphire eyes met the cool grey of Cressida's and she wrinkled her nose, as if what she was about to say disgusted her. "Books like these are meant to be loved, not packed away on a shelf out of reach. And not surrounded by hard lines and sterile whites. Books aren't just things you own, they own you. Unless you're just completely full of shit and only display them to trick people into believing you're more sophisticated than you are."

Cressida clenched her jaw hard to keep her quivering chin from giving her away. Patients weren't supposed to see her flinch. Her breath came in shallow drags. She was overreacting. Surely, this girl was just another patient lashing out at their therapist instead of confronting her own problems. She couldn't know that Cressida's blood was pounding in her ears, that her skin was on fire, or how hard she worked to hide her disdain for those books. It had to be all in Cressida's mind. Max would have told her to get ahold of herself.

Cressida unclenched her fists and turned her palms to the ceiling. She rested the backs of her hands on her lap and willed calm through her body. Patients came to Cressida for her to reflect back at them like a mirror: one-way and impenetrable. They didn't want to know her, and she was happy to oblige. The relationship they craved was about relinquishing control and the thrill of not caring about anything or anyone but themselves. Just for a moment. This girl was no different. "You obviously feel very strongly about the books. Talk to me about how they make *you* feel."

"They make me feel like I shouldn't be here." Vee's eyes flashed but she made no move to leave.

"Why is that?"

Vee shrugged and crossed her feet on top of the coffee table, the coveted Virgil forgotten in her lap.

There was gum stuck to the bottom of her battered sandal. Cressida's eyes locked on several red hairs- her hairs- protruding from the smudge of flattened gum. Hair and glitter. Vee must have tracked it from across the carpet. And now she was sitting there waiting for Cressida to say something, to reclaim the power she seemed to have lost when Vee touched her books. Yet all Cressida could think about were those hairs on her carpet.

Cressida shook her head. "Tell me about your boyfriend. You said he thinks you're paranoid?"

"I'm not really in the mood to talk about it anymore."

Something had changed, as if Cressida had failed some unspoken test. Cressida leaned back against her leather chair. Her instincts were off with this girl. She scratched her temple with the back of Max's pen. Perhaps the lack of sleep had finally dulled her wits. "Well, that's up to you, but you must have come here looking for some kind of answers."

"Maybe I was just curious about this place." Vee nodded her head toward the sea, sensing its presence without seeing, as if even indoors she could feel it calling to her.

Disappointment bloomed in Cressida's gut like a relentless weed. Some people couldn't resist the spectacle of the asylum. Like children to the pied piper, they were drawn to its sorrow, to its grotesque grey spires jutting out from among the cheery seaside town like the horns of the Kraken. They'd make any excuse to get inside. Vee had seemed different, genuine, but maybe she was just another thrill seeker looking to cross an urban legend off her bucket list. Cressida sighed and placed the notebook on the side table on top of the moleskin planner and laid Max's pen over both. Dissapointed twice in one morning. What a day.

Vee watched quietly as Cressida slid the pen down to the center of the notebook until the angle between it and the top edge was precisely ninety degrees. Cressida coughed and sent a piece of glitter sparkling into the air between her and the girl, catching the morning light and then falling to the carpet beside the coffee table. Vee giggled.

That was enough.

Max wouldn't have allowed such behavior. Cressida had other patients who needed her time, who needed a real connection. Patients who needed *her*. Cressida stood, nearly toppling the leather chair behind her. The girl was mocking her, stealing her time, and violating her things. She stepped around the table to where Vee was sitting and without a word, held out her palm for Vee to return the book. Her fingers trembled in the air between them.

Vee smiled before handing it over, unfazed by Cressida's unprofessional reaction. Maybe even pleased. There was a small gap between her front teeth. It was the kind of thing an orthodontist should have fixed, making her flawless. But on this girl it didn't seem like a flaw. Or maybe it was her flaws that made her so infuriating, and so fascinating.

The smell of dust, salt, and something sweet—maybe strawberries—filled the space around them, and Cressida turned away to keep from sneezing. She walked back to the shelf and stretched onto her toes. The girl had seemed so delicate as she drifted into the office, but she must have been tall because Cressida could barely reach the space left by the book without climbing onto the lowest shelf to hoist the volume back into its rightful place. Vee had made it seem so effortless.

Cressida's sleeve brushed the undisturbed surface and the white silk came away coated with dust as thick and dark as ash. She was overwhelmed with an urge to wash her hands. Her skin itched and Cressida wondered if the dust and glitter had invaded her pores. She jammed her hands into her pockets and turned back to the girl.

"So where were we?"

Vee was sitting further down the sofa from where she had been a moment before, her long, turquoise fingernails tapping against the wooden arm, exactly the way Hamish's had an hour earlier. Yet the two patients couldn't be more different. Hamish's constant and dependable presence had been replaced by Vee's fidgeting hands and darting eyes. Where he had yearned for Cressida to define him, to ground him in reality, Vee refused to conform. She was mesmerizing to watch like a traffic accident waiting to happen.

Cressida cocked her head to the side and regarded the girl with cool suspicion. Without breaking eye contact, Vee picked a piece of glitter from the sofa cushion and held it on the pad of her finger, examining it for a moment before she blew it into the air and into oblivion.

"On second thought, I don't really feel like talking at all today." Vee's bare skin scraped against the bottom of the cushion, as if she hadn't shaved her legs in several days. Something in her demeanor had shifted like the wind and suddenly she couldn't get away from the office fast enough. Her skirt billowed as she glided across the room, running her hand along the soft leather of Cressida's empty chair on her way toward the door, moving it just enough to throw off the careful angles. A smile crept across the girl's face as Cressida's narrowed eyes tracked her across the room.

The protective wall of professionalism and restraint that Cressida had painstakingly assembled had turned to dust. She could have asked the girl to leave, but that would have meant admitting defeat, that this girl was somehow beyond her help. Every day since the accident, Cressida had battled to regain control, both of her professional days and her empty nights. The senselessness of it all made her head spin. But surely Vee wasn't here to toy with her. She was just a normal girl with an asshole for a boyfriend and a penchant for wearing too much body glitter. Not exactly the stuff of nightmares.

Cressida crossed the room to where the girl stood waiting by the door, as if she was asking permission to leave. Daring Cressida to take charge of the interaction. Perhaps she needed a reason to stay. "Your session just started. You're welcome to leave, but I'm going to have to bill you for the full hour."

Vee shrugged and scraped her long nails along the dry skin on the back of her hands. "I'll just tell my boyfriend it was his fault. Maybe he'll stop making wild accusations about my mental health if he sees the cost."

Money wasn't Vee's weakness, but everyone had one. Cressida needed more time to find Vee's. There had to be a way to nail her down. "Well, if that doesn't work, you're always welcome to make another appointment."

"I might do that." She reached for the door handle but paused before turning the brass knob. "One more thing. All your degrees and the plaque on your door list your name as Dr. C. Dunhill."

Cressida raised her eyebrows beneath the fringe of her straight bangs. "That's correct."

"What's your first name?"

"Cressida." She'd stopped advertising her first name because patients were spending the first fifteen minutes of their sessions questioning her about its origin or trying to impress her with their knowledge of Greek mythology.

Vee smiled and nodded her pixie head. "I get it now."

There it was again, the feeling that this girl could see right through her. It was dangerous and exhilarating, like getting caught naked in the shower. "What do you get?"

"They're your parents' books." Vee pointed at the bookshelf over Cressida's shoulder. To *that* shelf. "That's why they don't belong." She beamed and the sun glinted off her dangling earrings. Red, orange and yellow beads cascaded down her neck like lava from a volcano. They looked homemade. The kind of project doctors assign patients in mental institutions to keep their minds busy.

"The books were my mother's." Cressida brushed her hair behind her ear, wondering what her lobes would look like pierced. Her mother would never have stood for such a thing.

"I knew it! Cressida, from *Troilus and Cressida*." She sighed. "I wish I had a story behind my name, but I don't."

"Viola. You weren't named for the character in *Twelfth Night*?"

"Oh God, no. The closest my parents ever got to Shakespeare was a Mel Gibson movie. I think maybe my mom liked listening to string quartets or something, but they never told me. She died when I was a kid."

"Well, maybe it's better that you don't know. My mother was all about subtext, and sometimes it's better that stuff stays buried." Cressida's voice sounded far away, like she was speaking to Vee from another plane. Or maybe from a dream. The exhaustion pulled at her limbs and she leaned against the wall for stability.

"That must make for interesting Thanksgiving conversation."

"She's dead." Cressida bit down on her cheek. She was revealing too much, becoming a window rather than a mirror. Completely out of control. She reached around the girl and opened the door to the hallway.

Vee didn't budge. "That's too bad."

"Not really." A bead of sweat tickled the back of Cressida's knee. The sun had risen higher in the sky and was now blaring through the bay windows and casting a molten glare throughout the office. Only Vee's slender body was spared by Cressida's shadow looming into the foyer. "If you like Shakespearean names so much, why don't you go by Viola? Why Vee?"

"It just feels more...like me." Vee bobbed her shoulders again and disappeared into the hallway, her skirt flapping behind her.

Cressida shook her head. It was possible this girl was all for show. Bright swirls of color masking a blank canvas. Beyond even Cressida's power to save. Yet her mind raced with possibilities. Even now she hoped the girl would return and prove her wrong. The nervous energy drained from the room and trailed behind Vee toward the front door, swept up in her skirt. It didn't make any sense, but Cressida's office felt emptier than usual now that the girl was gone. Emaciated. Hungry.

Cressida closed the office door and surveyed the room. Everything Vee had touched was askew, as if a tiny earthquake had shaken the room upon her arrival. Cressida's appointment book lay open on the side table, turned to the page for next week. She was sure she had not left it open. She walked around the back of the leather chair and turned the book around so she could read the words etched onto the page.

It wasn't Cressida's handwriting. It was larger, flowery and impractical, like the girl herself. There were loops in the V of Vee and it was written across the entire entry for next Friday. There was no room left for other appointments. No order. In a matter of minutes, Vee had left her mark on everything in Cressida's clean life. Reason would have her cancel the girl's next appointment, but her stomach lurched at the thought. There was no reason to see Vee again. Nothing to be gained. She hadn't asked Cressida for help, only taken what she wanted. Yet Cressida yearned for one more session. It wasn't logical. She'd allowed the girl and the glitter get under her skin.

Cressida ripped the page from the book and crumpled it to the floor. She paced the perimeter of the room, studying every object between the sofa and the office door. The Mason jar beside the planner was off center and the wingback chair was crooked, punching new holes in the Berber carpet. Cressida dropped to her knees in front of the heavy chair and repositioned it onto its usual dents. Then she fished the torn appointment page from beneath the chair, and flatted it against her hand. *There.* Everything was back to as it should be.

Still on her knees, she lowered her head to the cracked leather of her chair and breathed deep and low—as close as she ever got to praying. Oxygen filled her lungs, deep and cool, and she felt her blood pressure return to normal. A break. She needed a break.

A soft knock on the door interrupted her respite. It was only 7:30 a.m. Too early for her next appointment. The knocking intensified until it echoed across the room. Her heart still thumped in her chest and the irritation flowed like fire in her veins. She didn't like surprises. Cressida dragged herself to her feet and opened the door to find Roger's red face smiling back at her with his horse teeth and wooly bear caterpillar eyebrows. He was wearing a Lycra top stretched across his wide chest and shorts that revealed the smooth muscles of his thighs. In one hand was a bike helmet and in the other a half-empty bottle of yellow Gatorade. Dr. Roger Banks believed cycling to town every day would make him live forever. He probably should have known better.

"Good morning, Doctor Banks."

"Miss Dunhill. For the hundredth time, please call me Roger." He sighed and scuffed his shoe across the threshold of Cressida's office. "I just wanted to check in and see how everything went with Miss Marquis this morning."

Cressida stepped back into her office. "Yes, thank you for referring her to me. She seems like a handful, but I'm hopeful I can get through to her."

A satisfied smirk oozed across Roger's face. "Wonderful. I thought she'd be a good fit for you."

"Oh? Why do you say that?"

Roger grinned. "Because of her dreams."

"Dreams?"

"Yeah, when she called reception last week it was as if you were tailor-made for each other, given your unusual interest in dream analysis." His thin hair circled the bald spot on the top of his head like a whirlpool, Charybdis on his scalp, waiting to swallow her.

The thought of the Greek myth reminded Cressida of Vee's observations about her books and her chest tightened. "Oh. Right."

Roger tapped his skull with a finger and laughed.

The muscles in Cressida's cheeks hardened. Vee hadn't mentioned anything about dreams during their short session. Perhaps there was more to the colorful creature than just glitter and pretense. Perhaps Vee wanted help after all. Perhaps she'd be back.

"Yes, she and I will have a lot to talk about at her appointment next week. Thank you again."

Roger's fingers lingered on the wooden frame beside his head, stopping Cressida from shutting the door and retreating back into her office. "Speaking of dreams, I saved an article for you the other day. From *Scientific American*."

She had a subscription to the same journal. Roger knew that because he picked up the mail each morning. Cressida frowned. "Which one?"

"About the role of dreams in forming memories. Seemed right up your alley." He winked.

She had read study after study about head trauma and memory loss, but not one of them could explain why the accident had affected her ability to dream. Cressida dragged her hand across her tired eyes, their lids as dry and thin as paper. There had to be a solution out there somewhere. "That sounds great. Thank you."

"Great. I've got it in my office somewhere." He turned

sideways and held a hand out toward the hallway. "Care to join me?"

The familiar appeal of her worn sofa beckoned her, but curiosity and desperation urged her forward as it always did. She couldn't end up lost in the oblivion of her dreamless sleep forever, trapped and terrified, waiting for someone to find her curled up in the back of a cave. She nodded as she stepped into the hallway and closed her office door behind her.

CHAPTER 3

Dr. Roger Banks's office was a mirror image of Cressida's. Their identical closets met at the back, and there were matching bookshelves and bay windows framing the room. Back when the asylum had housed anywhere from twenty to fifty patients, these two rooms had served as dormitories. It was difficult to imagine rows of cots lined up along the walls that were now stacked with books, but Roger had framed black and white pictures in the entryway: poster-sized images of scattered souls wandering the rooms in white robes and slippered feet.

Though structurally the rooms were twins, Roger's dusty shelves were filled with awkwardly piled books, grouped together without thought or form. Pieces of his life were scattered around his office like breadcrumbs. There were crooked photos of his him and his wife on the summits of mountains and one of his wife in her wedding gown, all luridly displayed for everyone to see. Stephen King novels lay sideways on top of past issues of *Psychology Today* magazines. There were food-stained cookbooks splayed on top of the upright diagnostic manuals and medical references. His journals weren't even in chronological order.

It was pandemonium.

Roger's grand oak desk was littered with papers and the remnants of yesterday's lunch. He gestured for Cressida to sit in the chair across the desk and then brushed past her on his way to his own seat. The back of his hand grazed her shoulder and she could feel the damp heat from his body through her shirt. Deflecting Roger's impotent advances was the last thing Cressida felt doing after the morning she'd had.

She sat down hard in the chair and crossed her legs. The half smile she'd plastered on her face as soon as she opened the door wavered slightly, but Roger wasn't paying attention. Without a word, he swept some of the sheets to the floor and squinted at the others.

"Ah, here it is." Roger flipped over a small stack clipped together with a pink paperclip, and slid it across the desk toward Cressida. His eyes followed her hands as she reached out to examine the article.

The paper was from two years ago, and only marginally related to her research. It was about memory retrieval through dreaming and had very little to say about the actual mechanism of dreams. As usual. Her heart sank. "Thanks—"

Roger coughed and leaned forward over the desk, so close she could smell coffee on his breath. "Listen, I know you value your autonomy, but we really should schedule that progress meeting we've been skirting around. I am supposed to be supervising you, after all."

Cressida forced a laugh from the depths of her gut. This was the real reason for his visit. So depressingly predictable. Brown and grey and bland like the rest of her life. Was this the best she could hope for her life? She'd successfully avoided Roger's attention for months, ever since he offered to drive her home after hours one night.

"I'm doing fine, really." She hovered over her chair, ready to leave.

"Well, you've been working here for a while now and we've never really had a discussion about how you feel you're fitting in at the practice." He raised his eyebrows at the chair, and waited for Cressida to return to her seat.

Cressida bit the inside of her lip and sat back down. "I think it's going well. The patients are engaging and I'm able to keep the early hours I prefer."

"Yes, the great thing about living in a fishing town is there are plenty of people up before the sun."

"I agree."

"I've heard only the best reports about your competence as a therapist." Roger loomed over the desk, appearing much larger than usual. His pupils were dilated making his already dark eyes appear black. "But aside from the patients, how are you finding Silverside?"

"I stay pretty busy at work."

"I've noticed that you are spending a lot of time in the office. I'm worried you might be fixating on your job in a way that isn't healthy."

Cressida inclined her head, but didn't respond. Her head throbbed.

Roger walked around the bulky desk and stood beside Cressida's chair, blocking her quickest route to the door. His thick, coarse arm hair was visible through his white shirt. "Everyone needs a friend. Even therapists."

"I'm fine. Really." Cressida's throat tightened around the words.

Roger curled his tongue over his teeth as he smiled. "Miss Dunhill, this isn't a test. This is about reaching out."

"I have friends." Cressida pulled the paper clip from the article in front of her and straightened the metal, running her fingertip over the sharp end. Max would have told her to run.

Roger's hand fell against the back of her chair, inches from her ear. "You know, if you ever need anything you can always ask."

She was trapped. If Roger touched her, would she have the strength to jam the paper clip into his arm? He was taller than her, solid muscle deceptively hidden behind a layer of fat, but she was tough. And she had nothing to lose. "I don't think I need help."

Roger threw up his hands and laughed great chortles that reverberated in his chest. "No. I don't suppose you do." He retreated to the edge of his desk, his red face impassive.

The blood drained from Cressida's face and her body felt limp as though she'd sprung a leak. "I appreciate your concern, but I'm doing just fine."

"Just make sure you have something outside this place."

Outside was exactly where she wanted to be. She rose from the chair and bid him goodbye.

"Doctor Dunhill?" Roger called from behind her. "If you ever need anything, I'm right next door." He brought his fingers to his forehead and tipped an invisible hat toward her.

"I know," she said. "Thank you."

Cressida fled back into the hallway, her limbs as cold and numb as if they were made of gelatin. When she finally closed her office door between them, she bent forward and pressed her forehead against the polished wood, and her eyelids sagged. The restless nights had taken their toll on her sleep. Her anxiety was out of control. Roger wasn't dangerous. She was reading too much into his intentions. She squeezed her eyes shut. Exhaustion was bleeding her dry and soon she would disappear completely.

But not today.

Not today, Max.

Instinctively she crossed the room and collapsed into her leather chair. She reached her arm toward the side table, searching for Max's pen. Her fingers anticipated the cool touch of the metal, but found only rough paper and smooth glass. *Where was it?* She sat up straight in her chair, the muscles in her back hardened to stone. The pen was all she had left of Max. It had to be there. It couldn't be lost. Her stomach flipped. She'd already lost everything. She couldn't lose Max too.

She couldn't be left all alone.

In the dreamless dark.

The chair creaked as she hovered over the table casting an ominous shadow across the glass top. Her notepad was there, open to the empty page decorated with Cressida's scribbling and the words *Viola Marquis* scrawled across the top. The day planner was tucked beside it, the crumpled page containing Vee's appointment jutting haphazardly out the side. But no pen. Cressida checked between the pages of the notebook, under her legs in the chair, and between cushion and the arms.

On all fours she scoured beneath the chair and the coffee table finding heaps of glitter but nothing larger. Cressida's heart rate sped against her chest, hammering blood through her veins until she could hear nothing else. She tore at the glitter stuck to the carpet as if Max's pen could be hidden somewhere beneath. Max's pen was gone, just like he was. Dry sobs racked her chest and she slumped to the floor. Her cheek itched against the fibrous carpet, Hamish's mud, and Vee's glitter. It was all she had left.

Outside, rain beat against the bay windows behind Cressida, pulsing with the tidal winds, as if she was hearing the collective heartbeat of the small seaside town. The door rattled behind her and Cressida jumped to her feet. Her hands shook as she brushed glitter from her knees. The knocking was hurried, panicked, and she could see shadows pacing under the door. Someone was intent on seeing her.

Cressida pulled open the door to find Roger rubbing his knuckles and huffing from the exertion. His face was pale again and his eyes no longer opaque.

Not again. Cressida made no effort to shield him from her frustration. "What?"

"I'm sorry to bother you again, but I just received a call from St. Luke's." The creases beside his eyes deepened. "They need a consult on a young girl who's refusing to cooperate with police. I don't know the details, but I recognized the name. Sam Wolfe. She's a patient of yours, isn't she?"

The heat drained from Cressida's face and cold sweat tingled at her scalp. Sam was in the hospital refusing to talk to the cops. *That bastard finally put her in the hospital.* "I have to go. Now."

Roger nodded. "I'll drive you."

CHAPTER 4

Hospitals always smelled the same: stagnant chemicals, like hopelessness and sterilized death. Cressida steeled herself against it and followed the bleached white tiles to the nurses' station on the fourth floor. Leaning against the counter, navy blue pants pulled up high over his waistline, was a local police officer deep in conversation with a young nurse with curly red hair and a bored expression on her face.

Cressida approached the counter and cleared her throat. The nurse poked her head from behind the desk, but the cop didn't acknowledge Cressida's presence beside him.

"What do you say you let me back in there so I can do my job and stop darkening your doorstep?" The officer rested his elbow on the counter, his chin in his hand. He had almost black hair and a dark mustache that looked like it belonged on the set of a 1970s porno. A tuft of curled chest hair protruded from the collar of his uniform shirt.

The nurse pulled at a tendril of orange hair. "You know I can't do that. She has rights. She didn't do anything wrong."

The nurse craned her head around the cop's broad shoulders and smiled at Cressida. "Can I help you—"

The cop cut her off with a snort. "The Hell with that *she* business. I've known Bud Wolfe's kid his whole life, and a little make up and a dress isn't gonna change the fact that *he* attacked me. Don't make me get a court order."

Cressida stepped around him. "Excuse me, I'm looking for Sam Wolfe's room? I believe *she* is a patient here."

The nurse stared up at Cressida with hazel eyes and pursed lips. "And you are?"

"I'm Doctor Dunhill from the Silverside Counseling Group. I got a call saying Sam had been hurt, but I don't have all the details. Is she okay?"

The nurse leaned over the counter and shot a dirty look at the cop. "Are you her doctor?"

"No."

The nurse frowned. "We found your card in her wallet and assumed she was under your care. We hoped you could help us get through to her. She hasn't been particularly...cooperative."

"But she's conscious? Can I talk to her?"

The cop puffed out his chest and towered over Cressida. "Conscious? I'll say. Son of a bitch damn near scratched my eye out earlier." He pressed a fingertip to an angry gash above his left eye.

Cressida had seen much worse, and her head itched beneath her own bruise. Sam had good aim. Ignoring the cop, she once again appealed to the young nurse. "What room is she in?"

"403, but the doctor is with her now."

"Okay. I'll wait." Cressida leaned her back against the counter and folded her arms across her chest. She wished she still had her sweater.

The cop laughed. "Not so fun being kept out of the loop, is it?"

"Ignore him. We all do." The nurse rolled her eyes at the cop and smiled at Cressida. "Oh good. Here's Dr. Schneider now."

"Melody, can you make sure Miss Wolfe's chart is up to date?" The doctor was young and blond and reminded Cressida of Doogie Howser. He slid a manila folder onto the counter across from the nurse, who smiled and nodded.

The cop turned to the doctor. "Look, we need to get a statement from Sam, and he's not cooperating. We know he's in the system, but it's pretty clear someone beat the hell out of him, and given his...uh...lifestyle, we're considering this a hate crime. I just need to confirm the kid's story. I'm not the bad guy here."

The doctor bristled. "Officer Neal. Miss Wolfe prefers to be referred to in the female gender, and I believe she's earned it. I've already told you she doesn't want to answer any questions today. She isn't up to it, and I agree with her. You and I can both agree she's been through enough, and until she is no longer my patient, I'm going to look out for *her* best interest over yours."

Officer Neal rolled his eyes and turned to Cressida. "You need to convince...the kid...that talking to me *is* in everyone's best interest."

Cressida fixed the cop with a hard stare. "At this point, I'm not sure it is."

The system wasn't designed to protect people like Sam. Her father had visibly beaten her for years, but Sam had a history of running away as a teenager, drug use, and casual sex. Sam wasn't a pretty victim, and her father was a good old boy. He was probably drinking buddies with Officer Neal, here.

Officer Neal threw up his hands. "Fine, I'm going to get a cup of coffee. I could walk into that room and arrest him right now for assaulting an officer. He's over eighteen. But I don't need that kind of paperwork. Just get him—*her*—to talk." He stalked off down the hallway.

The nurse rounded the counter and appeared beside the doctor. She gestured at Cressida with her chin. "This is Doctor Dunhill. She's the psychologist whose card we found in Miss Wolfe's wallet."

The doctor smiled and stuck out his steady hand. "Nice to meet you, Doctor. Is Miss Wolfe a patient of yours?"

Cressida shook her head. "No, but she's not close with her family. Please, I only want to know if she's okay. What happened?"

Dr. Schneider took a step closer to Cressida, his posture softening along with his eyes. "We all just want to help, and I can see you do too."

"I do."

He chewed his lip. "Look, I can't officially give you access to Miss Wolfe since you're not family or one of her doctors, but she's asleep right now in room 403. If you'd like to just take a moment with her, for your own peace of mind, I wouldn't stop you."

"Thank you, Doctor."

Cressida's heart raced as she approached the door to room 403. Nothing had been right since Sam left, but maybe now they would get a second chance. Sam needed her now more than ever. She would come home, and everything would be okay again.

Shy, secretive, and confused, Cressida had felt an instant connection to Sam, the gangly boy with the long hair and smudged eyeliner whose place had shared a wall with her own. Cressida used to stay up late listening to him clomping around in awkward heels, watched him buy his first dress, and wept along with him during his gender reassignment consultation. They had been friends. Until she woke up one morning last week and Sam was gone. Without even saying goodbye. It didn't make sense.

In the sterile room, strands of sleek, dark hair fanned around Sam's head on the pillow, like snakes from Medusa's scalp. Her lips were swollen and split and her usually pink skin was blackened and tinged with yellow. Her long, slender nose looked broken. Her closed eyelids were fluttering as she dreamed and her chest rose and fell in time with the steady beep of the monitor. Cressida sat down in a chair beside the head of the bed. She leaned forward and touched the rough tape connecting Sam's IV tube to her arm.

The skin beneath the clear tape was pale and pinched. Cressida couldn't look away. It had to have hurt. Irritation pricked at her skin like needles. Surely, it was someone's job in this hospital to look out for Sam, to keep her from feeling uncomfortable or hurt or scared. It was such a simple thing to fix, unlike the rest of her pain. This is why Sam needed her. To shelter her from the real world, from the world that has never been kind to lost or broken girls. They needed to stick together. Cressida picked at the corner of the tape and it peeled easily away from Sam's skin. Blood rushed back to the pinched flesh.

Startled, Sam sat up in the bed. She grimaced as she focused her deep brown eyes on Cressida and her cracked lips pursed into something resembling a smile. "What are you doing here?"

Cressida propped her elbow on the waffled hospital blanket. "What are you talking about? Of course I'm here. Sam, what happened?"

Tears sprang to Sam's eyes and clung to her long eyelashes before dripping onto the butterfly bandage holding together the battered flesh of her cheek. She sniffed but didn't wipe the tears. It probably hurt too much. "I think you know what happened."

"Why would you go back to your father after everything he's done to you?" Cressida grasped the girl's hand and squeezed. Her bones felt delicate like the wings of a bird.

Sam pulled her hand away. "What choice did I have?"

"You could have stayed with me."

Sam turned her cheek and her voice cracked. "It doesn't matter anyway. Nothing will ever

be any different for me."

Cressida leaned further toward the bed and reclaimed Sam's shuddering hand. "That's not true. Once you get back home things will be better. The way they were always supposed to be. I'll help you."

Sam snorted and then winced in pain. She tugged her hand away from Cressida and folded it with the other across her chest. "No. You've done enough."

Cressida sat back in her chair. "You can't just give up. I won't let you."

Sam shook her head again and then turned her face toward the opposite wall. "I just want to sleep. Will they make me leave today? I want to stay here."

Cressida closed her eyes, but blood thumped in her temples. Sam was broken. She'd failed Sam. Failed to protect her. Her chest felt heavy, like someone had scooped out her insides and replaced them with sand. It wasn't enough. It never was. There must be something more she can do. "I can probably get you a few days in the psych unit for a suicide watch. I could get Roger to pull some strings with the hospital. It's not The Hilton, but the cops won't be able to bother you there. Is that what you want?

Her eyes widened. "You'd do that?"

"Absolutely. I wish I could do more."

"There's nothing more to do for me." Sam's eyelids were heavy and her whole body seemed to sink into the mattress, as if knowing she could stay in the hospital for another night or two had relaxed every muscle. How bad must it have been at her father's house?

"I'll come back tomorrow to check on you."

Sam's voice was barely above a whisper. "Don't." She closed her eyes and the beeping on the monitor slowed. Her lashes fluttered a few times and then stilled again as exhaustion and pain medication dragged Sam back into whatever dream Cressida had interrupted earlier.

Cressida hoped Sam's dreams would take her somewhere safe. Somewhere better than here. Maybe they would take her back home. To her real home. Cressida checked her phone. She had to get back to her office before her next patient arrived.

On her way out of the hospital, Cressida peered into each window along the hallway. Narrow beds filled the rooms, entwined with tubes and wires, surrounded by monitors, spotlights and instruments. Some of the beds were empty and others were littered with sad stories of people whose lives were supposed to lead them somewhere else. Ten years ago Cressida had been one of those people: confused after the accident, lost and hurt, and wishing she was anywhere else. Completely helpless. How had everything gone so wrong as to end up in a place like this?

Sam was probably wondering the same thing herself.

CHAPTER 5

When her office was finally empty, and the last of the daylight had receded back out the bay windows like the tide pulling away from the shore, Cressida slumped across the burlap sofa in her office. Today had been a long day and her weary thoughts were pounding incessantly in her head. She had failed Sam by trusting the system to care for a lost girl. Had she helped anyone? Even Hamish had left unresolved. Max's pen was gone, probably forever, and now she was left alone with her inadequacies.

Her head throbbed and her patients were hopeless and somebody had moved the fucking coffee table. Again. She groaned into the crook of her elbow as it draped across her face. Exhaustion called to her like a siren waiting to dash her against the rocks, and she was powerless to resist. She laid across the sofa, feeling her breath turn shallow and her heartbeat slow. She couldn't fight it any longer. Dreamless sleep is heavy and paralyzing, more like death than rest, and Cressida was never refreshed. Never reborn.

Then suddenly, the darkness lifted.

The couch fabric was itchy on her face and she tried to raise an arm to claw the skin from her skull. But she couldn't move. Snow fell through the twisted gash in the roof of Max's sports car. That car was the only thing Max had loved more than himself. Cressida's heart thumped, and her chest filled with an electric pain so intense she couldn't breathe. No. Not quite pain. It was something new, amorphous. She was *scared*. Everything sparkled: the snow, the shards of safety glass from the windshield, and Max. She was back at the scene of the accident that killed Max. She was remembering.

She hadn't seen Max's face in ten years, but there he was.

She had forgotten how beautiful he was, even in death. Strong and cool. Max's dark hair fell across his forehead and mixed with the blood oozing from his temples. It was black as oil, but flakes of colorful snow were dropping into the murk, melting and swirling into a rainbow. Not snow. Glitter. The bright white light bouncing off the snow fractured into a thousand colors, like Cressida was a prism, and she was surrounded by the most vivid hues she'd ever seen. It hurt her eyes, and as she shielded her face from the light, a figure stepped out of the shimmer. Yellow hair, emerald eyes, and turquoise nails. Light poured from the woman's silhouette. Cressida looked down for Max but his body had melted into a pool of liquid color.

No, not yet! She needed to see more.

But Max was gone, stolen again from her mind in the wake of the same accident. Yet this time something was different. There was more. The woman from the light reached out a hand and touched Cressida's shoulder, and instantly the pain in Cressida's chest gave way to a spreading warmth. *Peace*.

Cressida jerked awake and pulled her damp face away

from the rough sofa, her cheek raw and hot. Her blood pumped furiously through her veins. Her brain raged. Pulsing. Battering. Knocking. She rubbed her temples and ducked her head between her knees to dampen the sound. Her mind raced but couldn't catch up with the quickly fading images in her mind.

Flashes of light and color dance behind her eyes, but nothing tangible. Her thoughts whirred to a stop on Max's face. She could see him: eyes so dark they were almost black, the corners of his mouth which had just begun to crease, and the slight cleft of his chin. It was fuzzy and without context, but it was all there. She may have lost Max's pen, but something had given her back some of her memories. Not all, but some.

The knocking in her brain intensified, demanding her attention. Cressida lifted her head to the room. The bay windows sucked the heat behind her, and the cold dim of twilight seeped into the room in its place. Light trickled under the office door, past the shadow of someone's feet shifting back and forth in the hallway. Fists banged against the hollow door, rattling it in the warped frame. Cressida's heart crashed in her chest and Max's dead eyes burned into her retinas in rings like when you stare at an eclipse for too long.

Cressida's body felt like stone as her stiff muscles heaved her from the sofa and carried her to the door. She pressed her other hand to her chest, searching for the peace she'd felt in the dream, but she was empty once again. Memories pulled at the corner of her mind, like an answer to a riddle that was hidden just out of reach. *If something hadn't woken her, would she have seen what happened that night? Would she have seen how he died?*

Cressida shook her head and pulled open the door. On the other side, Vee's knuckles were chapped red from pounding and her blue eyes were darting frantically from Cressida's face to the front door as if she might change her mind and run away into the night. Rain dripped from her sodden pixie hair. She smelled like seawater as though she'd swam there. No longer floating, Vee's clothes stuck to her ribs, betraying how thin and frail she was beneath the waves of color: the same vivid colors that had warmed Cressida in her dream. Breath hitched in Cressida's throat.

The girl from her dream. Her first dream in ten years.

It was Vee.

The girl in front of her shivered. "I'm sorry to just show up like this." Her voice cracked from overuse, as if she'd been screaming into a pillow for the last several hours.

"Are you ok? What happened?" Another waft of salty air invaded Cressida's nose. Could Vee have been wet from the ocean instead of the rain? Unbidden, an image flickered into Cressida's mind, novel and uncertain, of a woman lying dead on the beach, surrounded by piles of wet fabric. Red, Orange, and Green. Like a vibrant shroud. The specter of the mermaid patient loomed large between them, but Cressida shook it off. Could this have been why she'd dreamed of Vee? To save her? But Vee didn't seem suicidal. She hadn't failed Vee yet.

Vee glanced down at her wet clothes like she hadn't realized she was wearing them. A shy smile peeked out from her bowed head. "It's raining again." She shook her head like an animal, and the volcanic earrings Cressida had admired earlier made a *tink-tink-tink* sound as they slapped against her neck.

Rainwater splashed onto Cressida's hands and the drops

rolled down her skin, unpredictable and unstoppable. Like the girl. Vee was the driving rain and the relentless tide, infiltrating everything and leaving tiny pieces of herself scattered in her path. There was still glitter sparkling in the lamplight, mud from Vee's shoes painting the carpet, and a damp breeze in the air. Vee was everywhere. Invading all her senses.

Cressida brushed the droplets from her hand and fixed her eyes on the shivering girl in front of her. "How can I help you?"

Vee's lips pressed into a hard line. "I needed to apologize."

"For what?"

Vee reached into the pocket of her skirt and held out her clasped hands as an offering of appeasement. "For this." She bowed her head in silence and waited for Cressida to accept her gift.

Cressida held her hands below Vee's without touching her dripping skin. Vee dropped a slender metal object into Cressida's palm and the light glinted off the silver clip at the top. Max's pen. Cressida opened her mouth to speak, but before she could say anything Vee slipped past her into the room and perched on the edge of the sofa, barely compressing the cushion, her muscles tensed and ready to run at any moment. Her presence was ethereal, fleeting. The cushion where Vee's wet skirt now rested was probably still warm from Cressida's feverish dream, but now the burlap darkened as the water seeped into the rough fabric. Vee had already permeated everything else.

Vee wrung her hands in her lap. "It's just this thing I do sometimes."

"What?"

"Take things that don't belong to me. My boyfriend says it's a cry for help."

Cressida's head was spinning in the wake of her dream. It was surreal that the girl was sitting in front of her. She fought to focus. "Is he right? Is it a cry for help?"

"No. It just happens. Like my hands have minds of their own." She shrugged without lifting her eyes.

Cressida just stared at the wet girl huddled on the sofa, glistening just as she had in the dream. It was as if Vee had been birthed from Cressida's mind and dropped outside the door, as wet and afraid as the day she entered the world.

Vee met Cressida's gaze with tears welled in her blue eyes, darker than they were that morning, like the sea before a storm. Without the billowing fabric and wild blond hair, Vee seemed more vulnerable. More real. Cressida hadn't noticed before the way Vee's face was slightly wider at the top, like a heart. Or how wide her shoulders stretched across her body. Or how the bones of her shoulders protruded from beneath twitching lean muscle. Her skin was tanned down to her sculpted nails. Those ridiculously impractical nails that touched everything.

Cressida drew her own shoulders back slightly and lifted a hand to her cheek. Vee was taller and thinner across the middle than Cressida, but with almost no curves. Cressida was gifted with what her mother used to refer to as *a womanly figure*, but with the height difference the two women probably weighed about the same. They weren't so different. Beneath the clothes and the colors, they could have been sisters, cut from the same tragic cloth. Except everything about Vee exuded warmth, where as Cressida was carved from ice.

Cressida had never known anyone like Vee before.

Maybe if she had, things would have turned out differently.

Max would have said that was nonsense, that she was born this way. Cool. Calculated. Calm. Like him. Cressida's pulse slowed, and she set the pen back onto the side table where it belonged. She drew a deep breath. Cressida had Max's pen again and everything was back to normal.

Almost.

CHAPTER 6

Cressida smiled at the shivering girl in front of her and held out her hand toward the office. "I don't have another client until tomorrow. Would you like to finish this morning's session now?"

Vee looked down at her soggy clothes. Her skirt sagged along her waist, revealing the bones of her hips. There were visible bruises on her pelvis, the kind one would expect to see if someone fell against a hard surface. Or was pushed against one.

Cressida was reminded of Sam, lying in the hospital, battered and alone. There had been no one else to protect her, and Cressida had failed her. She wouldn't let it happen again with this girl. Not when the bruises were right there in front of her face. Although, Vee had mentioned earlier working on her father's fishing boat for spare cash. Maybe she'd slammed against the side of the ship during a storm. Cressida would need to be sure.

"Vee?" Cressida prompted.

The girl shook her head. She didn't want to talk.

Vee's teeth clacked together as she shivered on the sofa.

Something had taken this enigma of a girl and turned her upside down. The glitter and mud could be cleaned, but Vee must have appeared in Cressida's life for a reason, as if she was the answer to an unspoken question. Cressida needed to understand.

"You know, Vee, I've got an old sweatshirt lying around, if you want to borrow it."

Vee cocked her head and smiled. "Are you sure? I don't know if that crosses the doctor-patient boundary rules." Odd coming from the girl who had knocked on the door soaked in rainwater and tears of contrition, palming a stolen pen.

Vee's eyes sparkled. She had crossed the first boundaries by stealing from Cressida and showing up unannounced, and now she was tempting Cressida along with her. The girl wasn't interested in traditional therapy. She wanted to break barriers. But Cressida had waited ten years for her memories of the accident to return, so maybe this girl's unconventional presence in her life was the catalyst she needed.

"I won't tell if you won't." Cressida glanced over her shoulder at the pen resting beside her notebook on the table. It wasn't policy, but therapists had done a lot worse.

She closed the gap between them in three confident steps and rested her hand on Vee's shuddering shoulder. Her skin was hot and damp beneath Cressida's stiff palm—had the room been a couple degrees cooler, steam would have risen from Vee's fevered body. Cressida pulled her hand away and continued past the sofa to a small closet in the back corner of the office. She pulled a charcoal-colored hoodie from a metal hanger and held the clothes out to Vee. Dull and dank, Cressida might as well have been offering Vee the uniform of the committed, a cotton-clad prison sentence. At least it was dry.

Vee rose from the sofa and held out her hands. Cressida's grip tensed on the sweatshirt. Max would not have approved of Cressida rewarding a patient with kindness after she'd violated her therapist's trust and the sanctity of her office. Goosebumps covered Vee's arms and her earrings trembled against the veins of her neck. She was freezing. Cressida relinquished the sweatshirt as Vee tugged the garment to her chest. "You just happen to have spare clothes lying around your office?"

"You never know when a patient might turn up in need." Cressida smiled. "Or when you'll get caught in a downpour."

Vee's skin glowed from exposure to the harsh wind and rain. Only pain could bring out such beauty. Each day since the accident, Cressida had felt numb. No pain. No splendor. Everything in her life was dismal, like a piece of her had died along with Max. Maybe it had. For years she'd yearned to recover those final moments, to understand how she'd become the person who awoke in the hospital that day. Alone. But until recently there had been only darkness. And now a glimmer of hope stirred in her belly.

Vee ducked her head into the baggy sweatshirt and the grey washed out Vee's skin and made her seem older than before. It was a reverse metamorphosis: extravagant to pedestrian, butterfly to caterpillar. Even her eyes had paled from blue to a denim grey. She looked like Cressida only with short, blond hair. "It suits you."

"Thanks." Vee smiled again and the chip in her front tooth was irritatingly charming. Max would have said imperfections were meant to be corrected, not admired. Yet, this girl was different. She was awash with the splendor of fallacy, of humanity. She was everything Cressida had never known but always craved: warmth and light and love.

The girl pulled her arms into the sweatshirt. Her limbs

pressed against the soft material like a baby pressing against its mother's womb as she shimmied out of her tank top and dropped the sodden garment to the floor. Vee was naked beneath the grey sweatshirt, but Cressida was the one who felt exposed. The expensive silk draped across her arms, cold and impersonal, felt paper thin.

Cressida looked at the floor, her eyes fixed on the wet shirt dampening the pale Berber carpet where mud and glitter still clung to the fibers. She'd forgotten to clean them, or maybe she liked the reminder of how Vee had changed her life. Cressida's nerves were electric, and she wanted to know all of the girl's secrets.

Cressida lowered herself back into the leather chair across from Vee and squeezed her pen tight between her fingers. "You mentioned that your boyfriend thinks you steal items as a cry for help. Can you expand on that a little more?"

Vee's chin disappeared into the folds of the sweatshirt like a turtle into its shell. "He thinks I have a problem with dramatics."

"Because of the stealing? Or is there more?"

She flopped back onto the sofa. "I don't know. You'd have to ask him. Though he'd probably just tell you to fuck off."

Cressida didn't flinch at Vee's aggressive language. This morning, confidence had wafted from the girl's pores like the glitter she spread throughout the office. Now, stripped of her exuberance, she was bared. And it was clear she didn't like it. Cressida scraped Max's pen across her notebook. *Boyfriend.* "Do people usually do whatever he says?"

"Some of them."

"What about you? Do you always do what he tells you?"

"I'm here, aren't I?

Cressida touched Max's pen to her lips. "What do you think he'd say about that?"

Vee chewed the inside of her cheek and a half-smile crept over her mouth. "That therapy is a waste of my time and I have him to talk to and that should be enough."

"Do you think it's a waste of time?"

Vee's eyes bored into Cressida's. "I haven't decided yet."

Cressida's fingers twitched. Perhaps Vee wanted to be dazzled, but there was no way to beat a patient at a battle of wills unless you changed the game.

Cressida stood and dropped her notebook into the seat with a loud slap. "Well, there's nothing more to talk about until you do."

Vee's mouth twitched into a smirk. She spread her fingertips over her knees and wiped her palms along her skirt. "That's it?"

Cressida pressed her lips together and stepped aside to clear a path from the sofa to the door. "That's it. I've kept an appointment for you next Friday at five. You have a week to decide if therapy is worth your time."

Vee stared up at Cressida, her lips pursed. Cressida had called her bluff. Vee stood, walked to the door and paused with her turquoise nails, the color of tarnished brass, tapping on the knob. Her head dropped. "You aren't what I expected when I came here," Vee spoke with her back to Cressida, her words bouncing off the wooden door.

Curiosity overcame Cressida's better sense. "What were you expecting?"

"Someone as old and haunted as this place." Vee chuckled, but Cressida couldn't help but think of Roger pacing the halls of the old asylum for the last twenty-five years.

"Are you disappointed?"

Vee cocked her head. "No. I'm glad it's you. I feel like I

can relate better to a woman my age. Like you and I could just be friends." She laughed again but the smile didn't reach her eyes.

The girl was baiting her, but Cressida bit down hard on her tongue. She needed to hold her ground. "That sounds like a good place to start on Friday."

Vee nodded and opened the door. The light from the hallway spilled into the office, casting a long shadow over the room. Glitter sparkled in the glow— on the carpet, the chair, even the walls— and then it was gone. Vee was gone. The office was dim and colorless again, the plain walls and neat bookshelves fading as if today had been just another day. But Cressida knew better, as she had known with Max.

Nothing would ever be the same again.

Vee didn't think Cressida was haunted by this place, but she had her demons too. The first time Max had touched her she'd begged for it. His hands were firm and steady and remorseless. He'd taught her to focus her obsessions, her needs. But now she needed Vee. Rain rapped on the bay windows, matching the clock on the wall tick for tock, like a metronome counting down the minutes until she could go to bed and wait for her next dream, her next memory. Somewhere in her subconscious was the answer to the question that had eluded her for a decade.

What had really happened the night Max died?

CHAPTER 7

The hospital was a very different place on a Saturday afternoon. Children raced through the hallways, their sleep-deprived and grief-stricken parents pleading with them to slow down. The waiting room was filled with coughs and sniffles and bruises and bandages that couldn't wait until Monday morning. The desk on the fourth floor was piled high with charts and folders, and nurses buzzed around like bees gathering nectar. No one noticed as Cressida passed by the counter unattended and followed the pale blue stripe painted along the sickly yellow walls toward room 403.

Bolstered by confidence and the first restful sleep she'd had in years, Cressida smiled as she passed patients in the hallways. Today was the day she would convince Sam to come home with her: the day she would start to put her life back together. She and Sam would stay up late talking about their dreams, their plans, and Vee. What would Sam think about Vee? Excitement churned in Cressida's stomach.

The door to Sam's room was propped open and even the air around it smelled different than it had the other morning. Less stale. There was a hint of something floral floating on the wind as nurses and doctors rushed past with heavy carts and beds. Lavendar? Maybe lilies. Cressida should have bought flowers for Sam. She would have liked that.

Cressida's heart sank.

What if Sam was angry that she hadn't come back to visit that night? She might be jealous of Vee. Cressida paused outside the room and peered through the window. She wanted to know what kind of mood Sam would be in when she arrived, but something was wrong.

There was a petite girl—maybe in her early twenties—leaning across the bed, blond curls spilling over her shoulders onto the same scratchy waffle-print blanket Cressida had touched on Friday. The blonde's head was resting on the shoulder of an older man, perhaps twenty years her senior, with frosted tubes protruding from his flared nostrils and a hospital gown open enough at the front to reveal a smattering of coarse grey chest hair mingling with the girl's shiny ringlets. His eyelids fluttered as he slept and the girl's head rose and fell with each labored breath he took. He had one of her hands clasped tight against his chest. She was using the other hand to read her phone.

Cressida stepped away from the window and checked the number on the door again. 403. This was supposed to be Sam's room. At least it had been yesterday morning.

The strange girl in the room looked up at Cressida with swollen eyes, her cheeks were splotchy and carrying the faint indentation of the blanket. The man in the bed could have been her father, some beloved relative stricken down unexpectedly while she was away at college, but there was something in her eyes, a deep pain and fear that told Cressida it was more than that. She'd felt that fear before when she woke in the hospital ten years earlier only to learn that Max had died.

Surely the hospital would have called if something had happened to Sam: complications, internal bleeding, clots, aneurisms, hemorrhages. The possibilities swarmed around Cressida like an angry mob. Or maybe her father had found her again, taken her away this time for good. Somewhere Cressida could never find her. She bent forward and rested her elbows on her knees to keep from sliding to the floor. The blue tile swirled and faded between her feet. She couldn't breathe, mouth open and gasping for air, her lungs screamed to be filled. But she was empty.

Completely.

Again.

Sam was missing, and she felt the pain of loss all over again.

Cressida turned away from the mourning girl in the room, the painful window into her own haunted past. Her senses burned with memories of the day she woke in the hospital. Her head was still bandaged and the gauze felt like sandpaper against her skin. Her breath tasted like hospital food and morphine, but her wrists still carried the faint scent of perfume. It was acrid and chemical and much too old for her nineteen-year-old taste, but Max had liked it. She'd known he liked it because she'd seen the desire in his eyes when she'd reached across his chest in the car that night and pulled his pen from his breast pocket while he drove. The touch of the metal against her fingertips was the last thing she remembered before waking up in the hospital.

Dark and alone.

A familiar voice pulled Cressida back to the hospital. "Are you ok? Do you need help?" It was the redheaded nurse from yesterday.

Cressida raised her eyes and met the nurse's concerned stare. She couldn't speak, but she nodded her head slowly, cold sweat dripping along her temples. She steadied herself against the wall, but her head was spinning.

"I think maybe I should get you a bed." The nurse crouched in front of her with her hands outstretched, like she was afraid Cressida might bite.

Cressida forced herself to her feet. She drew a deep breath and felt the blood rush back to her face. Her voice rasped in throat. "No. I'm fine."

The nurse looked down at Cressida and her brow pinched. "I remember you. You're the psychiatrist who was in here the other morning. Doctor Dunhill, right?"

Cressida wiped dirt and probably thousands of antibiotic resistant bacteria from her hands onto her pants. "What happened to Sam? Did she move rooms?"

"No. She checked out AMA this morning."

"Alone?"

"I believe so, ma'am."

"I don't understand." Cressida squeezed the bridge of her nose between her thumb and forefinger. "Did she leave a message?"

Pity clouded the nurse's pretty green eyes. "I don't think so."

"She just left?" *Again.*

"And in a hurry too. She grabbed her clothes but left the rest of her things here." She scratched her arm through her green scrubs. "Would you like to take them for her?"

Cressida nodded and the nurse disappeared behind the desk, returning with a clear plastic bag. Inside was a leather wallet, Cressida's business card, and Sam's ancient cell phone with the flip top and the cracked screen.

The Sam she'd known was really gone this time. Cressida had wanted Sam to be different. To be real. But once again she'd been fooled. Outside, rain beat against the windows of the hospital, pulsing with the tidal winds, as if she was hearing the collective heartbeat of the small seaside town.

THE NEXT MORNING, damp streets shimmered in the early light. Not even 9:00 a.m. and already the weekend tourists had descended on Silverside, splashing through puddles in their stiff flip-flops and sunglasses with the tags still on. Sundays were always the worst. They were the mornings when she and Sam would stay in and read together: Cressida thumbing through the latest Pynchon or Roth or Koontz if she was feeling particularly adventurous, and Sam salivating over fashion magazines and self-actualization doublespeak. Sam always said she didn't have the patience for fiction, but Cressida found real life far more tedious.

Especially now that she was thrust into the masses with nothing better to do on a Sunday morning than wade through a sea of blank faces, searching for something to distract her from the gnawing worry that the dream she'd had the other night had been nothing more than a fluke. A temporary seizure that shocked her memories to life only to feel them slowly fading away again. The article Roger had given her mentioned a connection between dreams and long-term memory retrieval, but it all seemed too easy at the time. Now it felt like cruel and unusual punishment.

Cressida squinted down a narrow street lined with junk shops and high-end boutiques. Her throat tightened as she was knocked off kilter by anonymous shoulders, hips, backpacks, and at least one horse-sized dog on a jangling chain.

She spun on the sidewalk, the dizzying mob swirling around her like an eddy. This was a mistake. She shouldn't have come here. Sweat dampened the back of her t-shirt and trickled under the waistband of her jeans. Anxiety clenched her stomach and she doubled over, ducked beneath the seething crowd. Then she was there, weaving among families and surfers, long black hair tied up in a bright scarf, and wide feet stretching a pair of platform wedges. Cressida only saw the figure for a second before a boy rushed passed and slammed her to the pavement, but she was certain it had been Sam that ducked into a trinket shop across the street.

When the crowd subsided, Cressida heaved herself from the steaming sidewalk and into the road. Maybe Sam hadn't gone as far as she'd feared. She needed an explanation for why the girl that used to be a boy that used to be her friend had abandoned her again. She deserved that much. Her heart thudded in her chest. The door to the shop jingled as she pushed through it, away from the bustle outside, and into a cluttered room that smelled of lavender soap and oldies playing over tinny speakers. In contrast to the crowds still visible through the glass door, the shop was eerily devoid of life.

The cashier's counter was abandoned and the only movement was the slight swaying of *I Silverside* t-shirts on the rack, as if someone had brushed past in a hurry. Cressida clenched her fists tight and followed the rustling where she found the girl with long, dark hair standing on tiptoes and running her fingers along the novelty shot glasses on the back shelf. She was straightening them into a row. Cressida froze. Sam had never shown signs of OCD when Cressida had known her. She looked more closely at the girl in front of her and something else didn't make sense. Sam was several inches taller than Cressida, and wearing heals she would have stood well over six feet tall. A remarkable height for any woman. This girl was merely average.

Cressida's hands went limp. She'd been wrong. Again. Her tired eyes and damaged mind were playing tricks on her in the worst way. She turned away to leave, but bumped into a display table knocking stacks of books to the floor with a loud thwack.

The girl wheeled around and nearly toppled off her platforms. "Are you alright?"

"Yeah, sorry about that." Cressida stooped to gather the books.

The girl bent down beside her. "Can I help you with something?"

Cressida looked down at the books in her hand. On the front cover, in all its Gothic glory, was a sleek black and white photograph of the building where she worked. It was titled *The True Story of The Mermaid Asylum* and it was reduced to clearance along with about forty of its brothers and sisters. Nobody wanted a real story when fiction was so much more fun, and she smiled because Sam would have hated that she was right.

There was nothing in this store for Cressida. "No. Thank you."

"Well, just let me know if you see anything you like."

Cressida placed the books back on the table and dusted off her knees. "I will."

On her way to the front door something caught Cressida's eye, glittering in the front window like a dancing light. She approached the display case and located the source of the movement. A pair of beaded earrings was trembling in the wind from an electric fan oscillating through the store, and every time they turned a different colored bead would catch the sunlight and flicker. Blues and greens flowed into each other and tumbled like a waterfall. They looked exactly like the pair that Vee had worn they day they met, only a different color. Cressida raised her hand to her virgin ear lobe.

The jewelry was flashy and impractical, form over function. The fan blew past the earrings again and the beads tinkled like bells, soft and sweet, and Cressida knew that she had to have them. She turned back to the girl with the black hair. "How much are these earrings?"

The girl craned her neck over the racks of overpriced memorabilia. "Which ones?"

"The blue and green beaded ones."

The girl smiled. "Oh, yes. Those are very popular. Thirty bucks."

It was more than Cressida usually spent on superficial items, but she had to have them. It was as if her subconscious was trying to break free. She didn't have it all figured out yet, but she knew it had something to do with these earrings.

Cressida reached into her back pocket and pulled out her wallet. "I'll take them."

CHAPTER 8

Cressida bent forward in her leather chair to scrape a square of glitter from her patent leather pumps. Friday again. It was the end of another week, and the air in the office smelled like mothballs. The crimson hue of dawn had faded from the office and the bay windows were cast into shadows. Brown and grey once again replaced pink and orange, and there was an old woman creaking on the sofa across from her. Her head barely reached above the back of the sofa and her grey hair blended into the cushions. Gone was the halo of promise the sun brought each morning, and instead cold death stared her in the face, and it was complaining about arthritis.

"And when it rains, there are days I can barely get out of bed. And it rains all the time." The old woman's skeletal hands shook as she flexed her fingers. Purple veins stood out against paper-thin skin and her fingernails were the cloudy yellow of jaundice.

"The Pacific Northwest is known for its rain, Mrs. Coulter."

"My daughter thinks I should move to Phoenix." Mrs.

Coulter sucked her mouth into a scowl that seemed to devour her already wrinkled face.

"But you don't want to move?"

"No. My Warren is buried here. We lived in Silverside our entire lives."

Cressida's patience had disappeared with the sun. Cressida's hands shook as she brought a mug of cold coffee to her lips. Dark circles had greeted her in the mirror when she woke that morning, and she could feel them pulling against her cheeks now. "So you have to die here too?"

"It wouldn't be right to leave him."

"Who?"

"Warren." Mrs. Coulter's dry eyes sunk deeper into her face, but there wasn't enough moisture left in her body to spare for tears. The ghost of her husband was haunting her. The shimmering image of Max's pen flickered in front of Cressida's eyes and then faded again to black.

"But he's dead, and you're in pain."

Mrs. Coulter's ancient body hunched forward, her joints grinding in their sockets. "This is the life I chose. I just wish my daughter and her new husband could understand that."

The clock ticked with agonizing leisure as Mrs. Coulter unburdened herself. Each minute felt like hours, as if Cressida had sunk into another endless, dreamless sleep, only this time she couldn't wake up. When Mrs. Coulter finally rose from the sofa, she inched her way from the office back toward her empty house. The moment the door closed behind her, Cressida collapsed onto her side on the sofa. It was still warm from the old woman's body, and Cressida pressed her face into the burlap. Her ears throbbed where the beaded earrings dangled from her newly pierced flesh. They tickled against her neck with each breath. The glitter that had stuck to her body for a week had finally fallen away and scattered across the carpet.

It had taken days to restore the office to its pristine condition after Vee had turned it on its ear. She had done everything right, put everything back the way it was the day of the dream, and yet her mind remained locked. No new dreams. No closer to remembering how Max died. She'd been meticulous, but something was wrong. Cressida had reread all the articles on dreams and recovered memories, but none of them reported the effects waning over time. There had to be a reason she hadn't dreamed again, that she still couldn't remember the details of the accident.

Cressida cracked her knuckles and checked the clock on the wall again: 5:15 p.m. Another mystery gone unsolved tonight. Vee was an unpredictable force as powerful and dangerous as any hurricane. She had no idea whether Vee would come back at all, or whether her boyfriend would convince her that therapy was pointless. Or worse, punish her for the betrayal. The bruises on Vee's hips had been as purple as the gashes on Sam's face. They were fresh. Cressida gulped another mouthful of stale coffee and shuddered at the bitter taste. Maybe she shouldn't have pushed Vee so hard. She could lose her the way she'd lost Sam. Only this time there was so much more at stake.

At 5:24 p.m. there was a quiet knock at the door. Cressida jumped from the sofa and banged her knee on the coffee table, knocking a box of tissues to the floor. Her leg screamed in pain as she limped across the room. On the other side of the door stood a smiling Vee, dressed all in red and tugging at her hoop earring. Vee dropped her hand from her ear and hugged both arms around her narrow waist, probably covering the bruises hidden beneath her blouse. "I'm so sorry I'm late."

Cressida bit the inside of her cheek to hide her smile. She should have been annoyed—it was unprofessional and unacceptable to show up twenty-four minutes late to an appointment—but she wasn't. "Don't be. I'm glad you came back." Cressida held out a hand to Vee, who grasped it with a grin. Her skin was too soft to have spent many days working on a fishing boat, and the bruises had been too incongruous. Her story didn't fit.

"Me too. This place creeps me out, but there's something about it that I can't resist." Vee smiled and walked past her into the room as if she'd been there a thousand times before. Her blond hair glowed almost yellow in the evening light and her teal fingernails danced over the shelves as she passed by. It felt right that she be there. Like the asylum itself was calling to her, craving her light and cheer in its cavernous insides the way an addict's veins burn for his next fix.

Cressida held her hand out toward the sofa, steering the wandering girl to her rightful place in front of the wingback chair. Where she could properly assess her. "So where would you like to start today?"

Vee flopped onto the sofa and dust and glitter whooshed from her clothes and hung in the air around her in a sparkling cloud. She pulled her feet onto the cushion beside her and shrugged. "I don't care."

Curiosity tingled to Cressida's fingertips. She had so many questions for the girl, but all of them required Vee to trust her enough to open up. "What made you come back today?"

Vee looked at her hands in her lap and rubbed at a dark bruise on her wrist. Cressida hasn't noticed it there on Tuesday. "You. You're different from everyone else in this fucking town."

She should talk to Vee about the bruises, formalize an escape plan in case of emergencies, maybe even report the bruises to Roger and the local authorities. But then she'd lose control. They'd turn Vee's case over to social services or the police. She might never see the girl again. And for what? The police had done nothing to save Sam. There must be another way to protect what makes this girl special.

Cressida lowered herself into her chair. "Last time you were here you mentioned your expectations for therapy, that I wasn't what you expected. Why don't we talk about that?"

Vee's cheeks flushed pink. "I guess I pictured some old guy with a white beard asking me about my parents and my first sexual encounter."

Cressida laughed. "You watch too much television."

Vee shook her head, eyes roaming Cressida's bookshelves the way a man's eyes wander over a woman's body. "I prefer books." Her voice was sultry, almost carnal, as she gazed at the neatly stacked spines.

This was Cressida's chance to bond with the girl. The books might serve as a gesture of good faith—a way for her to connect with the elusive girl beneath the glitter.

Cressida stood up and approached the shelves. "I want to show you something I think you'll appreciate."

High up on the same row as *The Aeneid* was a black velvet box about the size of an encyclopedia volume. The box was sealed with a gold latch that Cressida flipped up with her thumbnail. She carried the velvet case on her open palms as if it were an offering for the gods frequently depicted in the very books on the shelf where it had been, and set the display box in Vee's lap. There was not a speck of dust on this book. It was meticulous and preserved and safe.

Vee rested her hand against her chapped lips. "Can I?" Vee whispered, barely audible through her fisted hand.

"Books are meant to be loved, right?" Cressida repeated back Vee's words from that first session. Mirroring her. Illustrating for her that Cressida could understand her on a deeper level. She handed Vee the velvet box and sat down on the sofa beside her.

Vee's eyes were wide as a child's on Christmas morning. She lifted a tattered book encased in plastic from the black box, holding onto the sides of the binding the way one might do with a record to keep from scratching it.

Vee ran her turquoise-tipped fingers along the plastic dust jacket. "It's beautiful. You said these books belonged to your mother?"

Cressida's voice was low and reverent. "Yeah. This one is Troilus and Criseyde by Geoffrey Chaucer. It's not a first edition, but it's worth quite a lot of money."

"That's amazing." Vee peeked inside the book and let out a satisfied sigh, long and low and almost sensual. The book meant something to Vee. To Cressida it was only dust and ash: her mother's legacy branded on her at birth. There was nothing of her in that book. There never was, but it had haunted her childhood like a recurring nightmare.

"Yes. My mother was quite the collector." In her mother's mind, children were dangerous balls of chaos threatening the order of her literary world. Books were not meant to be loved. They were meant to be respected, and in some cases feared. Like mothers.

"Is this where you got your name?"

Cressida fixed her eyes on the book and nodded. "Unfortunately." Her voice was laced with disdain.

Troilus and Criseyde was the story of a young girl sent away from her betrothed and her home by her father, and who despite promises of everlasting love and fidelity, quickly takes another lover. It was the ultimate tale of the capriciousness of women and the devastation that inevitably results from trusting them. It was an anti-romance. The preeminent story of the jilted lover and his forgotten paramour. Cressida's mother had treated the book like a cautionary tale of things to come for all young girls.

Her mother had doled out the literary name along with its predestined legacy, and then used it to control Cressida. There was nothing could do in life to make up for the weakness of her namesake. Girls were flawed and easily tempted, like Eve and Pandora. They weren't to be trusted. It was their original sin, and something for which, in her mother's eyes, she could never atone. Cressida used to believe her future was out of her hands, already written, like one of her mother's ancient stories. Until she met Max and he taught her to take command of her life.

Vee flipped the pages carefully and then furrowed her brow. "I've never read it."

Cressida huffed. "It's basically the exact opposite of Romeo and Juliette. Instead of dying in each other's arms, Cressida gets bored of waiting for her lover and sleeps with someone else. She disappoints everyone."

Vee's blue eyes were less cloudy than they had been a moment before. "Maybe your mother just thought it was a pretty name."

"My mother never saw anything pretty in me or my name." Cressida cracked the knuckles on her right hand as if she could crush all thoughts of her mother in her palm.

She'd never been more than a life-like doll her mother could pull from the closet and dust off before important functions, a name she could toss out in conversation to demonstrate her literary prowess and dedication to her field.

Vee closed the book carefully and replaced the plastic dustcover. "Well, these illustrations are amazing. Really something special. Something like this belongs in a museum." She sat up and laid the velvet box on the coffee table. "Thank you for sharing it with me."

Cressida nodded. "Thank you for bringing back my pen the other night, and for making the right choice today."

The muscles in Vee's arms tensed as the focus turned back to her, and she sat up straighter, crossing her legs. Something wasn't adding up for Cressida. Vee had stolen Max's pen to gain her attention, returned it as an excuse to see her again, and kept her follow up appointment this afternoon. Yet she refused to let Cressida lead the session. It was as if she wasn't looking for answers so much as spreading chaos: touching everything around her, infiltrating it, and leaving it forever changed. Just like she had in Cressida's dream.

Slow recognition chilled Cressida like ice through her veins. Vee wasn't just a part of the dream, she created it. Cressida had dreamt for the first time shortly after Vee's first session. She was the only thing Cressida hadn't been able replicate from the night of her dream was Vee: her effervescence, her easy disregard for rules and conventions, and her gratuitous color. No matter how hard she tried, Cressida couldn't eliminate the glitter Vee spread around her. It stuck to everything, invisible most of the time until the right light shone on it from a particular angle. Then it blinded Cressida with color. She couldn't escape it. Vee was unlike any patient Cressida had seen before.

Vee was the reason for the dreams. She had to be.

Afraid to breathe as if she might scatter Vee into the

wind, Cressida waited, her throat closed and her hands squeezed tight enough in her lap that she could feel her pulse in her fingertips. Every sound hammered in her ears like thunder. Her subconscious had awoken after years in the dark to warn her to keep Vee in her life.

Vee's voice chimed through the noise in Cressida's head, reminding here that there was a real person sitting across from her and not simply a riddle. "I want to be a writer someday." The words floated light in the air as if she'd spoken them into the wind.

"Why not now?"

"My boyfriend, Rex, says we need me to keep working. He's in school and can only work part time. So I have to earn enough to pay my bills as well as most of his." Vee rolled her eyes and crossed her arms in front of her, slumping against the back of the sofa.

There he was again, this man holding her back, stripping her of her autonomy and her dreams. And possibly putting Cressida's dreams at risk too.

And now he had a name.

CHAPTER 9

Cressida coughed. "His name is Rex? Like a dog?"

Vee inhaled sharply like the words struck her across the cheek and then she scowled. "Yeah, I guess so. He wouldn't appreciate the comparison much though. He doesn't have the best sense of humor." She scratched the back of her hand leaving red welts under her painted nails. The girl was nervous. This man whose opinion Vee clearly hated and yet valued enough to seek therapy was her weakness, her vice.

"You don't live together?"

"No, Rex says he needs his own space to study and concentrate while he's still in school."

Cressida scratched the bridge of her nose and furrowed her brow. What kind of asshole makes his girlfriend sling fishing nets to pay for an apartment where he won't let her live? The bruises on Vee's wrist and hips were more concerning than Cressida had originally thought. Maybe this was the real reason Vee had come to Cressida. With men like Rex, it usually wasn't difficult to uncover their dirty laundry. "We have doctor-patient confidentiality, so we can call him whatever we like. It can be our secret."

Vee giggled and sat back on the sofa, crossing her legs toward Cressida. "Deal."

Cressida leaned closer to the girl. "And anything else you might want to tell me about him will also stay between me and you."

Vee's eyes were wide. Innocent. "Like what?"

Cressida tipped her chin toward Vee's fidgeting hands. "Like where you got those bruises on your wrist."

The girl snorted and rubbed her wrist. "This is nothing. I got my arm caught in a tow rope the other day."

Cressida bit her lip. It was certainly possible, based on what Vee reported, that she'd been injured on her father's boat. But Cressida didn't believe it. If Vee wouldn't admit what was happening, then Cressida couldn't be expected to report it. She still needed proof. "Well, just keep it in mind if there ever is something you want to tell me. Or if you feel like your life is in danger, I'll be here."

"Thanks. I will." Vee chewed her lip and scratched her nail across a loose seam on the sofa, worrying the thread until it came loose under her finger.

Cressida frowned. "So, what is Rex studying?"

Vee shook her head and yawned. "I don't want to talk about him anymore right now. It's been a long day and I haven't had dinner." The sofa sank beneath Cressida's weight when Vee jumped to her feet. She wiped her hands on her skirt and sighed. "I should probably get going."

"What? You're leaving early again?" Once again, Vee was leaving in the middle of a session—without explanation. This wasn't the way things were done. The sick feeling of abandonment she'd felt in the hospital on Saturday swept over her again. Cressida crossed her arms. Her face was hot with annoyance and the revolting sensation of desperation.

Vee shivered. "I'm just not really sure this whole therapy thing is for me."

"Because you don't want to talk about Rex?"

Vee shook her head and her earrings glinted in the light. "No..."

"I think you're here because you need to talk about him."

"I'm not sure why I came here." The girl looked down at her feet as they scuffed against the carpet, but she wasn't leaving.

"You told me you came here because you could tell I was different from the rest of the people in town."

"I did."

"What did you mean by that?"

Vee cocked her head to the side. "You really care, don't you?"

"What do you mean?"

"About me."

Cressida stood from the sofa, ready to shadow the girl's next movements. "I want to help you. Like all my patients." But Vee wasn't just another patient.

"I'm sorry for wasting your time." Vee's eyes were dark, almost midnight blue. She hugged her arms around herself and looked over her shoulder at the door. The streets were black outside the bay windows, the last of the afternoon heat draining from the room as if Vee was planning to take it with her. Rain battered against the glass and Vee's skin prickled over the bruises on her arms.

"Do you live far?"

"About half an hour's walk from town." She took a deep breath and shook her limbs, as if priming her muscles for a long journey.

"You walked here?"

Vee peered down at her clothes and smiled. "Well, tonight it looks more like I swam here." The gloomy mood that had gathered in her eyes was gone and replaced once again by her playful side. It was as if there were two of her inhabiting the same skin. She was pure and uninhibited, yet filled with a sadness that stagnated just below the surface.

Cressida followed Vee to the door. "Are you sure you want to go? We still have time left, if you want to stay and wait out the rain."

"You get used to this sort of thing if you spend enough time here." She hovered in the doorway and then a wicked smile crept across her face. "Can we just start over next week? I promise to do better."

"Sure."

The prospect of a clean slate was appealing, but it was a lie. Just like the glitter that infested Cressida's office, once Vee came into her life there was no erasing it. No going back. Cressida chewed the inside of her cheek. It didn't make sense. Twice this girl had turned up for an appointment only to leave after ten minutes. Could it be that she felt the kismet between them as well?

"Good." Vee nodded her head then breezed from the room like a soft breath, floating silently into the night.

Cressida stood staring at the closed door for several minutes, half expecting the capricious girl to change her mind again and return. In that way Vee was more like Cressida's mythical namesake than she was herself. Only the gurgling of Cressida's empty stomach finally convinced her to abandon her watch. The stillness in her office was stark in contrast to the bustle of Vee flitting about like a firefly, and its emptiness was deafening. Her eyelids hung heavy in their sockets, but she wouldn't sleep again. Not until she figured out what made this girl so special and how to protect it.

The office was too stuffy. She needed to get out, so she grabbed her keys from the hook beside the door and switched off the lights, casting the room into darkness and sending the sparkling of the glitter into oblivion.

THE CRAB SHACK was a popular sports bar lodged in a converted beach house, the balcony spreading onto the sand along with the sound of enthused fans that echoed across the sea. Sam had talked about taking Cressida out to the bar several times, but they could never commit to a plan, and Cressida had never thought to pursue it. Tonight just felt like the right time to correct that wrong. Cressida huddled over a small table in the corner of the outside seating area, so close to the beach that sand littered the floor by her feet and she would have been able to hear the ocean if it weren't for the commotion of the busy restaurant around her. She'd been lucky enough to stumble upon the seat just as an elderly man wearing a faded university of Oregon baseball cap had vacated it.

Tall poles with oil lamps burned overhead, but what little heat they produced was whipped away by the coastal winds. Most of the tables were full and the waitress was frazzled. The hair in her pretty French braid was loose on one side as though she'd been tugging it out of frustration. She tossed a menu onto Cressida's table without stopping on her way to deliver a plate of nachos to three boisterous men two tables over. They sounded like sea gulls hollering into the night. Cressida's head buzzed with the voices in the restaurant and her hands shook as she grasped the menu.

She should have been home reading a book, not here among the living.

She'd made a mistake.

The room erupted with such force it threw Cressida back to the aftermath of the accident: the scraping and twisting of metal, the hissing of the Jaws of Life as the police pulled her from the wreckage, and the terrible shrieking emanating from one of the nearby cars that night. She shivered in the dark. The memories she'd sought for so long hacked through her mind like knives. Shredding, tearing. There was blood everywhere. It was too much. Why now?

Cressida slapped her menu to the wet table, but she couldn't hear the sound over the roar of the other patrons. Her chair scraped silently across the composite decking and the blood whooshed muted to her brain. She couldn't see the front door through the kettle of sports fans circling her table like vultures. Through the sea of jerseys and college affiliated sweatshirts, a billowing figure in red appeared, wavering like a mirage. She weaved her way through the crowd, blond hair glowing in the firelight from the heaters.

Vee's blue eyes searched the space around Cressida without seeing her. Perhaps she was waiting for the abusive boyfriend. From somewhere deep in her gut, Cressida shouted Vee's name. The force of it took Cressida by surprise and she had to steady herself on the table to keep from tipping into the mob. She had no idea why she'd done it. Why she'd drawn attention to herself like that. It would have been so easy to remain shrouded in anonymity, to watch Vee for the rest of the night. Maybe even catch a glimpse of how Rex hurt Vee. Maybe if she was there to stop it, the police would do their jobs. Probably not.

Something else had awakened in Cressida last week along with her memories; after years of neutral observation and analysis, she wanted to experience something for herself. She wanted to know Vee the way she'd thought she'd known Sam. The way Max had known her. This could be her second chance.

"Hi!" Vee squinted in the low light and then grinned. "What are you doing here?"

"Dinner." The effort of speaking more than a word at time across the room was unappealing.

Vee broke free from the hoard and leant against Cressida's table. She lowered her head so her mouth was only inches from Cressida's ear. "I've never seen it so busy. The Blazers must be doing well tonight. I can't find a table anywhere."

Cressida looked into Vee's round face and pleading eyes. Every cell in Cressida's body was screaming to leave the crowded bar, but then she might never see Vee again. And maybe if Vee was with her tonight instead of with her boyfriend she could heal for at least one night without any new bruises. Cressida could keep her safe for a while.

"Why don't you sit with me?" Cressida shouted.

Vee pulled out the chair opposite Cressida and slipped her legs under the table. She leaned toward Cressida and smiled. "Thank you." She pulled the menu across the table and flipped it over. "So, do you follow basketball?"

Cressida snorted but the sound was lost in the crowd. "Not at all."

Vee's mouth fell open like she was laughing but the sound was carried away on the wings of the gulls. "Oh good. Me either. Rex loves it. He goes out every week with his friends to watch the games." Vee seemed to shrink. Her shoulders hunched over the table and her hands balled in her lap.

Cressida cringed. The world is full of assholes who leave

their marks on women one way or another. Rex wasn't special, but his power over Vee was worrying. The more Cressida saw the girl, the more she realized Vee was in danger. She was in danger of being hurt, and also of losing that colorful spirit that made her more than just another girl from Silverside whose life held her hostage. Like Sam. Cressida couldn't figure out why anyone would *choose* to be a woman in this world.

Cressida tapped the tabletop. "So you said you've been here before?"

Vee's pupils misted over and she stared glassy-eyed into the darkness over the ocean. "Yeah, it's our special place. Rex and I came here on our first date." She twitched and brought her eyes back to Cressida like she'd just remembered where she was. "So the guy I talked to on the phone in your office said you're particularly interested in helping people deal with weird dreams. Must be really interesting."

Cressida shook her head. "You'd be surprised how predictable most people's dreams are." For most people, dreaming was as natural as breathing, and just as easy to take for granted. For Cressida, it was the ultimate mystery.

"Really? Oh, not mine. You wouldn't believe me if I told you some of the things I've dreamt. What about you? Are your dreams predictable?" Vee's hands were folded on top of the table, her turquoise nails laced together to tight that Cressida couldn't tell which finger was which.

Cressida's voice was hushed like everyone in the room was listening to their conversation. "I don't dream." It was barely audible.

Vee sat back in her chair, her forehead creased. "At all?"

"Nope. Not for ten years." *Until last week.*

"It must be hard for you to listen to other people's dreams then, huh?"

In another life, the girl might have made a good therapist. “Sometimes.”

“So you dreamed before ten years ago? How does a person just stop dreaming?”

“I was in an accident.” The doctors told Cressida that the dreams might return someday, but the subconscious is fragile and easy to fool. When it came to dreams, doctors were just poking around in the dark anyway.

“I’m so sorry.” Vee’s face was long and the corners of her mouth turned down with concern. She let the menu drop in front of her.

Cressida shook her head and smiled. “It was a long time ago.”

“I bet it still feels like yesterday.”

Blue eyes met steel grey, but their thoughts were interrupted by a collective gasp from the sports fans in the bar. Cressida dropped her eyes to the table and pulled the menu toward her. Beneath the table, Cressida’s legs were shaking. “So is the soft shell crab good here?”

“I don’t know. I don’t really eat seafood.” Vee smiled and her shoulders raised toward her ears apologetically.

Cressida looked up from her menu. “Wait, didn’t you say you worked on your father’s fishing boat?”

“Yep.”

“And you don’t eat seafood?”

“Nope. Can’t stand the smell of it. I bet you can infer all sorts of things about me from that, right? Like about my childhood or something?” Vee’s mouth pulled at the corners. Her eyes were wide and a little fearful. The color faded from her face and she sat before Cressida, a ghost of the girl that brightened her office that evening. Subdued by something in the moonlight.

Maybe what Vee needed was a friend, someone who

existed outside the walls of an institution. "I don't analyze patients over drinks."

"Well, we don't have any cocktails *yet*." Vee laughed again, this time the musical tone carried across the table like bells.

Cressida tapped the menu. "That's one problem I *can* solve tonight." She raised her hand and flagged the scattered waitress to their table.

Vee's icy eyes reflected the light from the oil lamps above their heads. They burned with more light than seemed possible from such a small flame. Beside them, Cressida's eyes must have looked like those of a corpse.

CHAPTER 10

Several apple martinis later and the color had returned to Vee's cheeks. The sickly green liquid sloshed from the shallow glass and splattered against Cressida's white blouse.

"I'm so sorry." Vee's melodic voice slurred. "I'll wash it for you next week."

Cressida's hands flew to her shirt as she tried to shake off the green stains. Cressida's ears heated. "Next week?"

"At my appointment." Vee ran her index finger along the rim of her glass, collecting sugar like a humming bird.

"Right." Cressida sipped the virulent cocktail, and the inside of her nose burned. It tasted like Jolly Ranchers and fire. The room drifted in and out of focus. Her fingers were sticky from wiping her shirt, now hopelessly splattered like a piece of modern art. Maybe it was time to buy something with a bit more color. Something that would hide the stains.

"We rescheduled for next week, right?"

Cressida pinched her chin between her thumb and forefinger. "Well, not officially. Honestly, I didn't think I'd see you again after this evening."

"Really? Why?

"Because you don't seem entirely comfortable discussing some of the less pleasant aspects of your life. Until you're ready to speak candidly, I can't help you."

A crease formed between Vee's eyebrows. "Candidly? Rex usually tells me I'm too blunt."

"There's a difference between gregariousness and honesty."

Vee's mouth hung open slightly and her tongue passed slowly across her bottom lip. Then she smiled. "See! I knew you were different. I'm really glad I ran into you tonight."

Cressida cracked her knuckles. This was dangerous territory. Maintaining professional boundaries was the first thing psychologists were taught in clinical training. But Vee was more than just a patient in crisis. "Me too."

Vee beamed. "I guess it was fate. So do you come here often?"

"Never."

"I guess there's a first time for everything!" Vee laughed and then the smile flickered from her face like the flames of the overhead heaters in the wind. "But you can still be my therapist after tonight, right? There's no rule against getting drunk with a patient?"

"Well..."

Vee rested her elbows on the table and her chin in her hands. "Please."

"Sure. Why not?" Cressida's lips stuck to her teeth as she smiled. The alcohol was desiccating her—soon she'd look like Mrs. Coulter, creaking back and forth on her sofa and complaining about the rain. For some reason the image made her laugh.

"Good." Vee giggled along as the bar erupted into shouts

and jeers then fell to a disappointed murmur. The game must have ended.

Vee stared at the television across the room and the light flickered in her eyes. At some point in the last half hour, fire pits had started burning on the beach and the smoke wafted across the table between them.

Vee's eyes welled and she turned back to Cressida with trembling lips. "I think Rex is cheating on me."

Cressida straightened up in her chair. Perhaps Vee was ready to listen to reason about the man. "Then why don't you leave him?"

Vee's shoulders sagged and the fire in her voice cooled along with her eyes. "Well, I don't exactly have any proof."

"Then how do you know?"

"I had a dream about it, and my dreams almost always come true. But Rex thinks I'm full of shit, and what if he's right?"

A gush of air escaped Cressida's lungs. She abhorred the idea of agreeing with Rex, especially when he could exert his power over Vee at any moment to end their therapy. "Dreams are just our subconscious telling us things we already know, Vee."

"I don't know what I know anymore. That's why I came to therapy." Vee rubbed her wrists without intent, a nervous twitch, and there were two neat scars running up the inside of her arms. Cressida hadn't noticed them in the artificial light of her office, but under the moonlight they stood out purple and angry against her pale skin. *Rex wasn't the only one who'd hurt Vee.*

"Besides the dream, do you have any reason to think he's cheating on you?" An electric sensation buzzed through Cressida's chest. Burning, seething rage. Rage at Rex for hurting Vee, at Vee for letting Rex drive her to the point of cutting her wrists, and at herself for inviting these feelings back into her life after she'd just lost Sam. Life was simpler when it was black and white and dull. Anger was the enemy of control. Max taught her that.

But maybe Max had been wrong. Sometimes anger could reclaim power too. If Vee was angry enough at Rex to leave him, she might finally be safe.

Vee shrugged again. It was a terrible habit. "He's hiding something. I just feel it." She puffed her cheeks out and released a sharp breath. "And, boy, if he knew I was talking to you about him, he'd never let me come back."

Cressida couldn't let Rex talk Vee out of therapy. She had to break the hold he had over her somehow. She leaned across the table until she was face to face with Vee. "Do you want to find out for sure what he's up to?"

ROGER BANKS'S 1992 Volvo Station Wagon was damp inside like the window had been cracked all night, humidity clung to the dash, and the windows steamed with each breath Cressida and Vee exhaled. Light trickled through from the streetlights above and reflected off the raindrops that rolled down the windshield, flickering and dancing as if the droplets were alive. Cressida pulled down the driver's side sun visor. A key fell into her lap. One of the benefits of living in a small town is people still behave as if it's 1950. Roger was as trusting as he was foolish—Cressida had seen him leave his keys in the car every night for three years.

She glanced up at the darkened windows above their offices. Roger and his wife were probably asleep in their separate twin beds. He wouldn't miss the car until morning. That gave them hours to stake out Rex's house and still return the car before dawn. Besides, he had told her that if she needed anything she shouldn't hesitate to ask. He wanted to help her. That's what he kept saying every time he'd looked down her shirt. Roger would forgive her this little trespass as she had forgiven his.

Cressida jammed the key into the ignition and the car shuddered to life. Cressida didn't drive. She had a license, but hadn't actually been behind the wheel of a car since before Max died. She didn't remember much about that night, but she knew shouldn't have been there.

"Nice car." Vee shivered in the passenger seat. The heater was wheezing exhaust into the cabin and Cressida had to open a window to keep from killing them both.

"Yeah, it runs."

Cressida eased the car out of the parking space and onto the winding coastal road that ran through the middle of town. The roads were mercifully quiet. There were no headlights to blind her and no other cars to drift into. Her fingers clenched the steering wheel until her knuckles blanched and she felt the steady vibration of the asphalt grinding against the tires. It hummed in her brain, like the deafening drone of her dreamless sleep. Numbing. Punishing. Except this time she could hear the soft sound of Vee humming tunelessly to herself as she stared out the window like a child.

Sweat dripped between Cressida's back and the cracked leather seat. The feeling was achingly familiar. It had been hot in the car that night with Max too. Sweat dampened her hairline as the images danced through her mind. He'd taken his eyes off the road, just for a second, to turn down the heater. Cressida's heart crashed in her chest. She bit down hard on the inside of her cheek, willing the memory to stay with her a little longer, but it was gone. The memories were coming now even when she was awake. Why?

Seemingly oblivious to her extraordinary effect on Cressida, Vee nonchalantly lifted her foot onto the dash and pointed out turns and stops from memory. Vee was at ease, her smile shining through the dark. Already happier than she'd been at the bar—because of Cressida. Cressida drew a deep breath and relaxed her hands on the steering wheel. Her pulse steadied. This had to be the right thing to do.

A few minutes later, Vee pointed out the window to a small house with a deep porch and blue shutters. "This is Rex's place."

The porch light flickered over rusty lawn chairs and a dirty grass mat. The neighbors were so close they could have shared drinks from each other's porches. Maybe they did. There were beer cans rolling along the flaking wood deck, some new and some old enough that the sun had faded their labels.

"He said he would be studying with friends until late so I should sleep at my place tonight."

Cressida pulled the car along the curb opposite Rex's house and parked a few houses down so they could see his front door. She turned off the engine, killing the dashboard lights, and they were cast into darkness. "Is his car out front?" Cressida nodded toward the street in front of the house.

"No, I don't see it. Maybe he's still out. Maybe we should go. Rex will be pissed if he catches me spying on him." Vee pulled her phone from her pocket and checked the time. It was nearly midnight. She yawned.

"It's dark and he's never seen this car before. Are you afraid he'll hurt you if you confront him about the cheating?"

Vee's voice dropped and she rubbed her wrist like she had in the bar. "No. He's not like that." Her chest rose and fell in long, deep motions, and the windows were already foggy with her breath.

Cressida reached across the car and cranked the passenger window slightly open. "Otherwise we won't be able to see anything."

Vee wrinkled her nose. "How long do we sit here?" Cressida could just make out her chipped front tooth through her parted lips. Her blond hair was flattened to her head and her dark roots showed through in the dim light. It was still beautiful, like a snowcapped mountain after a storm. Cressida wondered what she would look like with blond hair. Something to brighten up her world the way Vee had brightened her office.

"We'll sit here as long as we have to."

"I don't know if this is such a good idea." Vee rubbed her eyes with the back of her wrist, slumped into the seat.

Cressida lifted her hand to the keys in the ignition. "It's your call. We can leave right now and pretend we were never here."

Vee squeezed her eyes shut. "No. We're already here. Let's stay just a little longer." She laid her head against the faux wood trim on the door. She hiccupped. "So where is your family now? You said your mom passed away, and I got the impression you weren't close. What about your dad? Brothers and sisters?"

Vee's eyes fluttered. She probably wouldn't remember most of what they talked about by morning, and a distraction might help warm Vee's cold feet. Cressida pressed her back against the driver's seat. "No brothers and sisters, and my dad left before I was born. I never met him. It was just me and my mom, and honestly, most of the time it was just me."

Vee knitted her brow, her lips pursing as she considered what to say next. "You must have had some good times together though, right? I mean, she sounds like she was an interesting woman."

Cressida's stomach hardened beneath the seatbelt. "I barely knew her."

"What about the good times? You must have had fun together sometimes." Vee closed her eyes like she was speaking from her dreams. Cressida wouldn't have pegged her for an optimist.

"She liked to feed the birds." Cressida spat the words into the stale air of the car, the bitter taste of bile and resentment on her tongue.

"That's nice." Vee hummed on the verge of sleep.

Cressida waited until Vee's breath slowed to a steady rhythm before she continued speaking to the cold, black night. "When I was six she spent an entire weekend erecting feeders in the backyard. Every kind of seed a bird could hope for. I thought it looked like a fairy garden."

"Mmmm." Vee shifted against the door, the seatbelt pulling against her beaded earrings.

"But then the squirrels found them. Within hours there were dozens of squirrels decimating the seeds and scaring the birds away. Mom was furious. I asked her why she didn't want to feed the squirrels too, but she said they weren't what she wanted, and she always got exactly what she wanted." Cressida gripped the steering wheel until her knuckles were white. "That night she refilled the feeders again, and when I woke up the next morning the yard was clear. Not a squirrel in sight."

Vee sighed in her sleep. Her foot lolled to the side on the dash and her arms wrapped around her leg.

Cressida's heart thumped in her chest and adrenaline surged through her veins. She'd never told anyone this before.

Not Sam.

Not even Max.

"Then later when I was playing in the sand pit under our back deck, I found them. Dozens of fuzzy corpses, their black eyes glassy and staring. They covered the ground, some of them still writhing, until the whole pit looked like it was breathing its last breath."

Cressida sighed into the emptiness. Vee remained motionless.

"She didn't warn me. She'd poisoned the seed. She knew the squirrels would get there first, and she hated them for being stronger than the birds. More successful. Mostly she hated them for not being birds. When I told her what I'd seen she just handed me a shovel, told me to clean it up, and retreated back into her reading. She had to work, and my tears were wetting her book."

The car fell into silence and Cressida released the steering wheel, her fingers still curved angrily around an invisible foe. Her chest heaved and she could still smell the acrid scent of fear and dead flesh. In her office she was always in control. Empress over the sea of dirt and sand. Until this minion of mayhem, sprite of chaos, had come fluttering into the room and suddenly everything was blown away in a breath of sea air and the scent of strawberry shampoo.

Vee was breaking her open. Cressida's power had been shattered into thousand pieces and whisked away with the glitter that fell from Vee's clothes. Cressida's head ached and her eyes were heavy. Vee muttered in her sleep, but Cressida couldn't understand her dream language. Instead she stared at the door of Rex's house, willing it to open, so she and Vee could move on with their lives.

Rex didn't interest Cressida.

Vee was Cressida's bird and he was merely a squirrel in her feeder.

CHAPTER 11

Cressida slouched in her seat and wrapped her arms around herself as the chilly evening wind whipped along the street and in through the open car window, stinging her face pulling her back from the brink of sleep. Cressida's eyelids thickened and cold sense of foreboding settled in her gut. Ominous and overwhelming. Goosebumps rose on her skin as a particularly icy blast filled the car, thick and wet like ice. Or snow. Cressida opened her eyes. She was suspended upside down in the car as black flakes fell over her head and soiled the white blanket beneath what should have been the roof of the car. Now all that remained against the ground was a gaping hole of twisted metal and freshly upset earth.

More black spots fell to the ground above Cressida's hanging head. No, not black. Deep red; the color of blood. She was back at the scene of the accident. Beside her the passenger seat was empty. Vee was gone. Crumpled against the door was a huddled figure, dressed all in white and curled into the fetal position with her head hidden under her arms. It had to be her. Pain seared through Cressida's head as she struggled to free herself, to reach Vee. But she was trapped. The blood dripped faster until the ground below was completely saturated. Cressida's head began to spin and her vision tunneled over Vee's body. Then something shifted. The girl's arm fell away from her head revealing sleek, red hair.

Cressida jerked her head forward and cracked her forehead on the steering wheel of Roger's Volvo. The snow was gone and Vee was snoring in the seat next to her. The dream faded, but Cressida could still hear the surprised grunt that hung on Max's lips when she'd touched him, the squeal of tires, and the shrieking of twisted metal. Her memories shimmered like holograms and then zapped out of sight again. Max had been surprised when she'd leaned across the car toward him. Surprised and excited. Cressida rubbed the lump forming above her right eye and rolled up the driver's side window.

The figure lying on the ground under her hadn't been Vee after all, but Cressida. And she'd been Max. Cold, bleeding, and helpless. Chills ran down Cressida's spine. Even her nightmares were laced with importance, tiny shards of memories slicing their way through her mind like some kind of bloodletting ritual. The car was spinning around her and as hard as she tried, Cressida couldn't remember the last time she'd felt so afraid. Of what? The dream? Nightmares were the price one paid for the privilege to dream, the ancient coins with which to pay the boatman on the river Styx. She'd told her patients the same thing hundreds of times. The fear was something else.

Beside her, Vee ground her teeth in her sleep and the sound reverberated down Cressida's spine. She held her breath, afraid the slightest movement would wake the girl. What time had Vee been up that morning, tossing nets and hauling fish for her father? For Rex. For people who didn't care at all about Vee's dreams. But Cressida could care for this girl. On some level, she already did. After all, what is real commitment if not the intertwining of hopes and dreams? And Cressida's dreams had both came in close proximity to Vee. It couldn't have been a coincidence.

The capricious girl was the antidote to Cressida's suffering, a healing elixir, but one which was barbed with poison. Vee could disappear at any moment, leave therapy, move from Silverside, or fall victim to some horrible act of domestic violence, taking with her all hope. She couldn't let that happen.

Vee snorted and straightened up in the seat, rubbing her cheek where the lock had imprinted into her flesh. She rubbed her eyes with the back of her wrist. There were fingerprints welted into the soft skin beneath her hands like she had gripped her arm too tight in her sleep. The dawn burned on the horizon, turning the sky from black to blue, crimson to gold. Rex's ramshackle house stood on a hill, surrounded by trees and overlooking another row of houses below, and in the distance, the blue sparkle of the sea. The large windows framing Rex's house were still dark and lifeless. Dusky waves crashed in the shadows, waiting for the sun to bathe them in color.

"Did I miss it?" She croaked.

"He didn't come home."

"Oh." Vee's mouth tightened and she looked out the window at his silent house. She frowned.

"That could mean—"

"I know." Vee's chin dropped to her chest and she looked at her hands. Her turquoise polish was chipped and ragged.

Cressida turned the ignition, startling a cat from under the car. It skittered down the street. "Next time we'll bring snacks and coffee."

Vee smiled, but there was no humor in her eyes. "This was probably a bad idea anyway."

The fuzzy edges around Cressida's mind sharpened to attention. "Hey, don't give up so quick. When is his next study night?"

"Not for a while, but he's supposed to be watching the game with some friends next Friday." She rubbed her eyes sleepily.

"Then I'll see you in a week."

Vee laughed. "I guess Rex was right to be worried about me going to therapy."

"I guess so. It's hard to feel sorry for the guy though."

"You know you don't have to do this, right?"

"Yes, I do." Cressida tapped her hands on the steering wheel. "Where can I drop you off?"

"I can walk from here. It's only a couple blocks." Vee checked her phone and her mouth twitched. "So should I just text you about Friday."

Cressida caught a glimpse of her reflection in the rearview mirror. Her hair glowed red in the sunrise. "How's seven? We can just meet at my office."

"Perfect! Should we count that as my appointment for next week too?"

"If you want."

"Great. See you then." Vee sprung from the car and into the fresh air.

The wind pulled at the grass and swirled sand along the street as Vee rushed into the distance. Cressida smiled as she drove away. The colors of the morning shimmered off the rain soaked streets and warmed the car. Perhaps she would even go for a run that morning.

BY THE TIME she pulled the Volvo into its usual space the birds were chattering in the trees, the dew was sparkling on the grass, the flowers were opening toward the sun, and Roger was standing beside the car wearing Lycra pants, a purple sweat band, and a concerned scowl.

The sound of thumping filled Cressida's mind. The slow, rhythmic beat of her heart, filling her muscles with oxygen. There was glitter in the passenger seat and glitter on her hands. There was no escaping it. Borrowing the car and bringing it back before dawn had been a perfect plan. It shouldn't have gone wrong. She shouldn't have let it. Shouldn't have fallen asleep.

Fucking Rex. If he had just come home like he was supposed to then Cressida would have woken up earlier. Rex would have been history and Cressida wouldn't be trapped inside her boss's car staring at the ocean while he slammed his palm against the window. She didn't make mistakes like this. Ever.

"Miss Dunhill? What in God's name is going on?" Roger Banks's face glistened with sweat and anger as he shouted through the glass.

Cressida turned off the engine and eased out of the station wagon. Her shirt was wrinkled and she was wearing the same outfit he'd seen her in the day before. "I am *so* sorry."

"Well, I sure as heck hope so. I was about to call the darn cops." He pressed his face close to hers and the sick, metallic odor of fear wafted off him in waves like the ocean.

"I...was with a patient."

"In *my* car?" His hand flew to his forehead and mopped sweat into his thinning hair. Strands streaked across his ubiquitous bald spot. Cressida's mother used to rake her fingers through her hair when she was angry, until she got sick and it started coming away in gobs.

This was really his fault. He should have been more careful about where he left his keys, and who knew about it. She stood taller. "There was an emergency."

"What kind of emergency? Was it the same friend as before? From the hospital?" His shoulders dropped an inch and his jaw relaxed. He always cared too much. No wonder people took advantage of him.

"No. Everything is fine now. One of my new patients was in crisis."

"New patient?"

"Yeah, that girl you referred to me last week. She turned up in the middle of the night soaked to the bone. There were signs of previous suicidal gestures. I feared the worst."

Roger had been a medical student at the institution when the mermaid patient died.

His muddy eyes lit with recognition and years of wasted empathy. His shoulders drooped forward and he watched his shoe scrape the floor. "Poor girl." He raised his eyes to Cressida "Are you ok, dear?"

Cressida handed him the key. "I'm fine. Sorry for worrying you."

He grasped her shoulder. "No, no. You're not going to get away that easily."

Cressida's mind jumped to Vee's bruises, to Sam lying beaten and broken in a hospital bed, and to Rex. Her body tensed, ready to fight. "What?"

"Having a patient threaten suicide is a grueling experience for the patient and the therapist. Especially a young one, like yourself. I think now might be a good time to sit down for one of those counseling sessions we talked about."

"Oh, no. I'm fine. I'm sure you have lots to do this morning." If she'd been wearing sneakers instead of heels she might have run. She looked down at his tensed calves. He probably would have caught her anyway. Instead she pulled her arm free of his grasp.

Roger tipped his head toward one of the second story windows of the asylum, nestled beneath the peaked eaves and the sun-bleached shingles. The curtains twitched. Apparently Cressida wasn't the only one being watched. "I was going to go for a run, but my morning is pretty open. I don't want you burning out too soon. This is what supervisors are for."

Cressida shook her head. "I don't need therapy."

"I'm not saying you do. This job can take a toll on anyone's emotional wellbeing, especially when faced with difficult patient situations. You've had a rough week. Sometimes we just need a chance to release some pressure." His voice was soft like he was singing a lullaby.

Cressida shivered. "You know, I've had a long night. I should probably just get some sleep."

Roger pocketed the key. "Are you sure?"

"Yes, sir."

Roger raised his eyebrows, and it might have been a trick of the dawn, but his cheeks seemed to redden. "Well, my door is always open."

Cressida nodded. "Thanks. And I appreciate your understanding about the mix-up with the car this morning."

"Don't mention it." Roger turned his back to his apartment. "But listen, next time you need to borrow the car, ask me first. Helen about had a heart attack when she saw it was gone this morning." He twisted around and ran off toward the beach, scattering sandpipers and scuttling crabs as his feet hit the sand.

Cressida needed a nap.

CHAPTER 12

Snow was falling onto Cressida's cheek as she lay frozen in her bed. The room around her was dim, colorless, and flat, like it was made of paper. Dark, grey clouds twisted along the ceiling. Instead of melting against her skin, the snowflakes burned her face, boring holes in her hard exterior. She held out her hand to grasp one and it seared through her palm. Yet there was no pain, only the dull throb of hopelessness.

More snow fell and burned away her grey flesh. Bright reds, deep blues, and vivid greens poured from her wounds like blood and spilled onto the floor. She tried to clean it up, but her hands had become formless balls of light--everything she touched erupted with molten color. The last of her dead flesh dropped away and she was naked, reborn into the cold and suddenly she was overcome with pain. Sharp, stabbing, like shards of metal being driven into her skull.

Cressida woke with her red hair swept across her eyes and her head buried between the cushions of her office sofa. Through the darkness she could see Max. The way the creases around his eyes deepened when he looked at her with longing. The way he stroked his index finger over his pen when he spoke to her, a subtle fidget, a tiny chink in the armor of his control.

The smooth metal of his pen had worn rough patches on the skin along the sides of his top knuckles, calluses formed from thousands of pages of clinical notes. She used to stare at them during her sessions, wondering what it would feel like to run her tongue over them. After ten years of staring into the face of the abyss each time fell asleep, her mind's eye was open again. The memories were flowing easier now. She remembered the look on Max's face just before the crash, his eyes wide with desire and his mouth twisted into an approving smile.

And this time there was something else. White lace as far as she could see and a long train flowing behind her. She'd been wearing a dress that night. She had forgotten just how beautiful it was.

And then there was Vee: her halo of messy hair, the way the bones of her shoulders protruded like wings when she shrugged her indifference, and the glow that always seemed to surround her. It was more than just the bright colors and gratuitous glitter. Vee's shine transcended the physical. It emanated from within her. From within Cressida's dreams. Things were just easier with Vee than they had been with Sam. More mutual.

Cressida rubbed her swollen eyes and sat up against the stiff headboard. The edges of her vision were starting to blur. She needed more sleep. More dreams. More Vee. She couldn't get enough. Cressida balled her fists in the sheets, testing her grip on reality, then leaned over to look at the clock beside her bed. Monday morning. For her patients, today marked the beginning of just another week to be swept away eventually like footprints in the sand. But for

Cressida, it was the beginning of the rest of her life, and only five more days until she'd see Vee again.

THE OFFICE WAS alight with the dawn, but Cressida turned on the lamp anyway and consulted her appointment book. *Monday 7:30 a.m. Olly Peterson.* A twelve-year-old with night terrors and an attitude to match. His mother said they went through four psychologists before settling with Cressida, and he'd scared them all. She'd been treating him for months. Cressida closed the datebook and laid it in the center of her closed notebook. She ran her fingers along the edges, perfectly framed, and sighed.

The office was always quiet on a Monday morning, but this morning even Roger was blissfully absent. She crossed the hallway, past Roger's closed door, and toward the bathroom. The office washroom was more of a tiled closet than a room. There was a small pastel pink pedestal sink and a matching toilet whose lid had gone missing before Cressida moved in. The surrounding tile was sea foam green and marked with the names of patients from the past and present, as well as some who came to visit the locally infamous Mermaid Asylum. Most of them were scratched and faded by now, forgotten the way legends often were.

The water ran brown from the tap for a few seconds before clearing the sand from the lines. Cressida splashed her face and smoothed her limp hair along her temples. Her eyes were wild and bloodshot, strung out on the memories she'd craved for so long. She was a mess, yet somehow it seemed her cheeks were rosier than they had been the day before. Somehow she was reflecting Vee's glow. She didn't understand it, but the dreams always followed the girl. The feelings Cressida experienced while in Vee's presence were more than just intoxicating, they were healing. Vee wasn't just part of Cressida's first dream. She *was* the dream. And for whatever reason Cressida's dreams were linked to her memories of Max. Without Vee, Cressida would be forced back into the darkness. She couldn't let that happen.

"FUCK MY MOTHER." Olly's lack of sleep was betrayed by the red rims around his green eyes, and the tremor of his hand as he sharply thrust his middle finger into the air.

Children were rarely so burdened. With most of her patients she hid behind the guise of the unaffected therapist, safe from their fears and their pain, but not with Olly. His life was filled with grownups who were afraid of him, or afraid to break him. But Olly wore a mask of his own: green hair, nose ring, and the stench of cigarettes to shield him from the fact that he, too, was marred.

"Fine. Fuck her, but you're here to talk to me. I want to listen." Cressida's usual leather chair sat empty. She perched on the coffee table, her knees nearly touching his. His face was thin like the rest of him. He didn't yet have the thickness of a man, but he had all the baggage.

"What's the point, lady? We've been talking for like... forever. I still can't sleep." He cracked the knuckles on his right hand and winced.

Cressida leaned in, giving him no room to withdraw. All children try to escape, starting with birth, but sometimes all they want is to be caught. "Because of the dreams?"

"Why the fuck do you think I'm here?"

Cressida's heart raced and her nerves were on fire. Here, in this room, she could make a difference. She could push people as far as she wanted, and it felt good. "Why *are* you here?"

"Because my stupid mother makes me come."

The slump of his narrow shoulders exposed his apathy as a bluff. Tremors in his hand, in his lip, gave away his fear.

"Then run. Why stay with her if all she does is piss you off?"

Olly froze, his eyes wide like an animal staring down the headlights of an oncoming car. "Well..."

Cressida folded her arms across her chest and straightened her back. This was what she did best, and this is why her patients returned to her week after week.

Olly's face was ashen as all the blood pooled to essential places, his heart too lethargic to pump it any farther. "I'm twelve. She'd find me."

"How does that make you feel?"

"Trapped like a fucking rat." He chewed the cuticle of his right hand, tearing a sliver of skin from the base of his fingernail and watching the blood pool and roll over his finger.

Cressida reached for the box of tissues on the coffee table and handed him one. The tough cushions of her sofa were great at hiding tears, but blood was harder to wash away. "Do you know what my favorite thing is about rats?"

The overhead light glinted off Olly's nose ring like glitter. Or maybe it *was* glitter. "What?"

"Rats are survivors. They'll do anything to stay alive, to keep moving. Even eat another rat." Cressida rose from the table and grabbed a wastebasket from beside her chair. She held it out for Olly to deposit his crimson-stained tissue, but he shook his head. Cressida set the bin by his feet and returned to her usual resting place in the leather chair.

The boy ripped at the edges of the tissue, shredding it

into narrow strips, studying the fibers as they pulled apart under his thumb. "Yeah, but some of the rats just get eaten."

"Only so the other rats can survive."

Olly scraped a shard of glitter from the cushion of the sofa and examined it on his fingertip. It glinted as red as blood against his pale skin in the morning light. He slowly brought his finger to his mouth and sucked the glitter off. One fewer piece of Vee left in the room.

Olly coughed. "My father wasn't a rat at all, then. He just fucking gave up."

Cressida blinked hard. "Is that how you see it?"

"How else can I see it? He ate a fucking bullet while his kid watched Power Rangers in the other room. What a pussy." The bloody tissue was balled in Olly's lap, shredded into a hundred pieces, like a nest: a place to nurture his growing resentment.

"You think he gave up on you?"

"I don't think he thought about me at all." He tossed the fluffy mound in the garbage by his feet.

"But you think about him. Is that what the dreams are about?" Months of therapy and this was the closest she had ever brought Olly to the edge, the genesis of his night terrors.

"He could have waited until I was at school so I didn't have to walk in and find the bastard covered in his own shit and brains." This was it, his last attempt to push away the memory by dehumanizing it. The anger in his face flickered for a moment to something else, something more primal and ugly and vulnerable: fear.

Cressida seized the opportunity by the throat. "And you're pissed."

"You're goddamned right I am. I was nine years old. I still brushed my teeth with a Star Wars toothbrush. I hate him for taking that normal kid shit away from me." Olly's body lurched forward and for a moment Cressida thought he'd been sick in the wastebasket, but instead he heaved long sobs into his lap.

"Good. You deserve to be pissed off."

Olly sat up, snot mixing with tears and dripping past his pierced upper lip. He didn't sniff it back. "My mom says I need to forgive him."

"The only thing you need to do is decide whether you're going to be the rat that survives or the rat that gets eaten." Cressida skin was on fire. She reached across to the side table and touched Max's pen. The cool metal was like ice against her fingertips.

The office door jittered and then creaked open. Olly's mom, a tiny mouse of a woman with brown hair and a flower pinned to her blouse, prodded her head into their space. Olly snapped his head from between his legs, grabbed a tissue from the box, and blew his nose hard and loud into the silence. The moment was gone, and his hands were no longer trembling. Cressida released a sharp breath. She'd been so close.

"Am I early?" Mrs. Peterson smiled, though her eyes remained sad.

Oh, for fuck's sake. Cressida shook her head. "No. You're right on time."

Olly stood from the sofa and tossed his tissue into the trash. He shuffled past Cressida's chair, his pants hanging heavy beneath his hips, and laid his hand on the studded leather back of her seat. "See you next week." He pushed past his mother at the door and mumbled something about waiting in the car. Then he was gone.

Mrs. Peterson smiled apologetically and followed her son to the car. Cressida could see her empathy and pain written in the hunch of her shoulders and the creases at the corners of her mouth, but none of that was any use to her or Olly. Empathy couldn't save Olly any more than it could have saved Cressida, or Sam, or Vee. Cressida plucked Max's pen from the table and turned it over in her palm before storing it safely in the pocket of her black slacks. Anger, on the other hand, was a powerful motivator. She crossed the room to the desk in the corner and opened the laptop she kept there mostly for decoration.

How hard could it be to locate information on a man named Rex?

CHAPTER 13

The obsidian black bay windows framed the white face of the clock between them, capturing Cressida's attention yet again. It was finally Friday, and the day had been slow and torturous. Her neck ached from craning up at it all afternoon, watching the hands tick closer to 7:00 p.m. when Vee was supposed to arrive. Tonight she would uncover Rex's secret and prove to Vee that her suspicions had been warranted. Then there would be nothing standing between Cressida and Vee. Her palms were clammy and she wiped them across her wrinkled slacks. It was almost time. She needed to change.

Inside the small closet in her office Cressida found a pair of yoga pants and some tennis shoes left over from a canceled run with Roger last week. She stripped off her slacks, pulled on the yoga pants, and folded the dirty laundry into a neat pile. Her white button-down blouse was completely out of place next to her sporty bottom half. She should have kept the sweatshirt she'd loaned to Vee.

A timid knock at the door froze her thoughts. She yanked a shirt from the hanger and pulled it over her head.

Behind the door, Vee's slender shoulders were obscured by the groping arm of a man no taller than Cressida. His face was hidden behind stringy dark hair, thick eyebrows, and stubble around his jaw that looked like ants crawling over his face. He was Vee's polar opposite. Dressed in midnight jeans and a black T-shirt under a charcoal grey hoodie—Cressida's sweatshirt. He wasn't tall enough to reach over Vee's shoulder without tipping his body. It looked uncomfortable. Unnatural.

Vee's face was flushed like the first time she'd arrived in Cressida's office, and her earrings were tangled in her short hair. She wore a plastic smile when she greeted Cressida. "Hi, sorry we're late. Rex had a change of plans tonight."

Cressida lifted a hand beneath her red hair and touched the hidden earrings nestled against the nape of her neck. Hers and Vee's were a matching set.

Vee shifted. "I tried to call the office to cancel, but no one answered, so Rex suggested we just come down here together."

Rex's brushed the hair from his face and revealed a tired sneer, as if his face had been frozen that way for hours. He dropped his arm from Vee's shoulders held out his hand. "I'm Rex. Nice to meet you."

Cressida's blood singed her veins and she clamped her fists so tight her arms ached. This wasn't how it was supposed to go. She had planned everything out. The stake-out, the music she and Vee would listen to, the books they'd discuss. She'd even reread *The Aeneid*, and Virgil always gave her a headache. She and Vee were going to catch Rex in a lie, somewhere he wasn't supposed to be with a girl he wasn't supposed to know. Vee was going to thank her. But now Rex was here and everything was wrong. This was his doing.

Cressida couldn't think clearly. She let the air settle around his outstretched hand before she shook it. "Rex. Like a dog?"

His eyes narrowed and Vee coughed, but Cressida kept her eyes fixed on Rex's face. His jaw tightened and his Adam's apple bounced as he swallowed hard. "I prefer the fucking dinosaur."

Rex paused for several seconds before he slapped Vee on the ass and laughed. He was showing off for her like a peacock. It was disgusting, but how she would love to study him on her sofa sometime, to pull him apart bit by bit.

The plans Cressida had made might have been wasted, but that didn't mean she had to write off the entire night. Her fingers relaxed to her sides and a calm washed over her. She had been right about Rex all along. He needed to go. She could still show Vee what kind of man Rex was. Prove to her that she'd be better off without him. Cressida smiled.

Vee exhaled loudly. "We should probably get going."

Rex's eyes were locked on Cressida's breasts. "Is that my girl's shirt?"

Cressida lifted a hand to her bare chest. She could feel the scars from the accident dimpled on her skin, scattered haphazardly like buckshot. These were a part of the accident she'd never forgotten. She crossed her arms. The fizzling hatred returned to her gut. She wouldn't let Rex see her squirm. "I didn't have time to go home and change."

He scratched the back of his head and frowned. Vee's mouth was open, her eyes puzzled. According to Vee, Rex was used to getting his way with girls, and Cressida needed him to let his guard down. To reveal his true nature.

Cressida smiled sweetly and ran her hands awkwardly along the tie-dyed fabric and tilted her head. "Does it look ok?"

"You look great." Vee interjected, pulling on Rex's arm. "Now can we go?"

"You got it, babe." Rex wrapped his arm around Vee and pulled her toward the front door and away from Cressida. She closed the door to her office and followed them out.

THE CRAB SHACK was quiet enough to hear the soft music playing on the jukebox. The rabid fans had the night off along with the basketball team. Cressida suggested they sit outside on the patio, but Rex insisted they'd be more comfortable in the shadowy recesses of the bar.

Vee hung from his arm like a doll, limp and ineffectual and dull—nothing but Rex's plaything. *Nauseating*. It had already begun. He was stealing Vee's light. Behind their table, a group of middle-aged men drank oily stout. On Cressida's other side, a pair of college boys ordered another round of drinks despite the half-full glasses parked in front of them already. Probably in order to earn the attention of the moderately attractive waitress sporting silver hair, a studded collar, and designer motorcycle boots that had clearly never butted against the greasy foot pegs of a real bike. She looked like Steampunk Barbie, and they just looked desperate. But at least they were offering her something in exchange for her attention. Cressida watched Rex's stiff shoulders. Vee tensed whenever he moved.

Rex gulped the last of his beer and thumped the empty glass to the table. Steampunk answered the insistent clatter of his empty glass like it was a dog whistle. He sat back against his chair with a smug grin. The waitress slipped a fresh drink in front of Rex and lingered longer than necessary to ensure his satisfaction. She batted her heavily painted eyelids and twisted her fingers through her knotted hair. On her bicep, a dancing mermaid tangled around a ship's anchor stared, unblinking, begging Cressida to let her drown. This girl wasn't even alive when the mermaid patient had died. She probably thought the tattoo made her edgy, but what did she know about darkness?

"Are you sure I can't get you guys anything else?" The waitress's green eyes, perfect copies of the sorrowful eyes of the mermaid, never left Rex's smug face. He nodded his indifference, but leaned into her flirting.

"We're ok for now. Thanks, though." Vee placed her hand over Rex's forearm, but he slipped it away. How could Vee ever question whether this man was cheating on her? Clearly Vee was completely enthralled by Rex. His flirting with a waitress wasn't going to be enough to drive them apart tonight. Cressida needed to push him further.

"My girl thinks I drink too much. I'm surprised she even lets me out of the house to play gigs." He kept his gaze fixed on the waitress's joker smile. The college kids at the table behind them were staging a not-so-subtle coup complete with throat clearing and mug thumping, but their cries for attention fell on heavily-pierced, deaf ears.

"I knew I recognized you from somewhere." She snapped her fingers and pointed at Rex. "You guys played The Brig last week. You were amazing." Cressida pictured the mermaid on the waitress's shoulder rolling her eyes.

Rex grinned back and then yanked Vee's hand from her lap, squeezing it tight over the table. "See, babe? You should have come to the show."

Vee and the waitress winced at the same time but for different reasons. "I'm sorry I missed it." Vee glanced up at Cressida, her eyes searching, confiding, begging.

Cressida cleared her throat. "You know what?" She

smiled up at the waitress who dragged her eyes from Rex's face. "I think I will have another beer after all."

"I'll be right back with that. You let me know if you need anything else." Steampunk Barbie nodded her twisted head and dragged herself back to her job.

Vee mouthed *thank you* across the table and Cressida's heart jumped. She could tell Vee was ready to accept her help, to be saved. Sam had never appreciated Cressida's affection, acted like it was a burden, but Vee was different. Cressida had recognized that from the moment they met.

Rex was smiling and stroking his thumb across Vee's slender knuckles. "Too bad the guys weren't here to witness that. They would have gotten a kick out of it." His eyes were filled with lust—for the waitress, for fame, and for himself. Rex liked to think he was in control, but actually he was weak, pathetic, and hopelessly dependent on the admiration of others. Cressida smiled. This was how she was going to catch him. She just needed an opportunity.

Vee shifted in her seat, her arm awkwardly draped across the high table. "I always knew you guys would be famous one day."

"It's just a local club, babe." He released her hand and she slid it back into her lap.

"Well, *she* didn't seem to think so." Cressida nodded in the direction of the waitress who kept peeking at Rex while fielding questions from the college kids.

Vee drained her beer without breathing, and then coughed. Rex's eyes focused again on Cressida like he'd forgotten she was there. To him, women were simply mirrors through which to glimpse his own narcissism. Shadows danced across his unshaven face. "So what are you doing hanging around with your patients anyway, Doc? The

Mermaid Asylum making house calls now? As if that place isn't fucking creepy enough." He snorted.

He was drunk, but more than that, he was blind. "Vee and I are friends." *And he was on his way out.*

"Ain't that a violation of ethics or something?"

Isn't beating your girlfriend a violation of ethics? Cressida's shoulders tensed and she gritted her teeth. "No."

Vee's face looked almost green as she stared into her empty glass. She giggled.

Rex furrowed his neat eyebrows. They were too neat, as if he shaped them with tweezers. "What's so funny?"

"Nothing." Vee's giggles gave way to hysterical laughter.

Rex glared across the table at Vee. "Jesus, babe. Slow down or I'm going to have to carry you home."

Cressida leaned closer to Rex. "I'm sure the waitress will stay away for a while. Unless you catch up, Rex." She smiled sweetly through a clenched jaw, grateful the bar was too noisy to hear her teeth grinding.

"Yeah! What she said." Vee prodded Rex's mug, sloshing amber beer over the side.

Rex necked a long drink without taking his eyes from Cressida. "You see what I have to deal with?" He smiled like he was joking, but his eyes remained wild and unfocused. Unpredictable.

Vee shook her head.

Cressida did see what he had to deal with. A girl who deserved better, loving him when she had no reason to. He wanted Cressida to agree that Vee was the weak link. She wouldn't give that to him.

Cressida's voice was steady. "I see a lot of things."

"I'm sure you do." He leaned toward Cressida, eyes sharper than his wit. "In that place. I told Vee she doesn't need to see a shrink. She just needs to let loose every once in a while. Have some fun. No offense."

"None taken."

Rex pushed his mug in front of Vee and the beer sloshed onto the table in front of Cressida, spattering pale ale on her shirt. He snorted. "Oh shit. I'm sorry. But hey, Vee can wash it for you. Since it's her shirt anyway." His laugh echoed through the bar. Vee's face went red even in the dim light.

"Don't worry about it." Cressida didn't move as the cold liquid soaked through to her skin. A week ago, the mess would have had her heart racing. Now it was only a minor nuisance compared to the man sitting across from her, positioned between her and Vee and finally understanding what happened the night Max died.

Rex's lips tightened. "If Vee has a problem, she can come to me. Not some stranger." His jaw was tense and he sucked air past his teeth when he smiled. Every part of him shuddered with precarious restraint. Maybe he would snap, create a scene in public, and make the decision to leave him easier on Vee. She could stay with Cressida tonight. Maybe she would even move into Sam's old apartment. Perhaps with Vee so close the dreams would become even clearer. Cressida's stomach flipped.

Vee wrapped her hands around the sweating mug. The condensation dripped from her fingers to the table.

"What if she needs to talk about you?" Cressida spoke quietly, but Rex reared back as if she had shouted. Had she pushed him far enough to shatter his facade?

He flattened his hands against the wet tabletop, the tendons in his arm shivering with restrained agitation. "I guess you got me there," he spat then turned toward the bar. "I need to take a piss." Rex spilled from his seat and strutted toward the back of the restaurant. When he was out of earshot, Vee raised her head clasped her hands on the table. "Rex really is a nice guy, you know. He just likes to blow off steam."

"Don't we all?"

"Are you mad?" Vee knotted her fingers together. Her turquoise nail polish was almost completely chewed away.

Cressida sighed. "Mad?"

"I know it was just supposed to be us tonight, but I thought bringing Rex would be fun. I know I gave you a bad impression of him, but I can be very hurtful when I'm jealous." Vee rubbed her wrist. There were small fingerprints set in her pale skin. These were fresh bruises.

Cressida leaned close to Vee, whispering like she was begging Vee's permission. "Tell me he hurts you. I need to know."

Vee stopped rubbing and dropped her hands and her gaze to her lap. "That's nothing."

Cressida glanced over Vee's shoulder toward the bathroom. There was no sign of Rex or the waitress. They were hidden somewhere in the dark. Perhaps together.

"It's not nothing. You already told me he cheats on you. What else does he do?"

"It was just a stupid dream. He knows I'd never stay with him if he cheated on me for real. He's probably right that I'm just paranoid."

"How can you be sure?"

"I can't, but that's what it means to love someone, right? Having faith."

Faith was a word invented by hopeless optimists to justify the fact that they never learned from their mistakes. Love had nothing to do with faith and everything to do with sacrifice. Sam hadn't appreciated Cressida's devotion and now she was gone. Vee was supposed to be different.

"Vee—"

"It's fine. Really. Let's talk about something else." Vee raised Rex's partially full glass to her lips and closed her eyes.

Awkward minutes passed while Vee finished Rex's beer and he finished whatever it was he was doing. Vee shouldn't be so blind. She should know better, a woman who read the classics: Shakespeare, Chaucer, Tolstoy, Hawthorne. Centuries of stories about lust, betrayal, and the fickle nature of love. Cressida's mother taught her that, and it was the one thing for which she was grateful.

Cressida was about to ask Vee to accompany her to the bathroom when Rex appeared behind her chair. He hugged Vee around the neck and kissed her on the side of the mouth. "I'm sorry, baby. Forgive me?" The quivering rage had been replaced by ambivalence. Faking calm? Or maybe just waiting to get Vee alone so he could take it out on her.

"There's nothing to forgive." Vee kissed him back and he ran his hands through her short hair.

"And hey..." Rex pulled his face away from Vee and smiled at Cressida over Vee's tanned shoulder. "I'm sorry for being such an ass about Vee's therapy. I'm glad she has someone to talk to." He reached his hand around Vee to shake Cressida's hand.

Cressida smiled and grabbed her glass instead. "Cheers."

"Cheers." Vee mumbled.

Rex returned to his seat across from Cressida. She rested her elbows on the table and propped her chin on her hand. "So Rex, Vee tells me you're in school. What are you studying?"

"Music composition. Just something that lets me play with my band and call it school work." Rex's eyes slowly focused on Cressida's cool face, then dropped to her exposed chest. Cressida's skin burned. She wanted to cover up, but she wouldn't give Rex the satisfaction.

"Rex is a really amazing guitarist." Vee practically swooned in her seat.

Cressida sat up straighter and clasped her hands on the table. "That's really impressive."

Rex's chest swelled with pride. Then he belched. His hand rested on Vee's bare knee. He was an easy mark.

"I've never had any musical talent whatsoever, but I've always been in awe of people with natural abilities. They make it look so easy." Cressida purred.

Vee peeked at Cressida. Her lips were chapped and pale, almost the same color as her face. The girl batted her eyelashes. "That's the mark of a great musician. They make you think it's the easiest fucking thing in the world, when inside it's tearing them up."

Every boy who strums a guitar in a dank garage somewhere thinks he's a poet.

Cressida hummed her feigned approval. "Oh, that's really beautiful." She smiled at Vee. "That must require a lot of practice. A lot of time spent honing your craft. Long nights."

Rex hiccupped into his mug. "Well, anything fucking worth doing—"

"I think I'm gonna be sick." Vee clasped her hand to her mouth and stumbled for the bathroom.

Cressida stood. "I should probably go with her."

Rex waved his hand dismissively. "She'll be fine. Sit down and have a drink with me." He laid his hand over Cressida's arm, gently but with clear purpose. With Vee gone his eyes were bold and focused. "You know we've been together for ten years. She'll never leave me."

Cressida pulled her arm free of Rex's grasp and pushed back from the table. "Maybe next time."

The night hadn't gone as Cressida had planned, but she wasn't ready to give up. There would be other nights. Cressida trailed the girl in the flowing skirt into the bathroom. Rex couldn't reach Vee there but Cressida could, and there was nothing he could do about it.

CHAPTER 14

Cressida's apartment was a pink pearl tucked into the dismal grey sand of the Oregon coast. In the early morning hours, she could hear the diesel hum of the fishing boats along the horizon, the clanging of rusty bells, and the creaking of nets being slowly reeled in. The rooms were small, but Cressida didn't need much space —big apartments meant more empty walls to decorate. Cressida had gotten a great deal on the place because she preferred to face the parking lot instead of the fickle waves beating the coast with salty fists.

Cressida's door was on the top floor, and she could just see it from the sand below the three flights of stairs as she approached. The two apartments under hers had been empty since she moved in. It was quiet. Peaceful. Cressida had never needed much sleep and in the middle of the night, from her front window she could imagine she was the only sentient creature for miles, an empress surveying her kingdom of vacant boxes and slumbering homes.

The three apartments on the ocean side of the building were always full, teeming with life and love and noise.

College dropouts and aging surfers, suffering artists, and families just passing through came and went with the tides. Cressida didn't bother to learn their names. They could be gone by morning. The top floor apartment though, the one that shared a wall with Cressida's, had always belonged to Sam.

But now there were no footsteps on the other side of Cressida's wall, no hesitant knocking in the middle of the night, no friend looking for a shoulder to cry on. Only silence. Cressida unlocked her front door, drugstore bag swinging from her arm, and left the parking lot drowning in the lonely night.

She crossed the sparse living room—white tile floors offset by a dark leather sectional sofa and a bookshelf filled with all the volumes Cressida hadn't wanted in her office. Back issues of journals, her bound dissertation, and fiction. Her favorites were Albert Camus, Thomas Pynchon, and Chuck Palahniuk. To Cressida, *Fight Club* was the pinnacle of romance. The culmination of a despised soul ripped open and occupied by another. Oh, to have the ability to wake up in a new place, a new body, and a new life. It was beautiful. It was healing. It was everything Max had offered her.

Cressida left sandy footprints on the tile as she made her way through the apartment, tossing her keys onto the small kitchen table with a clank that echoed down the narrow hallway to the bedroom. Her flesh was marred with goose bumps usually hidden by one of her modest blouses. But Vee's shirt left nothing to the imagination. It was as scant as the décor in her bedroom: all sharp lines and stark whites. All except for a single antique vanity nestled in the corner. The bedside lamp was on, casting a sickly yellow glow over the white comforter and hard tile floor. As she passed the chipped vanity, her thin face bulged in the ancient glass until she was recognizable only by the halo of red hair protruding from her neck like a fiery mushroom cloud. The mirror was hideous, but it belonged to her mother and it had always been there, even when her mother was not. Things were so much more permanent than people.

The plastic from the shopping bag stuck to Cressida's fingers as she released it onto the bathroom vanity. She ran her fingers through her hair and watched it waver in the mirror. Spotless—unlike her. Her hands trailed along her throat, to the scars along her neck and chest from the accident. The smooth bumps were numb under her fingers and she could almost hear the windshield shattering, smell the blood rising with each heartbeat, and feel the searing pain as the glass sliced through her skin.

The heavy fabric of the borrowed shirt clung to her ribs. Vee was off somewhere with Rex, but there was still a piece of her that he couldn't take away. Cressida's hands reached the hem of Vee's shirt and she pulled it over her head, then dropped her pants to the floor. Lithe and strong beneath the scars, Cressida stood in front of the mirror, exposed. A blank canvas ready to be painted. Vee would understand her love, her admiration. She would appreciate Cressida's effort in a way Sam never did.

From the bag on the vanity she pulled a box of hair dye and a pair of shears. Cressida inspected the cool metal blades and ran her finger along the sharp edge. It sliced easily through the skin. Blood trickled over her hand and down her arm, deep red against her pale skin. The pain sent shockwaves through her brain, igniting memories of hurt and suffering she experienced growing up: the time her mother held her head under the water until her vision had tunneled and her lungs screamed for death, the first time she had sex when she was twelve and alone with one of her mother's students. And Max. The exquisite pain that molded her life flooded out of the small wound on her finger and filled the room with vivid color.

CHUNKS of her red hair glowed, nearly iridescent, under the bright bathroom lights. Itchy strands stuck to Cressida's wet feet as she stepped out of the shower. She bent to the floor, dripping wet, and swept the hairs into a neat pile with a towel. One by one she pinched them between her fingers and threw them into the garbage can. With each piece of herself that she discarded she felt lighter, different. Was she changed? She regarded her reflection in the bathroom mirror.

Blond elegance gazed back at her, blending into the white tile behind her. Almost camouflaged. She ran her fingers through her short hair, pulling away any straggling loose strands. The girl in the mirror smiled, strange and yet familiar. She ran her fingers over her breasts and her nipples hardened. Beneath her stomach—smooth with taught muscle—the last remaining red hair gathered. One hand slicked through her short blond hair and another entangled among the red.

Her back arched, pushing her breasts toward the mirror. Under the blinding light of the white bathroom she stood, a perfect dichotomy of fire and ice: a true Chimera. She sighed as her fingers reached deep inside her and coaxed a long, sorrowful wail from the girl in the mirror. Her face flushed. She ran her free hand down her throat to her chest and over her scars. She pinched hard on her nipple until the pain made her cry out. Her vision darkened. She moaned as her body pulsed with the electric shudders of her orgasm.

Spent and shaking, she slumped over the sink. Tears streamed down her face, catching the bright bathroom lights and refracting them into a thousand colors.

Cressida walked on shaking legs back into the bedroom and stooped before the vanity where her clothes laid wrinkled on the floor. She folded the yoga pants and set them in front of the wavy mirror. Vee's tank top smelled of beer and sweat, and faintly of strawberries and the ocean: Vee. Cressida held the wrinkled shirt to her naked body, feeling the soft cotton over her rough skin. She opened a small drawer at the top of the vanity and pulled out a velvet box exactly like the one containing Troilus and Criseyde in her office. She flipped the little gold latch.

Cressida lifted out a heavy object wrapped in a floral silk scarf: cornflower blue and covered with red hibiscus flowers. It was the kind of thing women in the '50s would wear to keep their hair in place while driving along winding California highways in a convertible. Something straight out of a Hitchcock film. She was glad she hadn't buried it the with the others.

Cressida draped the scarf around her neck and felt the cool silk trailing down her back. Wrapped among the silk was Sam's gold watch. The face was cracked from where it had landed on the hard floor after bouncing off Cressida's head and it no longer kept time, but there was still a message engraved on the back. *Happy Graduation. We are proud of you, son.* The watch was gaudy and impractical and probably worth a fortune. The second hand twitched impotently between two notches.

Cressida traced her thumb along the letters engraved along the back—cool metal covered with scars. She wrapped the watch back in the scarf and laid the bundle beside the box. Then she folded Vee's tank top into a tight square and laid it on top. She trailed her fingers over the tie-dyed cotton one more time and then closed the box, sliding it once again into the drawer. Safe. Protected. Close. Cressida walked naked to the bed and slipped under the crisp sheets, barely upsetting the tightly tucked corners. The chilly blankets pulled against her shoulders, pinning her to the bed like a 1000-thread count straitjacket.

CHAPTER 15

Dawn had long since passed when Cressida opened her eyes to the blinding sun streaming through her open bedroom window. Her limbs felt as if they were floating beside her, and the sounds of her dream still swirled through her head: laughter mixed with cries, pleasure with pain. Her heart ached, yet she was renewed. Waves crashed along the rocks outside, children laughed as they ran to avoid the surf. Saturday again. The beach was loud and crowded, crawling with tourists from Portland, hiding their pale skin behind floppy brimmed hats and chalky sunscreen. So many people, but it just made Cressida feel lonely.

She and Sam used to sit in the window overlooking the sea and watch the world dance by below, together but separate. She'd thought they had been born kindred spirits, forced into identities that didn't match their insides. Both unloved by their families. The day *he* became a *she* to the rest of the world gave Cressida hope. Sam never saw it that way.

Cressida lifted her head from her pillow, the pale cotton

bleached from last night's hair dye, and ran her fingers through her newly cropped hair. This Saturday would be different though. She wasn't completely alone. She had her memories, she had Vee, and she had something she needed to take care of.

From her closet, Cressida selected a long grey skirt and an ocean blue blouse that still had the tags attached; the most colorful thing that she owned. She made the bed, smoothing the corners and replacing the ruined pillowcase with fresh white linens. The room was awash with light, bouncing off the crisp bedding and getting warped by the mirror on the vanity. But something was still missing. She retrieved the scarf and the watch from the vanity, pulling the watch loosely over her narrow wrist. She wrapped the silk around her head and tied it beneath her chin.

THE WIND WHIPPED past the blue scarf concealing Cressida's short hair, and a pair of oversized sunglasses shielded her eyes from the stinging salt in the air. The tide was out and the sand along the beach was full of bubbling holes, temporary homes to tiny crabs that only existed when the moon pulled the sea from the shore—an entire world under Cressida's feet.

Children with buckets dug deep pits that filled with water with each passing wave, dogs barked and chased the irritated sandpipers, and tourists huddled under blankets away from the damp wind.

The beaches in Oregon were not like the beaches in California or Florida. They were harsh and grey and wild. Cressida breathed deep and it reminded her of the first time Vee came into her office smelling like the sea. Not the way

Hamish smelled of cigarettes and fish guts whenever he visited, but the subtle hint of ocean air, the way the clouds smelled fresh before a rainstorm.

Cressida stood in the mouth of the cave—not a natural cave, but rather a deep alcove formed by the stilted foundation of the old Mermaid Asylum that loomed over the rock cliff above. It was Cressida's favorite place in Silverside. A space all her own, full of forgotten objects and buried memories. The sand was damp from that morning's high tide. Around her feet were neat rows of piled sand, like tiny unmarked graves.

Some of the finely cultivated mounds were upset by wind, or the waves, or the occasional nosey crustacean. Cressida tied her skirt around her thighs and knelt down among the cold seaweed and frothing algae to straighten the rows once again. Each pile of sand she patted down felt familiar and comforting, like coming home after a long journey. She scooped a new hole at the end of the row closest to the stone wall at the back of the shelter.

Her right wrist was heavy from the gold watch and she slid the metal clasp over her hand without loosening it. The broken watch thudded to the ground at the bottom of the hole. Tears fell from Cressida's chin, further dampening the already wet sand and splashing off the cracked face of the watch. She'd always hated this part. Saying goodbye. But at least she would always have a piece of Sam this way. Hidden and safe where no one would find it. She pushed the loose sand into the hole and shaped it into another mound exactly like the rest. Forever anonymous, but never forgotten. Cressida smiled as she pulled herself to her feet and wiped the muck from her knees.

At the back of the cave, Cressida found an old wool shawl. It was threadbare and damp from the tides and sea air, but Cressida picked it up and held it tight to her chest. It smelled musty and the fibers of the wool had become stiff and itchy from the salt. She wrapped the shawl around her shoulders and hugged the cold wool to her. She felt freer already. There was nothing left to focus on except Vee.

Back on the beach, the wind whipped the silk scarf against her neck. This was the part of Sam she was going to keep. It just felt right. A few minutes later Cressida found herself glancing up the rock cliff beside her to the street in front of Rex's house where she and Vee had sat on Friday night, bonded in their common goal and united in their crime. A winding path led up the stone face of the cliff, twisting and turning its way to the sandy streets above. Cressida crossed the beach like one of the first creatures to venture onto land, pulling farther from the formidable tides. She climbed a set of ragged stone steps carved into the stony bank onto the street above. From the higher ground Cressida could see the house with the deep porch and the blue shutters. Rex's bachelor pad. The wind had blown his discarded beer cans off the stoop and scattered them along the street where they bounced along the asphalt with hollow clatters.

Cressida swept a few loose strands of blond hair back beneath the scarf. Hidden away like a glorious secret. Imbued with the power of anonymity, she crossed the street and walked along the sidewalk in front of the small house. Music drifted through the open front window and mixed with the persistent squall of the seagulls bickering over discarded French fries. She lingered in front of the house listening to the metallic twang of the electric guitar fumbling its way through the solo from "Purple Rain."

The music stopped abruptly and loud voices filled the emptiness. Shrill and angry, a woman's voice hit registers

Cressida had only heard a few times in her life. Her mother had never yelled. Silence was a far more sinister weapon to use on a child. Cressida had once been locked in a room for three days for stealing a Barbie doll from a friend; not because it was a crime, but because it was a useless piece of sexist propaganda. Solitary confinement—nothing but the doll and peanut butter sandwiches shoved under the door. Cressida had pulled the hair from the doll one strand at a time to quell the boredom. The next week, Cressida's mother had forced her to return the Barbie to its rightful owner, naked with a bald head and a little baggie full of plastic hair. That little girl had screamed when she saw what was left of her toy.

Then there was the sound of the screaming the night of the accident that still echoed in Cressida's mind, pulled from the recesses of her memories by the dream. A woman: not Cressida's mother, but Max's wife. She shrieked that night, not because Max was dead, but because Cressida laid crumpled beside him in familiar white chiffon and lace. The memories washed over her like the tide, clearer than they'd ever been before. Cressida could feel the soft fabric of the dress against her skin, the way her breasts had struggled against the corset that had been fitted for someone else, and how clean and smooth the flesh of her chest had been. Not like now.

Cressida had done it all for Max. For the look on his face when she leaned across his lap wearing that dress, smelling of that vile perfume—the perfume he'd once bought for his wife. She'd done it for his sigh when she'd taken his pen from his pocket and unzipped his pants, all while wearing his wife's wedding gown. It was all coming back to her in waves like the sea. Everything Cressida had ever gotten from Max she had stolen.

The little house with the blue shutters shook with that same primal sound: the cry of hatred in the face of hopelessness. It was the cry of the unloved. Cressida sat on a bench along the sidewalk across from the neighboring house and closed her eyes, listening to the symphony of rage. Glass smashed inside the house, and then the front door banged against the frame. Vee looked smaller from that distance. Her white sundress billowed like a great sail, as if she could fly away on the morning breeze. She sat down on the top step of the porch and buried her head in her hands. There were several red marks standing out against the pale flesh of her forearm, one for each finger.

The house behind Vee was cast back into silence and the rest of the world seemed to respect the moment. The relentless birds circling dead fish on the beach were mercifully quiet, the children had grown tired of dodging the waves and were now burying themselves in the sand while their parents took photos on their phones. Even the wind had slowed and stopped the sand from scratching along the street. The stray cans from Rex's porch lay still, baking in the sun. It seemed Vee and Cressida were the only two people on Earth.

When the music resumed inside the house, Vee stood up and walked down the steps toward the sidewalk, toward Cressida, sweeping the tears from her cheeks.

Cressida brushed yellow hair from her forehead and straightened the scarf, concealing her newness. This moment needed to be about Vee. The girl's steps pounded into the pavement like the beat of Cressida's heart. When she was close enough to touch, Cressida smiled, but Vee passed by without hesitation, a wave of strawberry-scented sea air ruffling the scarf around Cressida's head. It was as if Cressida didn't exist.

Air drifted in and out of Cressida's lungs, her heart pumped blood and oxygen to her body, but she felt nothing. She watched Vee hurry away from her toward town, her flip-flops throwing up tiny drops of sand with each step.

Cressida's mind raced. Had Vee finally made the right choice and left Rex? Was she on her way to Cressida's office now to tell her the news? How could she not have noticed Cressida standing there? She must have been too blinded by grief. Poor girl. A breakup from such an intensely dysfunctional relationship could require months of therapy to heal. She and Vee would be together every week for the foreseeable future, and Cressida's dreams would continue to light the way to her past. Cressida dragged her eyes from Vee's retreating figure and turned back to the house.

A lamp flicked on in the window and the music resumed. He barely missed a beat. What kind of an asshole breaks up with his girlfriend and then goes on playing Prince like nothing happened?

A few minutes later the music stopped and Rex appeared in the doorway, searching. He raked his fingers through his hair. Then he slammed the door and jogged to his car before peeling out. Cressida wondered if he was going after Vee or headed somewhere else to release the pressure. He, too, passed by Cressida as if she was nothing, like she was empty. Empty like his house.

A gull shrieked overhead, breaking the silence and jarring Cressida to her feet. Her transformation had been so complete that she had become a shadow, masked in plain sight and indistinguishable against the background chaos of the real world. She should have gone back to the office, waited for Vee to show up at her doorstep. But she couldn't resist the pull of the vacant house. She wanted to know why they had fought. If it was really over. Her face was blank as she walked up the steps where Vee had sat moments before. Cressida drew a deep breath and imagined she could still smell her presence—salt and surf and sweet. She approached the front door, turned the knob, and disappeared inside.

CHAPTER 16

The house was dark thanks to small windows and the low-hanging craftsman-style porch. Given the ramshackle outer appearance, the inside was surprisingly cozy, with hardwood, a large area rug and an overstuffed sofa slung with extra blankets. The walls were covered with concert posters and photos of Rex's band, an older woman Cressida assumed to be his mother, and even one of a shaggy old dog. No pictures of Vee. Maybe he didn't want his other girlfriends to know he was a cheater.

She stepped around pieces of shattered vase and three dying tulips to a grand staircase with large wooden banisters. The upstairs bedrooms were small and decorated with ornately framed pictures of boats and seashells, like something from a cheesy bed and breakfast.

Rex's bed was enormous: a California King with a metal frame. No headboard. Large beds are kind of thing men think will make them more attractive to women but actually announces their indifference, their desire to retreat to the furthest corner once their appetite has been sated. The blankets were twisted and half the pillows lay strewn about the room. The furniture in the room was mismatched like it had been picked up at estate sales. Cressida opened the closet door and fanned through the white plastic hangers.

Practically every item in the closet was black: faded T-shirts from bands she'd never heard of, dark jeans, and a couple cheap button-up shirts that were still crisp from the package. It was easy to see why he had been attracted to Vee's colorful personality. Cressida's cheeks burned. She didn't like having anything in common with Rex. Buried deep in the back of the closet were two dark grey suits and a handful of brightly colored shirts with matching ties slung over the shoulders, still in plastic from the dry cleaner. They didn't belong here any more than she did. She pushed the hangers back into place, concealing the expensive suits with vintage grunge.

Cressida closed the closet and pulled open the top drawer of a faded green dresser along the wall beside it. Inside was a jumble of women's clothes, a toothbrush, a box of tampons, and a dog-eared copy of Palahniuk's *Choke*. The spine was cracked and the pages were bent and yellowed. *Books are made to be loved.* Vee's voice seemed to waft from the pages along with the dust. Cressida had read Palahniuk before, admired his unapologetic outlandishness, and recognized her own solitude in the parade of misfits he brought to life. She understood his characters—Tyler Durden, Tender Branson, and Victor Mancini—even respected them, but never loved.

She pulled the clothes from the drawer, running her fingers along each item before precisely folding each article and replacing them in the green dresser. Green. The color of jealousy, of coveting. Rex confined Vee to a tiny drawer, her wants and desires compartmentalized among her wrinkled panties and musty clothes. She sent the sad drawer and its contents back into the shadows.

On top of the dresser was Rex's wallet, curved and worn from the contours of his back pocket. He must have left in a hurry. His driver's license listed his name as Rexton Harris III. The child of privilege shirked his family obligations and becomes a rock musician. How clichéd. Beneath several credit cards were concert ticket stubs, a pile of receipts, a condom, and a cocktail napkin from the Crab Shack with a phone number scratched across it. The steampunk waitress, maybe?

From downstairs, the front door clicked on its hinges and the air itself changed, like someone had opened a window during a storm. She stuffed the wallet in the waistband of her skirt and pulled her shirt down over the bump. A physical representation of Rex's entire life whittled down to the second dimension. The hairs on her arms and the back of her neck stood tall, craning to see who would be coming up the stairs, deciding her fate. Footsteps tapped along the living room floor and then quieted as they landed on the soft rug. Cressida stood frozen to the spot in front of the dresser. There was no point in running. The house was too small to hide.

Rough soles scraped against the hard steps—louder, closer. Her stomach tensed. Out of dozens of times she had broken into Max's house, tried on his wife's clothes while she was at hairdressers, massage appointments, and book club meetings, Cressida had never been in danger of getting caught. She was always careful, meticulous. Except when she'd let Max find her, but that had been part of the game. The first time had been innocent enough. She'd found a necklace in the sofa cushion during one of their sessions and put it on. She'd had no idea to whom the jewelry belonged; Max hadn't told her it belonged to his wife until after he'd fucked her on the sofa. It was the first time he'd touched her. She'd been sixteen years old, and she'd begged him for it.

The footsteps stopped at the top of the stairs. *Move. Do something.* Cressida's feet felt heavy like she was wading through sand. She pushed the bedroom door aside and came face to face with Vee's wide eyes and slack jaw.

"Cressida? How...I mean...what are you doing here?" Her forehead wrinkled like it had in the bar when Rex was talking to the waitress.

Ice flowed through Cressida's veins and she released a slow breath. "I came over to check on you after last night and the front door was open. I was worried someone had broken in."

"Oh." Vee crossed her arms and her eyes paused on the scarf wrapped around Cressida's head like a snake. "But what are you doing up here?"

Cressida's throat was dry. She stiffened her fingers at her side. "I thought maybe you were in bed."

Vee's eyes scanned the room behind Cressida. "Where's Rex?"

"He's not with you?" The wallet stuck to her lower back with sweat: dead cow skin rubbing up against living flesh.

"No." Vee shifted her weight to one foot. The fire she'd had in her eyes the day they'd met had faded to pale embers. *Rex had stolen Vee's flame, and if Cressida didn't get rid of him he would steal her dreams as well.*

"Is everything ok with you two?"

"Yes. No. I don't know. What the hell are you doing in here?" She stamped her foot like a toddler.

"The front door was open and I was worried about you. I thought maybe Rex hurt you."

"What? No. I mean, things got a little heated between us this morning, but that was nothing. Just a little argument." Her shoulders relaxed, but only a fraction of an inch.

"Heated how?" Cressida took a step forward and grasped Vee's elbow. The last thing she needed was for Rex to come home and find her in the bedroom. Or notice his wallet was missing.

Vee's arm softened under Cressida's grasp. "He told me I embarrassed him last night." Vee allowed herself to be led back downstairs. "And some other stuff. He was being completely ridiculous."

"Like what other stuff?" Rex hadn't exactly hidden his wallet containing the waitress's phone number. Vee could have easily found it while cleaning up the room, and she'd know he was just a spoiled rich kid who wanted the world to think he was a tortured genius. An artist. But he would never be David Foster Wallace or Ernest Hemingway or even Kurt Cobain. He was just some asshole who wanted was to hide Vee away in a drawer.

Vee pulled her arm free of Cressida's grasp. "Stuff about you. He thinks it's weird that you're suddenly hanging around all the time." Vee picked at the paint on one of her nails and the red polish peeled off in a long strip.

"That's crazy. We're friends."

Vee pulled another strip of paint off her fingernails and let the red scraps fall to the floor. The flakes of polish floated onto the living room carpet like bloody snow. "Yeah, that's what I told him—"

"He didn't believe you?"

Vee raised her eyes to meet Cressida's. "He thinks... you're weird. I told him he was full of shit."

Cressida stretched her fingers along her skirt. Rex had

played his hand too early. Hadn't done his research. "Some people just can't live with the things they don't understand."

Vee's eyes widened as Cressida lifted the quote straight from the pages of her Palahniuk book. "I'm sure he's just looking out for you, but how sad is it to have to deconstruct everything, to analyze it to death?"

Vee's mouth twisted "That's funny. There's a very similar line in one of my favorite books. It's what made me want to be a writer."

Her favorite. The girl needed to be wanted, loved, and fought over. Cressida smiled. "*Choke*, right?"

Vee's eyes sparked "You've read it?"

"Once or twice."

"Palahniuk is a genius. What I wouldn't give to crawl inside his head and poke around."

Cressida pushed a stray hair back under the scarf, overcome by a sudden urge to cover up. The scars on her chest burned. "I know the feeling."

Vee smiled and slumped back on the sofa beside Cressida. "I saw him once, you know."

"Who?"

"Chuck Palahniuk. Rex and I were visiting his parents in Portland and we saw Palahniuk ducking into this tiny restaurant hidden under a bridge downtown. It was dumb luck that I saw him at all, and it was like fate telling me to follow my dreams of becoming a writer."

"And did you?"

"No." Another strip of nail polish dropped onto the Rex's sofa.

"Why not?"

"We had somewhere to be. We were just passing by."

"When was that?"

"A couple years ago, right before Rex went back to

school. So everything got put on hold." Vee shrugged and Cressida bit her lip.

"You shouldn't let Rex take away your dreams." *And he certainly wouldn't take Cressida's.*

"Maybe." Vee's mouth twitched. Her eyes turned down at her hands and she picked at her last perfect nail.

"Either way, we should do something to take your mind off him. What do you say we borrow a car and head into Portland for the day? If you want to be a writer there's no better place to start."

"I can't today. Rex and I are supposed to be having dinner with my parents." The sun peeked out from behind some clouds and caught a few specks of glitter clinging to Vee's hair. Tiny shards of color among the sea of white that had enveloped Vee. If she had come into the office today, would Cressida have even noticed her among the sea of sand and dirt?

"Then let's just go somewhere and read. I'd love to show you my book collection." Sweat pooled under Rex's concealed wallet and dripped down Cressida's lower back.

Vee's jaw set and she stood from the sofa. "I should probably stay here and wait for Rex." She walked to the front door and opened it. The sun poured into the room like liquid gold.

"Ok. I'll see you at your appointment on Friday. Five-o-clock?" Cressida lifted herself from the sofa and stood beside Vee. On closer inspection, Vee's hair was a little longer than Cressida's, and her roots were dirty brown along with her eyebrows.

"Yeah, I'll see you then."

The girl didn't want to be saved today. There was still time.

Vee's hands trembled as she held the door. She was

nervous. Rex must have scared her more than Cressida thought.

"If I don't see you before."

"Definitely. Thanks for coming to check on me. Bye." Vee pressed her lips into a tight smile as Cressida stepped out of the house and closed the door as soon as Cressida was past the threshold. The distance between them felt thicker than the hollow wooden barrier. Cressida's pulse slammed through her veins louder than the door.

CHAPTER 17

An alleyway ran behind the row of houses, each connected with a driveway. Cressida walked along the neighbor's alley until she found a place where she was out of direct view from the street but could see Rex's front door and living room window clearly. Cressida pulled the scarf from her head, tugged the silk around her neck and it tightened across her throat. There were garbage cans surrounding her and upturned recycling bins stacked against the neighbor's vinyl siding. She pulled a bin from the stack and set it on the pavement like a bench. And watched.

Nothing.

She passed the time rubbing the napkin with the Crab Shack waitress's phone number between her thumb and forefinger. The first two digits of the number wore away as the sun crossed the middle of the sky and bore down on her shoulders. The back of her neck was not accustomed to direct sunlight and she could feel the virgin flesh turning pink.

Inside the wallet, folded unevenly and tucked away

beside the napkin was a wad of receipts. Taxi rides, quick lunches, and hotel receipts from The Pearl District in downtown Portland. It was more the kind of thing one would find on a businessman than a rock musician. One of the hotel receipts was dated the same night that Cressida and Vee had waited for him outside his house. Rex was so full of lies that there was barely room for anything else. Cressida stuffed the receipts into her bra and sorted through the rest of his wallet.

Inside the flap, behind his platinum American Express card was a tattered photo of a girl. Dirty blond curls formed a halo around the chubby face of a girl in her late teens or early twenties. She was turned away from the camera, looking over her thin shoulder, long hair falling down her back. She was tiny, more hair than body, and her blue eyes jumped off the photo. They were the color of the ocean on a clear day. *Vee.* Cressida turned the picture over. Smudged letters reading "I will always love you" looped across the back of the picture in giant curly handwriting. It was an odd thing to find among the evidence of Rex's deceit.

Cressida tucked the picture in her bra with the receipts and clutched the wallet to her chest. Sooner or later Rex would realize it was missing. And Vee would know Cressida took it. She had to put it back.

Rex's car pulled into the driveway just before 5:00 p.m. *Cutting it close for dinner.* He stormed into the house and slammed the door behind him. Cressida moved from her recycling bin bench and approached the house. From outside the living room window she could hear muted voices talking. Not fighting. Several minutes went by and no one yelled, no one left the house. Cressida braced herself against the side of the house and peeked into the living room window.

Vee's arms were around Rex's thin neck and she was shaking her head as she talked. Her lips were full and pink and her cheeks flushed. Rex groped at Vee's hair and pulled her face to his. Cressida's scalp tingled and itched. Vee didn't fight him off, but kissed him back with the same reckless flare she'd used to ruin Cressida's datebook and upset all her furniture. This wasn't the Vee from her dreams. This girl was selfish, mercurial, and confounding. She moaned as Rex pushed her over the arm of the sofa, her dress bunched over her hips, and he leaned hard against her from behind. He reached around in front of her and hooked his finger into her open mouth. She closed her lips around his dirty intrusion.

Vee was supposed to be angry, uncover his cheating. She was supposed to leave him and get her color back, bringing herself and Cressida into a new world full of life and beauty and vibrant dreams. And Vee didn't even care where he'd been.

Rex tossed his jacket to the floor and unzipped his pants. Then he was inside her, pleasuring her, possessing her. Vee closed her eyes and bit down on his curved finger, daring him to split her open. Vee obviously craved intimacy, the kind of love that transforms you and remakes you. She just didn't know where to find it. She probably hadn't gotten enough attention from Daddy and now mistook attention for love, and pain for affection. *Sad, starved, naive little Vee looking for someone to define her.*

Rex groaned and stilled against Vee's battered hips. He slapped her ass and she melted onto the sofa with a combination of euphoria and self-loathing etched onto her face along with the pattern from the cushion. Rex zipped his pants and disappeared into the kitchen as Vee tugged her clothes back into place and then turned on the television. No one changed for dinner.

They weren't in a hurry. Vee had lied to get Cressida out of the house. Was she pulling away? Cressida's stomach lurched. The same thing had happened with Sam. Just when they had gotten close, when Cressida had started to feel safe, she'd disappeared. Cressida had done everything right this time, and still Vee didn't understand. It had to be Rex's fault; he was ruining everything. A few minutes later the lights dimmed in the house and Vee and Rex rushed to the car, Vee's dress still twisted, her hair plastered to the side of her drawn face. Cressida stood still watching the cloud of dust from the tires rise to the sky.

Vee was his that night. Not Cressida's. Rex had remade her into his plaything—dull and lifeless. And already Max's image in Cressida's mind was fading, overshadowed by the gratuitous images of Vee's face contorted with lust and self-deprecation. Cressida retched into the bushes beside the house, darkening the soil with her bile.

Wiping her mouth, Cressida headed up the steps and paused on the porch. The sun was going down over the ocean, turning the blue waters red like something from the book of Revelations. Fishing boats pushed the boundaries of the Earth like they would spill over the edge of the world. It was easy to see why the entire town of Silverside revolved around the sea, and why people seemed powerless to resist its pull. When everything else faded away and only the sound of the waves crashing remained, walking out into the sea and giving yourself over to it was like being reborn.

A car drove past in front of the house and Cressida tensed, but in the silvery light of dusk the driver might have mistaken her for Vee and he waved without suspicion. Cressida touched the jagged edges of her hair and smiled back.

She turned the knob and crossed the dark living room by memory, stumbling only over Rex's leather jacket still crumpled beside the sofa. Cressida picked it up from the floor and slipped it over her arms. It was still warm, almost alive.

Upstairs, the bedside lamp cast a pale glow on the messy bed. Cressida stuffed her hand in the pocket of the leather jacket and pulled out a folded piece of paper. It was a flyer for a band called The Ampersands playing at a dingy club called The Brig later that week. Written diagonally across the top of the canary yellow paper were the words "*Tina's - Friday 11:00 a.m.*" It was almost too easy.

She laid the wallet back on the dresser and retrieved the Palahniuk from the top drawer. The rest of the items were undisturbed since she last saw them. Book in hand, she sat down on the foot of the bed so her feet were flat on the floor and then laid back, watching headlights from neighboring cars cast long shadows on the ceiling. Everything was warm. Comfortable. Like she belonged there.

The leather jacket creaked as she scooted backward toward the pillow. The sheets were soft against her cheek, probably a high thread count. Not the kind of thing you expect to find in the bed of a starving artist.

A car door slammed outside and footsteps grew louder on the pavement. She held her breath, waiting for the sound of the front door squeaking on its hinges, muted voices coming back to search for a lost wallet and discover her. Cressida wrapped herself tighter in the leather, running her fingers over the cold, soft skin. The footsteps did not stop at the door.

Cressida cracked the book and turned to one dog-eared page, devouring the words as hedonistically as the sex addicts in the book. Cressida imagined Vee laying in this bed, touching herself while reading *Choke*, a story about someone who needs to be saved so badly that he constantly puts himself in danger. Vee's hands on her breasts, sliding over her trembling stomach, her neck arching back as she finally touches her aching center. There was no Rex, no bruises. Only Vee's hands, her eyes squeezed shut, and her free hand tugging on her blond hair. Hair just like Cressida's. The daydream was so vivid that Cressida didn't realize that she too was masturbating, the lines between fantasy and reality as thin as the pages of the book.

Her sweat dripped into the lining of Rex's jacket and onto the sheets below her. She stretched her arms above her head and loosened the clenched muscles of her core. Her legs still trembled from her orgasm and her hand smelled of sex and leather. She closed the book. Her heart rate slowed to a steady beat pulsing in her head like the rise and fall of the ocean.

Cressida's legs were unsteady as she walked to the dresser, replaced the book in the drawer and left it slightly ajar. She then placed the Rex's wallet, upside down and open, near the edge of the dresser. From inside her bra Cressida produced the slightly damp cocktail napkin with the phone number and dropped it into Vee's drawer. The band flyer was also wet from her sweat and had left a yellow stain on her skin. She let it fall to the floor behind the dresser, only the corner visible from where she stood. It would look like an accident when Vee found them. Rex being careless with his wallet the way he had been with her heart. Her blood rushed through her veins and goose bumps rose across her chest. She patted the receipts and the photo of Vee in her bra. *Still dry enough for the box in her vanity.*

The bedding was still mussed from her antics when Cressida left the bedroom and padded downstairs in the dark. She dropped Rex's jacked on the floor by the sofa where he would look for it. Hopefully he'd smell her the next time he put it on.

Outside the stars were bright over the dark ocean and the moon illuminated the street. Cressida walked home along the beach as the tide came in, the waves reaching closer and closer to her feet with each surge. She picked up her pace until she was running along the sand, the sound of her steps speeding along with her pulse. The beach was changing as she passed, the miles behind her no longer recognizable, her footprints swept away by the sea. Everything being reborn. Cressida smiled in the dark.

CHAPTER 18

The office was stuffy on Monday afternoon, one of the rare humid days of the year when Cressida wished she could open the grand bay windows at the back of her office. The remnants of her lunch were putrefying in the wastebasket beside her wingback chair. The entire room smelled like pastrami.

She could barely eat. Her phone had been cruelly silent all day, and the one time it did ring it was only Mrs. Coulter calling to cancel her appointment for later in the week. Something about an open house. So either her arthritis was flaring up and she was too proud to admit she couldn't get out of bed, or her daughter finally convinced her to move to a drier climate. Either way, it freed up an hour. Cressida pulled her datebook into her lap and rolled Max's pen between her fingers. She frowned as she crossed Mrs. Coulter's name off her schedule. *Such a mess.*

Her entire office was different since she'd started spending her free time on Vee. She hadn't dusted in a week and while the glitter had mostly dissipated, the mud she'd ground into the carpet was still there, glaring at her while she sat in her appointments. She never quite got her chair back into the same position since the day she met Vee either, and the entire room looked just slightly askew. But the most notable difference in the space was Cressida herself. Her new red shirt blazed through the dull room making everything else seem paler. Her hair was the topic of several discussions that day, including one twenty-minute negotiation with a paranoid patient who refused to even enter the room, and a sideways glance from Roger on his way into his office.

Then there were the dreams. Her entire career had been colored by her simultaneous fascination with the process of dreaming and her inability to actually relate to her patients who wanted to talk about theirs. But no more. Her mind was alert and active. Every minute of every day was a challenge, some new puzzle to be solved. She felt lighter, as if cutting her hair had lifted a hundred pounds from her shoulders. Now she billowed exactly like Vee's skirt had done the first day she arrived in Cressida's office.

Cressida's thoughts were interrupted by urgent knocking at the door of her office. She didn't have another patient for half an hour so she jumped out of her chair, knocking Max's pen to the floor in her haste. Her breath hinged in her throat. There was only one person she wanted to see on the other side of her door. She could hear Max tutting at her for acting like a graceless child, running through the house and knocking things from shelves in exuberance. Cressida had never been allowed to be that child. But now the jubilation bubbled through her blood, collecting in her chest right behind the peppered scars from the accident. The scars Cressida thought could never heal. She threw open the door and there, crumpled to the carpet, was a broken Vee.

Her slender body was bent and leaned against the wall,

like a bird with a battered wing. Her face was swollen and her eyes hidden behind thick lids. Ragged breaths shuddered through her chest and snot mixed with tears and dripped down her face. Everything about her was limp and listless--even her hair was flat. Had Cressida made a mistake by exposing Rex's philandering instead of reporting his abuse? Therapists have lost their licenses for errors in judgment before, and she'd already crossed so many lines with Vee. She should have been more careful. Yet upon closer inspection, although Vee's eyes were swollen and red, it was the first time Cressida had seen her without fresh bruises on her body. She wasn't hurt. Perhaps Cressida's meddling had saved her some pain. At least the physical kind.

Cressida offered a hand and pulled Vee to her feet. She was wearing the clothes Cressida had folded in the drawer at Rex's house. She must have slept at his place last night.

"What's going on? Are you ok?" She tried to disguise the anticipation in her voice with startled concern, but Vee didn't seem to notice either way.

Vee wiped her nose with the back of her hand and there was blood smeared on her wrist, the deep red darkening her pale flesh. Maybe she hadn't come away unscathed after all.

Roger poked his round face out of his office, eyebrow cocked in question, and his gaze landed on Vee's wrist. On the blood. He paled. Cressida waved him off, but he left his door wide open and she could practically hear him straining to eavesdrop. Hopefully she wouldn't have to endure another of his pointless friendly chats.

Cressida pulled Vee into the office and closed the door. She walked her to the sofa and sat her down. Vee's face was deathly pale apart from the red oozing from her nose and onto her clothes, and dripping onto the floor. The carpet.

Cressida handed her a tissue and sat down beside her. "What did he do to you?"

Vee pinched her nose and spoke with a nasal voice. "Who?"

"You know who." Cressida slapped her knee hard enough to sting through her skirt. "Tell me what happened."

The corners of her mouth turned down. "He's cheating on me. This time I know for sure."

She found the napkin. "How can you be sure?"

"Do you remember that horrible waitress who was flirting with Rex at the bar the other night?"

Cressida pursed her mouth and nodded.

"Well, I found her phone number written on a cocktail napkin today. It must have fallen out of his pocket or something." Her hands shook as she pulled the tissue away from her nose to check that the bleeding had stopped. It had, but her hands and chin were stained red.

"And you're sure there's no other explanation?"

"No. I also found a piece of paper with a woman's name on it and a date and time for meeting up. He's having an affair." She buried her head in her hands. The poor thing was so broken that she was actually mourning that asshole.

"So did you leave him?" *How could she not?* And now she and Cressida would be free to see each other as often as they wanted, to revel in their newfound intimacy, and Cressida could finally heal.

"No, he left before I got up this morning. Plus I wanted to talk to you about it first. I mean, you were there that night. Plus you're a therapist, so that makes you a double expert." She sniffed.

Cressida handed her a fresh tissue. "What happened to your nose?"

"That's nothing. I get nosebleeds when I'm stressed. I always have." Vee wrinkled her nose.

Bullshit. Cressida laced her fingers to keep from shaking the girl "Well, it sounds like you know what you want to do already. You don't really need me to tell you to leave him."

Vee clamped her eyes shut like she'd been doing her entire relationship with Rex. "I don't know what I want right now."

"I think you do, but you don't like the truth."

Vee looked up at Cressida with pitiful eyes, searching for answers but landing on Cressida's hair instead. It had taken her several minutes to look out from behind her self-absorption. "Oh! Your hair." Vee's hand raised to her mouth.

Cressida ran her fingers through her blond pixie cut. She remembered the first time she'd run her fingers through it in the bathroom at her apartment, and her pulse throbbed at the apex of her thighs. She pressed her legs together. "Do you like it?"

Vee's eyes roamed from Cressida's hair to her bright clothes and back to her steel eyes. Her hand was still covering her mouth but her eyes were wide like she'd seen a ghost. "I…um…you look so different." She dropped her hand. "You look like me."

Cressida laughed. Pride swelled in her breast and she could feel her skin starting to flush. Could Vee tell? "Well, you inspired me to make a change. The other day in my office you called me a fraud and you were right."

"I was?"

"Yes. I needed a change."

"Wow." Vee scratched her wrist with chipped red nails. "Well, it does look nice on you."

"It feels good. I knew you'd like it."

Vee hugged her arms around her chest like the temperature in the room had dropped twenty degrees. She looked confused. But who wouldn't be in her position? Cressida must now reflect everything Vee ever wanted to be: colorful, strong, independent, and whole. Everything Max had seemed to Cressida. It could be very intimidating, and Vee seemed lost. Cressida remembered that feeling. She could help Vee through it.

She nodded her chin at the girl. "So now it's your turn."

Vee's eyes widened. The whites around her irises were bloodshot. "My turn for what?"

"To stop being a fraud." Cressida stood up from the sofa and checked the clock on the wall. She had a schedule to keep, order to maintain. "Look, I have a patient coming in any minute, but can we meet up in an hour? I have a great idea."

A wrinkle set between Vee's eyes, but she had no fight left. "What do you mean I'm a fraud?"

"You'll see. Meet me here in an hour?"

Vee struggled off the sofa. "Yeah, ok. I guess so."

"Great." They walked together toward the office door. "I promise. This will make you feel better." She would help Vee find herself. The person *she* was supposed to be, and not just Rex's plaything. Once Vee realized how much thought Cressida put into that evening she would see how much better off she was without him. Cressida's nipples hardened. She shifted under her red blouse that she'd bought to go with her new hair, thankful her bra was hiding her dirty secrets.

"Thanks, Cressida. I'm really lucky to have met you." She smiled.

Cressida nodded. *She was right.* "One hour."

Vee disappeared down the hall, but before Cressida could close her office door Roger had his pretty hand blocking the frame. It was as if he'd been hovering in the hallway the entire time. Cressida knew his caseload had been steadily declining over the last few years, but she thought he'd at least have something better to do than micromanage her practice.

"Hi, Doctor Banks. What's going on?"

"Miss Dunhill." Apparently Roger had given up on their first name basis. "Was that the girl you mentioned a couple weeks ago? The *incident* with the car?" His thick eyebrows were arched above his eyes. Cressida had forgotten that Roger had never actually seen Vee in person, only spoken to her on the phone.

"Yes." The elation in Cressida's chest drained and a sickly chill passed over her cheeks.

"I'm a little concerned that she is becoming inappropriately attached to you, and that it could be putting you—and her—in danger."

"I don't think that's—"

"She was just sitting on the floor outside your office bleeding, sobbing, and beating on the door. I'm worried that she might be fixating on you." He rubbed the side of his nose with the back of his thumb. Even his itches were smug.

"She's just going through a hard time with her boyfriend. It's not a healthy relationship and I'm helping her end it." Cressida met Roger's eyes. He stared back. What was he after?

"Did she copy your new hair cut?" Roger touched his own bald head as if she needed a prop to understand the question.

Cressida laced her fingers together. "It's all part of her process. She's used to him controlling everything about her. She's using me as a crutch on her way to independence."

"All our patients are going through something difficult.

That's why they come to us. But sometimes those relationships can become toxic for both parties. It's easy to lose sight of that in this place." He waved his hand around the room. "I think it might be better for you to refer her care over to me and extricate yourself from her as soon as possible." He rapped his fingers against the door frame. *Roger wanted to save her from Vee. He had no idea.*

Cressida leaned close enough that she could make out the rough texture of empty follicles inside his bald spot and the dull pallor of dying hair along the edge. The vein in his temple bulged. "I don't think abandoning her care at this juncture would be in her best interest," she whispered.

"Is she in danger?" Sweat beaded up on his oily forehead and he wiped it away with the back of his sleeve.

"She denies any abuse, but between us, a disguise might not be a terrible idea."

"Are you sure?" His mouth dropped slightly and his eyebrows went limp. His body reeked of impotence.

"I am."

"Well, if you need anything from me, you know where to find me." He nodded back toward his office as if that needed clarification.

"Actually, Roger..." Cressida smiled and took a step toward him. "I do need to ask you a favor."

Roger's red face turned almost purple, the color of dead bodies when they're pulled from the water. "Yes?" The look in his eye was wild, almost masturbatory at the prospect of being needed.

"I need to borrow your car.

"For you or your patient?" His nostrils flared, and there were thick coarse hairs sticking out of his nose.

"It's a personal matter."

Roger sucked his teeth and the sound made Cressida

nauseous. "I'll have to check with my wife. She wasn't too happy the last time you borrowed it."

Cressida reached out and touched Roger's arm. His muscles flexed under her hand. "You've been so supportive ever since I arrived in Silverside. I finally want to take your advice about getting out of the office every now and then. I agreed to meet some friends in the city."

Roger opened his mouth and then closed it again. Cressida dropped her hand.

"I do think it's important to keep a well-rounded life." He sighed. "I'm sure Helen won't mind. But please fill up the tank on your way back. She hates when I run it down to empty."

Cressida smiled. "I promise."

"Let me grab you the keys." Roger turned back to his office and bounded through the door. A moment later he returned, face glistening, with his car keys in hand. He must have learned not to leave the keys in the car.

"Thank you, Roger." Cressida fixed her eyes on his as she said his name.

Roger grinned triumphantly. His unwavering desire to connect with people really did make him an easy mark. "Have fun tonight, Miss Dunhill. You're young. Enjoy it."

"I will. Thanks again." Cressida closed the door to her office and clutched the keys to her chest.

CHAPTER 19

"Are you going to tell me where we're going?" Vee was sitting in the passenger seat with her foot on the dash and the window open. The color had returned to her cheeks. She'd showered since her visit to the office and the scent of strawberries and ocean breeze filled the car.

"I'll tell you when we get closer." Cressida smiled. The wind rustled Vee's ice blue skirt against Cressida's red top, and to the world they must have looked like a tangle of blond hair and pale limbs. They could have been twins.

A road sign passed by the car in a green blur and Vee turned to Cressida with blue fire in her eyes. "Are we going into Portland?"

"Maybe."

"Why?" The excitement was practically lifting her from the passenger seat. Only the seatbelt was keeping her from floating away.

"Fine. If you want to ruin the surprise, we are going to have dinner at the restaurant you mentioned earlier. You know, the one under the bridge."

Vee scrunched her nose. "How did you find it?"

Cressida cocked her head. "How many restaurants do you think there are hidden under bridges in downtown Portland?"

Vee laughed and Cressida could practically feel Vee's heartbeat thumping next to hers. "You're crazy." *But she wasn't crazy. Not anymore.*

"And who knows, maybe we'll see someone famous this time too. Only we won't shy away." Cressida ran her fingers through her hair, shivering as the wind whipped across her face. It tasted like salt when she smiled.

Several rusty steel bridges spanned the Willamette River, connecting the two halves of Portland, Oregon like stitches on a giant wound. Tucked into the shadows beneath one of them was a tiny Cajun restaurant with patron saints and neon glowing in the windows. Inside, noise and color and spice surged to each corner of the narrow room. The lights filtered through tinted wine bottles and cast a rainbow of dancing flames over the long tables. Cressida's every sense was electric. Crowded restaurants often made Cressida feel isolated, like her voice would simply be drowned out among the sea of conversation. But here everyone sat together at grand tables, rubbing legs and shoulders with strangers. The room had a pulse. And she was in harmony with all of it.

As the hostess showed Cressida and Vee to their place in the center of the table, they scanned the room for familiar faces. There were more beards than business suits. All leather and pierced body parts. Twenty years ago this crowd would have ridden motorcycles and taken crystal meth. Now they rode recycled bicycles and slurped oysters from the half shell. Cressida nodded to a woman wearing an ironic T-shirt depicting Donald Trump's head superimposed onto the body of a baby with his diaper sagging below his chubby naked bottom and a finger pressed mischievously to his lips. The caption read: "I Trumped."

Vee sat across from Cressida, her blond head barely reaching the shoulder of the man beside her with an orange mullet straight from Bowie's The Spiders From Mars.

Cressida leaned across the table so Vee could hear her over the cacophony surrounding them. "No star sightings so far. Wouldn't it be amazing if we saw Chuck again?"

"I'm sure he has better things to do on a Monday night." Vee grabbed her water glass and picked out a lemon seed floating along the edge.

"What would you say to him if he were here?"

"Probably nothing."

"Well, you could always choke on your jambalaya. Maybe he'd feel obligated to help you." Cressida had always enjoyed that little quirk of *Choke,* and had often wondered if it would actually work.

"With my luck I'd probably just die." Vee smiled but her eyes were fixed on an invisible spot on the tablecloth, unseeing and unblinking.

"Nah, if Chuck didn't save you then I would."

Vee met Cressida's steely gaze and sighed. "I'm sorry I'm not very much fun tonight."

Cressida reached across the table and touched Vee's hand. Her skin was hot like she had a fever. "You've been exactly what you need to be."

Vee smiled, but pulled her hand into her lap. "You're a good friend. You just met me during such a weird time. And Rex. He used to be a lot of fun." Her eyes welled. "So did I."

The idea of leaving Rex had been born that afternoon, but Vee still had to cut the cord if Cressida was going to take control back from him. Cressida's dreams were dependent on Vee being a constant presence in her life. A willing participant. Rex had his claws deep, and Cressida needed to go deeper if she wanted to dig him out completely.

Cressida grabbed a crust of bread from the covered basket between them and scraped butter across it. "Some of the worst people I know have a fun side. Their ability to surprise people is part of what makes them unhinged." The bread sliced through the roof of her mouth as she ate, the metallic taste of blood mixing with the salty butter. She was so close to achieving her goal that nothing could distract her from Vee.

"Rex is an artist. He's always had an artist's temperament, but he isn't unhinged. He just forgets that his actions have consequences sometimes." Vee dropped her eyes and tugged gently at the end of her hair.

"Like when he hurts you?"

Vee's hand tensed and the tendons in her forearm popped. "He doesn't hit me."

The woman with the political shirt dropped her knife to her plate with a loud crash. She looked at Cressida with empathetic eyes and shook her head. Cressida stiffened her legs beneath the table, she wanted to kick the woman for eavesdropping, but privacy wasn't on the menu in a restaurant where strangers dine together like old friends. Instead she leaned closer to Vee and lowered her voice.

"I've seen the welts he leaves on your arm, the bruises on your hips."

"Those were nothing. Rex may be an asshole a lot of the time, but he wouldn't hurt a fly unless he had to." Her cheeks had paled. Vee lowered her gaze.

Don't lose her. "You don't have to pretend with me."

Vee looked up at Cressida. "I'm not."

"Then stop making excuses for him." The sound of Cressida's frustration reverberated down the long restaurant table.

"He said he was sorry."

"Was that before or after he banged the waitress?" Several pairs of eyes rose up from their creole delicacies to take in the dinner theatrics.

Vee looked around the room and her cheeks flushed, but she didn't whisper. Maybe she liked the attention. "After, I guess. I thought we were done with that. We had such a nice time together this weekend."

The image of Rex bending Vee over the sofa came unbidden to Cressida's mind. The way she'd sucked his fingers while he took her from behind, goading him on, daring him to hurt her. A nice time? He had used Vee. And Vee liked it.

Cressida reached across the table and grabbed Vee's hand, her palms surprisingly rough. The man with the Ziggy Stardust hair stared.

"That's how these guys operate. They are charming until they're not. Afterward they try to take it back by buying gifts, being more agreeable, or promising they will change. It's a cycle."

Vee dropped her chin to her chest. "It was just a dream. A hunch."

"What was?"

"Rex cheating on me. I never had any real evidence. Just a feeling that I couldn't explain. Until I met you, that is. You made it seem real."

Cressida shook her head. "It was always real. You just didn't want to admit it to yourself."

Vee's nose wrinkled and she rubbed it with the knuckle of her index finger. "What if I'm wrong?"

"You're not."

"You're always so sure of yourself. Of me. How do you do that?" The light from the candle between them flickered across Vee's face, casting shadows like bruises around her eyes.

Cressida grabbed another piece of bread from the table. "I have a very singular focus."

Vee chewed her bottom lip, her entire face falling toward her empty glass. "This whole thing makes me feel so stupid."

"You're not stupid. These guys are master manipulators."

A loud crash from the kitchen jolted Vee back in her chair and the shadows fell from her face. She sighed and shook her head. "I'm sorry. I'm such a bummer tonight."

"Don't worry about it. I'm your friend. This is what I do. And right now I can tell you the only thing you need to do is get as far away from him as possible."

Vee smiled. "Thank you. I knew there was something special about you the first time I met you. You don't need anyone to tell you what to do—you always know."

"I'm just reflecting your words back to you."

Vee's hand reached for her hair and she tipped her head to the side. "Yeah, I guess you kind of are."

Cressida mirrored Vee's movements like a mime and both women laughed, the sound of their amusement fading into the noisy background. It's funny how rooms full of people always seem to go quiet during the worst moments of a person's life, but have no problem drowning out the good stuff.

Vee's smiled faded. "I haven't been alone in ten years. I'm not sure I know how to do it."

"You're not alone. You have me." Vee needed to have someone to care for her. Someone to need her. To be addicted to her. And Cressida needed to dream.

"Just wait until I knock on your door at three in the morning because I heard a noise outside." Vee smiled and it almost looked sincere.

"It's been very quiet in my building lately. It could use a little excitement." Sam leaving was a disruption to her life, but it had been different than it was with Vee. Cressida hadn't dreamt with Sam. She had admired Sam, even envied her, but in the end Sam had turned out to be exactly like everyone else. She hadn't even said goodbye.

Cressida straightened her menu along the edge of the table.

Vee shivered. "I hate the quiet too. Some of my worst nightmares are about being alone in a dark room. Just totally aware and lonely."

Cressida knew exactly what she was taking about, except for her they weren't nightmares. They had been her daily routine until Vee showed up. Every night had been the same: nothing, nonexistent. "You know, you never really told me about the dream that brought you to therapy."

Vee rolled her eyes. "You'll laugh at me."

Cressida traced an X across her chest with her finger. "I will not. Besides, I'm sure I've heard worse."

"Well, it's not so much that the dreams are weird. It's that they come true."

Cressida's eyes glazed. As a therapist, advertising an interest in dream research is like posting a want-ad for telepaths, backwater psychics, and just plain crazy. She'd treated her fair share of *prophets* and so far none of them had converted her to their mystical thinking. "I doubt your dreams are actually coming true, more that you're just picking up on subtle clues in your environment that are imperceptible at a conscious level."

Vee furrowed her brow. "No, it's not like that. I dream about things I couldn't possibly know."

What people thought of as *"prophetic dreams"* were nowhere near as unusual as people believed, and were definitely not supernatural. Usually they were nothing more than a thinly veiled retelling of something they experienced without noticing. What was more surprising was how little attention they paid to the world around them. Cressida's fascination with dreams was centered around why people have them, rather than what they dreamt about. "Like what?"

"Umm, well there was Rex. I knew he was cheating on me." Vee turned her palms to the ceiling.

Even Cressida knew he was a cheater. "What else?"

"I've dreamt about songs and woken up to them playing on the radio."

"Most radio stations only have a catalogue of about thirty songs. Those are pretty good odds."

Vee's mouth pinched and her eyes set hard like sapphires. "I had a dream last night about your haircut." She folded her arms in front of her, satisfied that she'd made her point.

The smirk faded from Cressida's mouth. Had she been paying extra attention to Vee's hair that night at the Crab Shack? There had to be an explanation. "Ok, that's a little weirder. What was the dream about exactly?"

Vee dropped her eyes to the table and she picked at a piece of red candle wax stuck to the tablecloth. To the left, Ziggy and Trump looked on the edges of their seat, their half-eaten meals cooling in front of them on the table as they strained to listen. "Well, it wasn't exactly a haircut. I dreamt that Rex and I were floating in the ocean on top of two of those colorful pool rafts. Mine was pink and Rex's was blue. The water was perfectly calm and there wasn't a hint of land anywhere. A green seagull landed on Rex's boat and when he went to shoo it away it bit a hole in his raft. The bird flew onto my raft and I was sure it was going to pop it, so I didn't move. I didn't breathe. Rex was flailing around beside me but it was like he was behind a pane of glass. I couldn't hear him anymore. I reached my hand out to touch him and he melted into the sea until there was nothing left—"

"What does any of this have to do with my hair?"

"I'm getting there. So this green seagull hops up onto my shoulder and I can feel its claws digging into my skin. I close my eyes and wait to sink when the stabbing pain in my shoulder eases. I open my eyes again and now you're lying on my raft with me. You have my hair and my bathing suit. The only reason I know it isn't me is your grey eyes staring at me just as the bird had a moment before. You're pulling me toward you and I think you're trying to kiss me, but then you open your mouth as wide as a snake and try to eat me whole."

An uneasy knot formed in Cressida's stomach. There had to be a way to explain away the hair. She smiled through her clenched teeth. "And from that you took away that I was going to cut my hair like yours?"

Vee shrugged. "Well, obviously the rest of it is completely insane. That's how these dreams work for me."

"Right." Cressida chewed the inside of her cheek. They say everyone in a dream is an aspect of the dreamer. *Some part of Vee wanted to be devoured.*

"But don't you think it's amazing that I knew about the hair?"

She was missing the point, just as she has missed the point with Rex. "Perhaps it wasn't me in the dream at all." Or perhaps Vee was getting jumpy, just like Sam had. Cressida's stomach hollowed.

"What do you mean?"

"Well, maybe it was you all along and the fact that one of you had my eyes was just supposed to represent you seeing things my way. Maybe it was all about Rex and how I felt like he wasn't good for you." The real world was black and white, but dreams could be interpreted in shades of grey.

Her mouth was open and the wrinkle between her eyes was a chasm. "I never thought of it like that before."

"Dreams aren't always what they seem." Cressida pictured herself coiled around Vee, clinging to the girl for the sake of her own dreams. *And sometimes they are.*

The waitress approached Cressida from behind. Her hair was knotted into messy dreads and her eyes were two different colors. Long and thin, her face was covered with tattoos, but below the ink the skin was uneven and scarred with burns. Cressida touched her own scars through her blouse.

"Are you ladies ready to order?" The colors from the tinted wine glasses shone through the empty plug in her ear lobe.

"Yeah, I think so." Vee smiled.

They ordered their food, and the waitress moved down the line to serve the other patrons along the table. None of them looked remarkable enough to be movie stars or fringe writers, though it did seem like the kind of place one would have found Hunter S. Thompson passed out in corner or doing a line a blow in the bathroom. What a story that would have made.

Cressida nudged Vee who was picking wax from the

burning candle. "Well, I guess we'll have to come back another time if we want to spot a celebrity."

"Even if we don't, this was fun. I'm glad I finally got a chance to eat here."

"That's what friends are for," Cressida said. "Fun, and encouraging you to make good life choices." She raised her eyebrows.

"I know. You're right. I always said I'd leave if I ever found out Rex cheated on me. I promised myself."

"And now you need to promise me." Cressida fixed cold gaze on Vee's. "When you get home you need to tell him it's over."

Vee breathed deep and released the air across the table. The candle flickered and went out. Black smoke swirled around Vee's face, obscuring Cressida's view of her eyes.

"I promise."

CHAPTER 20

Cressida's bedroom was filled with the dewy glow of the dawn. The wind howled along the beach, whipping sand and salt along the side of the building. The "For Rent" sign that had hung in Sam's vacant window since she left clanged against the glass, a constant reminder that people changed, grew apart, and left her behind.

But today was not a day for mourning. The last few nights, Cressida's dreams had been filled with color. Even her nightmares had been spectacular pyrotechnic events filled with blood and gore, beautiful in their own way. The exquisite pain of remembering Max and the accident dulled to an ache for more. To experience the colors and the pain outside of her dreams. She wanted to feel things as deeply as Vee. She stared into the velvet box and ran her fingers over the picture of Vee she'd taken from Rex's wallet.

Shivers started at her toes and worked their way up her bare legs as the wind ruffled her skirt. Cressida wrapped the silk scarf around her shoulders. Everything about her floated and flowed with each gust of coastal wind. By the end of the day Rex would be gone.

Cressida hugged herself in the bent reflection of the ancient vanity mirror before peeling off the scarf and replacing the box in the drawer. Celebrations would have to wait. She had patients to see this morning and Roger's inevitable questions to dodge.

The sun peeked through the grey morning clouds as Cressida approached the dingy edifice of The Mermaid Asylum. At one point the clinic must have been beautiful, grand and welcome, its roofline as well as its aspirations reaching for the heavens. But now years of harsh winds, salt spray, and local legends had peeled away the shine layer by layer until all that was left was the hideous skeleton of an archaic institution. As last night's rain evaporated in the emerging sun, steam rose from the damp streets. Through the smokescreen came the eager face of Vee, tired eyes, unwashed hair, and a smile that could sink ships. Against her breast she clutched a basket like a newborn baby. Dressed in orange and yellow against the grey stone, Vee was the dawn embodied.

Cressida met her on the walk. "Vee?"

"I know it's early, but I just had to come straight here to tell you." There were red marks around her neck. Fingerprints.

"Tell me what?" Cressida's heart sank. Rex could have lashed out when Vee left him. Cressida shouldn't have left her alone.

Vee thrust the basket toward Cressida. It was wicker and looked like the kind of thing cartoon characters took on picnics. "I stayed up all night baking. I haven't slept."

"You came here to tell me you baked?" The heavy scent

of butter and domestication covered her usual freshness. She used to smell of the sea and of freedom.

"No. I baked because I was too excited to sleep." Her hands were trembling, and something caught Cressida's eye. The sun was glinting off something in her hand. *No, on her hand.* It was too big to be glitter.

Cressida reached out and steadied Vee's hand. There, on her left ring finger, was a modest-sized diamond set into a brassy gold band. "Oh."

"I'm engaged!" Vee shrieked and shifted her weight back and forth between her feet. Her energy poured from her like she'd sprung a leak.

Speechlessness was not a familiar feeling for Cressida. Her mouth gaped wider than a fish seeking air. "I…see that. How? When?"

"I talked to Rex last night, like we planned…"

Anger, on the other hand, was a feeling with which Cressida was well acquainted. Fire rose up into Cressida's throat scorching her words. "That was not what *we* planned."

"I know, but he admitted that he'd flirted with that waitress because he was jealous of you and felt left out. She gave him her number and he took it to be polite. But he never called her." Vee held her hand out for Cressida to inspect. "It's vintage."

Vintage was just another word for *used* and *cheap* which is exactly how Rex treated Vee. The sun caught the diamond again and it flashed in Cressida's eyes, taunting her with its presence. She wanted to rip it from Vee's skinny finger and toss it into the ocean. "I don't know what to say." She held tight to Vee's hand.

"Just say you're happy for me."

Cressida turned at footsteps behind her. Roger, huffing and puffing. Sweat poured from his head and soaked the back of his neon yellow Lycra shirt. His chest heaved as he fought to slow his heart rate. Sand stuck to his bare, hairy toes. "Good morning, ladies."

Cressida dropped Vee's hand and glowered at Roger. "Doctor Banks." The basket of baked goods formed a barrier between them. "Miss Marquis was just dropping off a thank you basket for the office."

Vee squinted at Cressida.

"And how are you doing, Miss Marquis? It's nice to finally meet you in person." Roger eyed the basket and the gurgling of his stomach could be heard over the sound of the waves.

"I'm good. Great actually. I just wanted to share some good news with Cress...Doctor Dunhill." Vee smiled and tipped her head to the side. The welts along her neck looked angry in the sun.

Cressida's head spun. She wanted to yell and scream and lecture Vee on the cyclical patterns of abusive men. She wanted to slap the girl and demand she explain what was going through that pixie brain of hers. But Roger's thick trunk was standing between her and her catharsis. He bent over in front of Cressida and stretched his hamstrings. Cressida turned away from the vile display of Roger's hairy lower back. "Vee, did you want to come inside for a session? I have a free hour."

"Actually, I think I'm going to get back home and make Rex breakfast in bed. I kept him up half the night last night too." Her enthusiasm was an annoying little fly buzzing past Cressida's head. If only she could swat it.

Cressida bit down on her cheek until she tasted blood. "We still have a few unresolved issues to talk about."

Vee looked down her nose at Cressida. Somehow she seemed inches taller, and years older, as if she'd bartered for stature with her future. In a way, she had. "Actually, I think our last session really helped me." She twisted the ring around on her finger.

Roger hovered beside them, breathing hard through his mouth. What the fuck did he want? Was he waiting for Vee to leave so he could tell Cressida how everything worked out for the best? If that was the case, he was dead wrong.

"Well, that's great news, Vee. I just have a couple quick billing details to iron out and then I guess this is goodbye." Cressida unlocked the front door to the office building and held it open for Vee. Roger slipped ahead of them and headed for his office.

Vee sighed. "Ok."

Though the sun had already sliced through the darkened clouds outside, the office was dim. Cressida hung her keys on the second hook beside the door and walked ahead of Vee to her wingback chair and sat down with a loud plop. Vee had screwed everything up, ruined their plan. Cressida grabbed Max's pen from the side table and gripped it so hard her nails dug into the bed of her hand. Vee loitered awkwardly in the doorway for a few seconds until Roger peered around his office door to make sure everything was ok.

Hesitantly, Vee shut the door further dampening the light in the room. Cressida reached over and switched on the lamp beside her chair.

"I know what you're going to say." Vee crossed the room, stepping around the coffee table without looking and sprawling across the sofa. A fire lit her eyes.

"We talked about this. He's not going to change." Max would have told her that Vee was addicted to the drama. That she needed to feel consumed, used. That's why she let Rex do those degrading things to her, why she let him wrap his hands around her neck, bruise her skin, and tarnish her character. Cressida's stomach turned and her cheeks burned. She had misread the situation again. Just like she had done with Sam. Max would have always known Vee would go back to Rex. He would have counted on the weakness of human nature. Darkness swirled around Cressida's head. She'd been weak and foolish and easily led, just like her mother and her name would have predicted.

"But he's changed. And it's all thanks to you. If you hadn't pushed me I never would have confronted him. And he never would have opened up about his feelings and how much he needs me."

"But what about our plans?"

"What plans?" Vee scratched the top of her hand leaving dry white streaks along her skin.

"Your therapy. Our friendship. We had plans." Her desperation shrieked from her throat like crabs being boiled alive. Cressida hated the sound of her own voice. Max would never have approved. Nor would her mother.

"We can still be friends. But I came to therapy because I thought my boyfriend was cheating on me. And now I don't have a boyfriend; I'm going to have a husband instead."

"Husbands cheat too."

Vee shook her head. "Not mine."

Cressida's heart thumped against her skull. There was a pain in her chest that reminded her of the accident, of the dreams she'd had since meeting Vee. Those memories were so close and getting clearer every night. She couldn't go back to the darkness, not after basking in such clarifying light. "So that's it then?"

Vee smiled and stood up from the sofa. She walked around to the bookshelves and ran her fingers over all the volumes. "For now." She turned back to Cressida. "We should get coffee this weekend."

"Coffee?" Words had lost all meaning.

Vee wafted toward the door. "Yeah, I'll give you a call. Thanks again for everything. You really were a big help." Her slim figure disappeared into the hallway. She was gone. Everything was gone. A dreary shadow hung over the office, the brown walls closing in on Cressida like she was being buried alive. Her lungs collapsed and she bent forward with her head between her knees. Sam was gone. Vee was gone. Max was gone.

She was alone.

Cressida sat in her chair with her back to the open office door for several minutes. The sun peeked out from the clouds long enough to cast a spotlight on the muddy rug below the sofa. Still gripping Max's pen in her hand, Cressida fell to her knees on the carpet and started scrubbing the stain with a Kleenex. The thin paper tore apart in her hands, but she kept scrubbing until her fingernails bled. A light knock on the door stilled her hands. The mud was still there, ground permanently into the carpet fibers. Along with Cressida's blood. She dragged herself to her feet.

When Cressida opened her office door she was greeted by Roger's shiny face in an expensive-looking seersucker shirt. The gentle pleats disguised his barrel-shaped torso and complimented his tailored pants.

Cressida scowled. "Doctor Banks."

"Please, it's Roger." His hair was combed and he was wearing cologne. "I'm going to be out of the office most of the day today, but I wanted to check to make sure everything was ok with Miss Marquis."

"Everything is fine."

He jammed his hands into the pockets of his pants and

rocked back on his heels. "If she's showing up unannounced with gifts it could be a sign that she has an unhealthy fixation with you. These things happen more often then you realize."

Her mother had warned Max of the same thing when she'd found the box of photos and mementos of him Cressida had hidden in her dresser. A foolish girl with a foolish crush on her mother's therapist, her mother had said, and she'd made Cressida watch as she burned each item. When her mother had told Max what she had found, he'd explained the concept of transference and how easily teenagers can be influenced by authority figures. Cressida had stood in the corner of Max's office that day feeling invisible. No one saw her. No one cared. And she'd used her invisibility to steal his house key. The first of many trespasses between them.

Cressida leaned against the doorframe. "I'm not worried. She's no longer under my care."

"Oh. Good for you. Were you able to find her a suitable replacement?" Roger pulled his hand from his pocket and wiped the back of his wrist across his forehead.

Cressida peered around Roger toward the front door. Rain was falling in sheets against the glass and somewhere out there Vee was getting soaked.

"Yeah, she had no problem moving on." Cressida's mouth tasted sour.

Roger nodded. "For what it's worth, I think you made the right call."

"Thanks."

"Well, I'm off. Court date. If you need anything just call my cell phone." He patted a lump in his back pocket.

"Court?"

"Yeah, I'm testifying in a competency hearing. Very dull affairs." He winked. "Not like a day around here."

The front door clanged open and Cressida smiled as her first appointment filled the hallway. "Ah, Mister Ellis. You're right on time." The thin, shifty man bristled when he noticed Cressida's short hair. Dark circles shadowed his eyes and there was a butterfly bandage across his crooked nose. He'd been fighting again, the curse of the wicked and the paranoid. He skirted past her into the office without touching anyone. Cressida nodded to Roger, closed the door and headed back to her chair, back into the brown, to drown in the sea of sand and dirt.

CHAPTER 21

Cressida gasped and sat up in bed. The dark curtains danced to the sound of the wind howling over the ocean below her apartment. The sheets were damp. Her hair was plastered to her forehead. Everything stunk of peroxide. Her heart thumped in her chest and her fingers were knotted in the bedsheets. Her body was stiff, almost like rigor mortis. She'd been lost again in the endless void of her dreamless sleep. Every nerve and every cell in her body was urging her to stay awake.

It was sometime during the dead hours of night, between when the last bonfire burned out on the beach and when the first birds woke in the morning. It had been three days since she last saw Vee and as many nights since she last dreamed. The thick fog of sleep hung over her head, but she refused to be pulled back into the haze. Sleep without dreams was like dying every night. Instead of drifting gently into a dream world, Cressida fell infinitely into nothing. Cold, dark nothing.

Her eyes burned as she pulled herself free of her bed and hauled on a pair of sweat pants and a sweatshirt from a pile on the floor. Her tense muscles ached like she'd run for miles, and her lungs burned for oxygen. Her reflection bent and swayed in the vanity mirror. Like she was floating beneath the waves. The luster was gone from her hair and even in the dim light she thought she could see the red roots jutting out from her scalp. The black velvet box lay open on the vanity, the contents scattered along the surface. The silk scarf was sprawled across the floor.

Today was Friday, the day she usually saw Vee, and her apartment seemed to be closing in around her. She wrapped the scarf around her neck, stuffed the picture of Vee into her pocket and tossed on sneakers over bare feet. Then she abandoned her empty apartment for the beach.

The tide was out and the sand stretched for miles in every direction in the moonlight. Crabs scuttled across the wet ground as Cressida slogged past their hiding places. The cold sea air drove the last of the sleep from her veins. Somewhere in the distance a sea lion barked, another creature awake when he should have been asleep. With each step she felt more alive, more connected. She ran in time with her heartbeat. Her chest was tight and her lungs burned, but she wouldn't relent. Wouldn't give up. Just like she wouldn't give up on Vee. There had to be a way to get her back in her life. To reclaim her dreams and finish uncovering Max's secret.

She ran past the alcove under the asylum without stopping. This wasn't the time to look into the past. She needed to protect her future. Her exhausted legs gave out on her just below Rex's house. Had her subconscious led her here on purpose? Urging her to check on Vee? Cressida leaned against the rock cliff to catch her breath, moss and kelp clinging to her palms. She climbed the winding path to the street above, conscious of each step she took so she wouldn't slip. There were more cars along the street than the last time she sat outside Rex's house. Music rolled over the shadowy streets. There were no lights inside the houses—except at Rex's.

It could have been that they weren't home or had forgotten to turn off the living room lamp when they went to bed, but Cressida could feel the light pulling her across the street. The house wavered like a mirage. She ducked into the alley between the houses and crept up to the window. Rex was sitting on the sofa with his guitar slung across his lap, his long fingers flitting over the strings faster than anything Cressida had ever seen. Rex frowned and stilled his hands. He shook his head. He began again, pulling inspiration from the instrument the way an artist does from a sunset. Cressida closed her eyes and listened until the music stopped. When she looked again, Vee was there in a loose Metallica T-shirt, her bare ass peeking out from below the hem when she walked. Vee rubbed sleep from her eyes and smiled as she approached the sofa.

Vee held out her wrists in front of her, her hands fisted beside each other. Rex shook his head. Vee scowled. She reached down and pulled the guitar from his hands, set it on the coffee table behind her, and straddled his lap with her half naked body. She pulled the T-shirt over her head and whispered something into his ear.

Cressida jumped at a crash behind her—garbage can. A cat sprinted out of the alley. She crouched lower outside the window, but no one in the house seemed to notice—Vee was holding her wrists in front of her again, her nipples hard and her hips grinding down onto Rex's lap. The skin behind her ears glowed pink, like her whole face was burning. He shook his head again, but she lowered her lips again to his ear. Rex flexed his fingers and his lips parted as he listened to whatever Vee had to say. Finally, he grabbed her arms and swung them around so she was laying beneath him on the sofa. He pinned her wrists above her head with one arm, the other pressed into the delicate flesh of her throat. Her blue eyes smiled through her grimace.

Rex leaned hard on Vee's arms as he unzipped his pants and pushed them to the floor. He kissed her mouth before pushing her face to the side, away from his, and her wild eyes flashed toward the window where Cressida was hiding. Slowly he and lowered himself between her spread legs. Her hips lifted to meet him half way. His fingertips dug at her as he thrust into her over and over, harder and faster. Cressida jammed her fingernails into her palms. This was how he marked Vee.

Vee threw her head back and moaned.

Rex pulled out of her and yanked her arms hard toward him so she was sitting up on the sofa. Her breasts rose and fell with her rapid breaths. He pinched her nipples so hard it made her entire body shudder, and when he moved his hands the skin of Vee's breasts was red and splotchy. Rex kneeled up on the sofa and wrapped his free hand around the back of Vee's head, pulling her face onto his erection. Her wrists free, she pulled her arms behind her back and looked up at Rex. He hesitated and the corners of his mouth twitched, but eventually he obediently reached around and grasped her wrists again. This time holding them tight behind her back. Vee's mouth widened and disappeared against his pelvis. Cressida could only see the back of her head as it moved back and forth, Rex's fingers digging into the back of her hair with one hand and her wrists with the other as he pushed harder and faster into her mouth. Cressida's stomach heaved and her pulse throbbed. Her blood pooled in the center of her body and she could feel herself getting wet between her legs. How could Vee let him treat her this way? She was disgusted by her own body's reaction.

Then it was over. Rex's hand went limp in Vee's hair and he dropped onto the sofa beside her, releasing her wrists. Vee sat up and rubbed her wrists where five perfect red welts had already darkened. She picked up her discarded T-shirt and wiped it across her mouth, then she leaned over and kissed Rex. She stroked his hair and lay down across his lap. Her chapped lips twisted into a satisfied smile.

Rex picked up his guitar from the table. His nimble fingers that a moment ago crushed into Vee's forearms moved delicately across the neck of the instrument. Vee closed her eyes.

Cressida slid to the dirt beside the house and buried her head against her knees. Everything was wrong. Vee was supposed leave Rex. She was supposed to feel eternally grateful to Cressida for giving her the strength to finally leave her abuser and they would be friends forever. Cressida was supposed to dream, to be whole again. She was not supposed to be standing outside Rex's house watching him bruise Vee again, and Vee was most definitely not supposed to enjoy it. Vee was ruining everything. Cressida's head spun as she stood on shaky legs. She walked home along the street, unable stand the thought of the sea filling her head with its incessant white noise. At that moment she longed for quiet, for solitude, and for dreamless sleep.

HAMISH SQUINTED at Cressida through weathered eyes. The office was quiet that morning with only the sound of Hamish's tree trunk of a leg bouncing against the sofa as he fidgeted. Roger would be arriving at the office soon bringing with him the smell of sweat and the burden of his pathetic concern. Her head pounded and her nerves were as frayed as the seams on her old sofa. Max's pen lay still on the side table next to her chair. She hadn't taken a single note on a patient in two days. She couldn't focus on anything other than the red marks on Vee's arms. She saw them everywhere: on the plain walls of her office, around Hamish's thick neck, and on her own skin. She pictured Rex's dainty hands around Vee's neck, him grunting with the effort of subduing her, and always Vee's perverse smile. Cressida shook her head.

"Are you feelin' okay today, Doc?" The swishing sound of Hamish's leg against the burlap cushions stopped. His bulky frame creaked forward. "Yeh look like death."

Cressida's lips curled into a passable smile. Hamish knew nothing of death. She visited it every night while he lay dreaming. "I'm fine. Just listening."

But she wasn't fine. She hadn't slept, hadn't rested since she stopped dreaming. Her appetite had vanished and she had developed a tremor in her right hand. Vee was gone and Rex had won. The bitter taste of defeat filled her mouth and she swallowed hard to keep from spitting onto her beige carpet. There had to be a solution to her problem, a way to dream without Vee, but she was too tired to think straight. All she wanted was to crawl into bed, but it held nothing for her except empty promises.

Why couldn't it be like it was in Rex's bed that day she snuck into his house? She'd possessed Vee within herself that day, and the dreams had come easily. But she couldn't risk getting caught, couldn't risk another misunderstanding like what happened with Sam. After all, that's all it had been: a misunderstanding and an overreaction. But she couldn't bear to lose Vee the way she'd lost Sam.

Hamish cleared his throat. "Robbie wants to bring some boy home fer dinner. Can yeh believe that?"

"That actually sounds really positive, Mister Hamish." Despite his fishy odor and tendency to track mud across her carpet, she looked forward to Hamish's appearance in her office each week. It was routine, safe, and calming: a problem she could actually solve.

"The wife is just so damn happy 'bout it too. She's been runnin' around baking pies and poaching salmon like we was feeding the crown prince. Haven't seen her so excited since the kids was little."

Cressida inclined her head. "Sounds like everyone is really trying to make this work. How are you feeling about it?"

Hamish shrugged. "It's only been a few weeks since we found out about his...er...preferences. I figured he'd give us more time before rubbin' it in our faces."

"Well, my guess is he's been waiting to share this part of his life with you for a lot longer."

Hamish wrung his hands together and his eyes dropped to his lap. "I just got used to the idea. Seein' it in the flesh is somethin' else."

Something sparked on the edges of Cressida's mind, but her thoughts were sluggish and she couldn't place it. "You think meeting his boyfriend will make it more real?"

Hamish nodded without looking up.

"Then I think this can only be a good thing, Mister Hamish, because it's real whether you see it or not. The sooner you can accept that, the better relationship you can have with your son. I assume that's the point of all this. Right?"

"Yeah, but I ain't sure I'm ready. Yeh know? What if I say somethin' stupid and Robbie ends up hatin' me anyway?"

Cressida leaned forward in her chair. "Then you'll try again. You don't give up on the people you love. And if you'd like we can role play some scenarios so that you'll feel more comfortable when the time comes."

Hamish glanced at a large plastic watch dimpling the flesh around his wrist. It was the kind of watch that still functioned after being run over by a truck. "Ain't we outta time?"

Cressida nodded. "Oh. You're right. We are out of time this morning. When is your dinner?

Hamish's face paled as he eased out of his seat. He drug the toe of his boot across the carpet. "Next Tuesday."

Cressida pursed her lips as she watched the fibers bend to his will. "Why don't you come in on Monday? I'm pretty open in the afternoon. I'd be happy to clear some time for you so you can feel better prepared."

His round face split into a genuine smile. "Sounds good, Doc. I don' know what I'd do without yeh."

"It's no problem, really. Just give me a call and let me know when you're available." She inhaled the smell of the sea and stood from her chair.

He patted her on the shoulder, his rough hands like sandpaper against her silk blouse. The gesture was simple, fatherly, but it dug a pit in Cressida's stomach that reminded her again of Vee. Hamish was changing, venturing outside his comfort zone for the sake of his son. Everyone around her was becoming something new, something special. She saw it every day, helped people see it in themselves, but it would never be real for Cressida. She would never change. Not without Vee.

Her tired mind paused again over something Hamish had said. Something about seeing his son's lover making his sexuality seem more real, forcing him to accept it rather than sweeping it under the rug. Perhaps Cressida hadn't done enough to force Vee to accept the fact that Rex was a liar and a cheater. She'd hinted at it, given Vee ample reasons to suspect, but perhaps what she needed was solid proof. Something to make it real. No more wild accusations and suggestive coincidences. She needed something more concrete. Undeniable.

Then Vee would understand. She'd come back and so would Cressida's dreams and her memories of what happened the night Max died. She knew in her gut that she'd changed that day, and maybe if she could just remember it clearly, she'd finally be able to understand her own creation story.

CHAPTER 22

Paper from the receipts Cressida had taken from Rex's wallet crinkled in her palm as she pushed through the crowd of bouncing sports fans in front of the bar at The Crab Shack. Their collective energy was greater than that of the Blazers who were once again failing to delight basketball fans across the state. The bar, on the other hand, was handily raking in money from disgruntled zealots intent on drinking away their vicarious loss. Capitalizing on pain and weakness was a standard business practice. After all, life was a bloodsport. There was no point in pretending it was anything but.

Cressida reached the front of the mob and slapped her hand to the counter to draw the bartender's attention. A mermaid tattoo winked at Cressida from behind the taps of domestic beer and watered-down soda. The waitress from the other night. Her name tag said Elise, and her lip piercing said *fuck with me and I will cut you*. Without looking up she smiled, her lips pulling at the metal ring in the middle of her bottom lip. "Can I help you?"

"I don't know, maybe." Cressida's ears rang as Elise

pulled the tap and foamy beer hissed into a soap-stained glass. "My friend got really drunk last week and lost his wallet so we're retracing his steps and trying to see if anyone found it or remembers seeing him with it."

Elise glanced at Cressida between pulls of the tap. Her face froze, a blush rising in her cheeks. "Sure, I remember you." She dropped her head and wiped the dry counter with a cocktail napkin. The very same kind she's used to give her number to Rex. If Cressida could get her to admit she'd fucked Rex, maybe Vee would reconsider marrying him.

"You were with the guitarist from The Ampersands and that redheaded girl."

The waitress thought she was Vee. Cressida smiled. "Right. So I was just wondering if you noticed him with his wallet that night. So we'll know if he lost it before or after we were here."

Elise scratched the root of one of her silver hair twists. "I don't really remember."

Cressida leaned over the bar until she was close enough to see the color of the girl's eyes. Mossy green. "But you *did* talk to him that night, right?"

"Look, I see what's going on here. I thought you guys were together, but he invited me to his show this weekend, so I gave him my number." She raised her hands above her shoulders. Her fingernails were chewed to the quick. "He never called. I swear."

"Did he say he would?"

"No, he didn't say a word. Look, can I give you a piece of advice?"

Cressida nodded.

"If you're having to haul your cookies all over town to check up on where your man has been then maybe he isn't worth the trouble." Elise whirled around and started taking orders down the line. The mermaid on the waitress's arm seemed to chuckle her disdain. *Even this girl could see that Rex was a liability.*

Cressida turned her back to the bar and dug the receipts back out of her pocket. Rex was hiding something and if he hit on a waitress while he was out with his girlfriend then he must have done it somewhere else too. Cressida flipped through the taxi receipts and lunch checks. No one was going to remember him in such anonymous places. She paused over the hotel receipts. There was no reason for Rex to be renting hotels midweek when he was supposed to be studying with friends unless he was cheating. She needed proof though. Something undeniable. Something better than the waitress's phone number or a meeting time. Cressida kicked the stool next to her.

A shadow fell across the papers in her hands and Cressida looked up to find a tall, blond man in a green University of Oregon sweatshirt towering over her like a jolly giant, a beer in each hand. He was younger, probably in his early twenties, with broad shoulders and a nose that looked like it had been broken a few times. He was probably a promising high school football player who went to college on a four-year scholarship to be a glorified punching bag for the guys with bodies like a Mac truck. Silverside was the kind of place where unwanted people washed up.

"Did I hear something about The Ampersands?" He leaned against the bar and set one of the beers down beside Cressida.

"Yes. Do you know them?"

"Yeah, they played a party a buddy of mine threw a few months ago. They were awesome, and boy did they know how to get the party going." He nudged the beer closer to Cressida's elbow. She picked it up and thanked him by clinking it against his own bottle. "Are you like a groupie or something?"

Cressida took a long drink from the bottle. The beer tasted like rotten fruit, decay, and death. She thumped the bottle back onto the counter and fixed the young man with her darkest grey stare. "I used to date the guitarist."

"But not anymore?" He winked like he'd said something clever.

"Nope. Not anymore."

"I can't imagine it's easy dating a musician. A nice girl like yourself should be with someone who knows how lucky they are to have you." He smiled and his teeth were perfectly white and straight. Somewhere an orthodontist was driving a sports car thanks to this kid's parents.

"You know, my friend was always telling me the same thing. I wish I'd listened sooner."

"Better late than never." His face was so smooth Cressida doubted he'd ever had to shave a day in his life. He was like a giant Gerber baby with a six pack and a drinking problem. "My name's Brett. What's yours?"

Why couldn't her mother have named her Jane or Susan? Something short. Something sweet. Something easy to forget. Fucking bitch. Although...

Cressida smiled at him. "My name's Viola. It's nice to meet you." She smiled and scratched the top of her hand, because that's what Vee would do. Her nails were short but they still left white streaks across her skin. She hadn't dreamed since Vee left, but maybe if she could inhabit her spirit for a night, she could learn to dream on her own. Maybe it could be like it had been in Rex's house again.

Brett looked over his shoulder and the thinning crowd behind him. The game must have been over. "Well, Viola, it seems my friends have left me. Want to get out of here?" He flashed his million-dollar smile again. It was dazzling.

THE FIRST TIME Cressida had understood the power of becoming another person was the night Max saw her wearing his wife's necklace. She'd gone from standing invisible, despised, and alone in the corner to an object of influence and lust in seconds. For so long she had inhabited the persona of the disappointing daughter and despised youth that any reprieve from the loathing was a welcome distraction. She hadn't loved Max's wife, and neither had he for that matter, but Cressida had loved the way it had made her feel to be someone different: her skin awash with new sensations and new fabrics. And once she'd seen the effect it had on Max, she became someone new for him each day.

She stole small things: perfume, stockings, the occasional blouse. It became part of her routine. She would arrive at therapy as Cressida: cold, gnarled, and scabby. But as soon as Max closed the office door she stripped away layers of pain and hatred, the years of life with her mom, and the physical and emotional scars, and replaced them with silk. She would stand before him, naked, open, and new, and he would touch her. It was the only time she felt content. Like she owned him.

As Cressida and Brett walked hand-in-hand along the beach she had that feeling again. Her clothes hung differently from her shoulders, her arms lighter and stronger, her smile more genuine. When Brett looked at her he saw Vee. When they arrived in front of his house and he kissed her, he was kissing Vee.

Cressida closed her eyes and thought about the look on

Vee's face that night she'd watched her and Rex on the sofa. Vee was like her, trapped and bound by her identity. The battered girlfriend. But in those moments with Rex she was free. Free to fuck, free to scream, and free to cry. Cressida wanted to scream too.

She followed Brett up the short walkway into his small house. There were beer cans and pizza boxes on the sofa and laundry littering the floor. It was pin-drop silent in the house so either Brett's room mates were out or they were fast asleep.

The only furniture in the room was the double bed covered with a homemade quilt sewn from old T-shirts. Brett was a good boy, with nice parents and expensive dental work. He wasn't Rex, and he wasn't Max. But still, he looked at her with awe and desire, like she controlled the stars. She sat down on the edge of the bed and pulled at Brett's belt buckle. It slid easily from his waist and landed on the floor by her feet. She watched his eye widen as she unbuttoned his pants and hooked her thumbs over the waistband of his boxer briefs, pulling both past his knees. He was already hard.

With Max it took time. He would slowly strip away every piece of Cressida's clothing until all that was left was her stolen identity. Only then would his excitement peak.

Brett stepped out of his pants and fumbled with Cressida's top. He yanked it over her head and dropped to his knees in front of her. Cressida's skirt rustled as he ran his hands up the inside of her legs and back down to her ankles, dragging her panties along with him. Then he disappeared under the folds of her skirt, his fingers and mouth making their way up her legs until they reached the neat tuft of red hair at the apex. Cressida laid back on the bed and stared at the ceiling. Brett's tongue lapped against her, warm and wet, but all she could picture were the marks on Vee's wrists after Rex fucked her.

Cressida tugged his shoulders, calling him up to meet her on the bed. She reached her arms above her head and held her wrists together. "Hold me down."

Brett's eyes narrowed. Max's eyes had looked that same way when Cressida had stepped into his car wearing his wife's wedding gown the day of the accident. She remembered it in vivid detail. She'd been someone else that night that he died too.

"Do it."

Brett hovered over Cressida with one hand on her wrists and one between her legs, pushing, searching, needing. He spread her lips and filled her with his thick fingers. The hand caressing her wet center was so strong, so solid, yet the one holding her wrists was soft and tender. He wanted to worship her. She wanted him to mark her.

"Get the belt," she whispered into his ear and he obeyed, his eyes searching hers for reassurance.

"Are you sure?" He straddled her half naked body and held the leather belt in his hands.

"Yes, and make it tight." She scooted up along the bed until her hands bumped the metal headboard.

Brett threaded the belt through the metal bars and then tightened it around Cressida's wrists. Her arms stretched above her head, pulling at the muscles of her back and shoulders. Her fingers tingled and her entire body clenched. She could feel the sheets dampening beneath her. This was what Vee felt. "Now fuck me."

Pushing her skirt over her stomach, Brett positioned himself on top of Cressida's trussed body, his eyes as big as his erection. She cried out as he pushed inside her, the leather from the belt digging into her wrists as her body struggled to find rhythm with his. Cressida closed her eyes and pictured herself from above: blond hair, bunched skirt, and strong man pounding away at her womanhood. She was the heroine in her own story. She was Vee. The scars that peppered her chest disappeared and her grey eyes flickered deep blue in her mind. Brett pressed down hard against her pelvis as he ground her into the bed, his thick fingers digging into the soft flesh of her hips. Her arms ached but so did her insides, and with each thrust the spark in her gut burned hotter. Slowly the sensation spread through her stiff body until finally it burst into flames. She screamed, long and loud and like no sound she'd ever made before.

He pulled out of her and covered her skirt and her bare thighs with warm, sticky liquid before collapsing on top of her. His bulky chest crushing her lungs until there was nothing left inside them, like the rest of her. Cressida closed her eyes and felt her heart beating fast against his heavy body, the lack of oxygen blurring the edges of her consciousness.

Brett unhooked the belt. His cheeks were red as if he was embarrassed of what he'd just done. "Are you ok?"

"I'm fine." Cressida pulled her wrists to her chest rubbing each one in turn.

Brett and wiped her thighs with the bottom of her skirt, but before he could say anymore she rolled onto her side to sleep. Her skin tingled. Brett laid down awkwardly beside her and wrapped his arm around her protectively. People were always trying to protect Vee. They all wanted to save her. Even Cressida.

She smiled and drifted slowly into oblivion.

CHAPTER 23

Cressida sat up wheezing for air, the spreading numbness of sleep clawing at her chest beneath her bare breasts. Beside her the man she'd fucked as Vee lay curled into a ball like a child, naked and murmuring into his hands, oblivious to the sickly sweet smell of sweat and sex. The belt he'd used to tie Cressida to the bed hung limp across the headboard. It hadn't been enough. She still couldn't sleep, couldn't dream. She wasn't Vee. And somewhere out there, Rex was using her up. Cressida's limbs were unsteady as she stepped out of bed, aching from Brett's rough grip and from the relentless grasp of her empty sleep.

She grabbed her wrinkled top, pulled it over her head and glanced around. No clock. Cressida tiptoed through the door into the hallway, sandals in hand. She'd never spent the night with Max, never had to sneak out of his house while his wife slept—theirs had been an organized affair, clean and hidden.

She wasn't going to get out unseen tonight. There was a

light on downstairs, and voices, laughter and celebration, coming from the living room. *Dammit.*

Quietly Cressida descended and walked into the living room, shielding her eyes from the harsh lights with the back of her hand. On the ratty sofa sat two men, boys really, every bit as large as Brett and taking up the entire length of the furniture. Both wore Silverside Community College sweatshirts and their broad shoulders touched as they twisted the video game controllers in their hands. One of them with long dark hair pulled into a ponytail, bronze skin, and an even darker beard dropped his controller to his lap and threw up his hands in defeat. He tugged hard at his coarse facial hair and then looked up and met Cressida's eyes. His irises looked almost black in the glare of the television.

"Hey, Ian, check it out. Brett actually talked a girl into coming home with him." He nudged the boy next to him on the sofa: pale ivory skin, freckles, and hair almost as red as Cressida's had been before she dyed it.

Ian's eyes were almost the same color as Vee's, but they didn't sparkle. Most likely they were dulled from booze and boredom. He smiled without making eye contact. "Hi. Sorry if we woke you up. Dev here is a louder loser than he is a lover."

The dark-haired boy scrunched his nose. "Don't fucking say the word *lover*, man. It's creepy. You're scaring the nice lady." He nodded at Cressida who hadn't moved from the entrance of the living room. "You wanna sit?"

Cressida wanted to leave the overgrown man-children to their video games and their tasteless jokes and their banal college experience. They were trapped in this backwards seaside town attending community college instead of accepting their inevitable vocation as crabbers, fishermen or dock workers. They were pretending to be something they weren't. Something they weren't born to be. But then, so was she.

Cressida smiled and sidled up to the sofa, twisting the straps of her shoes between her fingers. The living room window was cracked and she could feel the ocean breeze rustle her skirt against her legs. Her hips were sore from Brett's insistent fingers and she lowered herself gingerly onto the sofa beside Dev to keep from wincing. Cressida pictured the bruises she had seen on Vee's arms—much like the ones she would certainly find on her body tomorrow. She'd done everything right. She'd been Vee. Yet her sleep had remained fevered. Desolate.

Dreamless.

Ian shifted his body toward Cressida. "So what did you say your name was?"

"Viola."

He grinned. "Like Gwyneth Paltrow in that Shakespeare movie?"

Cressida cocked her head. "Umm..."

Dev whirled on his ginger friend. "What are you doing watching Gwyneth Paltrow movies, you pussy?" He jabbed Ian in the ribs and turned back to Cressida with his eyebrows raised as if he was inviting her to join the assault.

"I watched it with my ex girlfriend, you dick. Besides, I wasn't talking to you."

Dev met Cressida's gaze. His eyes were bloodshot. "How did you and Brett meet anyway?"

Cressida's eyes followed Dev's hands as he folded them in his lap. He yawned. Whatever was keeping him up all night was slowly wearing off.

"We just met tonight actually. At The Crab Shack." She'd failed twice that night: failed to catch Rex cheating on Vee and failed to conjure enough of Vee to resurrect her dreams.

She dug her short nails into the soft flesh of her wrist. She wanted to claw the skin from her bones.

Ian leaned closer. “You go to Silverside Community?”

Her fingers froze against her arm. Silverside. It was possible one of these guys knew something about Rex. After all, they went to the same school, and Brett had mentioned The Ampersands playing at a friend’s party. Perhaps the night wouldn’t be a waste after all. Cressida shook her head. “Nope. How do you guys like it?

She glanced over her shoulder to the stairs. No sign of Brett. She hoped he would sleep until morning and she could disappear without the awkward goodbye. Though chances were she would run into him again. Small towns were the enemy of anonymity, but maybe she could use that to her benefit with Rex.

Ian puffed out his chest to show off the logo on his sweatshirt. “Dean’s list and everything, baby.”

Dev’s eyes rolled into his head, but Cressida shifted on the sofa to face Ian. “Wow, that’s impressive. What are you studying?”

“Working on an associates in business. I’m going to PSU next fall.” Pride glowed through Ian’s practically translucent skin. He was probably the first person in his family to do anything other than work the shipyard.

Wind rippled across the floor and cooled Cressida’s bare feet. The coffee table in front of them was littered with coasters from bars around town and she shivered as she leaned forward to line them up neatly against the edge of the table. With each edge she straightened, Cressida’s heart rate slowed. The questions burning at her tired mind began to cool. “Portland State is a great school. Congratulations.”

Dev’s head was lolled against the back of the sofa. He was dead weight. Ian, on the other hand, was pink with excitement. She crossed her legs, her skirt riding up over her knees. Ian shifted on the sofa trying to get an unobstructed view of her bare thighs. Dev's head drooped to his chest and then snapped back up.

"I'm gonna have to go to bed, man." Dev hauled himself off the middle of the sofa and dragged across the carpet to the stairs. "Later." His large feet thumped on each step until he reached his room and closed the door.

Through the front window, the sun was lightening the horizon from black to midnight blue, fading the stars along the edge of the world. The video game controller Dev had abandoned lay across the sofa between Cressida and Ian, its cord sprawled over the stained fabric like a dead snake. She reached over and coiled the cord around the controller, pulling it tight against the curved plastic. Ian's remark about the college and associate degrees was nagging at Cressida's mind. Rex's story about his music degree wasn't adding up, but her brain was too foggy to find the inconsistency.

Ian wrung his hands in his lap and took a deep breath. "You know, I should probably get some sleep too."

"Oh, that's too bad."

Ian dropped his gaze to his lap. "I've got class in the morning, otherwise I'd stay. Brett has great taste in women." His already pink face blushed scarlet.

Cressida reached over and pushed his shoulder playfully. "You're sweet."

"It was really nice talking to you." He stood from the sofa but Cressida reached out and took his wrist.

She smiled. "Before you go, I wanted to ask you a question." Ian's lips parted and he glanced down at her hand. She pulled it back and ran it through her hair. Vee's hair. "I have a friend who wants to go to SCC to study music composition. Do you know anyone in the program?"

Ian squinted. "Music?"

Cressida nodded. "Yeah."

"That doesn't really sound like the kind of thing SCC does. It's more about GEDs and transfer degrees for people who need to freshen up before going to a university. Maybe she's thinking of Portland State or Linfield?"

Cressida's skin tingled along her spine. Rex's story about studying with his friends had never made sense to her. She should have known he was lying. "Oh. I must have misunderstood."

Ian nodded at the stairs. "Are you staying or going?"

"Going, I think." Cressida slipped her feet into her sandals and followed Ian to the door. "Could you tell Brett I had to get home? It's nothing personal."

Ian reached for the door handle and brushed Cressida's arm with his. "What an idiot," he muttered under his breath.

"What?"

"I was just saying Brett is an idiot. He must have done something really annoying to send a pretty girl packing at five in the morning." He pulled the door open and held it for Cressida. Outside, the sky was changing from blue to gold. Ian's hair looked even redder in the budding dawn.

Cressida walked into the doorway and turned. "It was nice to meet you."

"Ditto. I hope to see you again, Viola."

"Me too." Once she figured out what Rex was doing when he said he was in school, she would be that much closer to getting her own Viola back. Her eyes were heavy, but Cressida knew there would be no rest until the dreams returned. Only endless empty nights. Vee needed Cressida to save her from Rex, but even more than that, Cressida needed Vee. She needed to possess her, learn to become like her, let her colors wash over her, so Cressida could dream again.

The front door clicked shut behind Cressida and she walked to the edge of the street. The ocean was sparkling in the distance. Whales spouted water high into the air, a lighthouse flashed into the fog, and fishing boats left their docks eager and ready to pull some crab traps. Hamish was out there among the throng of vessels, his big hands tugging ropes and slinging fish. There was something comforting about that fact. The entire town of Silverside came alive with the sun, its inhabitants drifting from their beds to their jobs with the same fundamental predictability of the tides. *Except Rex.*

Cressida had no idea what Rex was doing at that moment. But she did know that he had lied to Vee. He'd told her she had to keep working for her dad to pay for a school he never attended. He just wanted to keep control over her, or maybe to know where she was at all times. He was willing to sacrifice her dreams for his own selfish pleasures. The receipts from the Portland hotels Cressida found in Rex's wallet sprang to mind. If he wasn't in school all day or studying all night...

He was doing something. Or someone.

Cressida turned down the street and walked toward her apartment. She needed to find out more information about Rex's extracurricular activities, and if asking the local folks wasn't going to yield anything useful she would go straight to the source.

CHAPTER 24

Rex's band, The Ampersands, were playing a show in a club called The Brig, a nautical themed dive bar built around an old shipwreck that had been dragged onto the beach decades before and never disposed of. The stage was hewn straight from the hull of the ship, and all around the establishment were salvaged pieces of the wreck repurposed into trendy new doors, windows and tables. Last year a reporter from *The Oregonian* stopped into The Brig for a drink on his way home from a wedding near Cannon Beach and ended up writing a sparkling review about its masterful combination of history and innovation —like Silverside itself.

After the article was published, Silverside was overrun with hipsters and yuppies arguing about whether or not the ship should have been donated to a museum while they sipped their ten dollar drinks. It was a huge revenue boost for the town, but soon the novelty wore off, as novelty always does, and The Brig returned to its humble beginnings of drunk fishermen and sweaty metal-heads.

On that Sunday night the bar was thinly populated with

a strange mixture of students from the University of Oregon who considered themselves bohemian for setting foot in the salty bar and steampunk locals who cursed the very tourist trade that kept their tiny town from sinking into oblivion. Green and yellow flashed against black and white and leather under the vicious stage lights.

Cressida slipped past the hardcore fans in front of the stage and headed for the bathroom. She splashed water on her face. Her eyes were almost transparent against the fluorescent lights around the mirror, like they were empty, merely a shell waiting to be colonized. Her tight white top dipped down to her cleavage and her black skinny jeans clung to her hips. She clutched her hand over the peppered marks on her chest and they burned under her touch. She wrapped Sam's silk scarf around her neck and draped it across the scars, hiding them from plain sight. Yet with every gust of wind she was reminded that she would never rest again unless she healed the damage caused by the accident. And if her degree in psychology taught her anything it was that the deepest scars affect the mind, not the body.

In the distance a microphone squealed to life, and Rex's smug voice boomed through the wooden frame of the bar. "Thanks for coming out to party with us tonight. We're The Ampersands." His unpretentious introduction was a surprising feat of restraint from someone who craved such constant admiration as he seemed to.

Cressida checked her teeth in the mirror and then pushed through the bathroom door into the swell of music flooding from the stage. There were several round tables dotted around the bar behind a sparse row of fanatics jumping and slamming into each other. Cressida slid into a chair on the far right of the stage where Rex was fingering his guitar with such concentration he hadn't noticed her arrive. She watched as his skillful hands pinched and squeezed the neck of the instrument with force and grace and love. She pictured his hands wrapped around Vee's neck, dragging her just to the brink of pain and then letting her ride the wave back. Just then Rex's eyes lifted to the crowd and landed momentarily on Cressida. She held her breath, waiting for the recognition to light his expression, but he just winked and dove into a dizzying guitar solo.

Rex glanced at Cressida several more times throughout the first set, but his face remained impassive. Either he didn't recognize her or he wanted her to think that she wasn't important enough to remember. When the band broke for an intermission Cressida watched as Rex sashayed to the bar for a drink. The waitress from the other night, Elise, stood beside him flapping her mouth rapidly at his ear. The mermaid tattoo on her arm jiggled as she gestured excitedly. *What a sycophant.* Rex nodded his head. But he didn't smile.

Elise scowled when Rex turned his back to her carrying two bottles of beer, her face more twisted and ugly than the drowning mermaid on her arm. Elise looked past Rex toward Cressida, who snapped her head down to avoid eye contact. Elise would out her to Rex if given half a chance. He might even tell Vee, poisoning her against Cressida for good. Once again she'd ended up without the power. All she could do was wait.

Cressida stared at her hands, counting to one hundred before looking up to see whether Elise had noticed her. If the waitress had spotted her then so could Rex. Her mind raced. She might have underestimated Rex's observational skills. At that moment she couldn't remember how many times he'd looked into her eyes at the Crab Shack. Once? Maybe twice? She should have paid better attention. She sucked a deep breath, the muscles in her legs tensed and ready to run. If she left now, maybe Rex wouldn't see her up close and she could deny ever being there if Vee asked.

Too late.

Black boots came into view beside her own, chunky and scuffed. Cressida raised her grey eyes and was met by swirling brown irises and a crooked smile. Rex set one of the beers down on the table in front of her and twisted a chair so the seat faced him and the back was between him and Cressida. He lowered onto the chair with his arms folded across the metal back.

"Hey, there. I couldn't help but notice you sitting here during the show. You look lonely." His jaw was soft and his eyes were a little unfocused, his pupils dilated. Drunk. Or perhaps he was just in his element, the music whittling away his defenses like an aphrodisiac.

Cressida picked up the amber bottle and clinked it against Rex's beer. "Thanks. I guess I'm not lonely anymore."

Rex leaned over the back of the chair. "You look familiar. Have I seen you in here before?" The crease between his eyes deepened as he tried to pull her face from the recesses of his memory and failed. Vee must not have told him about Cressida's haircut. She'd kept that secret. And now Rex didn't recognize her as Vee's friend. Vee's therapist.

Cressida gazed into the bottle. "This is my first time."

"Ooh. A virgin, huh?" He bared his teeth like an animal on the prowl.

The familiar hatred bubbled up in her stomach, burning and welcome and...alive. "I guess I am." She forced a laugh. "Please be gentle."

Rex threw back his head and barked a hideous laugh. "I like you. What did you say your name was?"

Cressida paused and ran her fingers along the scarf hanging over her chest. "I didn't."

Rex's eyes trailed after her hands and over her breasts. "A woman of mystery, huh? I like that." Rex jumped to his feet so quickly Cressida flinched. Wild and unpredictable, Rex was a god here, and he knew it.

"I have to get back up on stage. Don't move. I'll be back."

Cressida nodded her head and took a swig from the beer bottle. Vile. It reminded her of eating the spoiled food her mother served as punishment for not doing the grocery shopping after school. Those days, her mother wanted her to fail. Wanted her to be a disappointment, and to be frustrated by her own incompetence. Every bite of each rotten meal was a triumph. Brute strength was irrelevant. Some rats refuse to die.

She took another sour drink of beer through gritted teeth. This was a fight she would win as well.

TWO FINISHED SETS and three beers later, Rex was more than generous with his time and his money. Cressida nursed her drinks while Rex pounded them. He was the lead singer of the band, the king of the bar, the alpha male. It was probably what Vee had seen in him in the first place. That kind of obvious power was intoxicating. Not that it made her happy. Vee needed to learn about real power, the kind of power that can change you.

Rex slapped his hand down onto the table. "I can't stand it," he slurred. "You have to tell me where I know you from." His hand crept across the sodden table until it found Cressida's. His rough fingertips, calloused from hours of pinching chords, brushed across her knuckles so lightly she could have imagined it. Gentle, beseeching. It was not the touch of a barbarous man.

Cressida slid her hand into her lap. "You really don't remember?"

"Ah ha! So I'm right. We have met. I can't believe I wouldn't remember someone who looks like you. You look exactly like my girlfriend." He smiled and leaned back against his chair, the king on his throne. "Does that freak you out?"

Cressida leaned her face close to Rex. She could smell the beer on his breath and the earthy musk of his leather jacket. She wondered if he could still smell what she'd done while wearing it. "No, I think it's kind of hot."

He cocked his head. "Why's that?"

"Because when you meet someone new who reminds you of someone you care about it's like falling in love all over again. You get a second chance to remember the things you once found so irresistible about them, but have since grown tired and trite."

Rex's jaw was slack and his eyes were locked on Cressida's. It was the first time he'd really seen her all night. His murky brown eyes gleamed, something molten and evil. The rotten fruit from the tree of knowledge. "I know you." The words were labored and hushed.

Cressida just smiled.

"You're the therapist. The one who wanted to hang around with Vee." His face was puzzled but not afraid, made brave by the hour and the alcohol. He didn't push away from the table, didn't stand or shout. He was conceding his power.

Cressida's skin tingled. "What about me reminds you of Vee?"

"The hair." Rex nodded at Cressida's head.

"Then touch it. Remember what it felt like the first time

you touched her." Cressida pulled her chair closer to Rex. Damp heat radiated off his body.

Rex leaned forward and put both hands on either side of Cressida's head, just above her ears. Slowly he began to thread his fingers through the hair along her temples, pressing against her scalp with the same force he'd used to coax music from his guitar. He wasn't just touching her, he was worshipping her. Worshipping Vee. Cressida closed her eyes and parted her lips as a small moan escaped. Rex drew a sharp breath through his gritted teeth as he laced his fingers behind Cressida's head and pulled her face toward him into a rough kiss. It was the opposite of reverent: sloppy, hurried, and it dragged Cressida off her seat.

Rex pulled away but kept his hands on Cressida's hair. "Fuck. Why are you doing this?"

"Because I can." Cressida slid from her chair and swung her leg over Rex until she was straddling his lap. "Is that ok?" The scarf around her neck moved with Rex's rapid breath. Vee didn't believe that Rex would cheat on her. Cressida was going to prove her wrong. Once and for all.

Rex pulled the scarf aside and exposed Cressida's chest and scars. She held her breath letting him absorb her at her most vulnerable, most helpless, and her most messy. Rex's hands dropped from her hair and snaked around her waist, pulling her down hard onto his lap. The seam of her jeans dug into her groin.

"We need to get out of here," he rasped.

Cressida leaned forward and whispered in his ear, "My place isn't far."

CHAPTER 25

The tide was out when Rex and Cressida stumbled up the stairs to her third floor apartment. The *For Rent* sign in Sam's window flapped in the breeze, banging against the glass like it was trying to give Cressida a message. She ignored it. Inside the apartment Rex slung his jacket over one of the dining chairs and took Cressida's steady hand in his trembling one. It reminded her of the boy she'd taken to prom her senior year in high school, the boy she'd wished was Max and who'd cried when she fucked him. Rex pulled her into his body, pinning her arm between them. There, in front of her books—her mom's classics, Max's psychological manuals, and Vee's favorite, Palahniuk—Rex pushed his tongue into her mouth. He tasted like beer and guilt.

"Where's your bedroom?" He said when their lips parted.

Cressida twisted around so her back was against the book shelves and pulled Rex to her by his vintage Audioslave T-shirt. "I want to stay here."

She wanted to stay among the books. For so long, they

were the closest thing she'd had to dreams, to a connection with the sentient world. Now she was no longer the girl her mother cursed her to be, existing only to advance a more important story. Tonight she would write her own story. She'd create her own dreams.

Rex pushed her until her shoulders bumped against the spines of the books. She knocked several books from the shelf as she grabbed the wooden surface for support. He pressed his mouth hard against hers, banging her head against a hardback volume. Fifth shelf, halfway down: probably Shakespeare. Dull pain spread through her skull, red hot and liquid. Is this what it felt like to be Vee?

Rex hit his knees, unbuttoned her jeans, and jerked her pants and underwear to the floor. Cressida kicked them aside. Her legs quivered and she was wet the way she had been that day watching them from the alley. She wanted him to take her the way he'd taken Vee.

Rex ran his nose up the inside of her leg until it rested on top of the soft patch of red hair between her legs. He blew air against her and it ripped through her body like a tornado. Her legs shook. She braced herself against the shelf to keep from falling.

Littered on the floor around Rex were all her favorites: *Fight Club*, *Choke*, *The Stranger*, *Desperate Characters*. All books about people yearning to make a connection, and here she was with Rex between her legs, running his tongue along her clit and making it all possible again. Everything was working out perfectly. Vee would have to believe her this time, and then she would come back. She would shine back into Cressida's life like the dawn and with the sunrise would come the dreams, and Max. A loud moan echoed through her sterile apartment. Cressida barely recognized her own brazen voice. *Harder.* Another book crashed to the floor.

Rex grabbed Cressida's hips and stood. He unbuckled his pants and dropped them to the floor. Cressida wrapped her arms around his neck. Then he grabbed her hips again and shoved her against the shelf, the sharp wooden edge digging into her back and marking her skin. *Vee's bruises.* The sound of paperbacks fluttering to the floor filled her mind but she couldn't see them—she only saw him. His long, black hair fell over one eye and he leaned into her. Stubble scraped her chin as he kissed her, and he tasted sour. Rex lifted Cressida's feet from the ground and she wrapped her legs around his waist. Then he was inside her, harder and longer than she would have guessed. With each thrust he filled her emptiness to the brim. He dug his fingernails into the flesh of her hips and knocked more and more books from the shelf. She closed her eyes and pictured Vee's battered hips. One more thing that bound them together.

Rex drove his tongue into Cressida's mouth with the same force as he slammed against her hips. She could feel sweat dripping down the backs of her legs and her hands gripped the wood hard as she bounced up and down. She squeezed her eyes closed. She wanted to come, wanted to let go the way she had seen Vee do that night, but she couldn't. Something wasn't right.

Finally, with a deep groan Rex stilled, his fingers releasing Cressida's backside and her feet dropping to the earth once more. She slid to the floor and sat among her books with her back against the bottom shelf. She was breathing hard and her heart pounded in her chest. The scars along her breast were white against her flushed skin. They looked like stars fading in the dawn. Rex hauled up his jeans and sat down beside her, his erection still settling against the stiff denim.

His eyelids were heavy and his breath rasped in his throat. "Now can we find the bedroom?"

Cressida stood up against the shelf and took his hand. She stepped over the fallen books, the dog-eared roadmap to her old life, and pulled Rex behind her to the bedroom. For once she was glad all her neighbors were gone. Once in the room, Rex flopped onto her bed and was snoring in seconds. Cressida undressed and slipped into bed beside him. Her mind was filled with flapping book pages, shelves slamming against their pegs, and flesh slapping together. *Tomorrow everything would change.* She smiled to herself as she fell asleep beside Vee's fiancée, covered in his handprints, his smell, and his fluids.

It was dark, but not the kind of dark that usually claimed her when she slept. It wasn't empty. There were screams echoing in her mind, a sharp pain in her chest, and something else: a sick heavy sensation in her stomach like it might drop out the bottom of her body. As the screams became more focused, Cressida tried to isolate each one. There was a baby crying, hungry, scared and alone. There were her mother's panicked cries when she found a graduate student huffing away on top of her twelve-year-old daughter. There were Cressida's wails when her mother had locked her in her room for two weeks after until she knew she wasn't pregnant. There was the muted sound of Cressida's fear as her mother had held her head under water, and the world had started to lose focus. And finally there was Max's wife, screaming when she saw her dead husband lying in the mangled car beside a teenage girl wearing her ruined wedding dress. That scream was the loudest and it reverberated through the pit in Cressida's stomach. The pain she understood, but the sick feeling was new.

She rolled onto her side and drew her knees into her chest. What the hell was that? Cressida opened her eyes and looked at the mess she had made. Would Max have approved of her resourcefulness or would he have been appalled by the chaos she created when she embodied Vee? The sun was starting to peek through the open curtains. Olly and his mother would be waiting at her office in a couple hours. She slipped out of bed and walked naked to the living room. Books were cast about the room, splayed out and abandoned like bodies in a war zone, their pages akimbo.

One by one, she lifted the books to her naked breast and carried them back to their respective shelves. The musty smell of the pages lingered in her nose and on her tongue, faint yet familiar like an old friend. She smiled as she lined them neatly in a row, running her fingers along the spines, tickling them. All except Paula Fox's *Desperate Characters*. That one must have been under her feet last night--the cover was bent and broken. Not satisfied simply to watch, the book had demanded to interact, to reach out from the pages and physically alter the world outside. Fitting. Cressida smoothed the cover under her fingers and slipped it back onto the shelf beside Neil Gaiman and Mervyn Peake, gritty realism bumping up against escapist fantasy.

The floorboards creaked as Rex appeared in the doorway to the living room. His hair was sticky from sweat or last night's hair gel and his five o'clock shadow was way past midnight. He rubbed his crusty eyes with the back of his wrist.

"What the fuck happened last night?" he asked as he watched Cressida reassembling her apartment in the nude.

He didn't remember their little tryst. Cressida looked down at the last few books by her bare feet. Everything was almost back in place, but she needed to be the one to tell Vee about the affair first, not Rex. If he suspected Cressida had seduced him on purpose, then he would go straight to Vee with the accusation. She needed to control him just a little longer. "I'm not sure."

"Did we?" Rex looked down at his own clothes. He'd fallen asleep in his jeans, but his fly was still open.

Cressida pulled at her fingers. "Yeah."

"Fuck. I don't even remember how we got here." He scratched his stiff hair. "You were at the show last night, right?"

Cressida raised her eyes to meet Rex's panicked brown gaze. His brow was knit and his hands were trembling. He didn't want to get caught. But then he probably shouldn't be fucking around on his fiancée. "The last thing I remember is you buying us a fifth round."

"Oh, Jesus." He pressed his fingertips into his left temple. "No wonder I feel like someone's playing the fucking drums in my head."

She smiled innocently. "I remember that I enjoyed the show. You guys are really good."

"You can't tell Vee."

"About going to the show?"

"About any of it."

Cressida reached over and grabbed a blanket from the sofa and wrapped it around her like a cape. She was a superhero. Untouchable. "I'm not sure I could lie to her. Won't that only make it worse?"

"No. She can't find out. She'll freak."

He was coming around to hiding from Vee, but it needed to look like it was completely his idea. "It was an honest mistake. We were drunk."

Rex stumbled to where Cressida was standing. He put his hands on her covered shoulders and held her at arm's length. His fingers dug hard into Cressida's muscles the same way he'd bruised her hips the night before, but this wasn't an act of aggression or catharsis. He was desperate. Gone was his confidence, his swagger, his playboy strut. He was more naked than Cressida.

"You don't get it." Rex's voice cracked as he spoke barely above a whisper. "She will *not* be ok with this. She'll hate us both. Please. Don't say anything."

Cressida's shoulders were screaming for release, but she stood perfectly still absorbing the pain and thinking about all the times Rex's hands marked Vee's flesh. This time it was Rex that quaked, and he seemed to shrink in front of her. He would take this secret to his grave if she let him.

"Ok, if you really think it's for the best. I won't tell Vee." Cressida's cheeks tightened as she fought off a smile. She had thought it would take weeks to gather incriminating evidence on Rex to show Vee, but this worked out so much better. Vee couldn't deny Rex was cheating on her now.

Rex's hands dropped to his sides and he headed for the door where his boots lay toppled against the frame. Messy and scared, he looked nothing like she'd have imagined a man capable of such duplicity. How had Vee not caught him in the past? He patted his pockets, glanced back at the couch —now out of alignment with the chair—and his jacket. "I should really get home." He retrieved the keys and his coat. "I have an early class."

Cressida's ears pricked. *Liar*. She nodded her agreement that it would be better for him to leave sooner rather than later. There was still a lot she had to do before her first client that morning. Starting with her wreck of an apartment. Everything smelled of Rex and booze.

Her hands quivered as Rex gathered the last of his things and hurried down the stairs toward the parking lot. She watched him go from the living room window. He pulled his phone from his pocket and pulled it to his ear. Maybe he was calling Vee to check in after not coming home. Or maybe he was calling the girl he was really supposed to meet last night. Rex rounded the corner of the parking lot and disappeared down the winding coastal road.

But not toward his house. Where the hell was he going? Cressida stretched her neck to follow his shadow, but he was gone. There were only so many places to hide in their small town. It would be easy to follow him, but she had patients to see that morning: people whose dreams were supposed to fulfill her.

CHAPTER 26

Everything seemed darker than usual. It was dawn, yet the storm clouds outside were so thick it looked like midnight. Wind whipped the rain against the glass and it sounded like thousands of tiny fists trying to break down the window

Olly Peterson hunched forward on Cressida's office sofa, his face in his hands, no head visible save for the hair that spiked between his black fingernails. One chipped middle fingernail was painted blood red. He looked like the joker from a deck of cards. The stale odor of cigarettes permeated the space. It would take days for the smell to dissipate, long after Olly had drifted from her thoughts. He raised his head.

Cressida held Max's pen between her fingers. It felt heavier than usual, almost rough as it rubbed against her fingers. Olly's boots scraped along the carpet, his teeth ground against his fingernails, and the clock thundered against the wall. There was no light, no color, save that stupid fingernail that Olly kept chewing.

Lightning flashed through the room bringing everything

into temporary focus: the dark circles under Olly's eyes, the tremor in his hand, and the sweat on his forehead.

"I talk to him in my dreams sometimes. My dad."

Cressida froze Max's pen against the page. "What do you say to him?"

"I tell him I fucking hate his guts, and that sometimes I want to slit my own wrists just so I can go to Hell and kick his ass." Olly's voice cracked.

This was wrong, wrong, wrong. She'd had patients break down in her office and threaten violence and suicide before, but not Olly. Never Olly. He'd always remained strong, resilient like her.

"Do you often fantasize about suicide?"

"No, but it would be just what that fucker deserves."

Cressida raised her eyebrows. "You'd kill yourself just to punish your father?"

"No. I don't know." Olly slumped back in the sofa and chewed his black nails.

"What about your mom?"

Olly spit a shard of black fingernail into the air and Cressida watched it fall to the carpet. "What about her?"

Cressida forced her eyes away from the dead body part burrowing into her carpet. Olly's suicidal baggage mixing with Vee's copious glitter. Dissonant. "Do you think she deserves to be punished too?"

"No."

"And what about you? Do you deserve to be punished?" She leaned toward him. "Do you deserve to die?"

"It doesn't matter what I deserve."

Cressida stood up from her chair and walked around the coffee table until she was standing over the sofa where Olly sunk deeper into the cushion. She handed him a tissue from the box on the table and sat down on the corner. "It absolutely does matter. You can't exist, or not, just to affect other people. You have to live for you."

Olly stared straight ahead, avoiding eye contact. "You sound like my mom with all her pop-psychology *love-your-self-first* bullshit."

"Maybe I do, but I've put too much of my time and energy into you to have you give up now. I thought you were going to be the rat that survives."

Olly stared at the floor, his face as white as the churning sea. Cressida's heart thumped in her chest. Olly couldn't let his coward father dictate his life any more than Vee could let Rex dictate hers. And Cressida wasn't going to lose either of them today.

Olly raised his eyes to Cressida's. "You know he talked to me? Before he did it, I mean."

"Your dad? When?"

"I went into his office because I couldn't find my fucking iPad, and I saw him sitting at his desk with the gun in front of him. I'd never seen it before. I didn't even know he had a gun."

Cressida scooted to the edge of her seat, her heart thumping against her chest. "What did you say?"

"I just stood there like an idiot. I didn't say anything." Olly hugged his arms around his thin chest. The long sleeves of his black shirt bunched slightly revealing a neat row of cuts along his forearm, all lined up like hash marks. She thought of Vee's scars and the ones on her own chest. Self-loathing could come in many forms.

"What did he say?"

"He said he was sorry. I didn't even know what he was talking about. I thought he meant he didn't know where my iPad was. I was a fucking moron."

Cressida handed Olly another tissue which he snatched from her hand and crumpled into his fist.

"You were nine years old."

"I should have known what he was going to do, but I just walked out of that room, shut the door behind me, and went off to play Minecraft. I was putting together fucking block castles while my world was falling apart." Guilt and sorrow had aged him—Olly was jaded beyond his years. Someday he would make either a great poet or a dismal killer.

Cressida moved so she was sitting beside him on the couch. "And what do you think that means?"

"It means it's my fault. I could have said something. I could have called Mom. But I did nothing, and five minutes later I heard the shot."

"Have you told your mom about this?"

Olly shook his head as if trying to jolt the thoughts from his mind. Someday this trauma would all be a memory confined to dreams and nightmares.

"No, I didn't tell anyone else. What good would that do?"

"It might help her understand what you're going through. And it might help you to share it with her."

Olly's eyes widened like he was standing on the edge of a tall cliff and Cressida was about to push him over. "She'd fucking hate me forever."

"Why?"

"Because I should have saved him." Olly dropped his head to his hands again, his shoulders convulsing with sobs.

Cressida stayed still beside Olly, waiting for his breathing to slow. She might have reached out to touch him, wrapped her arm around his shoulder, comforted him. But she didn't. It would have been unnatural, and Olly would have felt it. "You couldn't have saved him, but you can save your relationship with your mom."

"I can't."

"You can. Sometimes you have to risk rejection to really connect with someone." Wasn't that true? Maybe Vee would hate her for telling her about Rex. Or for sleeping with him in the first place.

"I told you. Isn't that enough?" His wide eyes were wet and pleading.

"It can be for now."

A soft knock at the door followed by the harsh fluorescent glow of the hallway announced Mrs. Peterson's arrival in the office. Olly clamped down on his tissue and straightened against the back of the sofa. His whole body froze like he was holding his breath.

"I'm sorry. Olly, we should really go or you're going to be late for school." Mrs. Peterson stood in the doorway silhouetted by the cruel yellow light from the hall. Over her shoulder, Roger's door was still closed. Cressida had noticed his car was missing when she arrived at the office earlier. He must have been tied up in court again.

Mrs. Peterson was wearing a pale green dress suit with her Century 21 name tag pinned to the lapel. Her hair was wet and flattened to her head and the makeup she'd probably applied in the car that morning was melting down her cheeks. She must have had an important showing today, but what horrible conditions in which to try and sell a house. No wonder her checks for Olly's therapy were always late. Silverside was the location of the worst event in her and her son's life. It must have been difficult to convince people to move in when all you want to do yourself is escape, and Mrs. Peterson wasn't a born saleswoman. *She cared too much.* She probably would have made a good match for Roger.

Olly sniffed sharply and then coughed to disguise the sound. He took a deep breath and stood, shoulders still slumped. Cressida had not yet saved Olly from his demons. There was still time.

But she could save Vee from Rex, and herself from the anguish of a shattered past. As Olly walked toward the door he muttered thanks under his breath. Cressida nodded at the back of his head and at Mrs. Peterson, smiling as warmly as she could in the dark, cold office. They closed the door behind them and Cressida was cast back into the shadows.

The rest of Cressida's patients that day canceled their appointments due to the storm that had settled over Silverside like black death. She watched through the window as wind gusts swirled the clouds around like an ominous nautilus shell. Emotions worked the same way, raging through people like hurricanes, stirring them up, causing immense collateral damage, but never really moving them forward. Olly was stuck in a purgatory of guilt and shame and fear, and it was tearing him apart. But for what? His father was weak and selfish and ineffectual. Like Sam had been. Love only clouded judgment, and both Cressida and Olly would be better off without it. Dreams, on the other hand, were the eye of the emotional storm, the point of clarity and serenity among the chaos of feelings. One could not exist without the other.

CHAPTER 27

Cressida took her lunch to the alcove below The Mermaid Asylum. On her way down to the beach she stopped and collected the mail. It was usually a responsibility that Roger assumed, but he'd been so busy with testifying lately that he'd neglected it to the point of overflow. She left his mail on the floor outside his office door and headed out to the cave. The makeshift lean-to was private, but still within view of the raised parking lot so Cressida could make sure no one turned up looking for her or Roger in the storm. The cave looked very different in the light of the day. A ratty sweater was stuffed into the metal cart collecting sand and mildew. Decades of cigarette butts and discarded anti-psychotic medication lay fossilized under Cressida's feet among the packed mounds she'd cultivated into neat rows. She could almost feel the pulse of their collective tortured souls.

Cressida dug an old needle out of the sand and pushed the plunger. She set it on the metal cart along with a couple of photographs that were still in pretty good shape. She could never bring herself to bury these mementos along with the other patient's belongings she'd found when she first came upon the alcove. Something about the photos moved her. One was of a tall brunette leaning her back against a tree and holding a book open in her palms, smiling through sparkling eyes at the person holding the camera. It was a look that came from some combination of surprise, irritation, and love. It was too beautiful to be buried under the sand.

Cressida flipped through the bills and circulars, tossing them one by one onto the wet sand by her feet. Then her fingers froze over a hand-written envelope: no post mark, no return address, just the name *Cressida Dunhill* scrawled in tiny, sharp lettering. Cressida tore into the paper and pulled the letter from its hiding place. Her eyes fell to the name at the bottom of the single page. Sam. The muscles in her jaw set and she held her breath as she devoured the words pressed into the page with the same dark, scribbling script.

Dear Cressida,

I know what you're thinking. Who writes letters anymore these days? But it almost poetic. Plus, I haven't got a new cell phone yet, so don't bother trying to track down my number. In fact, don't bother looking for me at all. Seeing you in the hospital made me realize I needed to put a stop to this. I can't keep looking over my shoulder for the rest of my life. I've done enough hiding for a lifetime. I won't do it anymore. You were always there when I needed a hand to hold or a shoulder to cry on. You consistently went above and beyond what anyone would expect from a neighbor or a friend, and for a while it was comforting. But part of me always knew you weren't right. You were never comfortable in your own skin. I think it's what drew me to you in the first place. But we both know you need help. And it's not something I can give you. I can't be your hand to hold or your shoulder to cry on, and I certainly can't be your new skin. I am not the answer to your problems. I can't change you or save you. What you want isn't friendship, it's obsession. It's creepy and it's suffocating. I can't be your pet project anymore. I'm done pretending for everyone else. I was wrong to go back to my father, and I won't make that mistake again. But I will also not be coming home to you. If you ever cared about me at all, please leave me alone. Don't come for me. Don't look for me. Don't even think about me. I am gone.

Sincerely,

Sam

Cressida turned the sheet over in her hands, looking for more, but there was only that: a single page of messy writing after years of friendship. A gust of wind whipped the thin paper from her hand and pinned it against the side of the cave. *No. Not yet.* Cressida fell to her knees in the sand and snatched for the letter, but another gust blew it out of the shelter and away down the beach. Huddled there in the shadows of the cave on her hands and knees, Cressida dropped her forehead to the wet sand. *Gone.* She'd said it in her own words, and now it was true. Surely real love wasn't so easy to change. She would never have left Max. She would have done anything to keep him with her. Her hands shook and she fisted them into the sand beside her, gritty damp boring deep under her fingernails. Obsessive? Creepy? Sam had been the one who was so quick to abandon her best friend who had only come over to borrow some clothes. Cressida wasn't the one who needed help.

She lifted her head from the earth. Cressida never asked Sam to fix her, never asked her for anything until that day. But that's how it was with people; they were perfectly happy to take and take, but as soon as Cressida needed some understanding suddenly she was crossing a line. Sure, she'd let herself into Sam's apartment with the key Sam kept under the mat for nights she was too drunk or exhausted to dig through her purse for her keys. How was Cressida supposed to know Sam would come home find her there, in bed, with Sam's favorite dress floating over her like a blanket and the silk scarf snaked across her body? She was always planning to return the clothes. She was just so tired.

Cressida's hand drifted to the dwindling knot on her temple. The bruise had long-since healed, but she could still hear the sick sound of the solid metal colliding with her skull. How could she have anticipated her friend would scream and hurl a heavy watch at her head like a lunatic? The buckle had caught Cressida in the temple and left a mark for over a week, but even then she wasn't angry. She'd been ready to bury the past even before the blood washed away.

She'd been willing to forgive Sam, to work through the difficult times, and come out closer on the other end. To change along with their dynamic relationship. But the next morning Sam was gone. She'd never appreciated Cressida's admiration, her love. And just like that Cressida's world had grown dull and quiet. Until Vee. Sam's letter was simply further proof that she had never understood Cressida, never seen beyond the surface. They could never have achieved the kind of intimacy that Cressida had felt with Vee. They could never have shared dreams. Sam thought she was leaving Cressida, but the truth was Cressida had already moved on. She was glad the letter was gone; it saved her the effort of burying it among the rest of her failures.

Tears stung her eyes along with the salt from the wind, and Cressida crawled back into the depths of the cave to finish her lunch. Across the narrow spit of beach, the waves churned in the purple storm. No fishing boats on the horizon this morning. Not a single person on the beach.

Sand ground in her teeth as she took a bite of her sandwich, but she didn't care. The wind whipping across her face smelled like Vee. Sam wanted a fresh start, and so did Cressida. Max would have wanted that for her.

That night Cressida would tell Vee about Rex's cheating, and Vee would see the lengths she was willing to go to for her friend, to protect her. Vee would forgive her. She had to. This time there would be no misunderstandings. And then the dreams would return, bright and colorful like they had been that first day. Everything would be ok. Seawater clouded Cressida's eyes as she stared into the wind toward the parking lot where a lone figure huddled against the rain, red skirt stuck to her legs. She looked small, like she could blow away with the wind. Cressida's breath caught as the girl disappeared around the edge of the building.

Vee.

It was as if Vee had sensed how much Cressida needed her at that moment. But had Rex folded and told Vee the whole story? He could have ruined everything. He just couldn't leave well enough alone. Hate singed Cressida's veins. Some rats don't know when they become food for the survivors, even as they are being devoured. Rain battered against the sand outside the shelter. The waves crashed like thunder in time to her frantic heartbeat. *This was not the plan!* Lightning flashed on the horizon illuminating the clouds in violet and grey.

Vee reappeared in the parking lot, her dress clinging to her flesh as if all her skin had been peeled away, leaving her with the crimson sheen of muscle. Base and raw. She leaned into the wind to keep from toppling backwards, but did not retreat the way she'd come. Where was she going?

Vee followed the path from the parking lot down to the beach, stepping carefully on the mossy rocks to avoid slipping in the rain. She reached the sand and kicked her sandals aside, digging her toes into the beach. Vee's hair was dark when it was wet and plastered to her face, and she bent forward against the wind. She approached the wild sea, struggling forward step by step, letting the waves beat against her legs. Her skirt floated, circling her in the water like blood ready to attract a shark.

Wind battered against Cressida's ears, filling her head with unrelenting static as she hurtled herself toward the water's edge. Maybe Rex hadn't told Vee anything about last night. Maybe she was here because she, too, missed her connection with Cressida. Missed their friendship. Cressida shouted Vee's name, but the wind threw it back in her face along with the seawater. Cressida looked around the shelter for something she could use to get Vee's attention and her gaze landed on the heavy leather cuff restraint.

She pulled it from the sand and felt the weight of it against her palm. *These were the kinds of bonds that were not so easy to break.* Cressida pulled back her arm and threw the cuff as hard as she could into the storm. It landed with a thud in the sand about two feet behind Vee, but she heard it and wheeled around. Vee's face twisted when she saw Cressida, the wind now blowing at her back, pushing her toward the building. Toward Cressida.

And she looked more menacing than the storm.

CHAPTER 28

Vee's blue eyes were almost grey against the stormy backdrop. She stopped at the edge of the shelter and crossed her arms against her wet shirt. Her eyes were rimmed with red from salt—maybe tears. Cressida smiled. Vee stood deathly still, unwavering.

Cressida took a step toward Vee. "I didn't expect to see you today. I'm sorry I wasn't in the office when you knocked."

Vee ground her toes into the sand. "I wasn't here to see you."

Cressida recognized the look on Vee's face. She'd seen the same one on Sam's face before she threw the watch. It was fear. But surely Vee wasn't afraid of Cressida; the only one she had to fear was Rex. "What's wrong?"

"It's just...well, it's about Rex. I know how you feel about him. So I thought I'd talk to Doctor Banks instead."

Cressida held out her hand. "Don't be silly, Vee. We're friends. You can tell me things."

Vee shook her head. "I don't need a friend today. I need a therapist. I think I'm going crazy."

Cressida raised her hands in front of her like she was approaching a skittish animal. "I can be both. I can be whatever you need me to be."

Vee's nostrils flared, her jaw working. Finally, she met Cressida's eyes. "Rex didn't come home last night or this morning, and he's not answering his cell phone. I used the tracker on his new iPhone and it says he's in Portland, but he's supposed to be in school today. I thought we were past this."

Cressida wrapped her arms around Vee's shoulders and pulled her into the shelter, beckoning her back to the asylum's discarded past. Beneath her feet were all that remained of the pieces of Cressida's life that had come before her, all failed where Cressida was determined to succeed with Vee. It would be different this time. And Vee wouldn't end up just another mound in the sand. Cressida hugged her. Despite the rain and the seawater, the girl still smelled like strawberries. "I'm so sorry, Vee."

"I mean, I'm sure there's an explanation, but I just thought things would be different between us now that we're getting married." Vee sniffed.

"Some people never change," Cressida whispered into Vee's ear. "I knew you'd see eventually, but I needed to show you before you wasted any more of your time."

Vee pulled out of Cressida's embrace and fixed her with a hooded stare. "Show me what?"

"That Rex isn't good enough for you. That he doesn't deserve you. That you were right about him all along."

Lightning lit the clouds behind Vee's head and the hairs on Cressida's arms stood on end. The diamond on Vee's finger glinted in the pale light.

"What are you talking about?"

"He cheats on you, Vee. He always has and you've known

it all along, but you didn't want to trust yourself for some reason. I wanted to give you proof."

"What kind of proof?" Vee's voice was barely audible over the roaring of the storm.

Cressida met Vee's puzzled glare. "I did it for you."

Vee's eyes widened and the corners of her mouth twitched down toward the sand. The color drained from her usually rosy cheeks. "Did what?"

This was her moment. Cressida felt a tingle rip through her body like electricity. "I went to Rex's show last night, just to see if I could catch him hitting on someone or anything that I could offer you as proof that he's a lying asshole."

"Okay..." Vee's feet were buried in the sand to her ankles making her shorter than Cressida so she had to look up to meet her eyes.

"He didn't recognize me at first and he bought me a drink. He wanted my attention. My *affection*." Cressida could feel Rex's hands on her hips as he lifted her against the bookshelf in her apartment. The sound of the wind and the waves was reminiscent of the flapping pages of Cressida's books, spilling over them as they fucked, tearing her old life apart and making way for her new one.

Vee's mouth was open. "What did you do?"

"I didn't do anything. He wanted it. He asked to leave and go somewhere more private."

"Cressida, what the hell did you do?"

"You weren't getting it. I tried to show you with the phone number and the flyer with the girl's name on it. I left them for you to find, but you didn't believe it. You were going to marry him."

"What are you talking about?"

"You were supposed to leave him. To take back your power. I set it up perfectly for you."

Vee took a step backward, stumbling over the wet sand. She stood with the rain pounding against her back, the muscles of her legs fighting the wind to keep her from falling into Cressida. *Stop resisting.* "You broke into Rex's house that day. You weren't there by accident or to see me."

"I was doing you a favor."

Vee's hand covered her mouth. "And the hair. You're out of your fucking mind."

"No. I'm not the crazy one." Cressida stepped into the rain after Vee. The torrent flattened her hair to her head, a mirror image of Vee's. They were so alike. *How could Vee not see that?* The dry sand from the shelter whipped around them and sparkled with each bolt of lightning, just like the glitter that still coated Cressida's office. Vee's vibrant color. But there was no more color in Vee's gaze—only helplessness and panic.

"Get away from me."

Cressida was losing her. There would never again be color in her life. Everyone left her: her mother, Max, Sam, and now Vee. Why? What about her was so broken that no one could ever fix her? The answer rested in the ground with Max, but even her memories had been taken by the accident. She'd done everything right, everything for Vee, but it didn't matter. Everything had turned again to sand and shit.

Cressida took another step toward Vee. "I can't."

Vee stepped back, eyes wide, her head shaking rapidly from side to side. She was going to take it all away. Again. Just like Sam. Cressida couldn't stand the thought of holding another letter in her hands, this time from Vee, in whom she'd placed so much hope. She wouldn't let that happen.

Cressida shouted against the howling wind. "I did it so we could be friends. Be together."

Vee stopped shaking. "So you fucked my fiancé?! Do you know how completely fucked up that is?"

"I did it for you."

"Bullshit."

"I did it for *us*."

"Did you enjoy it? Did you like pretending to be me?"

Cressida reached out to grab Vee's shoulders again, but she ducked farther out toward the sea.

Cressida followed. "It wasn't about enjoyment. It was a means to an end. This end. I did it all for you."

"How was he? Was he gentle or do you like it rough too?" The tide encroached and there were only a few yards of sand between them and the rippling ocean. Vee backed up until the water lapped at her ankles, washing away the sand and dirt only to bury her feet again when it retreated.

Cressida followed her into the tide and reached for her hand. The Pacific Ocean water was freezing. "It doesn't matter. Now that you know the truth we can just move on."

Vee's voice rose to a shrill cry. "Move on to what?"

"To the way things are supposed to be. Us being friends. You'll be better off without him."

"I can't do this right now." Vee pulled her hand away with such force she lost her balance and she landed on her hip in the surf. She rolled onto her hands and knees as the water swelled up over her elbows and thighs. She gagged spit sea water back into the ocean like it was poison. She squinted up at Cressida with white hot hatred.

Cressida leaned down to help Vee onto her feet, but the girl shook her head violently as another wave crashed into her side. Fierce and unyielding, Vee had never looked more powerful. The abhorrence in her eyes reminded Cressida of her mother. The way she'd glared down at Cressida while she held her head under the water over and over. The way she'd laughed when Cressida had begged her to stop. Sneered as she choked. Vee had no idea what true hate looked like.

Cressida crouched beside Vee, her skirt slapping against Vee's and clinging to her soaked skin. "Let me help you. Everything is going to be ok now."

"Get away from me, you crazy bitch." Vee's voice boomed louder than the thunder. It was a sound that didn't belong to her. "I don't want anything to do with you ever again."

A shiver tore down Cressida's spine like a bolt of lightning. The wind quieted along with the rest of the world as cooling numbness spread through Cressida's body. Dull. Dead. She'd been wrong all along. Again. Vee was just like Sam, like her mother: toxic and dangerous. Vee staggered upright in the rising surf, the water reaching above her knees and pushing her forward before sucking her back again with each wave. She stepped around Cressida and started wading to the shore, her red dress splayed around her like a pool of blood in the water.

Cressida lunged for Vee and caught her wrist. She pulled Vee's arm back toward her revealing the yellowing bruises along her forearm from were Rex had held her arms down that night on the sofa. "You'd choose him over me? This is what he does to you and you'd pick him?"

Vee spun around, twisting her wrist in Cressida's grip. "What? This?" She laughed and it sounded like the wind shrieking in the tempestuous background. "This is nothing. He does this because I *want* him to."

Cressida squeezed Vee's arm, reddening the healing bruises. "You like when he hurts you?"

"No one can hurt me." Her face was stone, but her eyes

betrayed her. She was bluffing. She could be hurt, but Vee loved it, got off on it. The only person Vee needed to be protected from was herself. Vee needed the pain the way Cressida needed to dream. It was a sickness from which she would never recover. She needed to be punished, purified. Made to see that only Cressida's love was true.

"Why don't you just leave me alone and go back to being a loner in your creepy psycho office? Fucking stalker. I bet your boss would love to know what you do with your patients. They're going to take your fucking license." She jerked her arm free and turned her back to Cressida again.

This wasn't right. Vee was supposed to be thankful for all that she had done to save her from Rex. She and Cressida were supposed to be closer than ever and Cressida was supposed to go home that night filled with peace, ready to dream. To remember. She'd done everything right.

Some people just couldn't be saved. Her mother had known that all along.

Cressida's voice rose like the tide. "You were supposed to be different. Make me different."

Vee sneered. "I don't owe you anything."

Vee was ruining everything, leaving Cressida and taking her dreams with her, and now she was threatening to take her job too. To take what was left of Max. And for what? So she could protect her cheating boyfriend? This girl would not take everything she had.

Some rats were born to be eaten.

A hot, sick feeling surged in Cressida's stomach with the next wave and she grabbed the back of Vee's shirt and yanked. "You're just like everyone else."

Vee's head snapped up and a choked squeal flew from her mouth as her feet slipped out from beneath her. She crashed into to the sea at Cressida's feet. Waves splashed over her head, again, again. Relentless. Their eyes met briefly, cool grey hovering over ice blue like the clouds snuffing out the vibrant sky. Flashes of her mother's face lit Cressida's mind like lightning, her mouth twisted into a determined snarl as she'd ripped at Cressida's hair to keep her submerged in the tub. This was the only way to get through to a selfish, capricious girl. The only way to change her.

Her mother was right.

Cressida shifted her weight, testing her stability. Solid. Steady. She looked back at the shore, the cave, and The Mermaid Asylum. The only movement was from the waves on the sand, the wind in the trees, and the swirling of the deep purple sky. She brought her foot down hard on Vee's chest. The girl gasped for breath, but she found only sea spray and panic as another wave hit.

Now Vee needed her.

Cressida leaned her full body weight against Vee's breastbone, pinning her to the sand. Vee kicked her legs wildly and dug into Cressida's ankle with her long nails, but the icy water had numbed Cressida's skin. The seething ocean hid most of Vee's struggles beneath its white froth. If anyone had looked out their window they would only have seen a blond woman standing alone in the stormy sea like a water nymph or a goddess. Maybe it was Cressida who was changing.

The salt water stung as Vee's nails broke Cressida's skin, but it was nothing. Her nerves were as cold as the water. Dead. Cressida remembered the pain of the glass embedding in her chest during the accident with Max or the sick, thudding jolt of Sam's heavy watch colliding with her temple. Even in her final moments, Vee was giving Cressida back her memories.

It had been 3,715 days since Max crashed through the median of Interstate 84 and changed their lives forever. It had been 31 days since Vee breezed into her office and awakened her dreams, and only six since she tried to take them away. The wind howled overhead. Under the churning water, Vee's blue eyes were open and scared and unblinking. Just the way Max's had been. Her lips were as purple as the sky. Vee's slender arms drifted to the surface and swayed with the waves, the rain marring the beautiful image of her face, finally at peace.

No one will ever hurt you again.

Lightning lit up the sky again and reflected off the ring on Vee's limp finger. Cressida lifted her foot and snatched Vee's hand from the water. She pulled it to her chest and kissed each of the bruises along Vee's cold forearm. Her skin tasted like salt. Something dripped down Cressida's cheek and fell into the sea. Rain. Or maybe tears?

Vee's glazed eyes bore into Cressida, accusing, just the way her mother's had the night she'd died. Had Cressida forgotten that too? Thunder crashed overhead, but Cressida couldn't look away from the familiar dead, blue eyes. They were always the same: vacant and forsaken. Even on her death bed, foul and desiccated from cancer, Cressida's mother had hated her. The frivolous girl that sabotaged her career, stole her youth, and fucked her therapist.

Her mother had spat at Cressida with every drop of bile left in her and Cressida had covered her face with the pillow to stop her, just to quiet her, but as her mother thrashed weakly beneath her strong arms Cressida realized this was her only chance at a new life. She'd held the pillow in place until her mother's bony arms dropped to the side of the hospice bed.

Another wave crashed against Cressida's legs. The tide

was rising. She ran her palm along Vee's eyes to close her eyelids, to escape the memories reflected in their cloudy lenses.

Like some bold seer in a trance,
Beholding all his own mischance,
Mute, with a glassy countenance.
The Lady of Shalott.

Were they Lord Tennyson's words in Cressida's head or her mothers? She shook her head and the little beaded earrings tinked against her neck. It was over.

Now Vee looked like she was sleeping the same kind of cold, dead sleep that Cressida would have for the rest of her life without her. There would be no dreams to be haunted by Vee's empty stare. Resignation was as close to peace as she would ever come. Cressida pushed her friend farther into the sea and turned back to the shore, Vee's ring held tight in her fist.

CHAPTER 29

The sun peeked through the clouds just in time to set along the horizon. The street outside Cressida's bay window was shiny black obsidian cutting its way through the sand. The parking lot was flooded despite Roger's best efforts to sweep water away from the building with a push broom. Cressida sat rigid in her leather chair and stared out the window. Vee was gone and Cressida had failed: failed to save Vee, failed to protect her dreams, and failed to punish Vee the way Cressida's mother had punished her. There were no lessons to learn here. Nausea threatened to pull Cressida into the darkness of her mind, and this time there would be no rebirth.

When she'd first returned to the office, it had been silent, hollow like Vee's dead eyes had been as they stared unseeing at Cressida through the surf. But now the rhythmic scraping of Roger's broom kept her mind from wandering back to the ocean, wondering when and where Vee's body would eventually be found. Her bones ached and she could still feel the pull of the ocean, dragging her and Vee out to sea. She hadn't moved for hours. Not since she changed out of her soaked clothes into her only other outfit —the suit she'd worn the first day Vee arrived in the office. It seemed almost like an homage to Vee, not that she wanted to consider that. Or anything else.

The twilight lit up red and blue against the black streets and Roger's scraping stopped. The police had arrived. Someone must have found Vee, pulled her from the calm sea and searched her body for signs of life. Touched her bruised wrists looking for a pulse. Compressed her chest. Maybe even breathed into her mouth. But there was no point. Not anymore. Cressida's knuckles blanched as she gripped the arm of the chair to keep from succumbing to the dizzy spiral in her mind. Vee might even still be out there.

Cressida lurched forward and vomited into the wastebasket.

Surreal. After Sam had accused Cressida of stalking her and threw her out of the apartment along with the clunky watch, Cressida had waited for the flashing lights to appear below her apartment. She'd imagined them circling her home like sharks sensing her weakness, waiting to destroy her. But they never came. And the next morning Sam was gone, her final metamorphosis complete, and all that was left was the shell of her apartment and Cressida's admiration. But no one had come for Cressida.

Perhaps Sam had loved her more than she'd realized. It was there, even in her letter. Cressida had just been too blinded by Vee's light to notice the subtext. She should have known better. She'd studied literature. Vee was garish. Too obvious. She would have ruined everything, taken Cressida's dreams, her job, and her entire life. All for some man. At least Sam had spared her that final insult.

Would this be the end of her story?

Cressida held her breath and leaned forward in her chair, straining to hear the news through the thick walls of the asylum, but places like this were built for privacy. Voices murmured just outside of earshot, hushed and reverent. Her heart raced. The rational part of her brain, the part that fought to survive, wanted her to run. Away from the police, away from Roger, away from Vee—or what was left of her. But the same inexplicable force that had pulled her to Vee in the first place, that woke her dreams, that spawned a forgotten passion, rooted her to the spot. This was where she belonged.

A knock on the door sent Cressida jumping from her chair. She took a deep breath to steady her nerves and opened the door to Roger's damp face. His thin hair was plastered across his bald spot and his shirt was stuck to his skin, coarse chest hair visible through the thin material.

His lips were pale and stretched thin across his teeth. "You need to come outside right now."

Cressida's breath rasped in her dry throat. She swallowed and leaned her head out of the office, peering toward the front door. "Why? What happened?"

"They found a body on the beach behind the building. Again. I can't believe it's happening again." He squeezed the bridge of his nose between his thumb and forefinger, and his breath shuddered through his chest. As he walked away, he seemed to shrink in front of her and drift away just as Vee had when Cressida eased her lifeless body into the sea. Everything around her was drifting just out of reach.

Cressida closed her office door behind her and followed Roger to the parking lot, heart slamming into her ribcage no matter how she struggled to keep her breath even. *In and out.* Each breath in time with her steps. The situation wasn't hopeless. Surely the police wouldn't have sent Roger to fetch her if she was under arrest. She drew a deep breath and held it as she walked out the front door. No one had seen her walk down to the cave that afternoon. The beach had been deserted.

In the lot, steam rose from the wet street like a rolling fog. Two cop cars sent red and blue lights dancing in the puddles and coloring the wisps of vapors. It might have been beautiful if it hadn't been a harbinger of doom. Two officers stood in front of the cars. No guns drawn. The police were, at best, armed with suspicions and rumors, both of which were easy to dispute. The blood flowed again to Cressida's hands and feet sending a tingling sensation throughout her body as her adrenaline abated.

There was still hope.

The younger of the two police officers shook his head. "What are the odds, man? My last week in Silverside and I have to land a floater. This is going to mess up my whole week."

The older police officer ran his fingers along his thick belt and hiked his pants higher over his ample gut. A tuft of dark chest hair protruded out the top of his shirt and almost tickled his chin. His thick mustache twitched in the wind. *Officer Neal from the hospital.*

"It's probably just an accident. They usually are. Let's just get this wrapped up neat and tidy so we can send you off with a nice, clean record." He winked at his younger partner.

The younger cop nodded to his partner as Cressida and Roger approached, and Officer Neal tapped a finger to his forehead in a casual salute and walked around the back of the building. He hadn't recognized Cressida from the hospital. Maybe the haircut threw him. Either that or he didn't care. He was headed toward the beach where Vee's body must have washed ashore: where she might still be laying, bloated and stiff.

The thought of Officer Neal putting his ham hock hands over Vee's body made Cressida sick. She wanted to double over, but Roger was right behind her, breathing rapidly as he sidled up behind her. She should have weighed down Vee's body, or buried her in the sand, or hidden her away for the crabs to feast on later. *Stupid.* Cressida was trapped between the hideous beast of her own fallibility and the sucking pull of mediocrity: her very own Scylla and Charybdis. And there was nowhere to run.

Trapped like a rat. But what kind?

The tall, younger officer had a broad nose and broader shoulders. He would have been intimidating except for his peach fuzz mustache. He smiled at Cressida over the top of a small spiral notebook, and his fingers fumbled as he flipped a page. He seemed nervous. Despite his discomfort, his ingenuous eyes were soft and caring, not the face of a man who thought he was staring into the eyes of a killer. He looked up at Cressida again and, if she wasn't mistaken, a hint of scarlet colored his cheeks. "Ma'am, did you treat a young woman by the name of Viola Marquis?"

"Yes, she is a new patient of mine."

The young officer scribbled something into his notebook and responded without looking up. "When is the last time you spoke to her?"

"Tuesday, I think. She discontinued her therapy." Cressida took a step closer to the officer so her face was visible in the crisp beams of the cruiser's headlights. She might be a rat, but she wasn't about to be eaten.

His back stiffened in response to her close proximity.

Cressida's adrenaline surged and now she allowed her breathing to speed, wrung her hands in front of her and shifted her weight from foot to foot. "Roger said something about a body on the beach. What does any of this…I mean… why are you asking about Vee?"

The officer looked up from his notes. "You didn't speak to Miss Marquis this afternoon?"

Cressida froze, her mouth half open. Her lungs refused to fill and her eyes failed to blink. Could Vee have told someone she was coming to the office? If the cops had spoken to Rex first, he would have told them about last night. He would have given them a motive. "No." Her voice was barely audible.

The officer cleared his throat and flipped through pages of his notebook as if the answer to the riddle was buried between the scribbled lines of his notes. He knew something she didn't. He was in control. Cressida wanted to rip the pad from his hands and throw it into the ocean, but she couldn't move. Couldn't breathe.

"She didn't call your office this morning at 11:30?" He scratched his left eyebrow with the butt of his pen.

The police must have checked Vee's phone records. Air hissed through Cressida's teeth as she drew a breath through her clenched jaw. Vee had lied when she said she came to the asylum to see Roger. She had called Cressida first for help. The police must not have spoken to Rex. These were routine questions. "No, I ran home for lunch." She relaxed her jaw and, feeling bolder, took another step toward the officer. "Please…what happened?"

Cressida was close enough to smell spearmint on the officer's breath and to see the beads of sweat forming along his hairline. He looked up from his notes and gave a tight-lipped smile, almost condolences. "We're awaiting final confirmation, but we believe the body we recovered is that of Miss Marquis. Her parents reported her missing this afternoon and the description matches the body." His eyes met Cressida's and they were the same color as Vee's: blue like the ocean after a storm. It was as if the same sea that had taken Vee had delivered the officer to Cressida.

She brought her hand to her mouth the way Vee used to do. "That's awful. What happened? Was it an accident?" She turned around and looked at Roger whose face was red and swollen, his eyes haunted. He sniffed hard and his nose made a honking sound.

The officer frowned at Roger and then back at Cressida. "That's what we're trying to ascertain here. There was some evidence of a struggle—"

"A struggle? You think someone killed her?" Cressida's tongue was like sandpaper as it scraped across her mouth. Her fists were balled at her side.

The officer's face was impassive, cold stone, except for the twinge of his face as he chewed the inside of his cheek. "We just want to make sure we have all the facts before determining cause of death."

Roger nodded his head toward Cressida. "We understand."

The officer ignored Roger and focused on Cressida. In the lights from the cruiser, his eyes looked like fireworks. "Do you have any idea why Miss Marquis would have been on the beach in such a severe storm?"

"I have no idea."

"And you didn't see anything? Maybe when you left for lunch?"

"No, I'm sorry." Cressida looked down at her black pumps, now sodden and ruined. *Like Vee.* She fought away the urge to kick them from her feet. "I could barely see two feet in front of my face."

The officer nodded as he slipped his notepad into his

back pocket. “Well, ma’am, I think those are all the questions I have for you at this time. We’ll be in contact if we need anything further.”

Roger stepped forward until he was shoulder to shoulder with Cressida, years of repressed angst finally bubbling to the surface like toxic sludge. His sweat smelled bitter and metallic. “Did she kill herself?”

The officer flinched like he’d been caught doing something underhanded. Had he given away more information than he’d wanted? “Right now we’re just trying to piece together the hours leading up to her death. Just making sure we don’t overlook anything.”

Roger coughed. “It’s the same thing all over again.” He dropped his head into his hands. “What a waste.”

The officer raised his eyebrows, looking squarely at Roger for the first time since Cressida had arrived in the parking lot. “What do you mean, sir? Did you treat Miss Marquis as well?” He searched their faces, looking for clues. Waiting for someone to make a mistake. He was looking for Cressida, though he didn’t know it. Just like Vee had been. Her heart raced and an electric current worked its way down her spine.

Roger lifted his face and wiped perspiration from his forehead. “No, I didn’t treat her. I took her initial call and then referred her to Doctor Dunhill.” He nodded to Cressida. “But we’ve discussed her care on several occasions and I’ve witnessed some of their interactions outside the office. The poor girl was going through some very rough times.”

The officer retrieved his notepad and flipped to the next page. His eager note-taking reminded Cressida of a junior reporter determined to get the next big scoop. “What kind of rough times?”

Cressida interrupted before Roger could answer. “She

made a suicidal threat last week, but I didn't think she was serious. I discussed it with Doctor Banks and we decided that it would be best to transfer her care to another office." She met Roger's sideways glance with a smile and he nodded. It was best to keep the story consistent.

The officer scratched behind his ear with the cap of his pen. "Why is that?"

"Because..." Roger cleared his throat. "I know how hard it can be when a patient you grow fond of makes an attempt on their life. We're well-trained to cope with these situations, but suicide...it's not something you just get over."

The officer cocked his mouth to the side. "I understand, sir. So you're telling me is that she has a history of threatening suicide?"

Cressida nodded in agreement. Who was left to argue? Vee had been in therapy and two respected psychologists had confirmed she was unstable. It was an open-and-shut case, right? Exactly what the officer wanted on his last week on the job. So why the hell was this guy still scribbling in his notebook?

Roger stepped forward so his shoulder was between Cressida and the officer, shielding her. "Miss Marquis reported to Doctor Dunhill that her boyfriend was abusive and I personally witnessed her turn up to the practice, unannounced, looking very agitated. I suspected she was becoming overly attached to Doctor Dunhill. Which is another reason I suggested she transfer the girl's care."

The young officer raised his eyebrows. "I see." He scratched his pen across the paper then shoved the notepad back in his pocket. "We'll be in touch. If you think of anything that might help us piece together her final moments, please call us." He reached into breast pocket and handed Cressida a business card.

"Officer John Lahey," Cressida read out loud. She peered into his eyes and all she could see was the calm sea. *John.* It was a very strong name.

"Yes, ma'am. My cell number is on the back. You can call me any time." His voice was formal but his eyes spoke to her like friends. *Or maybe more. Could it be that he wanted to open up to Cressida, more than his profession allowed him?*

The sinking numbness that had settled in Cressida's chest when Vee died lifted slightly. Vee had been a mistake, an error caused by the confusion of dreams with reality. An unachievable fantasy. A liability. Max would have told Cressida to be more careful.

But maybe she just needed a safer partner. Someone stronger, more reliable. Someone who could protect her and her dreams.

Officer Lahey handed Roger a card as well and held out his hand. Firm and confident. "Thank you very much for your cooperation, Doctor Banks."

Roger grunted his response. Without another word, Officer Lahey turned and followed his partner's wide footsteps toward the beach, along the same path that Vee had navigated only a few hours before. Cressida watched until his head disappeared around the side of the building, and he was gone.

Roger turned to face Cressida. "Are you ok? This must have come as quite a shock. I wish I'd had time to prepare you." He squeezed Cressida's shoulder. Hard. Stronger than she'd have imagined.

"I'm fine. This is part of the job, right?"

"No. It shouldn't be. Not like this. If I was a superstitious man I would start to think this place was haunted." Roger's eyes welled. "You sure you're ok?"

"I appreciate the concern, but I think I just need to focus on my other patients. I could use a distraction."

Roger leaned forward and for a moment it almost seemed like he wanted to kiss her. She stiffened her spine and tipped back on her heels. "You remind me of myself when I was younger. How do you think I ended up chained to this place? You do what you need to do for you, and if that means you need to take a few days off you let me know."

Cressida braced for his advance, but Roger just patted her on the back awkwardly and walked past her into the office, leaving Cressida alone with the flashing lights and the sound of the waves.

CHAPTER 30

Shivers shook Cressida awake in her chair, her chest aching for air, but her lungs had forgotten how to breathe. Her skin was wet, her hair plastered to her head. She was drowning. All she could hear was the *whoosh whoosh whoosh* of the ocean in her head as if she held a conch shell to her ear. She threw her head between her knees, gasping, almost crying when the air finally came in blissful gushes, her exhales fluttering the carpet at her feet. And...glitter. A tiny speck between the carpet fibers. Cressida licked her finger and touched the shard of color. It was so small on her fingertip, yet last week it was the most important thing in her life. Not that it wasn't important now.

She held up her hand, admiring Vee's ring on her finger. The words *I love you, Vee* were engraved on the side. Vee's body might be lying in a morgue in Silverside Hospital, but Vee would never really be gone. Once the police had cleared the beach below the asylum, Cressida would lay what was left of Vee to rest in the cave with the others. She would live on inside Cressida, intimate and immortal. *Theirs was a true love.*

A faint knocking drifted under her closed door and made the hairs on the back of her neck stand up. The clock on the wall said 10:30 p.m. There was no reason for anyone to be banging on the front door of The Mermaid Asylum unless they had unfinished business with her. Was it the cops? Officer Lahey? Her stomach fluttered, but she beat it back down.

The knocking grew louder as she approached the door to her office, and more frantic still as she stepped into the hall. She walked slowly toward the pounding, squinting at the reflection of the room behind her in the glass. Were these her last steps of freedom? Her hand shook as she turned the metal latch on the door and the lock clicked open. Before Cressida had a chance to grasp the door handle, the glass swung out revealing Rex's shady face. His eyes were red-rimmed and tinged with burst blood vessels, like he'd been crying for hours. Or screaming. His leather jacket was soaking wet.

"Rex." Cressida looked over his shoulder to the parking lot. Roger's car was parked in its usual space, meaning he and his wife were asleep upstairs. *Witnesses*. She pushed through the door and stood in front of Rex on the grass welcome mat. "What are you doing here?"

Rex aimed an already bloodied fingernail at her "You. You did this."

Cressida flattened her back against the glass door. "What are you talking about?"

"You were her friend and her therapist. You were supposed to protect her. Instead you fucked with her head and you fucked with me and now she's dead." He lunged forward and slammed his hand against the glass beside her head. The vibrations tore through Cressida's body.

"I never told her anything about last night, Rex. I haven't seen Vee since Tuesday."

Rex slapped the glass again. "Stop lying to me, you stupid bitch! I know you told her. This is your fault."

No, this was Rex's fault. He was the liar. He had kept Vee from her dreams, her future, and from Cressida. He deserved to feel guilty whether or not he'd been the one to hold her under the waves. He killed Vee.

Cressida held out her palms. "You need to calm down."

"Don't tell me to calm down! The police are acting like I beat her." He jabbed a bony finger at Cressida's face. "You've been poisoning everyone against me this whole time. I know what you're up to."

Cressida pushed away from the door and stood as tall as she could. Sometimes when an animal attacks you cower, and other times you have to respond with strength. Even the lowliest rats know that. It all depends on the true nature of the rat, and how much they really want to fight. "Really? How do you know anything about me, about her? Where the hell were you all day while she was floating in the ocean?"

"That's none of your damn business. I know you told her because I just came from the morgue, and Vee wasn't wearing her engagement ring. There were marks like she'd ripped it off. She wouldn't have done that unless you told her that we slept together." Rex clenched his fists by his side, but didn't come any closer. He was all for show.

The ring.

Cressida's finger throbbed with the weight of a thousand pounds. She jammed her hand in the pocket of her slacks. Cressida lowered her voice to a growl. "Maybe she decided to leave you all on her own."

"No!" Rex shouted and it echoed down the street. A light came on above our heads in Roger's apartment.

Roger's head appeared through an open window, his bald spot shining in the moonlight, his eyes swollen with sleep. "Who's down there?"

Cressida stepped around Rex into the light from the window. "Everything is fine, Doctor Banks. I've got it under control."

Roger squinted. "Doctor Dunhill? Who's yelling? Do I need to call the police?"

Cops would complicate matters, especially if they knew Rex was here with her after Vee died. More so if Rex had told them they'd fucked. And he would. Probably. Though a tiny part of her sparked at the idea of seeing Officer Lahey again.

Not yet.

She held up her hands and waved them back and forth. "No. It's just Miss Marquis's boyfriend. He's upset and he wants to talk. I've got it under control. Go back to bed."

Roger's face disappeared but he left the window ajar. *Nosy prick.* She turned to tell Rex they should go inside.

He was already staring at her. No...not at her. At her hand. Where the light from Roger's apartment was glinting off the diamond ring. *Shit.*

"Why do you have that ring?" Rex's brown eyes were molten and black in the shadows. "You fucking killed Vee, didn't you, you psycho bitch?" His voice rose with each word.

Cressida's gut tightened and she took two steps back so that she was in plain view of Roger's window. She nodded up to the window and it was Max's cool, calm voice that left her throat. "I'd keep my voice down if I were you."

"Why the fuck would I do that?"

"Because you showing up here in the middle of the night shouting and intimidating Vee's therapist, making wild accusations, and waking up half the neighborhood doesn't look very good in court." She pulled the ring from her finger and slipped it into her pocket. Vee's flowing skirts never had pockets. Cressida could never have lived with such impracticality.

"What court? You're out of your fucking mind. You killed Vee and I'm calling the cops." He stepped toward her, yanking his phone from his pocket.

Not so fast. She held up her hand, a victor's smile playing on her lips. "That's fine with me. Let's both have a little chat with the police and see how things end up, shall we?"

Rex furrowed his sweaty brow. "What are you taking about?"

"Right now Vee's death has been ruled a suicide." *Hopefully. If she did her job correctly.* "But if the police think she was murdered, you'll be the one looking suspicious. You're the abusive boyfriend who made a sudden commitment to his deranged, terrified girlfriend right before she turns up dead. You reek of bullshit. Such a cliché. Then you show up here, threatening her shrink in the middle of the night?"

Rex froze.

Cressida jabbed her hands to her hips. "Who do you think the police are going to believe? Especially if they found out we fucked. If that sordid detail came out, you'd be on the hook for sure."

"We both would."

He was right, but he didn't have to know that. She squared her shoulders. "Doubtful."

Rex opened his mouth and closed it again as if the cogs in his brain were grinding to a halt. He doubled over and splashed vomit on the asphalt and splattered Cressida's shoes. She inched back. If her shoes weren't already ruined, she'd be pissed.

He retched several times before resting his elbows on his thighs and crouching over his puke.

Cressida clicked her tongue. "I think you should probably go home and sleep this off."

Rex shook his head at the ground. "I'm not drunk."

"Well, maybe you should be. That might be a better explanation for your behavior." Cressida turned her back to the huddled mess of a man, and walked back to the door. She paused with her fingers on the handle. "How about we agree that it's for the best if we don't tell anyone about this? You can understand the need for that sort of thing, right?"

"Wait."

Rex straightened up and wiped his mouth with the sleeve of his jacket. His face was as pale as the moonlight, his eyes as black as the night sky. He pointed to her pocket. "I want that ring back."

Cressida pulled the ring from her pocket and eased it onto her finger. "I want my friend back, but we don't always get what we want, do we, Rex?" She smirked and pushed open the door to the asylum.

She walked through the door and watched as the mirrored glass transformed Rex's gaping stare into her icy reflection. She locked the door. Though she could no longer see his face, she knew Rex was there, watching her through the one-way glass. She examined her hair in the reflection and fluffed it from the roots where a hint of red was peeking through like the first sign of spring through the winter snow. The ring glinted in the mirror. She pulled it off and examined the engraving on the band. *Sappy, bastard.*

Cressida unlocked her office door and stepped back into her dark office where she deposited Vee's ring in the Mason jar on her side table before curling up on the sofa. Rex was weak, but she wasn't walking home in the dark with him out there. But she was glad he'd come—now she knew that Rex hadn't told the cops about her. And now Rex couldn't tell anyone the truth, not without pointing the finger at himself.

Sometimes the truth isn't worth the hassle. That's what Sam decided when she'd moved in the middle of the night instead of reporting Cressida for trespassing. That's why no one questioned why Max had died with his fly unzipped in the car with a teenage girl. Death is more palatable than the things we truly fear.

People didn't want the truth. They wanted to sleep. They wanted to dream. But Cressida spent ten years without dreams, and she was ready to know what happened, the final piece of the puzzle. She shouldn't have been there with Max that night, touching him, arousing him, and wearing his wife's wedding gown. That wasn't what killed him, but she knew enough to know it hadn't been an accident either. She'd accepted the palatable story, like everyone else, for years. But no more.

Still, Rex was a nuisance. Cressida should have been rid of him by now, but he refused to fade into darkness. There was more to Rexton Harris III than a hideous name and a grungy garage band—he'd messed everything up, taken her dreams. She had to find a way to destroy him. Rat, squirrel, whatever he was, he was in the way.

Cressida was no longer doing this for Vee. *This was for her.*

CHAPTER 31

Roger Banks's portly face pressed against the bay window in Cressida's office. His sweat smeared the glass as did his cupped hands as he peered in at her. He rapped once. Twice. Cressida waved into the sunrise.

It was early. The sun had barely crossed the floor of the office to reach the sofa, and Cressida's body still felt dead and frozen from her dreamless sleep. Her bones creaked as she rubbed the shoulder she'd been laying on all night.

Roger's face disappeared around the corner and moments later there was a knock at Cressida's office door. Cressida smoothed her hair around her temples before turning the handle.

"I saw the lamp on from the street this morning and I wanted to make sure everything was ok." Roger's eyebrows were ruffled with concern. "Did you sleep here last night?"

"Yeah, I thought it would be safer than walking home. What with Vee's boyfriend making a scene in the parking lot and all." Cressida smoothed the wrinkled silk blouse she'd been wearing for the last 24 hours, but the wrinkles were set deep. Some damage couldn't be undone.

"That was probably a good idea. I should have called the cops last night." Roger's shoulders were pinched tight like someone had tugged them up with a string. He pressed the base of his palm to his forehead. "What was I thinking?"

Cressida smiled. "You were thinking I could take care of myself. Which I can."

Roger stopped flagellating and regarded her clothes. "Do you want to come running this morning? It might help clear your head."

"Thank you, but I don't have anything to wear." Cressida looked down at her disheveled blouse and slacks and shook her head.

"I'll drive you back to your place so you can change first. We have plenty of time." His eyes were wide and expectant.

There was no good reason to say no, even though all Cressida wanted to do was follow Rex to figure out what he does all day. Though...it might be smart to keep on Roger's good side, just in case Rex decides to grow a pair and call the cops. She smiled and looked down at her feet. "Are you sure it's not too much trouble?"

Roger grinned. "Not at all. Come on." He stepped aside and held his hand out so Cressida could step past him into the hallway. It was practically a curtsey. "The keys are in the car." Looked like Roger hadn't learned his lesson after all.

It was surprisingly humid that day and by about the third mile sweat poured over Cressida's nose and mouth causing her to cough and splutter as she heaved. Perspiration sprayed from her mouth in a fine mist as she trailed behind

Roger's tireless girth. Their route had taken them along the windswept shore, along the steep roads up the cliffside, through the winding streets that coiled tight around the office. And finally, they were done. The front door was less than 500 yards away, but Cressida puffed to a stop. Roger's turned around and jogged in place. Waiting.

Cressida's heartbeat thundered in her ears and her lungs couldn't draw enough oxygen. *Fuck running.* Goosebumps puckered her skin. She should have known better than to push her body so far after weeks of not sleeping. She doubled over and shook her hands to put out the fire that burned through her fingertips. It wasn't pain, but it was close. Something else.

Her breaths came in ragged gasps. Her legs screamed at her to run, but they could barely keep her from toppling onto the sidewalk. She could hear Roger talking through the haze of suffocation, but she couldn't make out what he was saying. Her heart was beating in her throat. *Thump thump thump.* She sat down on the sidewalk and lowered her head between her knees. She felt Roger's hand on her shoulder and every nerve in her body stood alert. *Fear.* It was fear she was feeling.

Roger put his meaty arm around Cressida and rocked with her as she fought to open her lungs. "Breathe. Just breathe." His words reached her slowly like sound through water.

Gradually, the air seeped further down into her lungs, cooling the fire that raged in her chest. Sweat dripped in her eyes. Her shirt was soaked through and her pants were covered in mud; she'd sat directly in a puddle.

Roger was still holding her up, his shiny face the picture of concern. His thick eyebrows creased and his mouth twitched as he searched her face for signs of recovery.

Cressida knotted her unsteady hands in her lap. “I’m ok now.” Her voice was hoarse from hyperventilating, but she could feel the blood returning to her cheeks. The cold, sick sweat of nausea was giving way to the warm sun on her face.

Roger pulled his arm back into his own lap, but he didn’t stand.

Cressida straightened her legs, testing the muscles to see if they would support her weight. “I don’t know. I guess I’m more out of shape than I thought.”

“Cressida.” Her name sounded wrong on Roger’s lips the way it always had on her mother’s. “That was more than just being out of shape. I think you need to take a break.”

“I know. I’ll walk the rest of the way back to the office.”

“That’s not what I meant. I mean I think you’re taking this thing with Miss Marquis harder than you want to admit. For Pete’s sake, it just triggered a panic attack.”

Cressida blew air through her lips. “That’s ridiculous.”

“Is it? You just lost a patient. You need to take time to grieve that loss.”

Cressida wrinkled her nose. “How do I do that?”

“Get out and do something that makes you happy, reminds you why you do this job.”

Feeling returned to Cressida’s legs and she stood unsteadily. She’d become a therapist to feel closer to Max after he died and she kept doing it out of habit. Almost like an addiction. She yearned to understand why she could no longer dream when every man, woman, and child that passed through her office could. She craved an explanation. She had failed with Vee and now the only thing that would make her happy is to pick Rex apart piece by piece.

Roger stood beside her. “There must be some friends or family you can visit for a couple days.”

“Well, actually...” The buzzing in Cressida’s veins went

silent, her panic replaced by icy determination. And a plan. "There is someone I've been meaning to visit in Portland."

"Great." Roger nodded his smug head. "Why don't you go do that today? I will cancel your appointments and handle any emergent situations. You just worry about you."

Cressida scuffed the asphalt with her sneaker. "But, Roger, I don't have any way of getting there." She looked down at her feet and scraped some the mud off her heel.

Roger looked over his shoulder toward the office parking lot. "Why don't you take my car? Helen and I don't need it today."

To find Rex in the sprawling metropolis of Portland, she'd have to follow him in the morning. "Oh no, I couldn't. Besides I'm not even sure my friend is there today. I'd have to call ahead."

"Tomorrow then."

Cressida grimaced. "I don't know, Roger. It's a huge imposition."

"Not at all. Listen, why don't you just take the keys now and bring them back to me tomorrow evening? That way you can take two full days off from this place and come back refreshed." His smile betrayed his desperation to help her. To save her. Maybe all of Vee wasn't lost.

"You're sure it's not too much to ask?"

"You didn't ask. I offered." He waved his arm toward the office. "Now, let's take a nice easy jog back to my office and I'll get you those keys."

"Yes, boss." Cressida smiled as Roger bound toward the building.

Cressida's legs were steady again and her pulse had slowed to the even beat of a war drum. She was going to figure out what Rex was hiding. Prove to herself that she'd been right all along, that Rex deserved to suffer. Then she could put Vee to rest inside herself for good.

By the time she reached the glass front door, Roger was holding it open. He ushered her inside by the small of her back and his fingers pressed the cold fabric of her shirt against her skin. Shivers crawled across her flesh as she slipped through the door and out of his reach. Roger had obviously made an effort to clear off his workstation; the piles of papers, books, and journals were now stacked two feet high on the floor beside the desk. On the top sat a cup filled with pens like Cressida's Mason jar, a couple photos of his round-faced wife, and another picture without a frame with tattered edges and a creased corner like it had been stuck inside a book for many years. She'd never seen this photo in Roger's office before. Cressida craned her head to get a better look.

The woman in the picture was tall with chestnut hair and bright blue eyes, eyes like Sam and Vee had. The woman had a mischievous smile that was eerily familiar, as if Cressida knew her from some other place. Or some other life. Roger opened the top drawer of the desk and pulled out the car keys. He followed Cressida's gaze to the photo on the desk.

"Do you recognize her?" His words echoed Cressida's thoughts.

"Yes, but why? Is she a patient?"

"She was. A long time ago." He set the keys down on the desk and ran his finger over the photo like he could reach through time and space.

Cressida's stomach reacted before her mind caught up and fluttered in her gut. The photo she'd found on beach the day Vee died. It was the same woman. "Is that...the mermaid?" Roger had kept her photo all these years because she'd died on his watch? "She was your patient, right?"

Roger lowered himself into his chair. His eyes were glazed and his mouth was drawn. "Lana wasn't actually my patient. Just a patient in the same hospital where I worked."

Cressida's brow creased. It didn't make sense. "Oh. I thought—"

"She was my fiancé." Roger picked up the photo and sighed. "I knew she was in pain, but I thought it was just her way of processing things. I didn't know how bad things had gotten until it was too late."

"Processing what?" Cressida sat down in the chair across from Roger's desk.

"Lana and I were hot and heavy from the moment we met. Made for each other. Of course, she ended up pregnant."

"Oh."

Roger shook his head. "We were happy as clams in the bay until we lost the baby. I came home from interning at the hospital to find the bed we shared soaked in blood and my beautiful fiancée gone. I found her sitting on the beach behind our house, the surf running red with her blood."

Cressida's skin crawled, but she couldn't move.

Roger took a deep breath. "We were devastated, of course we were. But we could have tried again. I tried to tell her that, but I couldn't reach her. She started talking about the sea and how she'd had visions of her past life as a mermaid. She thought the baby had been called back to the ocean because it didn't belong in this world. I thought it was her way of dealing with the loss." His broad shoulders sagged

No wonder he had blamed himself all those years, or why he had decided to become a psychologist instead of a physician. He wanted to understand where it had all gone wrong. Cressida leaned across the desk and patted his hand. His skin was clammy and soft. "I'm so sorry, Roger."

Roger looked up at Cressida, his brown eyes lost in the past. He shook his head slowly. "Everyone knows the rest of the story."

"I never knew how close she was to you."

"It's not something I share with most people." He leaned toward her, eyes earnest. "You need to take time to grieve this loss before it defines the rest of your life."

Cressida shivered. The way Max defined her? She wanted to run, away from Roger and from the sick feeling welling up in her stomach. Vee wouldn't define the rest of her life, and neither would Rex. *She wouldn't let them.*

"You're right. Thank you. And thank you for letting me use your car." Cressida stood, her legs solid and strong.

"You're very welcome, dear. And Helen and I would love to have you over for dinner tomorrow evening. Drop off the keys and stay for some food and company. What do you say?"

Cressida was cornered. There was no way out. The knot in her stomach dropped toward the floor. "I've already put you out so much."

"I insist. Six o'clock okay?"

"Great. I'll be there. Thank you." Cressida smiled through her gritted teeth and accepted the keys Roger handed her with all the strings attached.

CHAPTER 32

Dawn sparkled bright and clear over the houses on Rex's street as if the tempest of the days before had never happened. As if Vee could walk through the door at any moment. If she didn't know better, Cressida might have thought the whole thing had been a torturous nightmare. Except she still hadn't dreamed since Vee had abandoned her.

Cressida hunched behind the wheel as the first fishermen drove their cars to the docks. Soon baristas and bakery owners appeared carrying coffees in stainless mugs. Finally, when the sky had bloomed pink and purple overhead, business men in suits and ties started their morning commute into the city. Rex's car hadn't moved all night, but the lights in the house—on, then off—told Cressida that he was home. According to the flyer she found in his jacket last week he had to meet someone named Tina at 11:00 a.m. this morning. Hopefully he hadn't changed his plans because of Vee. *Not that he'd ever cared that much while she was alive.*

The sun was shining hot and bright by the time Rex emerged from the house with a bag slung over his shoulder.

He tossed the black duffel into the back seat of his car and slipped behind the wheel.

Cressida eased her car onto the street behind him, careful to stay far enough away that he wouldn't notice. She followed Rex's beat up car around the twists and turns of the coastal road to the highway. They passed by Cressida's office in the distance, the dank building standing out ominously against the cheerful residences and businesses around it. The asylum was a dark shadow on the quaint, sleepy fishing town. And now she would be that shadow looming over Rex. He'd brainwashed Vee against her, stolen Cressida's chance to dream, and threatened her job and her safety. He didn't deserve to move on with his life. To walk away unscathed.

The single lane road spread into a two-lane highway and flat coastal land gave way to mountains and evergreen trees. Cressida allowed two cars to slip between her and Rex creating a buffer between them. Her hands gripped the steering wheel until her knuckles turned white and her palms ached. Under the seatbelt her stomach churned. A headache chewed at her skull. It was the same road Cressida and Vee had driven last week to dinner in Portland. Vee's laugh echoed in Cressida's mind. They'd been true friends that night, but it was the last time she'd been able to reach the girl. After that, it was all about Rex. Cressida ground her teeth. It felt like a lifetime ago, but sleepless nights will do that. They warp time until nothing has any meaning anymore.

An hour later the high-rise skyline of Portland peeked out from behind the hills of trees. One grand pink building stood out alone, an angry phallus among the blanket of green trees and smaller buildings. Rex took an early exit. No city.

Where was he going?

He climbed a mountain road into the hills overlooking Portland and Cressida followed, hoping not to lose him for the forest. Or the cliff. Down below, the Willamette River cut through the center of the city and lights twinkled among the trees. There was nowhere in Silverside that offered that kind of perspective. Everything had to be faced head on. It was one of the things Cressida had liked about living on the coast. It felt like being down in the trenches of life instead of watching from the crow's nest.

Along the street, deceptively large houses leered at them through entire walls of glass. Beyond them was an unobstructed view of snow-capped Mt. Hood, jagged and alone against the trees below it. Each house on the street probably cost as much as ten homes in Silverside. Rex had no business being in this neighborhood. The car slowed. Rex pulled into the driveway of one of the larger estates. Cressida stopped several houses down, as Rex exited with his duffel and walked through the door without being greeted.

Rex's family came from money, but there's no way his affected little grunge band was earning the kind of royalties needed to buy a place like this. Unless Rex was making a little money on the side. Drugs. Gambling. Girls. *Could that be why he'd hidden his double life from Vee?*

Or maybe he was having an affair with a married heiress, burying his fiancée one day and himself in some rich cunt the next. Loathsome. Rex had hidden his life from Vee, held her prisoner in their poverty while he toyed with music, women, and fancy houses. He'd lied to Vee and he'd lied to Cressida. Because of him Vee was dead, and Cressida needed to know why.

A few minutes later Rex reappeared through the front door wearing a black suit and a bright yellow shirt with a silver tie. His long hair was slicked back into a ponytail. His shoes reflected the sun. He hadn't been in the house long enough to have met with anyone or performed any kind of service. What was he up to?

Rex's junky car pulled out of the pristine driveway and headed down the hill toward downtown. Cressida watched the gratuitous houses fade in the rearview mirror as she followed him out of the neighborhood and through the streets to a multi-story parking lot in the center of the Pearl District.

Cressida parked down the row and watched Rex start across the street where artisanal bakeries, used book stores, and high-end furniture shops screamed that they were at the intersection between yuppie and hipster. Rex grabbed a door and pulled with firm authority. Like he owned the place. *Entitlement runs deep.* The windows were mirrored and there were no commercial displays. It could have been a lawyer's office. Or maybe a private detective. Rex's family had money; perhaps they were digging around in their would-be daughter-in-law's suicide.

Cressida's thighs stuck to the seat as she climbed out and walked to the edge of the parking garage. Below the concrete wall, men and women milled around beneath the garage, talking on their cellphones, sipping their gourmet coffee, and thinking only of their insignificant little lives. They were nameless, faceless, and pointless. Cressida had felt that way until she'd met Max and he taught her she was someone of consequence.

Cressida took the garage elevator to the street level and crossed the busy traffic to the door where Rex had disappeared. The name on the front of the building was Harris, Becker, and Abbot. Everything else about the glass-fronted building was nondescript. A bitter taste filled Cressida's mouth as she pushed through the spinning door into a grand lobby. The inside was nothing like the boring shell of a building she'd seen from the garage. The floors were swirling pink marble and there was a tree growing in the middle of the floor—straight through the foundation of the building. The branches had been trimmed and formed a neat canopy along the vaulted ceiling, high above the heads of the patrons in the huge atrium.

Sun shone through hundreds of windows casting moving shadows on the floor through the broad leaves. Birds flitted between branches, but there wasn't a single drop of shit on the floor. Someone's only job was to clean up after these birds who had no business being there in the first place. How appropriate that Cressida should find Rex here. Where he didn't belong.

Along the right side of the room were several elevators and a semicircular desk behind which sat a young woman with black hair, green eyes, and fingernails so long they curved past her fingertips. She was as striking as the tree in the lobby and yet as superfluous as the birds since she couldn't possibly type with those outlandish claws. Not that anyone would care. So much can be hidden behind beauty.

Cressida stood for several moments watching the birds, waiting for them to poop or the girl to answer a phone. Anything to make the surreal lobby seem functional. On the wall beside the elevators was a directory with the names and office numbers of everyone in the building. Cressida walked toward it, her heels echoing through the room. One of the birds flapped its wings and ruffled its feathers at the noise. To the bird, Cressida was the intruder.

The top plaque read "Harris, Becker, and Abbot, LLP, Certified Public Accountants. Rex's father's name appeared at the top of the list beside the number of a corner office, no doubt. Deirdre Becker and Paul Abbot came next. *Of course his father owned the place.* Could the woman Rex was supposed to meet this morning work for his father? She scanned the names. No one named Tina. Buried near the bottom of the directory was a familiar name: Rexton Harris III, CPA. Rex had a title, an office, and a boring white collar job. He hid this life for the same reason he'd run from it for so long: because it was so very ordinary. Expected. Rexton Harris III fancied himself a poet, an artist, and this place was the pinnacle of corporate greed: an accounting firm complete with a sea of faceless strangers in designer suits sipping expensive lattes. Cressida reached up to touch the engraved lettering. How had she missed this?

Footsteps echoed in the distance and Cressida turned to see the young woman from behind the desk, with the bird-like talons and the painted smile. "Excuse me. Can I help you?" She couldn't have stood more than five feet tall. Her miniscule frame was dwarfed next to Cressida.

"Umm..." The lobby was so silent that her heartbeat drowned out the sound of the elevator dinging. Her heart jumped. She looked around the room, searching for an explanation for her presence and hoping this wouldn't be the moment that Rex emerged from one of the gold-plated elevators in front of her. The doors opened and three nondescript suits brushed past her on their way out of the lobby. They smelled like expensive cologne layered over last night's scotch.

The girl folded her arms across her ample chest and tapped her foot.

Cressida glanced back at the plaque beside the elevator. "I'm sorry. I think I might have the wrong building."

The girl rested her hands on her hips, her long nails

scraping against her pink leather belt like knives being sharpened on a block.

Maybe Rex had fucked her too. Was she Tina? No, why would he have to meet her at a particular time if they worked in the same building. They could just leave together. Maybe he'd ended the affair with Tina when he proposed to Vee, just like she'd predicted. The thought sat heavy in Cressida's gut. *It couldn't be that easy.*

"Okay, well let me know if there is anything I can do for you."

Cressida forced a smile. "Thanks, I will." Had she made a mistake coming here? Maybe there were no answers, no secrets, only staunch reminders of the girl she'd lost and the dreams she'd never have again. And what if Rex saw her there? Would he call the police? Roger knew she had the car, that she was coming into the city today. He would believe Rex. He'd put two and two together. Cressida couldn't breathe. She rushed past the girl, upsetting the birds, and flew through the door.

Once outside the building, Cressida rested her hands on the back of her head and sat down on the sidewalk with her back against the wall. Across the street were several shops, a delicatessen, and an unassuming coffee shop nestled below the parking garage, out of sight from the garage itself. *Tina's.* The name written on Rex's flyer hadn't been a person, but place. It could easily have been about some boring business meeting. She inhaled the crisp air, and rested her head against her knees.

Rex's biggest secret was that he had nothing interesting about him, barely anything worth hiding. He'd never been a rat. He was a cockroach all along, scared, insipid, and hiding in the shadows. He was weak, and it had probably turned his stomach every time Vee had laid herself at his feet, begging him to make her feel something. Tears pricked at the corners of her eyes, blurring her vision, and then he was there. Max. Cool, calm, and crystal clear. She remembered everything. Finally.

Max would have told Cressida to walk away now, to take the car back to Roger and continue on with her life exactly as it was before Vee. Controlled. But Max's need for order was what had killed him. He'd said they needed to stop seeing each other just because things had gotten a little messy, just because she'd taken his wife's dress. But he was hard when she'd leaned across his lap to take his pen. That she could remember. He'd wanted her to surprise him, to break his rules.

Sharp and clear, the memories unfolded in her mind for the first time in ten years. She was awake and yet she was dreaming about that day. Max's breath was shallow and excited when she'd taken him in her mouth. She'd finally taken initiative, broken the last and final rule he had for her. In that moment she'd taken control. He existed only for her, and she wouldn't let him leave.

Max had wanted to control everything: when they spoke, when they fucked, and when they broke up. But Cressida was done being under the thumb of Max and of her mother. She was ready to be somebody else for good, and Max could feel the shift. He came undone in her mouth as she jerked the steering wheel into the median, sending them both careening into their mutual destruction.

This was her doing. Her choice.

Cressida couldn't breathe. She'd fought for so long to learn the secret behind Max's death, behind the accident that shaped her into the dreamless creature she'd become, and now she finally understood. Max had altered Cressida's life by letting her take his, by sacrificing, the way she wanted to save Vee and Sam and Olly. Max had changed her, profoundly and permanently. The way Vee had changed her too.

Max had died happy, like Vee should have. Rex had ruined that for both of them, and she couldn't fix that, but she could take some initiative again. Own Rex the way she'd owned Max that day. Cressida pushed off the wall and onto her feet. She crossed the street and swung open the door to the cafe.

CHAPTER 33

The shop was small and narrow with a counter at the far end, and a tiny display case filled with stale-looking pastries withering under a heat lamp. It was the kind of place where quality was trumped by proximity and convenience. Most of the tables were covered in Apple laptops and reusable mugs made from recycled milk jugs. A white girl with dirty blond dreadlocks looked up at Cressida and smiled over her smart phone. Beneath her tatty hair was a Bluetooth earpiece and her smile quickly faded into a frown as she shook her head and shouted something about equities and trades into the ether. Cressida ordered a large drip coffee from a young woman with a round face and slightly upturned nose. She yawned and filled Cressida's order without a smile.

Cressida stepped over charging cables and hemp messenger bags and settled into the seat facing the barista, her back to the long counter across the front window. The coffee stung her fingers through the thin paper sleeve. She drank. Bitter pain filled her mouth, scorched her throat then her chest, spreading the warmth throughout her body. The sun beat down on the bare back of her neck. She missed her long hair.

By the time Rex jingled the little bell that hung from the cafe door Cressida's hair was dripping. He passed her table without a glance and approached the counter. This close, she could tell his black suit was finely tailored, the pants and sleeves hemmed to his specifications. His pants were long enough to touch the tops of his black leather shoes but not so long that they dragged on the floor, and his jacket sleeves were just a hair shorter than his shirt so that a hint of canary yellow peeked out from beneath the cuff.

Yet Rex still looked uncomfortable. He shifted back and forth as he ordered, then waited quietly for his drink. In Silverside, Rex wore his leather jacket as armor against the world, but here the suit seemed to be devouring him. Away from the salt and the sand and the permeating smell of rotting fish and dreams, Rex didn't shine. *He was nobody.* He perched at a table near the center of the shop and sat with his back to the door.

Another jingle announced the arrival of an older man in a tailored navy suit, but this man moved in his suit as if it was a second skin. His hair was silver, not grey the way Mrs. Coulter's had aged, but shining and vibrant as moonlight. The cut was neat and practiced.

The man stood in the doorway of the café, just taking in the room. Cressida imagined Max might have looked similar had he lived. He was the master of his realm in a way that Rex could never be.

Rex hunched lower in his seat without looking, as if he could sense the man's presence. The silver haired man tipped his chin to the barista and strode to where Rex was huddled over his coffee. The girl behind the counter dropped her eyes and the slightest hint of pink surfaced on her cheeks.

The man clasped hands with Rex then stood back expectantly, his perfect teeth bared in a smile worthy of an orthodontics add. Rex stood from his seat and for a moment it looked like he might take a knee in front of the older man but instead he embraced him like they were old friends. They were similar heights and builds. Similar coloring. Similar...faces. Rexton Harris Jr., accounting mogul and Rex's father. The house Rex had visited to change before heading to the office must have belonged to his parents. He was the prodigal son returned. Cressida pulled her hot cup closer to her on the table and leaned in to hear what they were saying.

Rex's father slapped Rex hard on the back and then pulled out a chair for him to sit. It was a gentlemanly gesture, but Rex sneered before thumping back into his seat. The elder Harris stood beside the table, giving him the high ground. "Glad you could make it, son." His words were friendly, but his tone was clipped.

Rex nodded into his mug and picked at something on the tabletop. Rex had made himself so small that his father looked right through him. Cressida used to do the same thing in her mother's presence.

"I'm glad you decided to grace us with your presence today at the office. It was very kind of you."

Rex didn't look up but his fists balled against the table. "I've been a little preoccupied."

"Well, it's high time you got your priorities in order." The older man's jaw set hard, the muscles in his face taught and the veins in the side of his neck stretched against his skin. "Why don't you go up there and order me a coffee from the pretty girl."

Rex flinched. "Dad, I'm not in the mood today."

"In the mood for what? For coffee?"

Rex lifted his head and stared at his father with the same molten eyes as when he'd confronted Cressida. "For your ridiculous head games and competitions. If you want her number, get it yourself."

Mr. Harris didn't blink at his son's outburst. He was cold as stone. "I don't want anything, son, except for you to stop moping around like a pussy and be a fucking man." His voice was calm and flat. Controlled. Like a good king should be.

"My just fiancé died, Dad."

His father huffed as loud as the espresso machine behind the counter. "Don't be a fool."

The back of Rex's neck reddened, but he said nothing. He wiped at his face. Was he crying?

Cressida's head throbbed. She pressed her fingers against her temples and took a drink of her slowly cooling coffee. It just didn't make sense. Rex hadn't lied to Vee because he was embarrassed of his wealthy family. He'd lied because she might have wanted to go with him to Portland. He'd been afraid that she would fall in love with the privileges and opportunities afforded to Rexton Harris III. He'd known she would have craved his life. The life he despised. The life he couldn't escape no matter how many basement clubs he played on his days off.

Mr. Harris crossed his arms. "It's time you start acting like the man you were born to be. Time you started living up to your name."

"I never asked for any of this." Rex clawed at the lapel of his suit, an imposter in his own life.

"You don't ask for your destiny, son. It's your birthright.

There are people who would kill to take your place at my table."

Rex instinctively reached his hand to his head to scrape his fingers through his hair but they tangled in his ponytail. He ripped the band from the back of his head and threw it to the floor. "Then let them have it. I don't want it. I never have."

"All this over some girl?"

Rex finally stood. "She wasn't just some girl. She was special."

"Rexton, she was a silly girl for a silly life. It's time you moved on, and the best way for you to do that is to move on with another woman. Or better yet, many of them. Now go up there and get that girl's phone number so we can talk about something else." Mr. Harris swept his hand through the air and finally took his seat as if nothing unusual had transpired between them. Maybe it hadn't. Maybe this was their usual.

Rex wasn't so different from Cressida. They both hated the names that were placed on them like weights on their shoulders, and they were both desperate to be someone else. *To choose another life.* The only difference was Cressida was willing to take what she wanted while Rex hid his shame behind rock and roll and a musician's swagger.

She realized too late that she was squeezing her cup. Hot coffee poured from the crumpled paper over the table and cascaded to the floor. The barista glared at Cressida. She swore under her breath. It was too late to run and there was nothing to hide behind, no menus or curtains. Rex and Mr. Harris both turned toward the sound of sloshing liquid and the panicked gasps from the owners of the nearby computer cables. Cressida stood from her chair in time to see Rex blanch. His mouth opened, but words didn't come out. Cressida left her cup on its side and turned her back to the room. She could feel dozens of eyes crawling up her spine as she pushed through the glass front door and rushed out into the street. Her heart pounded and she gasped for fresh air, but she couldn't stop running until she'd reached Roger's car.

CHAPTER 34

Cressida was late. Roger was expecting her and the car back by 5:30 p.m. but she couldn't drag herself from the shower. Red water circled the drain like blood as she washed the dye from her short hair. It would take months for her natural color to grow back out, but this would have to do. She'd made a mistake changing it in the first place, made a mistake with Vee. But there was no going back. *There never was.* The hot water fell in ribbons along her back, pounding over and over against her skin until her outsides were as numb as her insides.

She closed her eyes and listened to the hum of the water against her head, filling her mind with white noise. Her legs were tired and she lowered herself onto the floor of the shower. Crouched under the spray, Cressida let the water pour over her nose and mouth, felt the burn in her lungs from lack of dry air. She imagined how Vee must have felt drowning in the sea. She'd never screamed, never let the air escape from her lungs for something so futile. Or maybe she'd made peace with it. She said she'd wanted to feel something and maybe the last thought she had in this world was one of thanks to Cressida for giving her the gift of fear. The room seemed to ripple like the tide and Cressida held her breath until her vision narrowed. Choking, she reached up and turned off the shower and the sudden silence in her apartment was maddening.

She stood cold and naked in front of the mirror with none of the excitement she had felt the night she cut her hair. The glass was fogged and her edges were blurred, any color lost to the steam. She pulled on a bathrobe and rubbed a towel over her hair, bending down and shaking the water from her head like an animal. The first time she'd seen Vee do that she'd thought the girl had been free, boundless. But Vee had been just another trapped rat.

Cressida walked over to the vanity in her bedroom and pulled the velvet box from the drawer. Underneath Sam's scarf was the photo of Vee she'd taken from Rex's wallet. She ran her hands along the bright silk and thought of Sam. She was out there somewhere, fully changed. A new person. The most successful transformation Cressida had ever witnessed.

Pounding on the front door startled Cressida and the lid of the box nearly closed on her fingers. She frowned. Surely Roger wasn't worried about her already; the clock on the wall said 5:40 p.m. Only ten minutes late. She rushed to the front door to ask for another minute to get dressed. The knocking came again, louder this time, and Cressida was about to shout at Roger, but when she turned the latch the door flew open with such force it pushed her back into the apartment. Plaster fell from the wall and scattered over her carpet.

Rex stood in the doorway, his jacket gone and his yellow

shirt untucked. The silver tie around his neck was loose and slung over his shoulder like a noose. No longer was his suit ill-fitting and awkward—now it was disheveled, a messy sacrifice he had to make in the name of his family. A sacrifice that Vee had died for. Cressida had made Vee a martyr, which might have been the best metamorphosis anyone could have hoped for. *Would Rex do the same for Cressida?*

Cressida raised her hands in front of her and jumped back. "What are you doing here?"

Rex jabbed a finger at her. "You don't get to ask me that." He slammed the door behind him rattling the bookshelves and knocking paperbacks onto their sides. "Who the hell do you think you are?"

Cressida scanned the room for some kind of weapon. Rex stood between her and the kitchen and the bookshelves behind her were bare of any knickknacks except books. She took another step back and spoke softly. "I can see you're very upset. Maybe we can talk about it in my office tomorrow."

His eyes were wide. "Why? So you can kill me too?"

"Vee committed suicide, Rex."

"Bullshit. We both know what really happened, and did you really think that I wouldn't tell anyone just because you make some half-assed threat?" He stomped into the living room and pinned her against the back of the sofa. He stunk of alcohol and sour sweat. It was the smell of fear and desperation. It was the smell of death.

There was no way out, no way to overpower him. She was trapped by his madness. "Let's both calm down so we can think clearly. Can I get you a drink?"

"Do I fucking look like I need a drink?"

"Then let's sit down and talk." Her best chance was to distract him until Roger came looking for her, but she had no idea how long that would be. Rex would squeal then though, she was sure. He'd tell Roger about the ring. She should have buried it.

"Yeah, let's do that." Rex leaned away from Cressida and gestured for her to sit on the sofa.

She walked around to the front of the couch and sat down. Rex followed and sat on the coffee table in front of her.

Cressida chuckled. The sound had escaped her mouth and she tried to stuff it back in, but it was too late.

"What the fuck are you laughing about?"

"Nothing. It's nothing. I just sit exactly like that during some of my sessions. I was just thinking how ironic this is."

The crease between Rex's eyes deepened. His mouth was tight and pulled back over white teeth as perfect as his fathers. "Well you're not running the session this time, Doc."

"No. I know that. I'm sorry. What did you want to talk about?"

Rex wiped his eyes with the back of his wrist. "I want to know why us? Why her?"

"Vee came to me."

"Yeah, for help. And look what happened."

Cressida twisted her fingers in her lap. *Turn it around.* This was his fault—it's high time he knew it. And if he attacked her, she'd look that much more credible when Roger showed up. "She came to me for protection. Against you."

Air hissed through Rex's teeth. "I never laid a fucking hand on her that she didn't ask for. You're the one who fucking killed her." His voice cracked and he sniffed loudly, wiping his nose on his yellow sleeve. "Why did you choose her?"

Cressida glanced over her shoulder. The window facing

the parking lot was open, but she couldn't hear a car or see any lights.

Rex slammed his hand against the table. "Answer me!"

Cressida's voice stuck in her throat and she had to shout to dislodge it. "She made me dream again."

"She what?" Rex's mouth was open, his hand frozen to the spot.

The words poured from Cressida's mouth before she could stop them. "She changed me."

"How?"

Cressida frowned. "I don't know. She was gone before I had a chance to find out." Vee's eyes burned into Cressida's mind, open and frantic under the water as the life slowly bubbled from her body. In the end, she'd died like anyone else. Maybe the way Cressida should have years ago. She hadn't been special after all.

Rex sat forward again until he was inches from Cressida's face. "Gone? You mean you killed her. Why don't you just admit it?"

"Would that make you happy?"

"No. Nothing will ever make me happy again, but at least someone will have spoken the truth. At least I'll know what you really are." His brown eyes stared into Cressida's soul. They were so alike. Both of them rats. Rex was trying to survive.

He was trying to eat her alive.

"And what am I?"

"A killer. You see, you're not the only one who can stalk people. I did some googling after I saw you at the coffee shop this afternoon. This isn't the first time someone close to you has died."

Cressida's heart lurched. There were no official records

about her involvement in Max's death. It had been ruled an accident. His wife has made sure of that. Maybe there were a few newspaper clippings, an article in the local paper that mentioned a young patient, but nothing concrete.

Rex's eyes were wild and his hand shook as he pointed the chewed nail of his index finger in her face. He was out of control, operating on his most basic instincts: hunt and destroy. "Did you kill them too and make it look like an accident? That guy in the car? Fuck, you probably killed your mother too."

Cressida's voice came out hoarse and weak. "No."

"Bullshit. I understand the compulsion to kill a family member, but why Vee? She made you dream...that's good right?"

The sound of tires rolling over sand and gravel floated through the open living room window. Roger. Cressida stood, defiantly towering over Rex's surprised face. Fuck him. He had nothing over her anymore. "Because she chose you over me. We had a connection. Something special. We had dreams, and she just threw it all away for some guy who couldn't be bothered to tell her the truth about his life." She stepped up on the sofa and jumped over the back.

Rex leaped up from the coffee table and stormed after her. "What do you know about our lives? You barely knew her. You didn't have a connection. You were a fucking stalker."

"You're wrong." Cressida stumbled backwards toward the door. "And it doesn't matter anyway. No one will believe you. You're a liar and an abuser in everyone's eyes, and that's what counts."

"You're wrong. My father has money and I won't stop until everyone knows the truth about you."

Cressida smiled. "That's the thing. There's no such thing as the truth. I am whatever I want to be, whatever I need to be to survive."

Rex lunged forward as Cressida threw open the front door. He slammed into her and she tumbled backwards, tripping over the threshold and landing on her back on the stairs. Her head slammed against the steps with such force that stars exploded behind her eyes. A crack reverberated through the hall. A sharp pain shot up her leg, like thousands of knives carving her to pieces. She couldn't tell which direction was up—it was like being trapped in an undertow. Her lungs burned for oxygen as the impact of each step knocked the wind from her chest.

Metallic liquid gushed from Cressida's nose and lips. There was no room for air. She was drowning in her own blood. She landed flat on her back and the world stilled. Footsteps pounded against the concrete steps as she fell: Rex's from the top of the stairs, or maybe Roger's from below.

There were hands touching her, pulling her, urging her to stay with them.

Red and blue lights burned her retinas and voices murmured in her head. Rex's face was there, bruised and bloodied, his hands clasped behind his back. Maybe he had fallen behind her or hit the door frame on his way out of the apartment. Her vision darkened and then there was nothing. Sleep threatened to overtake her. Or death. Either way she knew that when she gave in the pain would be gone, floating below her like the sirens and the shouting. Disconnected. Nonexistent.

The last face she saw before the blackness finally overtook her was the young officer from the day Vee died. *Officer Lahey. John.* Cressida tried to smile at him but pain seared through her jaw, hot and vital. He'd shaved his ridiculous mustache and his blue eyes were searching Cressida's. Calling to her. They burned with azure flames and as the darkness closed in around Cressida she clung to the blue. The color. The building blocks of her dreams.

CHAPTER 35

"Can she hear me?"

"She hasn't woken yet."

"How long will she be like this?"

"It's hard to say. Ultimately it's up to her. She has to fight."

"Well, I'll stay with her until she wakes up. She has no other family."

Familiar voices hacked through the thick wall of sleep between Cressida and the world, but she couldn't place them. Her thoughts were sluggish and unsophisticated as she floated in some kind of limbo, some place between life and death. All at once, she could see the voices swirling in great colorful ribbons, entwining around her and lifting her toward a bright light. The light wasn't hot like the sun, but cool. Forbidding. A shiver ran through her body, raising goose bumps on her skin. She could feel them scraping against the ribbons of light that ensnared her. *Was she awake or asleep or something new?*

Without warning, the colorful ribbons holding her unraveled and she was falling toward a dark bed with metal bars along the side and soft handcuffs waiting to capture her. She opened her mouth to scream, but only pain shot from between her clenched teeth. She hit the bed with a thud and all the color and light blinked from the room, leaving only the cold.

Lights flickered in Cressida's eyes. A black haze lifted from her mind and the room crashed down around her. Fluorescent lights buzzed overhead, bright and burning, burrowing under her pinched eyelids and rousing her the pain in her leg, her head, her everywhere. The room around her was sick, pastel green and yellow, with a faded floral border along the ceiling. Everything was muted, soft, and tranquil: the sterile colors of the infirmed.

Cressida was lying flat on her back, arms pinned to her sides, one leg suspended in the air. She couldn't move her head. All around her were sounds, hospital monitors beeping, voices whispering, footsteps pounding. Memories swirled in her brain offering only glimpses of the last night before whisking them away again. Footsteps. Shouting. Rex's horrified face as he collided with her in the doorway, the world twisting as she fell down the stairs outside her apartment. And Officer Lahey had been there. Had Rex told him everything she'd admitted about Vee?

Cressida's fingers twitched and she moved her wrists, but they were held in place by soft brown cuffs. Was she under arrest? There was an IV in her arm and her head was fixed in place by a thick collar of padded plastic. Her left leg was immobilized by a full cast, elevated from the bed by a sling attached to the ceiling. To the right of the bed, Roger dozed in a chair, slumped forward with his chin on his chest. He snorted in his sleep.

Cressida tried to open her mouth to speak, to ask what happened, but her jaw wouldn't budge. Dull pain throbbed through her face with each rapid heartbeat. She couldn't move. She couldn't speak. This was the end, just like the dream she'd had. Or whatever that was.

Cressida tapped the bed with her hand as hard as she could to get Roger's attention but she couldn't get enough leverage with the restraints and the hospital blanket muffled the sound. Her heart pounded in her ears. The beeping on the heart monitor increased until an alarm sounded. She couldn't breathe. Her nostrils felt like pinholes, inadequate to move the oxygen required to sustain her life. She was dying. Drowning just like Vee. A gust of air tickled Cressida's feet and masked faces materialized above her, anonymous and portentous. Hands moved over her body, jostled and pulled. A multitude of strange eyes searched her face: brown, green, grey and pale blue.

"Miss Dunhill, can you hear me?" A man's voice boomed through one of the sterile masks. His eyes were dark grey like storm clouds over the sea.

Cressida blinked and fixed her eyes on the source of the voice. She groaned against her clenched teeth.

The masked man spoke again, this time a shout. "She's awake." He was looking at her, but talking to someone across the room.

Roger's face leaned close to Cressida. Purple semicircles bulged under his eyes and his bald head was slick with grease. "Cressida?" He smelled like bad coffee and stale cigarettes. Since when did he smoke?

She locked onto his eyes and blinked long and purposefully.

Roger smiled. "You're ok. Oh thank god. You're at OHSU in Portland. They transferred you last night."

Cressida pulled her arm against the thick cuff and then

dropped it back to the bed. Roger nodded and turned back toward the door. "Hey, can we get these things off?"

A nurse wearing a pair of ruby red scrubs the color of Vee's skirt floated into her field of vision. The hideous rip of Velcro tearing shocked her brain fully awake. Then she was free. Not handcuffed to the bed, not under arrest. Free. Rex hadn't told them about Vee. Yet.

She couldn't move her head, so she lifted her heavy arms in front of her face. Black bruises and scrapes covered the base of her palms. The skin was swollen and cracked and angry, but the pain was merely a dull ache. They must have given her the good drugs. She dropped her arms back to her sides.

She coughed and winced as the pain in her jaw scorched through her brain. It was white hot and raw and like nothing she'd ever felt before. No drug could numb that hurt.

"Try not to move," Roger said. "Your jaw is wired shut and you've had surgery to set your broken leg. When you didn't wake up they were concerned about a head injury which is why they transferred you here, but they think you'll make a full recovery."

Injured. But it was only temporary. Like a butterfly from a cocoon she would change again.

Roger rested his hand on the bedrail. His knuckles were also bruised and bleeding. Had he struck Rex after she fell?

The latch on the door clicked as it opened again. Roger held up his hand, indicating for the intruder to stop. "Not now. She just woke up and she's tired."

"I'll keep it quick, Doctor Banks." The man's voice was familiar, soothing. It was a voice from her dream.

Her dream. She had dreamed. How was that possible?

Cressida strained to see the source of the sound, but she

couldn't turn her head far enough. Roger scoffed and turned away from the hospital bed in disgust. He thumped back into the tiny chair and sulked. *He wanted to protect her from something.*

Bright blue eyes met Cressida's as Officer Lahey's pinched face appeared. He'd shaved his mustache since the last time she'd seen him, and his entire face looked different. He looked younger, more innocent. Idealistic, even. Like he'd gone back in time and unlearned every jaded memory he'd ever had.

He squinted down at Cressida as if she had a riddle tattooed on her forehead. "It's good to see you're feeling better. I'm officer Lahey. Do you remember me?"

Her heart monitor beeped frantically. *Shit. He's still a cop.* Cressida took a long breath and blinked her eyes. The pain lessened with each breath and her heart rate started to slow. Officer Lahey—John—sure didn't look like he was there to arrest her. And if he was, Roger would know and she would have seen it in Roger's protective eyes. This time Cressida was the victim. She was Vee, Sam, and maybe even Max. John wanted to save her.

"I won't keep you long, Miss Dunhill, but I do have to ask you a few questions. Is that ok?"

Cressida tried to nod, but the stabilizing collar around her neck held her tight. She blinked her eyes a few times trying to convey her frustration. She finally gave up and sighed through her nose.

John frowned and retreated from the bed, out of her line of sight. "Hey, is there any way we can get this neck brace off of her?"

A woman's voice shouted from a distance. Probably the hallway. "I'll have to talk to the doctor. Hang on."

Cressida stared unblinking at the grey ceiling and harsh

lights above her. It reminded her of the ceiling in her office, only here the floors and surfaces were sterile and bare, not filled with old books and stray glitter. Less mess to clean up.

Footsteps approached her bed. Two new faces appeared, haloed by the bright lights above. They peered into her eyes with a flashlight. They tested her reflexes. One of them ran a sharp object over the sole of her foot and she jerked involuntarily, like her body wasn't her own. The masked twins nodded to each other and then one of them unsnapped the collar around Cressida's neck.

Cressida turned to her head to the side and nodded tentatively at Roger who sat with his arms folded across his chest surveying the room. He smiled back at her and leaned forward over his knees. "Feel better?"

Cressida cautiously nodded her head, testing her range of motion and careful not to knock her jaw against her chest. She tucked her chin and lifted her head just enough to see the doorway where officer Lahey was shaking the doctor's hand. His blue eyes turned back to her and calm washed over Cressida like a wave, but different than it was when she held Max's pen. Warmer. *Everything was going to be ok.*

John's eyes glinted as he reappeared at her bedside. He flipped a page in his notebook with his pen. "Now, let's get this over with."

Cressida nodded and stretched her lips into a careful smile. The pain remained, but now it was a welcome reminder that she was still alive. Still changing and healing.

"On the night of April twenty-fourth, two nights ago, did you invite Mister Rexton Harris into your apartment at seven thirty-four Shoreline Drive?"

Her eyes narrowed. Cressida shook her head, slowly, carefully.

John scribbled into his notebook. "Did you let him in?"

Cressida shook her head again, stronger this time.

John lifted his blue eyes from his pad. "So, just so we're clear. Mister Harris entered your apartment without your permission?"

Cressida nodded. Rex had forced his way into her apartment, flinging the door open with such force it left a dent in the wall. There was proof.

"While he was there, did you argue?"

Cressida nodded again, her jaw screaming and her voice itching to escape her throat. It scratched at the walls of her neck like a prisoner in a deep dungeon.

John's blue eyes were fixed on the page as he scribbled, and he spoke without looking up from his notes. "About what?"

Air hissed from Cressida's nose as she sighed. This was important. John needed to understand why Rex was there. She needed him to see how unstable Rex was. How he'd lied about everything in his life: his job, his fidelity, and now this.

John looked up from his paper and shook his head "Oh. Sorry. Do you think you could write the answer?"

Cressida nodded, but she held her hand up with her first and middle fingers sticking up and the rest folded into a fist, like a peace sign.

John's eyebrows knitted together. "Two? You had two arguments?"

Cressida shook her head and slapped her hand against the bed. She held her hand up again with her two fingers raised. She shook them back and forth.

Roger peered over John's uniformed shoulder. He cocked his head to the side and then opened his eyes wide. "V."

"Huh?" John turned to Roger with a puzzled look.

"She's signing the letter V. The girl who died, Mister Harris's girlfriend's name was Viola. She went by Vee."

Cressida nodded and dropped her hand to the bed. The muscles in her arms twitched and pulled from the exertion. She sighed and closed her eyes.

John recorded the response in his notebook. "So you're saying Mister Harris came to your apartment that night to talk about his girlfriend, Viola Marquis?"

Cressida nodded.

"About her suicide?"

Cressida opened her eyes and shook her head slowly. She raised her hand and pulled one finger across her throat.

"About her being killed?" John's blue eyes were troubled. His forehead wrinkled.

Roger coughed from his chair. "I mentioned all this to you in my statement. Mister Harris was outside our office the other night yelling about how he thought Miss Marquis's suicide was murder. He kept going on about how Doctor Dunhill killed his fiancé and stole her engagement ring. It was nonsense. He was manic and out of control—clearly delusional and violent."

John turned his back to Cressida and spoke softly to Roger. "Was Miss Dunhill wearing a ring when you found her at the apartment?"

Roger huffed. "No, of course not."

The sound of John's pen scratching across the page filled the silence. Cressida slapped her hand against the bed, and both men turned their attention back to her.

"Is that what happened? He accused you of killing his girlfriend?"

Cressida nodded.

"Do you have any idea why he would think that?"

Cressida shook her head and closed her eyes tight. A

tear rolled down her cheek cooling the skin in its path until she reached up and wiped it away. Sam had cried exactly like that in her hospital bed the day that Cressida visited, when she'd leaned over Sam's bed the way John was hovering over hers right now. With that, the tears flowed more freely and Cressida didn't bother to sweep them away. Each drop that fell to the pillow under her head was cathartic, pure, and universal. Sam was still within her, dormant and waiting.

Roger hoisted himself between Cressida's bed and John's notebook. "I think that's enough questions for now. You already know what happened, anyway."

"This is just a formality, Doctor Banks, but I have to ask." John leaned over the bed so close that Cressida could smell his cheap aftershave and the faint odor of cigarette smoke. But there was no way John was a smoker. His fingers were too pristine, too meticulous. His partner must smoke in the cruiser they share. *What an asshole.* "Doctor Dunhill, did you have anything to do with the death of Viola Marquis?"

Cressida shook her head again with more force. *Please believe me.* She wanted Officer Lahey to tell her in his soft, smooth voice how everything would be ok.

"I'll let you rest now, Doctor Dunhill. Thank you for your time." He laid his hand on top of Cressida's. The pads of his fingers were calloused. "Between you and me, I think the kid is out of his mind, and there are several witnesses who saw him push you from the top of the stairs that night. The rest of these accusations are just his way of covering his ass. Don't you worry. We'll get him. And we'll put him somewhere he can't bother you anymore."

Rex was going to jail. Cressida closed her eyes.

Roger's voice drifted around her. "I think that's about all

she can handle for the day. If she thinks of anything else I'll have her call you."

Officer Lahey cleared his throat. "Oh, not me though. I'm transferring to Portland in a couple days. But I'll be sure to let Officer Neal know."

As the sleep pooled around Cressida, threatening to pull her under, she saw the face of John Lahey, his warm blue eyes smiling through the haze. She could feel the sun shining on her arm through the hospital window like a soft hand pulling her back into the light, keeping her safe from the black death of dreamless sleep. John's strong arm. He'd saved her that night from Rex and maybe he could save her from her dulled life.

Vee hadn't been the answer, couldn't fix her, but maybe she'd served a purpose. To lead Cressida to John. But now he was leaving. Even as the edges of her vision blurred she could feel his blue eyes burning into her soul. Bright, colorful, and eternal. *Like a dream. Vee was gone and there was no going back. Only forward.*

CHAPTER 36

The mahogany wingback chair creaked under Roger Banks as he dropped his heavy frame into the seat. From this vantage he could see the whole room laid out in front of him, meticulously organized desk in the corner on the right, bookshelves posed with impressive volumes that looked like they belonged in an ancient library or university, and two bright bay windows casting a harsh glare over everything in the office.

There was a coffee table in front of him with a half-empty box of tissues tipped on its side and a burlap sofa that reminded Roger of something he and Helen had seen at a flea market on one of their package vacations. It was either the camel-back tour through the Atlas Mountains of Morocco or the river-boat excursion along the Ganges in India. All Roger could remember from either of those trips was being eaten alive by mosquitos and the sound of Helen bartering relentlessly over fifty cents.

On top of the sofa were several cardboard boxes containing the contents of Cressida Dunhill's apartment. Her landlord had dropped them off early that morning and made sure to remind Roger of what a favor he was doing for his tenant by not hawking the laptop and tossing the rest of the items into the sea. Roger had tipped him twenty dollars for his trouble and then written down his license plate number, just in case. There had been more than enough excitement at the office to last him the next ten years.

The clock on the wall between the bay windows read 7:45 a.m. Normally Dr. Dunhill would have seen her first patient by now, but it had been over a month since anyone had used the office. For the first couple weeks patients trickled into the building looking for their trusted therapist only to find a sign on the door directing them to Roger. He did what he could for them, but there was a chemistry between doctor and patient that couldn't simply be traded like a baseball card.

One angry young man dressed all in black had practically beaten down the office door looking for Dr. Dunhill, and when Roger assured him she was no longer available he'd ripped several picture frames off the wall in the hallway. The next night someone had egged the front of the building and carved the word *rat* into the front door. That was also the night that Helen insisted they start locking their doors and windows before going to bed. Silverside had always been a quiet town, but Roger could feel the cold wind changing. Nothing stays dormant forever.

Beside the leather chair was a tall side table with an appointment book and notepad spread out across the surface. A thin layer of dust had settled on the books and Roger traced a dark line along the face of the planner. Beside the notepad lay a black metal pen with a silver band. Roger picked it up. It was heavier than he'd expected. He pulled the notepad into his lap and wrote the words *Cressida Dunhill's Belongings.*

When his young colleague had signed herself out against medical advice from the Portland hospital, he was sure she would be back to work within a couple weeks. She'd been a dedicated therapist, and one who went above and beyond the usual doctor-patient responsibilities. She'd cared. At least that's what he'd thought. He'd waited for weeks for her to return, but the rent on the building was too high for Roger to pay without taking on another partner. She just left without a word. Vanished. Sweat beaded along his forehead.

When Lana died he'd sworn he wouldn't lose anyone else to The Mermaid Asylum, and yet here he was taking an inventory and boxing up the belongings of another woman he'd failed to protect. And with Vee's death and Cressida's disappearance came the reporters interested in the growing myth of the cursed psychiatric facility. *No wonder patients were fleeing.* He'd lost three this week alone, but he couldn't blame them. And once the Rex Harris's trial began it would only get worse. Roger pulled himself free from the chair and the leather cushion wheezed as it re-inflated in his absence.

He carried the notepad toward the sofa and sat down beside the first box. He pulled Dr. Dunhill's laptop from the top of the stack and set it on the table. It didn't feel right to open it, so he catalogued it on the notepad and continued emptying the box. There were piles of books, many of them academic journals and hardback textbooks, but there were also dozens of novels. It would have taken hours to write them all down. He flipped through a particularly worn copy of *Fight Club* and wondered whether Dr. Dunhill had been a Brad Pitt fan.

The coffee table was stacked high with books and clothes, but no photo albums or frames anywhere. It was as if her life had only existed within the walls of this office and her apartment, like she herself had been institutionalized. Like Lana. When patients checked into institutions, they were asked to surrender all personal photographs and mementos of their outside lives. Cressida had done that without being asked. Roger shook his head and wrote *photos?* on the sparse list of belongings.

Roger peered into the bottom of one of the cardboard packing boxes and found a small, black velvet box tucked into the corner. He laid it out on the table and ran his finger along the gold latch. When he and Helen had travelled to England they visited the British Library and saw several ancient texts, all of which were housed in boxes such as this one. He flipped the latch and slowly lifted the lid. Sunlight glimmered off glitter which had been trapped in the folds of the velvet and gave the contents of the box a mystical glow.

On top of the box was a brightly-colored silk scarf. It looked like something Helen would have chosen from Bloomingdales, but he would have told her was far too expensive. Helen would never know that he hadn't bought this scarf new, and maybe then he could stop sleeping on the sofa. Roger lifted the scarf out of the box and unfolded it. His heart sank as he examined the elaborate pattern. There were pale droplets scattered along the scarf as if someone had dripped bleach along the silk. It was damaged goods.

He folded the delicate fabric back into a neat square and placed it on the table beside the box.

He wrote *scarf* on the notepad and peered deeper into the velvet box. He would have to think of another way to gain back Helen's forgiveness. The week he spent by Dr. Dunhill's side hadn't been easy on her. There were some crumpled hotel receipts and...an old photograph. He squinted down at the faded Polaroid. A young girl with short blond hair and bright blue eyes smiled back at him. Viola Marquis.

Dr. Dunhill had only known the girl for a couple weeks, but this photo was much older. The corners were frayed and the color yellowed. Roger stared at the photograph until his eyes burned and he lost focus. It reminded him of the photo of Lana he usually kept in his desk drawer, out of sight, where his wife would never find it. Photographs are usually proudly displayed, unless there is a reason to hide.

He slipped the picture into the front cover of *Fight Club* for safekeeping and tossed the empty cardboard box to the floor. Dr. Dunhill's entire life fit into this tiny office, and most of it stacked neatly on the coffee table.

The uneasy feeling he experienced while holding the photo of the dead girl only intensified as he surveyed the rest of the room. *Why were there no photos, no knickknacks, no memories among the books?* The air in the room tasted stale and he was overcome with an urge to run from the building and into the fresh air. Maybe he just needed to run, period. He hadn't been sleeping well lately and his later mornings rarely left time for his usual jogs.

He stood from the sofa and headed for the door. A little sun might help clear his head. The new therapist was moving his things into the office tomorrow, and Roger had a lot of work to do before then.

On his way past the leather chair, Roger tossed the notepad back onto the side table. It slid along the dusty surface and knocked a Mason jar full of pens to the floor. "Shoot."

Roger knelt to gather the mess. He collected half a dozen blue and black ballpoint pens and stuffed them back into the Mason jar. The heavy metal one he slipped into his pocket for safekeeping. It was too nice a pen to wind up at the bottom of a box in storage. As he ran a hand under the couch, he noticed a glint of light from under the wingback chair. Roger closed his fist around the source of the sparkle.

Roger sat back on his heels, opened his palm and peered at the tarnished gold band with a diamond set in the middle. It was an engagement ring. Roger had never heard Dr. Dunhill talk about a boyfriend or ever seen a man pick her up from the office after work. Roger brought the band close to his right eye and closed his left. In small script lettering on the inside of the band were four words: *I love you, Vee*. Roger closed his fist around the ring again, blocking the shine of the diamond.

Viola Marquis' engagement ring. Rex Harris had been telling the truth about Cressida taking it. But had Cressida actually...killed the girl?

Roger hauled himself to his feet, the ring heavy in his palm, and walked out of the office without looking back. His head felt caught in a vice. Cressida Dunhill was gone and so was Viola Marquis. There could be no bringing Viola back. And Rex Harris wasn't on trial for Viola's murder, but rather for the assault of Dr. Dunhill which Roger had witnessed with his own two eyes. The ring didn't change that fact.

A wave of nausea racked his body. He had defended Dr. Dunhill, fractured a knuckle punching Rex in the face after he pushed her down the stairs. Roger sat up long nights with her while she was in the hospital even after Helen accused him of having an affair. He'd done everything he could for her.

Was it all a lie?

Was she a killer?

Sand poured into Roger's dress shoes as he walked along the beach beside The Mermaid Asylum. He'd always hated that nickname, but today it seemed apt. He looked at the grey stone building rising up from the sand like shrapnel on a battlefield. He'd never noticed how ugly it was nestled beside the cheery bars and restaurants along the beach.

And no matter what he did to the outside, The Mermaid Asylum would always be proof that even their sleepy fishing town was vulnerable to devastation. And they were vulnerable too. But after Lana's death and his failure to save her, The Mermaid Asylum had become a part of him the way it was a part of Silverside. It was the last place she was alive.

He would always protect it the way he should have protected her.

Roger turned his back to the building and watched the waves crash against the sand, and felt the spray cool his face. This was where they found Lana, where they found Viola Marquis. He unclenched his fist and took one last look at the diamond, glinting in the sunlight. Then he pulled back his arm and threw the ring as hard as he could.

The people of Silverside didn't need to find one more piece of bad news washed up on these beaches. And Roger didn't need another reason to hate The Mermaid Asylum.

THE END

Don't miss the next book in the Mermaid Asylum Series:
Folie à Deux.

ANOTHER BODY WASHES UP on the shores of the Mermaid Asylum. The police rule it a suicide: the impetuous act of a woman obsessed with a dangerous legend. But Cressida knows better. Addictions aren't so easy to kill...

READ ON FOR A PREVIEW
or purchase a copy on

Amazon
Nook
iTunes
Kobo

"Human madness is oftentimes a cunning and most feline thing. When you think it fled, it may have but become transfigured into some still subtler form."

— Herman Melville, *Moby Dick*

PREVIEW: FOLIE À DEUX

Chapter 1

A SLIVER of sunlight streaked across the man's face as he leaned on his elbows over the bar. Neon lights shined up from under the lip of the bar and cast eerie pink and green glow on the rustic living wood surface. The whole Ponderosa Lounge was decorated to fit the intersection between nature and fashion. It was the hipster of drinking establishments, so typically "Portland" it was hard to take the place seriously.

The man squinted with only the left half of his face, like Popeye from the old cartoons. Except this man was no ship-shape sailor. Cressida had served him several times since moving to the East Burnside area, usually at some sort of corporate function: forced after-work cocktails with shiny black Amex cards and even shinier interns and secretaries. She'd known him before he'd ever said a word.

His name was Rob or Ron or Bob or some other single-syllable, forgettable name like that. He was a regular, and he liked to talk. A lot. It was a far fall from the flourishing psychology practice she'd left back in Silverside. Same banal complaints. Worse pay. She slid a black leather-bound menu across the pinewood bar. The whole place smelled like cheap vanilla Glad Plug-Ins. The sweet chemical smell permeated everything and no matter how many times Cressida showered it never really left her skin. The man rubbed at his nose with the back of his wrist, and she wondered how long before the clinging scent became part of her DNA. Another month? Maybe two.

Tending bar was only ever supposed to be a stopgap between psychiatric practices, but maybe now this life had invaded her every bit as much as Vee had done in Silverside. Maybe this was who she was now. Besides, what choice did she have? She couldn't go back. The Mermaid Asylum had claimed another victim. Vee was gone, and Cressida wasn't about to lose her dreams as well. Not again. Not after ten years. Ten years of deathlike, dreamless sleep, and she was finally awake. The Ponderosa might not be where she'd envisioned starting over, but at least everything was finally back in place after the chaos of Vee and Rex. Ordered and perfect. And if that meant spending the rest of her life smelling like a Yankee Candle, then so be it.

Cressida let out a slow breath and straightened the glasses below the counter. The tempered glass rims tinked together almost like music, and it reminded Cressida that she was supposed to turn on the usual background music when she'd opened that morning. It was just the two of them huddled together in the empty lounge and the silence was so complete that Cressida could hear the nose hair whistling in the man's nose with each shallow breath. She ran her index finger along the rim of one of the highballs and winced as her skin snagged against rough glass. It was chipped.

Okay, almost everything was perfect and ordered. Some things needed to be cleared out.

As if on cue, the man whose name she still couldn't recall cleared his throat and phlegm rattled deep in his chest. "Another vodka-soda, please." His fourth of the morning. It wasn't even eleven yet. Some people had no self-control.

"You got it." Behind Cressida was a mirrored panel framed on all sides by rough cross-sections of logs that looked a lot like giant corks. Shelves floated out from the glass and supported dozens of brightly-colored liquor bottles. She grabbed the Gray Goose and presented it to the swaying man as if she was a sommelier at a fancy restaurant. All she was missing was the white napkin slung over her forearm. She grabbed a dishtowel instead.

The man smirked his approval. He might have been about as deep as a puddle, but at least he had a sense of humor.

"Hey, I know you, right?" The sickly-sweet odor of mothballs and perspiration wafted with his breath.

Cressida pulled the busted glass onto the counter and nodded. "What do you think?"

He ran the tip of his thumb along his bottom lip. "Maybe you've just got one of those faces that always looks familiar. Like a doppelganger."

Cressida examined her warped reflection in the facets of the chipped highball glass. He had no idea how right he was. She'd kept her hair pixie-short like Vee's had been, but Cressida's natural red was the color of the grenadine sunset. Only the tips were still blonde from where she'd dyed it to match Vee's back in Silverside. The tiniest residue from her old life. Blended. Just like her. She dragged her eyes from her own reflection and plastered a fake smile on her face. "I'm hurt. You're only my all-time favorite customer." *Whose name wasn't worth remembering.*

The drunk man snort-laughed and he sounded like a truffle pig. "I like you. What was your name again?"

Cressida ran her fingers through her messy hair. Cascading down from her ears like waterfalls were the beaded earrings she'd worn every day since starting her new life. The new *her*. The sound of the earrings *tink-tink-tinking* against her neck reminded her of who she was inside. The rest was just for show. Or survival. "Viola. I've been working here a month, I guess I should really get a name tag."

"Viola." He ran is tongue along the inside of his cheek as though he was rolling the name around in his mouth before spitting it back out. He was drunk. Way too drunk on a Tuesday morning, and leaning heavily on the bar. He pulled himself forward off his seat. "Pretty."

"Thanks." She managed to disguise her eye roll by pretending to notice a cob web hanging from one of the exposed beams overhead.

The newly vacated stool behind the man squealed as it swiveled freely away and the sound echoed in the otherwise empty tavern. "Pretty name for a pretty girl. Did we ever... you know?"

"No." She swatted at the dusty web with the dishtowel. The sharp movement forced the man back onto his stool.

"Viola. Sounds familiar. Was your mom a Shakespeare fan?"

Cressida's lips twitched to a half smile. "Nah. It's more like a nickname. Came to me in a dream one night."

He twisted awkwardly against the wide oak bar and

retrieved his wallet from the pocket of his pants. "Changed your name, huh? You on the run? Maybe I oughta steer clear of the likes of you." He chortled at his own cleverness.

"Most definitely." Cressida scraped her thumb across the rim of the broken highball glass again, hard enough to cause pain. "So why don't you tell me what brings you in here so early on a weekday?"

He coughed and droplets of vodka-laced spit landed on the wood between them.

Cressida tensed, her fingertips curling back into fists, her left thumb throbbing against her palm. "Aren't you usually out later with the corporate crowd?

He flipped open his billfold and pulled a card from the stack. "She just threw me out. Me. Can you believe that?" *Probably.*

Cressida said nothing. She counted out her breaths by tapping her index finger on the bar. *One. Two. Three.* He wasn't done. He wanted to say more. She just needed to wait. She tapped again, as if she could coax it out of him like notes on a grand piano.

"She didn't even give me time to pack some clothes. Like she couldn't stand the sight of me for even another second. Fifteen years of marriage. Makes you wonder about a person." *Yes, it does.*

Cressida inclined her head. "Sounds like it came as quite a shock. Why do you suppose she would do something so impulsive?" The familiar sound of her therapist-voice swaddled her like a warm blanket. For years her job was the fix that allowed her to live an empty, dreamless life. Now it was more recreational.

The man cupped his hand over the credit card and slid it across the bar, smearing liquor and saliva along the way. He was wearing a moth-tattered sweater. In the hottest part of

September. And the baggy shoulders sagged around his thin frame, as if it wasn't even *his* moth-tattered sweater. He cleared his throat and nodded toward the row of liquor bottles behind Cressida. He pulled his hand back and wrung it together with the other. His nails were freshly chewed. "Can I get another one of those?"

Cressida turned over the card in front of her. Ben Bradley. *Ben.* She'd been way off. She was right about the corporate Am Ex, though. Ben probably worked in the same accounting firm as Vee's two-timing, psycho boyfriend, Rex. That is, before he'd gone to jail. These men with snappy names as short as their attention spans, they were all alike. Putting the broken highball glass to the side, she set a clean one on the bar between them and poured. The smell of vodka swirled together with the artificial vanilla like a chaser. It always gave her a headache, but it was better than Ben's mothballs or her old patients' odor of fish guts and desperation.

Ben scratched at the stubble on his face. There were holes in his facial hair larger than those in his sweater and just as patchy. "What's wrong with that glass?" He scowled toward the one in front of Cressida.

"Chipped. What's wrong with your sweater?"

The man tugged at the loose garment clinging to life against his bare chest. There was probably thicker hair there than on his face. "I had to borrow this from my neighbor."

Ice clinked against the side of the full glass as Cressida eased it toward him. "What happened to the shirt you were wearing?"

"I wasn't wearing one." *Here we go.*

The back of Cressida's leg ached. It had been about a month since the doctors here in Portland had removed the full-leg cast she'd been confined to ever since Rex had pushed her down a flight of stairs at her old apartment, and her skin was still sensitive. Any change in temperature or body chemistry would send tingles shooting down her calf like electricity. It was almost as if the pins they'd inserted were tiny lightning rods. Cressida shivered at buttoned the collar of her blouse another notch higher.

She leaned against the counter as she scraped at her jeans with the other foot. Even though it had only been a couple months, she had hoped to heal more by now. It was possible she had some kind of permanent nerve damage from the break, and that she'd have to remember Rex's smug face and greasy hair with every uneven step she takes for the rest of her life. She wondered what simple routines would remind Rex of her. Jail was the perfect place for men like him: cold, dark, and gray. Just the way Cressida's life was before Vee. Before the dreams. She bristled as she remembered the emptiness of her old life. Anything was better than drowning every night.

But Rex could suffocate for all she cared.

She shook her head. "So, Ben, I'll bite. Why weren't you wearing a shirt?"

"Well, I was trying to get it back on when she lost her goddamned mind."

"Who?"

"My wife." *Shocking.*

Cressida shifted behind the bar. "Because you were changing your shirt?"

"Well, no. Because of the reason it was off in the first place."

Cressida pulled a damp rag from the sink behind her and mopped at the bar. She didn't look at Ben's face, but she could imagine the sweat starting to bead up along his temples. "And why was that?"

His breath shook and there was a rumble that started low in his chest. A belch maybe. Or the vodka-soda bubbling up. He thunked back onto the barstool, and if it hadn't been bolted to the ground, they both would have gone careening to the sticky hardwood floor. His voice raised higher than was necessary to compensate for the extra six inches he'd just put between them. "It was just the one time. One time in fifteen years. Just a mistake." *Oh, Ben. Just like the rest of them.*

Now she was getting somewhere. Cressida stopped wiping the bar and held her gaze on Ben's face. "Just one time what?" She wanted him to say it. He was screwing some other woman and his wife caught him. Typical. All these men. All the same. Max's face materialized in her mind: beautiful, duplicitous, and pale with death. "What mistake?"

"I know I screwed up. I've been working late hours recently, and that's been taking a toll on her. But how often does an opportunity like this come along?" The pitch of his voice pinched Cressida's ears. If he'd been a woman, the world would have called him hysterical.

"What kind of opportunity?" That's what he was calling some idiot girl he'd duped into his wife's bed? Cressida wondered if the girl knew that. She held her breath and waited for the big reveal. His hands shook, and the guilt seeped from his pores denser than the booze.

"Soccer."

Cressida exhaled. She pinched her lips together to hide her surprise. "Soccer?"

"With the Timbers. It was a fundraiser event. A handful of us got to practice on the field with the team. Imagine. Me on a field with professional athletes. I mean, can you picture it?"

"No, actually." She pinched the bridge of her nose. "So your wife threw you out of the house without a shirt on because you took a long lunch break to play soccer with the Timbers?"

He dropped his head to the bar, his forehead streaking sweat on the freshly wiped surface as he peeled it back. "It was our anniversary."

"Today?"

A sob shuddered through him. "Yes. We had plans. I stood her up."

Cressida shielded her growing smile with the back of her hand. He was a pathetic mess, but at least he'd kept her guessing. People rarely surprised her anymore. She pretended to scratch her nose and wiped the smile from her face before dropping her hand to the counter. "Ben."

"She's never going to forgive me." He dragged his head from the bar and buried it in his hands.

Cressida pulled the glass away from his elbows. "Ben."

"What?"

She dumped the rest of the drink down the sink and grabbed the credit card from the bar. "Go home."

Ben dropped his hands from his face. "I can't."

"Yes, you can. Your wife is pissed, but she'll get over it." She ran the card through the register and printed the receipt.

"You don't understand. She's a piece of work when she's upset."

"You'd be surprised." Making a difference here seemed so much easier than in Silverside. Perhaps this was where she was meant to be after all.

Ben produced a pen from yet another pocket and signed the now sodden slip of paper. His hand shook as he handed it back to her. Okay, so he wasn't a cheater. He was still a drunken idiot. Cressida looked down at the damp receipt in her hand. And still a very good tipper.

"I'm going to order you an Uber," she said.

"But..."

"Just tell your wife you're sorry and that you'll make it up to her."

Ben pushed away from his barstool again and he steadied himself against the counter. "Thank you, Viola. I'm not going to forget you this time."

"You'd be surprised."

"Heh." He stumbled toward the tiny strip of light seeping between the double doors.

"Hey, Ben."

He turned around, his eyes widening for a second with the effort of staying upright. "Yeah?"

"Let her see you in that ridiculous sweater. She just might think you've been punished enough."

The doors jangled and bright light filled the room. Cressida squinted at Ben's silhouette and then went back to clearing off the counter.

Voices drifted across the bar.

"Shouldn't you be in school?" The words gurgled in Ben's throat as though he was fighting the urge to vomit. Four and a half vodka-sodas in, he probably was. Good thing that wasn't his sweater he was wearing.

A girl's voice chimed back. Louder. Stronger. "Shouldn't you be waiting for Godot, grandpa?"

Cressida snorted and smiled at the chipped glass between her hands. This was going to be good.

"You're not old enough to be in a place like this, young lady. I'll call the cops."

"You're drunk, old man. The cops have better things to

do. Haven't you heard? They're out making America great again."

"Who the hell do you think you...?"

"Hey, Ben." Cressida stooped down behind the counter and fished around in the storage cubby for her phone. "It's okay. I'll deal with her. Go home."

He mumbled something unintelligible and the doors creaked shut behind him. The bar was blissfully dim again and Cressida's eyes started to adjust. She straightened back up and standing where Ben had been a moment before, blocking the remaining light from the late morning sun, was a teenage girl. Her hand was on her hip and the other was holding a book. She was old enough to have read *Waiting for Godot* in English class but too young to really understand it. She was barely older than Lolita and in big trouble if she was even half as dumb. Her shirt had almost as many holes as Ben's sweater, but these were intentional. These flaws were sending a message. Scars on the outside to hide something on the inside. Her lip was pierced and her blue eyes were piercing. A tattoo slithered up one ankle.

Cressida grinned.

The girl stomped across the bar in leather boots that were only slightly heavier than the look on her face. She slapped a worn copy of *Fight Club* down on the counter, spraying dirty dishwater and stray alcohol around it in a mist. The pages were dog-eared and the cover was torn. She jabbed her hands to her hips.

"You're full of shit."

Chapter 2

. . .

"Always a pleasure to see you, Emmaline." Amusement twitched across Cressida's mouth.

The girl was made-up vicious. Even the lines of her eyeliner looked sharp as knives. "I am Jack's complete boredom." *This was going to be fun.*

Cressida raised her eyebrows in mock-innocent surprise. "You didn't like the book?"

"For someone with a literary name like Viola, you have terrible taste." The girl spun around one of the barstools but didn't sit. A messenger bag slid from her shoulder to the crook of her arm.

"I didn't choose the name."

A strand of the girl's ratty blonde hair stuck to her thick lipstick. "Still. People usually seem to live up to their names."

Cressida inhaled. "Or down."

The girl swept a hand across her face and pinned the stray hair back behind her ear. Her eyes narrowed and she leaned closer. She wanted to hear more. Cressida knew that look well. She'd broken down the walls of so many ambivalent patients before.

Seconds passed and finally Emmaline took the bait. "What does that mean? Why would I be surprised?"

Cressida smiled. Now she was hooked. "Never mind for today. So what didn't you like about *Fight Club*?"

Emmaline rolled her eyes and swung her heavy bag onto the counter with a thump. Frustration vibrated off of her like a tuning fork. She mumbled something about school.

Cressida put a few more inches of distance between them. It was like fishing: give and take, cast and pull. "I'm sorry. What did you say?"

The girl swallowed hard. "You told me it would change me. Well, I'm still the same."

"I said it changed *me.*"

"Well, it's dumb. Maybe you are, too." The girl's eyes widened, and she held her breath. Emmaline was testing her limits, trying to see if she could get a rise out of Cressida. *So textbook, it almost seemed forced.*

Cressida cocked her head to the side. "Oh, well since you make such an eloquent argument..."

The girl scoffed. "Fuck you. I don't have to justify anything to you."

Such anger. Over a book. And yet, she was here wanting to impress Cressida with her passionate pontification.

Fish fought harder once you dragged them into the boat, too. Max would have been drawn to this girl, fascinated by her irreverence. Just as he had been to Cressida at her age. *Angry. Dangerous. Alone.* That's what Max had written about her in his patient notes when they first met. So much for HIPPA. She'd found her file lying out on the desk one day while she was waiting for him in his home office. A plain manila folder pinned closed under his favorite Montblanc pen: sleek and black with a sharp silver fountain tip. Max always used that pen during their sessions. He never faltered, never misplaced it. That pen was probably worth more than anything Cressida owned back then. The night Max died Cressida had stolen that same pen, the one he'd used to define her for the rest of her life. That was the night she took her destiny into her own hands. She wondered what this girl was fated to take from her.

Max always had his own brand of ethics. And Emmaline would have fit right in. She was stupid and vulnerable because she didn't know just how stupid she was. The girl was just his type, and he would have crawled inside her head and made a makeshift bed there. He was the fucking

Goldilocks of transference. But Cressida wasn't Max. In fact, she wasn't even Cressida anymore. She was *Viola* now.

And this girl was begging to be understood.

There was a certain thrill involved in chasing down a person's demons, in wrestling them to the ground even when they threaten to fight back. Cressida had missed the power since leaving her practice behind at the old Mermaid Asylum.

Cressida laced her fingers together. "You want people to take you seriously?"

"Yes."

"Then you'd better learn to stay calm when you're challenged, when you're upset."

"What makes you think I'm upset?" Emmaline chewed at the cuticle of her thumb.

The nerves in Cressida's mending leg twinged. The cast was gone, but the bones would never really be the same. There would always be some kind of crack: a weakness. People were like that, too. Scars healed, but only on the outside. Rex hadn't stayed calm when he'd broken into Cressida's apartment and tried to kill her. Vee hadn't stayed calm when she'd threatened to report Cressida for ethical violations as a therapist. They'd both lost control and now they were both gone.

Order and discipline were the only ways to stay alive.

"Can I give you some advice?"

"Probably."

Cressida took a deep breath. "That get up..." She nodded toward the girl's dark makeup and slashed jeans.

Emmaline glanced down. "Now you sound like my mother."

"That's because you're not listening. Because you're sixteen and think you know everything." Cressida fixed her eyes on the girls'. "I am not your mother. I don't care if you dress like a cheap whore on Mardi Gras."

The girl flinched. "Seventeen."

"Fine. You want to send a message through your exterior? Great. Make sure you're sending the right one."

"And what's that?"

"A lie."

Emmaline paused for a moment like the words needed to burrow through layers of makeup and hairspray to get to her brain. "So the great truth about myself that I'm supposed to be projecting is a lie?"

"Yes."

"What kind of lie?"

"That you're a whole person." Cressida ran her fingers through her spiked hair. Vee's hair. Cressida wondered if she, too, was whole now.

"You're saying I'm not?"

Cressida locked eyes with the girl who seemed to shrink. "I'm not the only one who can see through you. One of these days someone is going to call your bluff and you're either going to have the guts to stand up for yourself or you're going to find yourself invaded."

Emmaline's cheeks reddened. "Invaded? What the hell does that even mean?"

"It means there are people out there who look for holes to fill. A new place to call home until they outgrow it. Like hermit crabs. And you, little girl, are full of more holes than your shirt."

Emmaline looked down at her clothes. "At least I'm not dressed like a nun."

Cressida didn't need to look. She could feel the pinch of her shirt collar against the nape of her neck, the itch of her scar-pocked chest brushing against the stiff cotton of her blouse, and the cuff of the sleeves as she pulled them down over the heels of her hands. This girl wore her scars like they were fashionable, but Cressida had long-since learned the value of discretion. That was the mistake she'd made with Rex. She'd let him see her scars and the way she needed Vee. She'd let him believe she was vulnerable.

Cressida brushed some dust from her sleeve. "It's hard to fill the holes you can't see."

Emmaline's mouth pursed but she didn't argue. With shaking hands, she smoothed a wrinkle out of her torn top. "Fine. I'm listening."

"Then why don't you tell me—calmly—what you didn't like about *Fight Club*? Think about it and tell me something worth listening to. Show me someone worth taking seriously."

The girl scratched at some makeup clumped in the corner of her eye. "Okay. Fine." She dropped her hands to the counter. "I thought it was overdramatic."

"Tell me more about that."

"Everybody's life sucks. Dude was just borrowing other people's problems because he didn't want to deal with his own. People get cancer. People get divorced. Some people can't stop drinking even when social services threatens to take away their only daughter." Her eyes welled. What looked like days-worth of makeup threatened to melt down her face along with the tears.

"Isn't that the point? Jack is the human condition."

"Yeah, but it's a cop-out. Most of us don't get to invent a new identity to avoid dealing with just how boring and fucked up our real life is. It's not that easy. The real *fight club* is just waking up every day and letting life kick your ass for a while. Then you go to bed, dream of a better life, wake up, and do it all over again."

"Been reading a lot of Bukowski lately?"

The girl rolled her eyes and the color in her cheeks deepened. "Do I look like someone who would read Bukowski?"

"You don't look like the kind of person who reads at all. I assumed that's what you were going for."

The girl sniffed. "For the record, I don't like Hunter S. Thompson or fucking Hemmingway either."

"Why does that upset you?"

"I'm not upset." Her voice cracked even as she denied her feelings. Being a teenager was confusing.

"If you say so."

Emmaline swiped at her phone for a moment and then turned it around to show Cressida the image of a book cover. "It was *Norwegian Wood*, okay? But that's not why I said that. That's just how I see the world."

Cressida slid the copy of *Fight Club* closer to the girl. "So you think Jack was avoiding his life and finding meaning in his boring existence by creating Tyler?"

"Yeah. Don't you?"

"No."

The girl stopped spinning the stool and slid onto the cushion. She rested her chin in her hands and blew a blonde hair, as stiff as straw, away from her eyes. "I think he was weak."

Cressida flipped to one of the dog-eared pages. "Why does weakness offend you?"

"Because what makes him so special?"

"He's not."

"Then why should I care?"

Cressida smiled. This was the type of debate she'd dreamt about having with Vee on some random, lazy Sunday morning. Until Rex messed everything up. He'd gotten in between them, cleaved apart what was always meant to be joined, and now Vee was gone forever. Dead. Like Max. All Cressida had left of both of them were her dreams, and a name. Vee. *Viola.* Every time she said it, excitement tingled to Cressida's fingertips.

She busied her hands with a dishrag, wiping the same spot on the counter until it shined. Polishing the exterior is the easy part. The rot inside has to be dug out. "The point is exactly that. He's not special. Everyone is made up of different fragments of personality. Sanity is simply the failure to see the line where one version of us starts and another ends."

"Okay. So?"

"Tyler was always there, hiding. Just because you can't feel your heart beating all the time doesn't mean you're not alive."

"Yeah, but Tyler isn't a bodily function."

Cressida closed the book and set it back in front of the girl. "Maybe. But I bet if you look hard enough, you'll find there are divergent iterations of you trading places in your body all the time. You just think you're in control. It's an illusion."

Emmaline picked up the book. "Yeah, but the illusion of control is better than nothing. The truth is worse."

"You're too young to be so jaded."

Emmaline slipped the paperback into her bag. "Maybe it's just one of my personalities. This one is a fifty-three-year-old divorcee with six cats and cobwebs in her cooter."

Cressida twisted her mouth to keep from grinning. "Did you just say 'cooter?'"

The tension in the room broke with the girl's grin. "Fuck you."

"You remind me of myself at your age."

"Well..." Emmaline ran her tongue over the silver ring in her bottom lip. Her tongue was dyed purple as though she'd eaten a Tootsie Pop for breakfast, and the contrast with the harsh metal piercing was striking. The impulsivity of a child butted up against the violent yearnings of an adult. It was a dangerous combination. This girl was low-hanging fruit, and for some reason the thought of her being plucked down infuriated Cressida.

The girl gnawed at her fingernails. "I still say, if you don't like your *fucking khakis*, the answer is to go out and buy a pair of jeans. Not to start a cult and blow up a building."

Cressida laughed.

The girl was angry and ridiculous, and she hadn't yet seen enough of the world to know that people blow things up every day. Figuratively, anyway. They just didn't usually understand why.

Ignorance is not bliss, it's numb. Pain is enlightenment.

Cressida had been numb for years after Max died and before she met Vee. Dull, desperate, and dreamless.

Somewhere inside Cressida, a spark of recognition ignited. "Em?"

The girl looked up. Her eyes were bloodshot. "What?"

"Why aren't you in school today?"

Emmaline zipped her bag hard enough that it fell to ground. "Are you serious? You're going to give me a hard time, too?"

"No. I just..."

"You're as bad as that guy when I came in. The one wearing the zombie Mr. Rogers sweater. Are you going to call the cops, too?"

"Of course not..." Cressida trailed off.

Emmaline bent to retrieve her bag from the sticky bar floor. "Why do you even care?"

It was a fair question and not one that Cressida had a good answer for yet.

Memories flashed in Cressida's mind with enough force that she held her breath. She was still getting used to the kickback of having any kind of visual memories. For so long her mind had been a black hole. Her head spun.

She could see Rex's hands clamped on her hips against the bookshelf in her old apartment. Volumes of stories she'll never read again—entire lives lost because Rex couldn't stay out of other people's business or their pants—pages flapping to the ground around them like dusty snowflakes. Books lying face down on her old apartment floor, pages akimbo beneath bent covers.

She saw Vee's face when Cressida admitted what Rex had done. Fear. Loathing. She saw the sneering pleasure on Max's face in the moment before his death, when she'd taken him in her mouth and taken the steering wheel of his speeding sportscar in her hand.

She saw her mother holding her head under water the way she'd held down Vee's. Dreams and memories are so intrinsically linked that Cressida could barely tell what was real and what she'd imagined. Each and every memory was overlooked by vacant eyes, cold and milky-white with death: Vee's eyes, Max's, and her mother's.

Glassy visages still stared at her even as she settled back into her body in the bar. Even while she watched this girl—who was so like herself and also so like she imagined Vee had been before Rex—flailing for meaning. Begging to be seen. Tyler Durden wasn't who Emmaline needed, but she'd come to the right place anyway.

Of all the gin joints in all the world...

"You know, I could get fired for even letting you sit back

here." Cressida uprighted a clean glass on the bar between them.

Emmaline smiled. Her blue eyes sparkled now. Not like the eyes still staring at Cressida from the back of her mind. This girl was very much alive: unpredictable, dangerous, and intoxicating. "I guess you're causing your own brand of mayhem."

The soda fountain hissed as Cressida pulled the tap back and filled the glass with Pepsi. "Sounds like you got more from the book than you think you did."

"It pissed me off."

"Maybe you needed to feel something."

Emmaline leaned back and crossed her arms. "Maybe."

Cressida jumped as the door jangled open. An old man shuffled on stiff legs across the bar and sat at one of the tables in the back. He groaned into the bench and cleared his throat. "I guess I should get back to work," she said.

Emmaline stood. "I get to pick the book next time, okay?"

"Sure. But only if you can convince me why I should read it. If you can learn to sell it, you can have anything in the world you want."

The girl shook her head. "You're weird."

"You have no idea."

Emmaline pulled her bag over her shoulder. "Hey, Viola..."

Goosebumps raised on Cressida's arm and she grabbed a menu from behind the bar to hide the shivers. "Yeah?"

"If anyone asks..."

Cressida waved the menu at the girl. "Yeah, yeah. I never saw you."

Emmaline stepped back toward the bar and laid her hands flat on the surface. "No." She leaned closer and her blue eyes locked on Cressida's. Her phone buzzed from her back pocket, but she didn't blink. "If anyone asks, I was here."

The old man in the back coughed again and Cressida furrowed. She nodded at the girl and turned away. There was something wild in the girl's eyes and it sent shivers up Cressida's spine. There was part of her that didn't like turning her back on that creature. Something familiar. But the door opened and closed and before Cressida had even reached the old man's table, and they were alone in the bar.

Chapter 3

There was water all around. No, not water. It was just air —empty space—but the air moved in waves like the ocean tide. Cressida closed her eyes and listened to the silence: No seagulls cawing or ship horns blasting. No lapping surf along the beach or scuttling of crabs on the rocks. Her mind was a vacuum. Her bed swayed and rocked and floated on nothing until it banged up against something solid. The jolt of the impact startled Cressida upright. Her blankets were gone and she was supine on a raft. It was exactly the kind of thing you'd expect to see in the summer at a pool—inflatable pillow and cup holders included—except this raft was blown up to the size of a queen bed.

There was so much light pouring around her that it heated Cressida's cheeks until they were dry and tight, and she could only crack one eye to see. Without blankets, she was completely naked and sitting up on the eerily levitating raft. She wiggled her toes and explored the body in front of her eyes. Not her body.

Cressida peered down at her bare legs. The scar on her knee, from where she'd fallen off the roof as a pre-teen trying to sneak out, was gone. There was no sign of the angry purple lumps on her shin where the doctors had pinned her tibia after Rex threw her down the stairs last month. The muscles in both calves were taught and equal, not wasting away on one side under thin, paper-like skin like the last time Cressida examined her legs in the shower. It was as if the attack had never happened. As if Vee had not died.

Her naked chest was smooth apart from a single raised freckle nestled just beneath her left breast. Long slender fingers with impractical turquoise nails curling out beyond their fingertips slid over her chest toward her neck. There were no scars. It was as if the accident with Max had never happened, as if the jagged shards of his broken windshield had never buried themselves in her flesh like shrapnel. It was as if she was whole again. Cressida ran her fingertips along her chest. She'd watched those same nails as they trailed over the spines of her books in her office the days she'd met with Vee. That day, she'd felt so exposed by the girl. And now, here she was, naked and inhabiting a dead girl's body, and she'd never felt more alive.

Cressida was dreaming again. Kind of.

Cressida pulled a hand close to her face, running the pad of her thumb over the sharp nails until something made her pause. These fingernails weren't just similar to Vee's that day in the office. They were exactly those nails. The tip of the middle finger was chipped almost in half with a jagged edge. It had kept snagging on the bindings and the sound had made Cressida's stomach turn. She'd resented Vee's relentless touch at the time and now those same hands were teasing something else out of her. It just wasn't clear what. Goosebumps spread over someone else's skin and Cressida felt them rise. These were not her hands, yet she could feel the sensation of touch beneath them as they moved.

Cressida's flesh tingled, and it wasn't clear if she was controlling this new body or not. Vee's hands were part of her and yet foreign at the same time. Some piece of Cressida rejected the intrusion, as she had before in her office, but she also welcomed the discomfort. She reveled in the conflicting pleasure and pain of being possessed and of possessing someone else. Vee was inside of her. Or rather, she was inside of Vee. The scars that usually peppered her chest were gone and replaced by smooth, virgin skin as cold and pale as snow. It was as if Cressida has been remade.

This was something new.

The raft bumped again and Cressida snapped to attention. She was still in her bedroom, floating about six inches from the floor that swelled and undulated beneath her as though it was made of gelatin. Beside her was a thick plexiglass wall, the kind of protective glass that one finds in prisons, hospitals, and mental institutions. Anything to keep out the condemned, the sick, and the infirmed. Her long nails click clacked on the glass as she touched the clear barrier. The raft drifted away and then softly nudged the wall again as if a current was drawing it in.

The room behind her was lit bright enough to catch her own reflection in the glass. Short blonde hair, blue eyes, and a wicked smile greeted her like a mirage in the glass. Vee. Cressida raised her hand to the glass and the reflection of her old friend did the same. She moved her hands in a circle like a street mime and smiled as the reflection matched her perfectly. Cressida closed her eyes and dropped her chin to her chest. The glass was cold on her forehead.

Loud thumps broke Cressida's thoughts and at first she thought the raft was slamming against the wall again, but when she opened her eyes, she saw Vee's furious face. Not the translucent mirror-Vee from a moment before, but the actual girl—in the flesh—banging her fists against the other side of the glass. Her mouth was wide and there were tears streaming from her bright blue eyes, but the only sound Cressida could hear was the pounding. Cressida raised her hand toward the wall and hesitated about an inch from where Vee's frantic fists smashed against the glass. There were streaks of sweat between them now. And a twinge of blood from Vee's battered knuckles spattered on the glass like a piece of modern art. It looked as though she'd been at it for a while.

How long had Cressida been asleep while Vee was fighting to get her attention?

The girl behind the glass never made eye contact with Cressida but glared at the wall as if it was opaque. Cressida inhaled and moved closer to the window, careful not to touch it again. For some reason that felt important. Her hand shook only a fraction of an inch from Vee's point of impact and she steadied her wrist with her other hand. For a moment Cressida was perfectly still.

Vee was wearing the same red skirt she'd been wearing the day she'd drowned. It billowed around her as if she was floating. Each time the hem of her skirt lifted, a dark swirl was visible along one leg. It started down around her ankle like a shackle, then serpentine up her calf like a twining vine dragging her down. Or a snake.

Tiny bubbles formed around Vee's nostrils and skittered up her face and into her hair. There was nowhere else for them to go. No air. Vee was drowning again.

Cressida eased her breath free and the window between

her and Vee fogged. There was movement behind the haze, but Cressida could no longer see Vee. A deep sense of emptiness filled Cressida's lungs, heavy and cold, the way the water must have felt in Vee's. Her heart hammered in her chest. It felt as though they were both dying. She needed to know what Vee was doing. Without thinking Cressida swiped her palm across the condensation and as soon as her hand—Vee's ridiculous nails and long, pianist fingers—made contact with the glass everything shattered.

A sharp crash ripped through the room and the entire wall splintered like a car windshield. Tiny little nuggets of safety glass rained down on Cressida like hail. Like it had that day in the car with Max. Rough edges scraped and tore at her skin. The weight of the glass pulled the raft closer to the floor as it accumulated around her. Water poured out of the room on the other side of the glass and splashed around Cressida's bed. It sounded like the ocean. The light dimmed around her and Cressida could feel the cold darkness of dreamless sleep pulling at the edges of her mind. She reached a hand up toward the place where Vee had been only a moment before, but there was nothing there.

No wall.

No Vee.

No water.

Just air.

When the raft touched the floor the last of the light evaporated around her and Cressida dropped back onto her pillow. All around her the tiny shards of glass melted to water and rained down, soaking her body, splashing against her closed eyelids, and plastering her hair to her forehead. Cressida opened her mouth to gasp and water filled her senses. Relentless and prodigious, the sound of the sea hummed in her mind. But this time there was something else. More banging echoed in Cressida's head. This time it sounded tinny and far away, as if it was being piped into her head from an old-fashioned radio. She opened her eyes again and wiped the wet hair from her eyes.

She was standing in the shower.

Stubby fingers with nails chewed to the quick materialized in front of her face. There were scratches down her forearms almost like claw marks. She'd had the same wounds on her legs from where Vee had dug her nails into Cressida's ankles as she fought for her last breaths. Luckily the doctors had assumed Cressida's injuries were all a result of Rex's attack later that week. These new abrasions didn't make any sense. The glass hadn't been real. Cressida tipped her head back and let the water run through her hair. Her legs ached and her back was sore. There was mud caked to her ankles and splattered up the back of her unevenly muscled calves. How had she gotten here?

Only a moment ago she was dreaming of Vee.

The knocking in her head started again, this time louder and more corporeal. *The door.*

Cressida stepped out of the shower and reached for her towel, but it was missing. She ran her hand down the sweaty wall and onto the floor, but the towel wasn't there.

More knocking.

Still dripping in little puddles around her feet, Cressida grabbed her bathrobe from the back of the bathroom door and scooted toward the sound. The windows of Cressida's tiny, first-floor apartment were still as black as night. It wasn't even close to dawn. She left the bedroom and walked through the open-plan living room and kitchen area. The clock on the microwave displayed 3:00 a.m. Something must be wrong. Cressida froze with her hand on the door handle. She peered through the peephole into the hallway.

What if Rex was out of prison?

What if the police had finally figured out she'd killed Vee?

The knocking stopped and this time there was just a faint scraping of metal on metal. The lock sprung free and Cressida leaned with all her weight against the door. Her heart sped in her chest as she focused her eye on a shivering shape of a human rattling the handle and pushing against the door with her bony shoulder.

Cressida swung the door wide. "Em? What the hell are you doing here?"

Want to know what happens next?
Pick up Folie à *Deux from all your favorite retailers:*

Amazon
Nook
iTunes
Kobo

ABOUT THE AUTHOR

Former cognitive psychologist turned suspense writer, Mary is a firm believer in strong, twisted female characters and unhappy endings. Her internet search history is not for the faint of heart.

As a freelance writer and humorist, Mary's essays have been featured on The Washington Post, Brain, Child Magazine, and Scary Mommy. She has also appeared on a Wisconsin Public Radio morning show discussing the psychology of parenting. Mary does not perform well at 5:30am.

Raised near Portland, Oregon, Mary now lives in central Illinois where the tallest thing for miles is corn. She shares a perpetually shrinking house with her three kids, two dogs, and two cats... and can usually be found writing under at least one of them at all times.

Join Mary's reader group
www.marywiddicks.com

Already a fan?
Join my street team here for exclusive access to books and stories before they're available anywhere else! Visit my website for more details.

ALSO BY MARY WIDDICKS

The Mermaid Asylum Series

Insomnia: A Mermaid Asylum Short Story

A Mutual Addiction (Book 1)

Born Under Fire: A Mermaid Asylum Short Story

Folie à Deux (Book 2)

Mermaid Asylum Book 3- Coming early 2020

Short Stories

Come Away With Me: A Short Story

Vice: A Short Story

Made in the USA
Middletown, DE
12 March 2020

86240924R00205